A KNIGHT'S KISS

Just what form of revenge was he going to take, Avery wondered. He certainly looked big, dark and dangerous, yet she felt no sense of impending peril.

"What do ye intend to do to me?" she demanded.

Cameron opened one eye and looked at her. Sitting as she was, her face barely topped the edge of the bed. "I intend to seduce you," he answered.

"Do ye now," she drawled. "And ye being such a braw handsome laddie, ye expect me to just swoon at yer feet? I would prefer ye dead, but we cannae all get what we wish for, can we?"

"Such violence. A wee lass like yourself shouldnae be so quick to promise mayhem and murder. 'Tis clear ye need to be tamed. Someone has let ye run too wild. Ye snarl and hiss at me now, but I will soon have ye purring."

"Such arrogance."

Glancing down at her mouth, Cameron decided he wanted to kiss her. As he started to lower his mouth to hers, he felt her tense, saw her beautiful eyes start to widen, and knew she had guessed his intent.

"Dinnae e'en think about it," she warned.

"Ah, but I *am* thinking about it."

Before she could say anything else, he covered her mouth with his. . . .

Books by Hannah Howell

ONLY FOR YOU
MY VALIANT KNIGHT
UNCONQUERED
WILD ROSES
A TASTE OF FIRE

The Murray Brothers
HIGHLAND DESTINY
HIGHLAND HONOR
HIGHLAND PROMISE

A STOCKINGFUL OF JOY

The Murray Daughters
HIGHLAND VOW
HIGHLAND KNIGHT
HIGHLAND BRIDE
(coming soon)

Published by Zebra Books

HIGHLAND KNIGHT

Hannah Howell

ZEBRA BOOKS
KENSINGTON PUBLISHING CORP.
http://www.zebrabooks.com

ZEBRA BOOKS are published by

Kensington Publishing Corp.
850 Third Avenue
New York, NY 10022

All Kensington titles, imprints and distributed lines are available at special quantity discounts for bulk purchases for sales promotion, premiums, fund-raising, educational or institutional use.

Special book excerpts or customized printings can also be created to fit specific needs. For details, write or phone the office of the Kensington Special Sales Manager: Kensington Publishing Corp., 850 Third Avenue, New York, NY 10022. Attn. Special Sales Department. Phone: 1-800-221-2647.

Zebra and the Z logo Reg. U.S. Pat. & TM Off.

First Printing: June 2001
10 9 8 7 6 5 4 3 2 1

Printed in the United States of America

Dear Reader,

Many of you have written to ask me what happened to HIGHLAND HEARTS, which was to have been published in March 2000. In a word, the Murrays happened—the brothers and then their spirited, can't-stay-out-of-trouble daughters. I decided to focus on the trilogy, to give Elspeth, Avery, and yes, little Gillyanne, all of my attention.

The good news is that HIGHLAND HEARTS, Tess and Revan's tale, will be published in February 2002. Little Gillyanne Murray will have her moment in the sun in October 2002, fully prepared to torment and delight her chosen hero with her unique charm in HIGHLAND BRIDE.

Many thanks for your interest and patience,

Hannah D. Howell

PS: The book you're holding in your hand, HIGHLAND KNIGHT, was originally entitled HIGHLAND RING, but my editor and I decided to change the title.

Chapter One

"Why have you brought the girl here?"

The hefty Sir Bearnard idly shifted his thickly muscled arm so that he could more firmly hold the limp girl he had captured, and warily eyed his liege lord, Sir Charles DeVeau. "I captured her on the raid," he answered.

"I did not send you out against the Lucettes to collect women. There are plenty lurking about the demesne who will readily serve the needs of any man."

"We did all you asked of us, my lord. I but found this woman as we rode away from the burning ruins of the Lucettes' keep, and I thought she could be used to pay a debt I owe."

"What debt?" Sir Charles rubbed his sharply cut chin with the long, ringed fingers of his left hand and tried unsuccessfully to get a better look at Sir Bearnard's captive.

"A wager I lost to Sir Cameron MacAlpin." Sir Bearnard frowned when Sir Charles laughed softly.

"Not only is the woman not much bigger than a child, dirty, and bruised, but have you forgotten that our large Scottish knight has taken a vow of chastity?"

"I did notice that he has nothing to do with the women, although many beckon to him."

"Well, do as you wish, but I think you will find that Sir Cameron would much prefer the coin."

"Mayhap if I offer him both of the women."

"Two women? I see but one."

"The other one was even smaller than this one, only a child. Sir Renford took her, for he has a liking for such tender ones."

Sir Charles shrugged. "Go. Try your luck. The man leaves us soon. He may be amiable to some bargain, may even know of some way to get coin for the wench. Just remember, if she causes any trouble, it will be you who pay the price."

Avery felt her captor bow slightly. Her insides were so twisted with fury, it was nearly impossible to remain limp as Sir Bearnard took his leave of the cold-eyed man he had been talking to and started to walk out of the great hall. This brute had just tried to destroy her kinsmen and all they held dear, and now he meant to use her to pay off some debt.

She could not believe how swiftly her idyllic visit with her mother's family had turned tragic and bloody. How many of her cousins had died beneath the swords of the DeVeaux? Had everything been destroyed? And where was her cousin Gillyanne? Gillyanne was just a child, barely thirteen. All these questions burned on the tip of her tongue, but she knew the brute carrying her to her fate would never trouble himself to answer them.

When Sir Bearnard finally paused before a thick wooden door and pounded on it, Avery winced. Each thud added to the painful throbbing in her head. The door opened and she softly cursed as the man walked into the room, callously banging her legs against the frame of the door. She tried to catch a look at the room he was entering, but her tangled hair obscured her vision. Then Sir Bearnard tossed her down onto a thick sheepskin spread before a hearth. The abrupt fall left her dazed, increasing the pain in her head until she feared she would swoon.

"And what is that?" a deep, rich voice asked in heavily accented French.

"A woman," Sir Bearnard replied.

"I can see that. Why should you attempt to give her to me?"

"I have brought her to you to pay my debt," Sir Bearnard explained.

"Even if I was of a mind to take her in trade," that cold, deep voice drawled, "she does not appear to be worth even half of what you owe me."

Avery gritted her teeth at that calmly delivered insult and decided she had feigned unconsciousness long enough. She brushed her tangled hair off her face and nearly gasped. The man standing next to Sir Bearnard and scowling down at her was huge. It was not that he looked so big just because she was sprawled on her back on the floor at his feet, either.

He wore soft deerhide boots and brown woolen breeches on his long, well-shaped legs. His white linen shirt was undone, revealing a taut, rippled stomach and a broad, smooth chest. It also revealed that his skin was as dark as that of many of the Frenchmen he served with. Avery mused that even she would look fashionably pale next to such a man. There was no sign of interest on his dark, lean face, no hint of any emotion at all. Framed by thick, raven hair that fell in soft waves to just below his broad shoulders, it was, however, an almost beautiful face. He had a firm jaw, high, wide cheekbones, a long, straight nose, and a mouth that even she found tempting despite the stern line it was pressed into. What truly held her attention was his eyes. Set beneath dark, gently curved brows and rimmed with disgracefully long, thick lashes, were the darkest eyes she had ever seen, black as coal and nearly as hard. She saw little chance of mercy or aid reflected there. Finally, she let him see her fury and watched his dark brows lift ever so slightly in reaction.

"I heard that you and your men were soon to leave us, Sir Cameron," said Sir Bearnard.

"In two days," Sir Cameron replied.

"I fear I cannot gather the coin I owe you by then."

"Then you should not have made the wager."

Sir Bearnard flushed a deep red. "It was ill-thought of me. But, you can gain something from the woman. Use her, ransom her, or sell her."

"You captured her in the attack upon the Lucettes?"

"*Oui,* just outside of the gates."

"Then she could be a peasant and worth nothing in ransom."

"*Non,* Sir Cameron, look at her gown. No peasant woman would wear such clothes."

When Sir Cameron bent down to examine her gown more closely, Avery gave in to the rage building inside of her. She kicked out at him, aiming to catch him squarely beneath his firm jaw, but he was quick—alarmingly so. He caught her leg, wrapping his long fingers tightly around her calf. Her skirts fell back, exposing her legs, and, to her dismay, he held her like that for a moment. She gasped in outrage when he suddenly lifted her skirts and peered beneath them, his fine mouth fleetingly curving in the semblance of a smile.

"Braies," he murmured.

Sir Bearnard chanced a quick look before Sir Cameron dropped her skirts back down. "Strange attire for a woman."

"So, you have not tasted of the gift you try to give to me," said Sir Cameron.

"*Non,* I swear it. I took her only to pay my debt to you."

Sir Cameron still crouched near her, still held her leg. He moved his left hand over her leg while holding it steady in his right. Avery seethed, her fury intensified by her helplessness. The man handled her as if she were a horse he was about to buy. What held her tense and afraid, however, was not offended modesty, but the fear of discovery. A moment later his long fingers slid up high enough to brush against the dagger sheath strapped to her upper thigh. She cursed. When he looked at her, his dark eyes briefly lightened by what appeared to be amusement, she just glared at him.

"I believe you, Sir Bearnard," Sir Cameron drawled as he removed her dagger from its sheath, released her leg, and stood up.

"*Merde.*" Sir Bearnard shook his head. "Never thought to search her for weapons. Just a woman, after all."

Avery kicked out at Sir Bearnard, but he quickly moved out of her reach, and she tugged her skirts back down. As Sir Cameron studied her weapon, the hint of a frown upon his face, a youth stepped over to him. She judged him to be about her age, eighteen or younger. He was as red as Sir Cameron was dark, tall, and almost too thin.

"Cameron, that is a . . ." the boy said in English, staring at the dagger and then at Avery in wide-eyed surprise.

"I ken it, Donald," Sir Cameron said in the same language, cutting off the boy's words.

Donald continued to stare at Avery and whispered, "She has eyes like a cat."

"Aye, and I begin to think she can be as feral as the worst of that breed." Cameron scowled at the door when someone began to pound on it. "I suddenly become most sought after," he murmured in French, glancing at Sir Bearnard.

"Bearnard, you fat bastard! I know you are in there," bellowed a deep voice.

"Ah, it is for you." Cameron nodded at Sir Bearnard. "Better find out what the man wants."

"Have I paid my debt?" Sir Bearnard asked.

"I am still considering the matter."

Sir Bearnard strode over to open the door and a large brown-haired man stomped into the room, but Avery was only interested in the small, thin girl he dragged in with him. "Gillyanne," she cried, and she started to move, only to be held in place by Sir Cameron, who gently but firmly planted one booted foot on her chest.

"You can have this little bitch back," Sir Renford growled, shoving Gillyanne toward Sir Bearnard. "She is diseased."

After one look at Gillyanne, Sir Bearnard hastily stepped away from her, his hands held out wide to avoid accidentally touching her. Gillyanne ignored both men and raced toward Avery. The girl came to an abrupt halt, squeaking slightly in fright, when Cameron drew his sword and pointed it at her.

"Ye would kill a bairn?" Avery demanded, too afraid for Gillyanne to be quiet or even play at being French any longer.

"She is diseased," Cameron said.

Avery stared at Gillyanne and slowly smiled. The girl's

fair skin was covered with blotches, welts, and spots. Her faintly mismatched eyes were puffy and reddened.

"Strawberries?" she asked her cousin. "He gave you strawberries?"

"Aye. Weel, nay," Gillyanne replied. "He had some in his chambers, and when he wasnae looking, I shoved a few down my gullet."

Cameron hesitated one more moment then sheathed his sword. "So, 'twas a trick." He took his foot off Avery's chest and frowned when the young girl threw herself into the slender woman's arms. "A deceit."

"Ye would think it more honorable if she allowed that French swine to rape her?" Avery snapped.

"She is just a bairn," muttered Donald, glancing toward Sir Renford with ill-hidden disgust.

"They speak English," said Sir Bearnard as he shut the door behind a cursing, departing Sir Renford.

"It would appear so," Sir Cameron replied. "I believe they may even be from Scotland."

"The Lucettes have a kinswoman in Scotland. Um, is it a good idea to let that diseased child touch the woman?"

"Do you fear her worth will be lessened? Do not. What ails the child cannot be caught by others."

"Will you take them both in payment, then?"

"I do not have much choice, do I? If they do not gain me anything, I can always find you again, can I not?"

Avery was a little surprised to see Sir Bearnard pale and nod jerkily as he said, "God speed you on your journey home, Sir Cameron."

"A Scot," Gillyanne whispered as Sir Cameron escorted Sir Bearnard to the door. "We are safe now?"

"I am nay sure," Avery whispered back. "He has accepted us in payment for a lost wager. That doesnae speak too weel of the mon. He doesnae look to be a verra safe mon, either. And, there is something about the name

MacAlpin which troubles me, but I cannae recall what it is.'' The door shut behind Sir Bearnard, and Avery lightly touched her cousin's face. "Will this soon ease?"

"Aye. It just itches."

"Let me do the talking," Avery advised as Sir Cameron strode back toward her.

Cameron stared down at the two tiny females he had just been given. He found the whole matter of bartering women very distasteful, but had realized long ago that he was one of few. The men he had been fighting with for the past three years had proven to have very little in common with him. He and his men had become increasingly isolated from the others they rode with, and that caused its own problems. Cameron just wished he had not had one final difficulty thrust in his way before he could reach Scotland, home, and, God willing, some peace.

The one he had been given first caused him the most unease. She was disheveled and dirty and did not seem to possess the maidenly decency to be afraid. She wore braies and carried a dagger strapped to her lovely thigh. He found her both beautiful and intriguing, and that alarmed him. It had taken most of his eight-and-twenty years to understand that women who stirred his lust brought him nothing but trouble. He did not appreciate this tiny golden-eyed woman reviving the fevers he had kept so tightly controlled for nearly three years. Not once in those long, cold years had he wavered in his self-enforced celibacy, but he was certainly wavering now.

Looking her over carefully, he tried to find something that explained why he was suddenly taut and aching, the blood pounding in his veins. She was tiny, would probably just reach his chest. She was also slender, not the lush-figured sort he had always reached for in the past. Her breasts were small, but high, firm, and temptingly shaped.

She had a very tiny waist and gently curved hips. He knew well that she had beautiful, slender, surprisingly long legs. That faint golden tone to her skin covered her whole lithe body. Donald was right. She did have eyes like a cat. They were not only a golden amber color, but vaguely tilted, enhancing their feline appearance. Set beneath dark, faintly winged brows and encircled by long, dark lashes, they filled her small heart-shaped face. A small, straight nose led to a full mouth. It was all nearly swamped by heavy waves of golden-brown hair that were flavored with glimpses of red and hung past her hips.

Dragging his fingers through his hair, Cameron rubbed the back of his neck and grimaced inwardly. She was a golden woman from the tip of her wild hair to her small, dainty feet. He could argue with himself until his tongue fell out, but he could not deny that she was exquisite. If he was going to hold to his vow of celibacy, he was going to have to stay very far away from her—something that could prove impossible as they traveled to Scotland.

"Who are ye?" he demanded.

Avery briefly contemplated lying, then decided it would serve little purpose. If nothing else, Gillyanne would not be able to hold to the lie for very long, being too young to indulge in any long or complicated deceit. "I am Avery Murray daughter of Sir Nigel Murray and Lady Sisek. One of the Murrays of Donncoill. This is my cousin Gillyanne Murray, daughter of Sir Eric and Lady Bethia Murray of Dubhlinn." She frowned when his expression changed from stunned surprise to hard anger in little more than a heartbeat.

"Cameron, wasnae it one of the Murrays who . . ." began Donald.

"Aye, it was a Murray," Cameron growled as he grabbed Avery by one slim arm and yanked her to her feet. "Do ye ken one certain Sir Payton Murray, mistress?"

"He is my brother," she replied, wondering what Payton could possibly have done to so enrage this man. She leaned away from him, feeling a sharp stab of fear when he finally smiled a cold, hard smile.

"Mayhap old Bearnard has indeed fully repaid his debt to me."

"My family and Gillyanne's will pay ye verra weel to return us safely to our homes."

"Oh, aye, they will certainly pay. 'Tis clear that fate smiles upon me at last. I am given one lass to ransom, and some fool I bested at dice has paid me with the sister of the slinking, cowardly bastard who raped my sister."

Avery gaped at the man, stunned by his insulting accusation; then pure rage swept over her. She called him a foul name, balled up one small fist, and punched him in the mouth. He bellowed a curse, but her attack and his lack of preparation caused him to stumble backward. A small stool caught him sharply in the back of his calves. He fell backward, taking her down with him. Avery landed on top of him so hard she felt winded, but she did not hesitate to grab his thick hair in both hands and bang his head against the floor. She hung on until the grip he had on her wrists grew too painful to bear, then abruptly released him. He let go of her to rub his abused head and she took quick advantage of her freedom. Even as she started to her feet, she punched him in the face again. She leapt to her feet and started to run, but he grabbed her skirts, yanking sharply.

A curse escaped Avery as she hit the floor hard. She quickly turned onto her back and, seeing that he was moving to try and pin her down with his body, she kicked him in the face. He cursed but kept on coming. Twisting, kicking, and pummeling him with her fists, she did her utmost to prevent him from pinning her to the floor.

Out of the corner of her eye, Avery saw a flash of

movement. A moment later, Gillyanne was on the man's back, her thin arms wrapped tightly around his neck. Avery punched Sir Cameron yet again as Gillyanne struggled to yank his head back.

"Donald!" Sir Cameron bellowed. "Get this hellborn child off me!"

It did not take Donald long to pull the tiny, cursing Gillyanne off Sir Cameron. It took even less time for Sir Cameron to firmly pin Avery down. She glared at him even as she realized that he had obviously done all he could not to seriously hurt her. That was a revelation she could ponder later, she decided.

"My brother is no rapist," she snapped.

"My sister says he is," Cameron replied in a cold, tight voice as he yanked her to her feet, her wrists held tightly in one big hand.

"And ye heard that false claim all the way here where ye serve these murdering swine, the DeVeaux?"

The way she said the name "DeVeau," as if it were the most heinous of curses, interested him, but Cameron decided he would have to wait to satisfy his curiosity about that. "My cousin Iain, who acts as laird of Cairnmoor in my stead, sent a runner to tell me the news. It has taken me a fortnight to clear myself of all obligation, but I am finally able to go home to deal with the matter."

Suddenly, Avery recalled where she had recently heard the name MacAlpin. She had read it in the last letter sent from home. Her mother had referred to "a small confusion" that needed to be cleared away between the MacAlpins and the Murrays. Since her mother had then gently hinted that she and Gillyanne might wish to linger with her French cousins, Avery had been writing back to ask exactly what "a small confusion" was when the attack by the DeVeaux had come. Now she knew and now she fully understood her mother wanting her and

Gillyanne to stay where they were. The rape of a laird's kinswoman was a serious crime, one that led to bloody battles over offended honor, one that could easily lead to a long, deadly feud.

"Have ye e'er met my brother or any of my family?" she demanded.

"I met Sir Balfour Murray at court once," Cameron replied as he dragged her over to the bed and picked up a set of wrist manacles from atop a large chest.

Diverted for a moment, Avery looked at him as he manacled her to the thick wooden bedpost. "Manacles at your bedside? Have trouble keeping the lasses in your bed, do ye?" She heard Donald gasp and saw a slight flush rise and fall beneath Cameron's dark skin, then wondered if it was particularly wise to so enrage her captor.

"I bought them to take back to Cairnmoor, for they are stronger yet kinder than the ones we use there," he spat out between clenched teeth, wondering why he felt compelled to explain himself to the impertinent woman.

She just shrugged and set her mind back on the crime he accused her brother of. "And just where was my brother supposed to have committed this heinous crime against your sister and your clan?"

"At court. Iain and my aunt took my sister there to try and arrange a marriage for her."

"And why wasnae this trouble sorted out there where the king himself may have aided in the settling of it?"

"Because my sister didnae say anything until they had all returned to Cairnmoor. They pressed her to accept a match with Sir Malcolm Cameron, but she kept refusing. Finally, she told them that she could marry no mon for your brother had stolen her chastity. If that was nay crime enough, she believes he has left her with child. Iain tried to settle the matter quickly and peacefully, but your brother denies the charge and refuses to wed my sister.''

''Ye surely havenae met my cousin Payton, then,'' said Gillyanne. He doesnae need to steal anything from a lass.''

''Aye,'' agreed Avery. ''Why should a mon exert himself to steal something that is offered to him by so many others, willingly and often?''

''Oh? And why should a lass shame herself with such a lie?''

''I dinnae ken. I have ne'er met your sister.''

''And I think ye are blinded to the mon your brother is.'' He grabbed Gillyanne by the arm and started toward the door.

''Where are ye taking my cousin?'' Avery made an instinctive move to go after him and cursed when she was roughly yanked back by the manacle on her wrist.

''I am taking her to get clean. Come along, Donald. I will send someone with water for ye to bathe and a clean gown,'' he added, giving Avery a brief, contemptuous glance.

''How can I bathe and dress when I am chained?''

''Ye seem to be a clever lass. I am certain ye will think of something.''

Chapter Two

Avery looked at her gown as the two maids who had helped her bathe and dress hurried out of the room. It was a lovely deep-blue gown, or it had been until it was sliced open down one side in order to get it on around the heavy manacle on her wrist. The dark lacing used to close it back up detracted from the smooth beauty of the gown. She wondered where that barbarian Cameron had found something so pretty. If he had bought it to give to some lover or kinswoman, it was now too ruined for that, and Avery found a small measure of satisfaction in that.

Glaring at the heavy manacle closed around her wrist, she tried yet again to pull her hand free of it, wincing as the rough edges scratched her skin. The chain linking her wrist to the bedpost was not even as long as the bed itself. She would not be able to move around much. Avery smiled coldly. It was, however, quite long enough to wrap around that black-eyed rogue's neck. When her tormentor stepped into the room, she idly caressed the heavy links of the chain, imagining his face turning blue as they tightened around his throat. She knew she ought to be alarmed by her own bloodthirstiness, but she was too furious to care.

"Where is Gillyanne?" she demanded when she did not see her cousin or the young squire return with Sir Cameron.

"I left her with the women," Cameron replied as he yanked off his shirt and moved toward a table where a large bowl of water stood.

"What women?"

"There are a few women who travel with my men."

"Camp fodder? Ye left a young lass with camp fodder?"

"They arenae whores. Two are wives and the other two will probably soon be made wives."

"Weel, I want her with me."

"Ah, me, I fear I cannae oblige you."

Avery watched him wash up and wished her chain was longer so that she could draw close enough to kick him. He sounded almost sweet, almost believably regretful, but the sneer was there to hear, whispering beneath the false courtesy. She did not think she had ever met anyone who made her so very eager to do them harm.

"She will be frightened and worried about me." Avery could tell by the look he sent her way as he dried off that she had failed to rouse any sympathy in him for a child.

"The women will pamper her. They were delighted to have her join them."

Cameron watched her closely as he sat on the edge of the bed and yanked off his boots. There was no doubt that she was furious. Her golden eyes were molten from the heat of her fury. Her small, long-fingered hands were so tightly clenched, the knuckles gleamed white. If she had a dagger she would cut his throat.

He moved to snuff out the candles, then went to lie down on the huge bed. Crossing his arms beneath his head, he glanced across the width of the bed to see her still standing there. Only one branch of candles remained lit, and they were on his side of the bed. The light from them made her eyes gleam despite the shadows she stood in. It only added to the feral air that clung to the girl. Then he looked over her slender body, saw how her gown was laced up the side, and almost smiled.

"Come to bed," he ordered.

"This bed? Beside you?" She shook her head. "Nay, I think not."

"Fine." He closed his eyes. "Stand there all night, glaring helplessly. I care not and it matters not."

The word *helplessly* made her snarl. If her chain were a little longer she could use that extra length as a mace to beat him. Avery savored the image for a moment, then sighed. Even if she had enough chain to flail him with, it would not work. She doubted Cameron would just lie there and let her beat him senseless.

What truly annoyed her was that he was right to call her helpless. At the moment, she was. He was also right to think it nothing but foolishness to stand there all night, but she heartily wished she could do it. There was no hint of the ravisher about him, but Avery knew how quickly a man could change from friendly to threatening.

Slowly she sat down on the floor and leaned against the side of the bed. Her head rested against a down-filled mattress, a luxury that surprised her. She idly wondered if it was his or if his hosts, the DeVeaux, had become so rich they could afford such pampering of their hired swords. It was tempting to crawl up on the bed, to sink her battered body into the soft folds of that mattress, but she fought the temptation. It would be the height of folly to crawl into bed beside a man she did not know, and one who felt he had a righteous grievance against her family.

She frowned and briefly peeked at his long body stretched out on the bed. He had not said how he intended to use her to gain that revenge that he felt was so just. Since he believed her brother had raped his sister, it was quite possible he thought to repay that insult in kind. Yet he made no move to touch her despite the fact that they were alone and she was chained to the bed.

Just the thought of someone accusing Payton of rape made Avery angry all over again. The fact that this fool believed such a tale made her positively furious. He could be excused in some way, she supposed, since the accusation came from his sister. However, before he dragged her into some act of revenge, he at least ought to make certain that the revenge was truly deserved.

And just what form was that revenge going to take, she wondered. The more she watched him, the less she thought him a man who would stoop to rape. He certainly looked big, dark, and dangerous, yet she felt no sense of impending peril. Avery hoped she was not allowing herself to be fooled or beguiled by his handsome face. If she relaxed her guard too much, she could be too slow to save herself if she proved wrong about him.

"What do ye intend to do to me?" she demanded, no longer able to silently endure the confusion of her own thoughts, and in desperate need of a few answers, no matter how chilling they might be.

Cameron opened one eye and looked at her. Sitting as she was, her face barely topped the edge of the bed. Despite the very adult look of anger on her face, she looked young, delicate, even appallingly innocent. There was a part of him that was thoroughly disgusted by what he was planning. There was also a part of him that was so strongly attracted to her fey beauty that it urged him onward with his plan, ruthlessly arguing away each newly born twinge of doubt. Revenge and desire combined too well to ignore or resist. And, he told himself in an attempt to soothe a pang of guilt, he would not hurt her. He would treat her far more kindly than many another would, given the same circumstances.

"I intend to seduce you," he answered, a little piqued when her expression of astonishment slowly changed to one of amusement.

"Do ye now?" she drawled. "And ye being such a braw, handsome laddie, ye expect me to just swoon at your big feet?"

He resisted the urge to glance down at his maligned feet. "Nay at my feet, lass, and I would prefer ye to be sensible."

"And I would prefer ye dead, but we cannae all get what we wish for, can we?"

"Such violence. A wee lass like yourself shouldnae be so quick to promise mayhem and murder."

"Add mutilation, for I am a wee bit inclined to that too."

" 'Tis clear ye need to be tamed. Someone has let ye run too wild. Ye snarl and hiss at me now, but I will soon have ye purring."

"Such arrogance."

Avery squeaked with surprise when he suddenly yanked on her chain. She struggled valiantly, but he still managed to drag her up onto the bed. When she found herself at his side, she tried to punch him in the face again, but he easily pinned her to the bed.

"Truth, my wee cat," he said, almost smiling as she glared at him.

"I am nay such a weakling or such a slut that I will bend to your wants with but a kiss and a stroke. Nay, especially not when 'tis meant only to shame my brother."

Avery decided the man was far too beguiling when he smiled, despite the fact that it was an annoyingly arrogant expression.

"Your brother shamed me and he wasnae gentle when he did it."

"E'en if Payton did as ye claim, which he did not, could not, and would not, it isnae your shame. It isnae a shame at all, except that of the bastard who committed the horror."

"My sister is nay longer chaste," he snapped.

"Are you?" Avery was not sure how it was possible, but she felt like laughing at his astonished expression. She knew instinctively that few ever saw that expression on his face.

" 'Tis nay the same," he said, beginning to think her thoughts were as odd as her looks.

Avery released a soft snort of pure contempt. "So speaks one of a breed who works so hard to steal a lass's chastity only to then condemn her for giving it up. And to speak of shame when a poor lass has had it ripped from her through nay fault of her own is the height of injustice."

There was a lot of truth in what she said, but what interested Cameron more was the anger behind her words. "This subject stirs a heat in you. I wonder why?"

"My cousin was brutally beaten and raped. Gillyanne's older sister Sorcha. Some of her father's enemies caught her and another cousin of mine. They beat and raped poor Sorcha and intended to do the same to my cousin Elspeth ere my Uncle Eric, Uncle Balfour, and Fither stopped them. Sorcha is soon to be a nun. Aye, and kenning the horror of such a crime, do ye really believe my brother would then inflict it upon another?"

Cameron had to wonder, but he did not say so. "Simply kenning someone who suffered such an insult doesnae mean the mon would e'erafter be unable to commit it himself. And, mayhap my sister miscalls it. Mayhap it was more seduction than rape, or she simply waited too long to cry nay. It matters not. He stole my sister's innocence and refuses to restore her lost honor by wedding her. So I shall have your innocence in penalty.''

"How romantic," she said, the sneer clear to hear in her husky voice. "I feel near to swooning from the power of your sweet flatteries and gentle wooing." She fluttered her eyelashes at him.

It surprised him, but Cameron came very close to laughing. Not only should he not find anything Sir Payton's sister had to say amusing, but he was not a man given to a lightness of humor. Lady Avery was so small and lithe, he did not dare rest his full weight upon her, but kept himself raised slightly on his forearms, yet she tried to flay him with words, threatened him, and physically assaulted him every chance she got.

Glancing down at her mouth, he decided he also wanted to kiss her. Her full lips were tightened a little in annoyance, but they still strongly tempted him. As he started to lower his mouth to hers, he felt her tense, saw her beautiful eyes start to widen, and knew she had guessed his intent.

"Dinnae e'en think about it," she said, pleased with the hard, cold tone of her voice, for she did not feel either at the moment—did, in fact, feel almost eager to taste his kiss.

"Ah, but I *am* thinking about it." He brushed his lips over hers, felt her bare her teeth, and warned, " 'Twould be verra unwise to bite me." He rested his full weight on her, firmly securing her beneath him, and captured her face between his hands. "I but mean to assuage my curiosity."

Before she could say anything, he covered her mouth

with his. Avery fought to ignore the warm, soft feel of his lips, fought to still the slow heat seeping through her veins as he gently nibbled at her lips. When she pressed her lips together to refuse the prodding of his tongue, he nipped her bottom lip. Despite all her efforts not to, she gasped, and his invasion was complete. One stroke of his tongue was enough to kill her plan to bite him. Avery found herself in a desperate battle against her own swiftly rising desire.

Avery was suddenly glad that she was pinned so firmly to the bed. She did not want this dark marauder to know how much she wished to rub her body against his. Or how she ached to touch his smooth, dark skin, to feel the warmth of his strong back and broad chest beneath her fingers. Or how her fingers also itched to be buried in his thick black hair, its rich softness tempting her as it brushed against her face. Avery just wished she could hide how her breath had quickened, how her heart beat faster, and how her mouth had softened so welcomingly beneath his.

As her passion soared, so did her fear. Avery did not understand. The man intended to dishonor her then toss her back to her family, hoping they would all feel her shame. He accused and insulted her brother, thus her family and her clan. He was a complete stranger to her, a man who had accepted her as payment for a wager. She should feel nothing except perhaps, disgust and fear. Instead, one kiss and she was inflamed. She wanted to tear off the soft leather loincloth he wore, wanted to touch and kiss every strong inch of him, wanted him inside her with a fierceness that made her womb ache.

When he finally lifted his head, she kept her eyes closed. Her mother had always teased her father about how easily she could read his lustful thoughts in his eyes. Avery had her father's eyes and strongly feared Sir Cameron would

be able to read her passion there. She winced faintly when
he grasped her chin firmly in one big hand, but still she
did not open her eyes.

"Look at me, Avery," Cameron demanded, not surprised to hear the husky thickness of his voice.

It astonished Cameron to feel so keenly alive with need,
his body throbbing with an unrelieved hunger. There was
nothing about Avery Murray that should stir his desire.
She was too slender, too impertinent, and too emotional.
Yet he wanted her with a need stronger than he had ever
felt before. The excuse that he had been celibate so long
any female body would do, rang hollow in his ears. She
called to something deep within him and he wanted to
see if she felt any hint of the same. He already knew that
her eyes revealed her feelings, and he was eager to look
into them. The fact that she was pressing them closed so
firmly her brow wrinkled only made him all the more
determined.

"Open your eyes, lass," he ordered again.

"I cannae," she replied. "I have swooned from an
excess of disgust."

Cameron would have deeply felt the sting of that insult
except for the fact that her voice was as thick and husky
as his own. She was clearly going to be stubborn, however.
A little subterfuge was definitely called for. He shifted a
little, easing his weight off her body just slightly, and
looked toward the door.

"Ah, Donald," he said, watching Avery closely, "why
have ye brought the wee lass back here?"

"Gillyanne?" Avery whispered, but, even as she
opened her eyes to look, she knew she had been tricked.
"Ye wretched, cunning bastard," she muttered as he held
her chin tightly, refusing to let her turn away from his
gaze.

Triumph sparked through Cameron's veins as he saw

the way her eyes glowed with the heat of desire. They also glittered with fury, although he was not sure if she was angry at him or herself. He expected it was some of each. It was easy to understand that the very last thing little Avery Murray would wish to feel for him was passion. In truth, although he savored the depth of the desire he felt and looked forward to heartily feeding that hunger, he was a little dismayed himself. Such a fierce, swiftly fired passion could easily become a complication he did not need or want. It would not change his plans, but it might be wise to practice some caution.

"Aye, that I am," he agreed almost cheerfully. "I am also the mon ye desire. Why not just give in now, lass?"

That display of mind-numbing arrogance nearly made Avery choke. Of course she desired him, although it galled her to admit it even to herself. He was an extraordinarily handsome man: tall, strong, and just a little dangerous. And there was a good chance that, as her brother Payton would so crudely put it, she was ripe. One also had to consider the possibility that the man was a very good kisser, skilled at turning a lass's mind to heated gruel. That he would even mention her mindless, traitorous desire for him or assume she would just give in without a whimper was what was so infuriating. Did he truly believe himself to be so compelling or her to be so weak?

"Why dinnae ye just crawl back under that rock ye slithered out from?" she said in a voice so sweet that she was surprised it did not make her teeth ache.

"And to think that is the same mouth I just tasted such a sweet welcome in."

"Ye delude yourself."

"Nay, but I think ye wish to delude yourself."

Cameron rolled off her, fighting his reluctance to leave the warm softness of her body. He sprawled on his back and crossed his arms beneath his head. A small grin fleetingly shaped his mouth when he heard her shift as far away from him as the bed would allow. He noticed she did not get off.

When he found himself regretting that he and little Avery had met under such circumstances, he cursed to himself. Those were dangerous thoughts. Not only could it make him hesitate in seeking justice and retribution, but he could easily begin to forget all that had made him choose celibacy. He had learned the hard lessons about the treachery of women, and he was not about to let some skinny lass with eyes like a cat make him forget them. He would soon end his long-endured celibacy, but he would never again let passion make him a fool.

Avery settled herself so close to the edge of the bed that the smallest of movements could easily send her plummeting to the floor. She hoped Sir Cameron was not a restless sleeper. Sheltering her gaze beneath her lowered lashes, she looked at the man who so effortlessly set her blood afire.

The dark look on his face made her frown. She did not really think he was sulking because she did not immediately succumb to his charms. In truth, she had given him an embarrassingly strong indication that she was very seducible. He should be looking annoyingly smug. Most men would be if they foresaw such an easy conquest. Instead, he looked as if he had just bitten into a very sour apple.

Her eyes widened slightly as she wondered if he found the sudden passion that flared between them as worrisome as she did. It certainly frightened her, if only because of how he meant to use it against her. It was too strong, too overwhelming, thus very difficult to fight. For her it signaled possible defeat. For him it could do the same, if in a different way. Surely it would be difficult to keep his mind and heart fixed upon revenge if his desire ran too hot.

For one brief moment, she contemplated using this fierce passion against him, trying to turn possible defeat into a weapon. Then she told herself not to be such a complete idiot. That sort of game required skill and knowledge, neither of which she had. Although she was not ignorant of what occurred between men and women and had even gathered a few facts from her brothers and cousins, she had not even kissed a man before this dark laird had captured her. A few practice kisses from her male cousins was the limit of her experience, and none of them had stoked a fire in her belly. Avery sighed and tried to get comfortable as she told herself to stay with her plan of hard resistance.

"If ye dinnae wish to sleep now, we could always return to our previous game," drawled Cameron.

"I dinnae think so, fool," she snapped. "I have a weak stomach."

"Ye really should study your opponent more closely ere ye whet your tongue on his hide."

"Is that a threat?"

"It could be."

"My, I am all a-tremble."

"Dinnae push me too hard, lass."

"Or what? Ye will hurt me?" She glared over her shoulder at him, a little pleased to catch the brief look of consternation on his face before he could hide it. "Ye have chained me, insulted my clan, and plan to dishonor me in some misguided attempt to avenge yourself against my brother. Pardon me if further threats and growls now fail to move me."

Cameron stared at her straight, slender back. There really was nothing he could say to that hard truth, so he remained silent. As he closed his eyes, he decided he was going to have to think of some new way to intimidate the woman. He would give some long, hard thought to some more creative and alarming threats first thing in the morning.

Chapter Three

"Avery!"

Gillyanne's call was enough to distract Avery from glaring at Cameron's broad back as he walked away from her. Although she was pleased to see her little cousin so obviously hale and unafraid, it only lessened her fury a little. For two days she had been chained to the bed, and now she was tied around the wrists and lashed to his saddle. If this was how she was to be treated, by the time she got to Scotland she would probably not care if her clan came to Cairnmoor and slaughtered every last MacAlpin there. In fact, she would probably cheer them on.

"Ye are weel, Gillyanne?" she asked her cousin, pleased to see the way Gillyanne glared at the ropes, then turned that look of fury upon Cameron. Even though the girl was too young and too small to help, it was nice to have someone on her side.

"Aye," Gillyanne replied. "The women coddle me, although they wouldnae let me come to see you ere now.

I think they would do almost anything for me save go against Sir Cameron's orders. The men, too. Although none have said so directly to me, I did chance to overhear a few mutterings which revealed not all of his lairdship's people agree with his plan. They are all verra keen to make Payton suffer, however.''

"He didnae do it."

"Ye need not plead his innocence to me. I ken it. He was one of the few amongst our cousins and brothers who would ne'er e'en redden our backsides no matter how we lasses tormented him. A mon who willnae e'en do that when ye fill his fine boots with pig dung isnae a mon who would hurt any woman.''

Avery grinned. "So that was you, was it?"

"Aye, his teasing had made me verra angry that day." She briefly shared a laugh with Avery, then scowled at the rope around Avery's slender wrists. "How fare you?"

"Weel enough. This enrages me," Avery nodded at her bonds, "but see how he has wrapped silk about my wrists beneath the rope? For all his black looks and growling, 'tis clear he will do his best not to really hurt me.''

"He means to seduce and shame you."

"Aye, there is that. He hasnae done so yet, if that is what troubles you."

"It did. Weel, all ye have to do is hold firm until our family can save us."

So simple, Avery thought, and she sighed. Cameron took every chance he could to touch her, tease her senses, stir her with heated words, and steal kisses. The fact that she had little will to fight off those kisses worried her more than she could say. At the moment, only her fury over being chained or tied gave her the strength to push him away. If Cameron ceased to bind her, that anger could lessen, and thus so would her ability to fight the temptation of the man.

"I will tell ye true, cousin, I am nay sure I can fight for that long." She smiled sadly at Gillyanne's look of shock.

Gillyanne cleared her throat and said, "He is a verra handsome mon."

"Oh, aye, verra handsome, though he is as dark as sin. And sin is what he tempts me to."

"Ye are nearly nineteen. Ye must have been tempted before and turned aside from it."

"Nay, I fear not."

"Do ye love him?"

"Gillyanne, the mon has chained me to a bed, tied me to his horse, and wants to use me to strike a hard blow at my family and drag poor Payton into a marriage he does not want. I would be a fool to love him."

"Not completely. He is wrong, but he does nay more than many another would do, believing what he does. And, 'tis clear he willnae wrest what he wants from you. So, if nay love, then ye are in lust."

"It would seem I am." She echoed Gillyanne's sigh.

Gillyanne patted Avery on the shoulder. "Ye can only do your best. I willnae fault ye if ye weaken. And considering how often our brothers and cousins weaken, they would deserve a sound thrashing if they faulted you." She shared a brief grin with Avery, then grew serious again. " 'Twould seem to me that ye must fight as hard as ye can, but dinnae fret if ye lose the fight. Mayhap ye may e'en find a way to take the sting out of the reasons why he means to bed you. And, we both ken that, some day, he will learn that his sister has lied."

"Aye, and then he will wish to do the *honorable* thing," Avery grumbled.

"Weel, if by then ye are in love as weel as in lust, 'twould nay be such a bad thing."

"It would depend upon what else he felt. Ah, and the brute returns."

Cameron caught the identical glares the two small Murray females gave him and nearly grinned. They had more spirit than some men he knew. If they but had the strength and height of a man, he would be in very serious trouble. Both of them looked far too eager to hurt him.

"Go back to the women," he ordered Gillyanne, and he bit back a laugh over the way she muttered some very colorful curses as she obeyed him. "When that lass finishes growing, she will cause some mon a great deal of trouble."

"Good," Avery said. "She will be a rich prize, and one should ne'er get one of those too easily."

"As easily as I got you?"

"True, I was tossed at your feet. Ye gained the weapon to use against my family verra easily indeed. Howbeit, ye will have to fight long and hard to wield it."

"Will I?"

He stepped closer, caging her between himself and his mount. The nearness of her was enough to heat his blood. If he read the flicker of warmth in her beautiful eyes correctly, it was enough to stir her as well. He prayed he was reading that look right.

The last betrayal he had suffered, the one that had caused him to retreat from the game of love, had left him uncertain of his ability to judge women. He had thought, in all his former arrogance, that he could read a woman's heart, could know that he and he alone stirred her desire. Time and time again he had found, not love, but faithlessness and betrayal, until it no longer shocked or surprised him, until he found himself turning his back on all women. What made his doubts even stronger now was the fact that Avery Murray was not like any other woman he knew. Was that heat in her eyes desire, or the urge to gut him like a pig? In Avery's case, he suspected it could easily be a bit of both.

"Aye, my bonny-faced cur, ye will," she snapped, furious with the weakness he had exposed within her—that blind, unthinking response of her body to his.

"And yet ye are already compelled to tantalize me with sweet flatteries."

Avery was torn between an urge to laugh and one to slam her knee into his groin. The urge to laugh was what troubled her, almost as much as her errant passions did. Humor, subtle or raucous, tart or sweet, had always appealed to her. She did not need anything else about the man to appeal to her. Before she could turn that anger against herself on him and assault him with a few harsh opinions, however, he tossed her up into the saddle and gracefully mounted behind her.

Cameron had barely nudged his mount into motion when Avery realized this was going to be a torturous journey. His big, strong body was pressed hard against her back. She was nestled between his thighs like a lover. His long arms encircled her as he grasped the reins. It was an embrace, and one she would have to suffer for hours at a time. Each movement of his horse caused their bodies to rub together in some way. They had barely ridden out of the gates of the DeVeau keep before she began to suffer from the potent effects of his nearness.

She tried to pull away. He pulled her back, holding her close in a firm yet painless grip. She tried to remain stiff, unyielding, but not only did that make her uncomfortable, it made her seat so precarious she could easily send them both tumbling out of the saddle. The image of Cameron gracelessly falling off his horse and sprawling in the mud was a pleasant one, but she could not ignore the danger to herself. She was lashed to the saddle by a rope that also bound her wrists together. She could all too easily

join him in his fall and find herself dragged along the
ground by a panicked mount. That would certainly steal
some of the joy out of Cameron's humiliation, she thought,
almost smiling at her own fanciful musings.

"I am glad to see ye are in a better mood," Cameron
said, catching the glimpse of a smile on her face.

"Aye, I was just thinking of how fine ye would look
facedown in the mud," she replied sweetly.

He quickly altered a chuckle into a cough. The woman
needed no encouragement of her audacity. Despite the
softness of the body pressed close to his, he realized there
was finely honed steel shaping that delicate backbone.
Even if he was right about the desire he could stir within
her, she was right to say he faced a long, hard battle to
gain anything from it. Cameron mused that, even if he
brought her to her knees with the sharp ache of wanting,
she would probably just try to crawl away.

"If I fall, ye fall with me," he said, not sure he meant
just a tumble from his horse.

"I ken it. 'Tis why I willnae try to kick ye out of the
saddle."

"Such admirable restraint."

"I thought so. Ye are keeping a close watch on your
back, arenae ye?"

"Aye, e'en though ye are weaponless and in front of
me."

"I meant, are ye watching for the DeVeaux? 'Twould
nay surprise me if the murdering oafs tried to take back
the blood money they paid you. Or decided they didnae
want ye talking about all ye saw and did whilst in their
keep."

"So, ye worry about my safety now."

"Such vanity. My wee cousin rides with us. I should
like to see her get back to Scotland unharmed. And," she

added in a hard voice, "if anyone is to gut ye, 'tis I who should have that privilege."

"Ye are a hard woman, Avery Murray." He gave an exaggerated sigh, then abruptly asked, "Why do ye so hate the DeVeaux?"

"They are murdering swine. They may have left many of my kinsmen dead."

"Mayhap, but I think the hatred ye bear them is an old one, born long before this most recent crime."

For a moment Avery contemplated telling him it was none of his business, but only for a moment. The long feud between the DeVeaux and the Lucettes was no closely guarded secret. Neither was the trouble the DeVeaux had caused her family in the past. The telling of the tale might even insure that the DeVeaux never had a MacAlpin sword on their side again, no matter how rich a purse was offered, and that could only be a good thing. She was heartily glad that, for whatever reasons, Cameron and his men had not been part of this latest treachery.

"It began with my mother," she replied, "although the DeVeaux had not always left my kinsmen in peace before that. Nay, they have always preyed upon the weaker, those with less might and coin. For peace and gain, my mother was forced into marriage with Lord Michael DeVeau despite all the dark things said about him. All those dark tales were truth. He was a beast, brutal and completely faithless. One night my mother found him mutilated and with his throat cut. She ran."

"Why? Did she do it?"

Avery could hear no condemnation in his voice. Although she had not described the true horror of her mother's first marriage, what little she had said was obviously enough. So, too, would Cameron have some knowledge of what the DeVeau men were like.

"Nay," she answered, "though she kenned all would

think she had. She had threatened such dire acts. No one would heed her about the horrors of her marriage, and she had often said she would end the torment herself if need be. My father helped her flee to Scotland. She had already been running and hiding for a year all on her own. 'Twas finally shown that others had done the murder to avenge a woman he had brutalized, and my mother was finally free. The hatreds were set firm by then, however. The marriage didnae bring peace but intensified the feud, and not all of the DeVeaux believe Mother is really innocent. Mayhap they dinnae really care, just wish to have someone to hate and fight with.''

''And mayhap they didnae like having their kinsmon revealed as the monster he truly was.''

''Aye, 'tis possible. They also didnae like the fact that my mother inherited so much. 'Tis small compensation for all she endured, and 'tis hers by right, but the DeVeaux hate to give up anything.''

''E'en coin paid to mercenaries.''

''Aye.''

''Dinnae fear. I had already guessed that. Our backs are closely watched.''

Avery just nodded. She wished she had some idea of the fate of her kinsmen. From what little information she had gathered over the past two days, the slaughter had not been as great as it had appeared to be. She could only hope that someone would send word to her mother detailing just how dearly the DeVeau attack had cost her family. It could be months before she learned anything, but at least she might finally learn the truth. Avery prayed it would be good news, good enough to banish the lingering horror of that day from her dreams.

By the time they stopped for a midday rest, Avery felt fairly confident the DeVeaux would not be a problem. Sir Cameron MacAlpin, however, was proving to be a

very big one. Riding in his arms all morning had left her
all too aware of her own weakness. She ached. It took
more will than she thought it should not to turn to the
man and tell him she surrendered, to order him to hurry
and find some place private so that she could show him just
how thoroughly she had capitulated. Her only consolation
was that she was certain Sir Cameron suffered as well.
Pressed as close to him as she was for the whole ride,
she had been all too aware of the hard proof of his desire.
She hoped it crippled the oaf.

The moment her wrists were untied, she hurried away
to seek a moment of much-needed privacy. It was not
easy, but she strove to ignore the huge, hulking man
plodding along beside her. Wee Rob was her guard, and
if the flush upon his cheeks was any indication, he was
as embarrassed as she was. Avery thought it a little odd
that this would actually make her feel, if not exactly at
ease, at least not so deeply mortified.

Once done, she returned to the others and searched for
Gillyanne. She almost smiled when she finally saw her
cousin returning from the trees, having obviously suffered
the same need she had. There was a big man trailing after
Gillyanne as well, and her cousin looked furious. What
was truly amusing was that the tiny Gillyanne's guard
actually looked a little intimated by the girl. It was not
amusing, however, to see that any attempt at escape would
require eluding two very large men.

"Are ye intending to listen to every wee word I say,
too?" Gillyanne snapped at her guard when she reached
Avery's side.

Avery could not completely repress a soft laugh when
both men hastily stepped back several paces. "They are
only doing as their laird commanded them to, Gillyanne."

"I ken it," Gillyanne said, "which is why I endured
it like the lady I am and didnae beat the fool o'er the

head with the first stick I could set my hands on.'' She took several deep breaths, then demurely clasped her hands in front of her skirts. ''There, I am calm now.''

''Does that truly work?''

''Sometimes, when I am not truly verra angry. As ye said, 'tis nay Colin's fault. Howbeit, that dark devil who ties ye to beds and horses best nay get too close for a while. So, how fare ye?''

''Weel enough,'' Avery replied as she hooked her arm through Gillyanne's and began a leisurely stroll, almost smiling when she heard their reluctant guards fall into step behind them.

''Truly? I thought ye might be a wee bit troubled. Just a sense I had.''

''And your senses are far too keen.''

''Aunt Maldie is verra pleased about that. Ye are nay without your own gifts. 'Twas ye who sensed the danger coming the day the DeVeau men attacked.''

''A lot of good that did.''

''We are alive. If we had been caught completely unaware, we may weel have perished in that first bloody onslaught. Aye, and our kinsmen were warned. Truth, it was too late for them to be completely readied, but, mayhap a few more had sword in hand than would have if ye hadnae sounded the alarm. E'en as we ran, we could hear the benefit of your warning.''

''We could?'' Avery was more than eager to hear that she may have been able to save a few lives.

''Aye. The first sound we heard was the clash of swords, nay the screams of the dying.''

''That followed.''

''Sadly, aye, it did. But that sound of sword hitting sword, chilling though it is, told us that someone was ready to face the DeVeaux, if only to hold them back so that others might flee and survive. Dinnae fret so. There is naught we can do but pray for the souls of the dead, and that there werenae too many of them.''

"I do so. Often," Avery murmured.

"We must fix our thoughts upon our current troubles."

"Aye. How to keep Payton free and unharmed."

"True," agreed Gillyanne, but then she fixed Avery with a steady gaze. "And how to ease your troubled heart."

"My heart is troubled, is it?"

"Aye. The lusting is bad, isnae it."

"Oh, aye." Avery shook her head. "My innards are knotted with it. My only consolation is that I believe his are, too." She exchanged a brief grin with Gillyanne, then grew serious again. "I dinnae believe I have the strength to fight it for verra long."

"Oh, dear."

"Aye, just so."

"Then we must set our minds to thinking of a way to steal some of the sweetness of victory from him."

Avery nodded. "I have already begun. One thing is to be sure to make Payton ken that my chastity wasnae stolen; it was given away freely and willingly. It will ease whate'er guilt Payton may feel."

"That will certainly lessen some of the bite of Sir Cameron's plans."

Silently cursing the way her pulse increased at the mere sight of the man, Avery watched as Cameron approached her and Gillyanne. It was understandable in a way. He was, after all, an extraordinarily fine-looking man. Somehow she had to turn what could easily prove to be a weakness into a strength, what could be made into an humiliation into a source of pride. It was not going to be easy, especially when his every look or touch turned her mind to warm gruel.

"But, first," she murmured so that only Gillyanne could

hear her, "I mean to make that mon ache, to make him want so badly that revenge is the last thing on his wee mind when I finally give in. I mean to drive him to the verra brink of madness."

Cameron's steps faltered a little when both Murray lasses suddenly smiled brilliantly at him. They were tiny, dainty visions of beauty, their smiles warm and real. Their unusual eyes sparkled delightfully with laughter. A man should feel pleased and a little vain to receive such looks. As he took Avery by the arm and led her to his horse, Cameron wondered why those pretty smiles gave him the strong urge to don every piece of armor he could lay his hands on.

Chapter Four

"We have become complacent, Gillyanne," Avery said as she and her cousin strolled around the edges of the MacAlpin camp.

"Have we?" Gillyanne paused briefly to study a little blue flower. " 'Tis a fine time of the year to be complacent," she said as she resumed her pace at Avery's side.

"True. Howbeit, I believe we have been lulled into forgetting we are prisoners—and Cameron's plans for Payton."

" 'Tis hard to recall such unpleasantness when spring warms the air. I am surprised ye can e'er forget it all when he binds you all the time."

"When 'tis done so lightly and with such care nay to harm me, I find I become accustomed, that my anger o'er the treatment fades. And that is what troubles me. I walk about in such a haze of lust I become oblivious to the reasons we ride with the MacAlpins."

"I thought your plan was to sink *him* into a haze of lust. 'Tis what ye said three days ago."

Avery sighed: "I believe I become too confused to ken if it is working. His temper is worsening, but is that because I torment him, or is he but an ill-tempered mon? Is it unrequited lust that sours his mood, or is it that his grand plan for vengeance isnae working with the ease he thought it would?"

"I think 'tis unrequited lust. To be truthful, we should say unfulfilled lust, for 'tis nay unrequited, is it."

"Sadly, nay. In truth, I begin to fear it may run a great deal deeper than lust in me."

"Then ye can do what cousin Elspeth did."

"Chase him until he catches me?" Avery laughed with Gillyanne, then shook her head. "I dinnae have Elspeth's skill. I cannae just ken with one kiss that he is my mate. I think he might be. 'Twould explain the mindless lust that besets me so quickly. 'Twould explain how I can feel anything at all for him, considering how he plots to use me against my own brother. Of course, it doesnae really matter, does it? What he plans makes any future with him impossible."

"Not necessarily." Gillyanne shrugged. "The end to this adventure could be less dire than ye think. Ye must decide if ye wish to try and win all, to make him want ye above all things. Aye, no matter how I look at it, the path ye must tread isnae a smooth one, but every turn in it doesnae lead to failure and heartache."

"Mayhap not. Howbeit, I do think we are making things far too easy for our captors."

"I dinnae think we can escape, Avery."

"I hold out no great hope for that, either, but that doesnae mean we cannae try." She met Gillyanne's gaze for a moment, and then they both smiled.

"Should we be clever or just bold for the first try?"

asked Gillyanne, glancing back at their guards. "Wee Rob and Colin are a fair distance behind us and caught firm in an argument."

"Weel, then, let us just be bold this time. On the count of three?" Gillyanne nodded and grabbed the front of her skirts, ready to lift them. Avery did the same as she counted, "One. Two. Three!" She bolted, not at all surprised that Gillyanne did the same, keeping close by her side as they ran.

Cameron cursed as a cry went up around the camp. He stuffed the map he and his cousin Leargan were studying back into his shirt even as he surged to his feet. The only thing that surprised him when he saw the Murray lasses trying to escape was how fast they could run.

"Curse Wee Rob and Colin," he muttered as he started to run. "I told them to watch those lasses closely."

"Ye cannae blame them completely," said Leargan, keeping pace at Cameron's side. "They are just wee lasses and they have been verra weel behaved."

"Which should have alerted us."

Leargan laughed. "Ye speak of them as if they are dangerous, cunning foes."

"Avery's mother managed to elude vengeful DeVeaux for a year, almost all on her own. Her father then managed to get them both out of France despite the huge rewards offered for their capture. Her cousin has just married one Sir Cormac Armstrong, a mon who managed to elude vengeful Douglases for two years or more."

"Jesu." Leargan was deeply impressed. "So, they may have learned a trick or two."

"Aye, and they are cursed fast on their feet, too. Ye follow the wee one."

"They are both wee."

"Go after Gillyanne. I will go after that other bundle of aggravation." Cameron ignored Leargan's laughter.

It enraged Cameron far more than he thought it ought, to see Avery running away from him. He suspected it was because he hated to think she was not as infected with blind lust as he was. Then he told himself not to let his own doubts blind him. She felt the need as sharply as he did, he was certain of it. And, perhaps, he thought, that was why she ran.

A grim smile curved his mouth as he chased her through the wood. He had no intention of letting her escape, not when he was so close to gaining what he craved. By the time they had stopped to camp for the night he had known that she was as twisted up with need as he was. Several times during the torturous ride, he had pulled a soft moan of want from her full lips, had made her shudder in his arms, and all with only the most subtle of touches. It was not thoughts of revenge that had him racing through the woods now, but a determination not to let the delight he was so close to gaining slip through his fingers.

Avery signaled to Gillyanne to veer to the right while she ran slightly to the left. They kept in sight of each other as they ran, but forced their pursuers to split up. Chancing a quick glance over her shoulder, she saw only two men: Cameron and his handsome cousin Leargan. If there were any others, they were lagging far behind.

Just as she began to think the game had been played long enough, for she was getting tired and Cameron was drawing nearer, she heard Gillyanne cry out. Avery immediately turned and ran straight for Leargan, who had caught hold of Gillyanne. She was briefly pleased when she saw how her sudden change of direction caused Cameron to stumble slightly before he could turn to follow.

Without hesitating, Avery hurled herself at Leargan. He cursed, let go of Gillyanne, and fell on his face.

Straddling his back, Avery grabbed hold of his dark hair and started to bang his head against the ground. When Gillyanne's cries of encouragement ended in a squeak, Avery stopped and looked around, not really surprised to see her cousin caught firmly by Cameron. Avery yanked Leargan's knife from its sheath. Tightly grabbing a hank of Leargan's hair, she yanked his head back and held his own knife against his throat.

"A trade?" she asked.

"Nay," Cameron replied. "Ye willnae hurt him."

"Are ye verra sure of that?"

"I hope ye are, cousin," Leargan muttered.

"Verra sure," Cameron replied. "Ye willnae hurt him, Avery, and ye willnae leave without this brat, either."

"Brat?" Gillyanne cried in outrage.

"Nay, I willnae." Avery sighed, released Leargan, and stood up.

Leargan stood up, brushed himself off, and held out his hand. "My knife, please."

Avery cursed softly and clapped it into his outstretched hand. When Gillyanne ran to her side, she took her cousin's hand in hers. She was not terribly concerned about punishment, although Cameron looked furious. He might lash her with angry words and secure her more firmly, but Avery realized she was completely confident that he would never physically hurt her.

"Did ye really think ye could escape?" Cameron asked as he grabbed her by the arm and started back to the camp.

"One can always dream," she murmured.

"And just where did ye think ye would go with no horses and no supplies?"

A good point, she mused, but she had no intention of letting him know she had only meant to plague him a little, even if that did leave her looking somewhat foolish.

"We thought we would throw ourselves upon the mercy of the nearest church."

"Aye," agreed Gillyanne. "We meant to claim sanctuary."

"Do ye really expect me to believe that?" Cameron cursed softly when both girls just shrugged. At the edge of the camp, they met up with the two guards and Cameron told the two red-faced men, "They are bonny and wee, but dinnae let that fool ye again." He shoved the two girls toward their guards. "They are cunning and more trouble than they are worth."

"Seek sanctuary?" Leargan said, laughter choking his voice as he and Cameron walked away.

"Wretched brats," grumbled Cameron. "They are up to something. They are too clever to think that escape could have worked. They kenned they would fail, which is why they fled empty-handed."

"Then why would they e'en try?"

"I wouldnae be surprised if 'twas done just to annoy me."

"Do ye think he has guessed our game?" Gillyanne asked Avery as they sat before Cameron's tent eating their evening meal.

"The thought that we merely try to annoy him may have crossed his mind," Avery replied, "but he willnae trust in that being the only reason. He will try to find some greater treachery behind it."

"He doesnae much trust women, does he?"

"He doesnae trust them at all."

"That doesnae bode weel if ye decide to try and win his heart."

"If he e'en has a heart to win," Avery grumbled.

"Oh, I think he does or ye wouldnae be having all this trouble. He just doesnae reveal it weel. Some men are like that."

"And some men dinnae wish to feel anything for any woman ever, and get verra good at locking up all feeling."

Gillyanne nodded, then frowned slightly. "But, he lusts after you."

"Lust cannae really be called a feeling, Gillyanne. Or rather, an emotion. 'Tis too easy for a mon to feel it for any woman. 'Tis nay from the heart is what I try to say. 'Tis nay from the mind or soul, either." She sighed. "Then again, it can sometimes become a crack in the wall a mon has built around his heart. But since I cannae see inside of Cameron to see if that crack widens, I must rely upon what I feel, and I am nay sure I can trust in that."

"I pray the mon I finally set my heart on is nay so hard to ken."

"He probably willnae be for you."

"Mayhap, although I have some difficulty sensing things if 'tis someone I ken weel or care about."

"Of course, for 'tis just when ye would like such a gift to be especially keen."

Gillyanne laughed and nodded. "Aunt Maldie says my gift may weel be working, 'tis just that I dare nay trust what I feel because my heart is involved. I think your heart is involved," she added softly.

Avery watched Cameron move around the camp talking to his men, and she sighed again. "Aye, I believe it is, yet I havenae e'en kenned the mon for a full week and he certainly isnae wooing me. It makes no sense. The only thing that keeps me from leaping on that mon in a lustful frenzy is the knowledge of how he means to use my weakness against my own family."

"A lustful frenzy?"

"Aye. There is nay other way to describe it." Avery watched Cameron walk off into the surrounding wood with his cousin and was not surprised at how her gaze remained fixed upon his taut, well-shaped buttocks, or how her palms itched to touch him there. "Several times today I wanted to kick him out of the saddle, but 'tis nay longer so that I can laugh at the oaf sprawled in the mud. Nay, I wanted him on the ground so that I could jump on him and start acting upon some of the crazed, heated thoughts which have tormented me."

"Then just do it."

"I ken we have talked of ways to take the sting from his plots of revenge if I do, but there is naught that can take the sting out of the fact that he beds me for revenge."

Gillyanne rolled her eyes. "Trust me, cousin. The verra last things that mon will be thinking when he finally beds down with you are Payton, his sister, and revenge. All ye need to do is make it verra clear that he isnae winning or taking; ye are giving. I dinnae mean ye should bare your heart's secrets to the oaf—just let him ken that ye are doing only what ye want and ye will ne'er let him use that against your brother or your clan. Now, he being a mon and as arrogant as the rest of the breed, he willnae believe ye can rob him of that weapon. Ye ken that ye can. Let that confidence guide you."

" 'Tis such a gamble," Avery murmured.

"Aye, but do ye want the prize ye can win bad enough to take it?"

"Oh, aye."

"So, how quickly do ye concede?"

"I cannae say. I believe I will torment him until I cannae take it any more." She laughed along with Gillyanne.

* * *

"They are laughing again," muttered Cameron, scowling at the two Murray lasses as he and Leargan returned to camp.

Leargan chuckled and shook his head. "They are unusual lasses."

"They are wretched brats who take great glee in making my life a pure torment."

"So, ye want her that badly, do ye?"

"I didnae say that."

"Ye didnae have to. Ye fair stink of it."

Cameron fought against the sudden whim to sniff himself and glared at Leargan. " 'Tis a good thing, isnae it. 'Twould be verra hard to get my revenge if the lass didnae stir me in any way."

"And ye willnae wait until ye can more closely study the situation at home, will ye?"

"My sister, my aunt, and Iain all tell the same tale. What difference would it make to hear it again, to wait until I am close enough to watch their lips move as they speak? Nay, Payton Murray will pay, and he will do right by my sister."

"And, if he does, will ye do right by his?"

"What?"

"Ye mean to seduce the mon's sister to force him to do right by your sister. If he does as ye wish, that still leaves one seduced lass without a husband. A lass who has done ye no wrong."

"I dinnae want a wife." Cameron resented the way Leargan had found the weak point in his plan.

"Yet ye dinnae accept that Sir Payton may not want one either. Ye are a contrary mon, cousin."

"Aye, and ye will soon be a mon weel covered in bruises if ye dinnae leave the matter alone." He nodded in satisfaction when Leargan said no more, yet he knew his cousin had not quit but had simply withdrawn from the argument for a while. "Ye take young Gillyanne back to the women," he ordered as they reached his tent.

The moment Leargan and Gillyanne had left, Cameron sat next to Avery and stared into the fire. He wanted to clear Leargan's words from his mind, but they refused to leave. There was that taint of unfairness to his plans. He could not deny that. He would demand Payton Murray restore his sister's honor with marriage, yet he would not offer the same. Telling himself such revenge was fair because Payton had refused to do what was right, and with his clan's full support, did not really ease that pinch of guilt. Yet he could not—would not—take a wife.

When Avery rose and went into the tent, he picked up the wineskin she had left behind and took a long drink. It was tempting to drink himself senseless. Not only would it kill his aching need for Avery, if only for a little while, but it would silence that nagging whisper of guilt. Unfortunately, yet another long day of travel faced him, and only a fool would try to face it suffering from the ill effects of a night of drinking.

Finally, when he felt Avery had been allowed enough privacy, he rose and entered his tent. The sight of her lying in his rough bed knotted his stomach with unquenched desire. He wanted to tear his clothes off, climb into that bed, and bury himself deep inside her. He wanted to touch and taste every slim inch of her golden body. He wanted to hear her cry out his name as her body trembled with release.

Not surprised to feel his heart pounding and his hands sweating, Cameron cursed and stripped down to his loin-cloth. He briefly washed up, crawled in beside her, and tied her wrist to his with a length of soft linen. Even in the darkness he could feel her glaring at him.

"Ye didnae really think ye could escape today, did ye?" he asked, shifting closer to her so that their sides were lightly touching. When he felt her tremble, he smiled grimly. He had no intention of suffering this torment alone.

"One must grab opportunity when it presents itself," she replied, cursing silently when she realized there was no room to move, that she had to endure the heady feel of his warm, strong body touching hers.

"Without food, water, blankets, or a horse?"

"Aye. We could have found most of what we needed as we traveled."

He ignored that boast. "And in a land filled with an old, powerful enemy?"

"It appears Scotland isnae exactly brimming o'er with friends and allies, either."

He rolled, pinning her beneath him. "I am not your enemy, Avery."

"Och, nay, of course not. How foolish of me. 'Tis friendship that has ye planning to shame me and use that against my clan."

"And if someone hurt one of your family, ye would forgive all and do naught but say a few prayers for his soul, would ye?"

"I wouldnae use the innocent to try and punish the guilty. Not that my brother is guilty."

Cameron sighed and kissed her. The way she so quickly and fiercely responded to him made him shake with need. Her nipples hardened, pressing against his chest and begging to be tasted. She arched against him, her whole lithe body revealing that she shared his passion. He was not surprised to find himself panting like a hard-run horse when he ended the kiss and raised himself up enough to stare down at her. There was some satisfaction in seeing that she was breathing just as hard. He knew he could take her now, that her own desire would betray her in his arms. It was madness to keep denying himself but he would do so. He wanted her to say "aye," needed her to be willing.

"How can ye keep denying what flames between us?" he asked, flopping onto his back at her side.

"What is between us is your need for revenge."

" 'Tis nay revenge that has me sweating and shaking like a mon with the ague. Or ye."

"Me? Nay. I am as cool and calm as a placid loch on a still summer's eve." She ignored his contemptuous snort of amusement "Ye willnae use me to hurt my kinsmen."

"Just one—Payton."

"I will fight as hard to save my brother as ye will to save your sister. Good sleep, Sir Cameron," she added quietly when he made no reply; then she struggled to cool her heated blood so that she could rest.

"Ye will give in, Avery," he said after several minutes. " 'Tis too strong to fight for long."

"Mayhap," she conceded, 'but I still willnae let ye use me against my brother."

Cameron could not believe how excited he got over the word *mayhap*. It was no concession. Yet, it was more than she had offered so far. Closing his eyes and forcing his body to calm itself, he reached out for sleep. On the morrow he would increase his efforts to break her will, press her until that *mayhap* became an aye. He just prayed that he did not drive himself completely mad in the process.

Chapter Five

Her hands were free. Avery could not believe it. It had been two nights since she and Gillyanne had made Cameron chase them down, and as she had expected, he had become more vigilant. He had also become more determined in his seduction. Those two nights had been long, torturous ones, filled with self-denial. The days had been just as bad. Both of them were exhausted from the fight. And that, Avery decided, was why she was sitting on his horse, her hands free of restraints. Cameron was obviously too tired and distracted to tie her up properly. She was glad she had not given up testing her bonds each time they were tied.

Avery looked around and finally saw Gillyanne standing near the other women. If she could get the girl's attention, they could make a run for it. Gillyanne knew how to mount swiftly, and this time they would have supplies. Avery wondered why she was just sitting there wondering about it and not already galloping toward Gillyanne. The answer to her hesitation could be summed up in one word, she thought in self-disgust: Cameron.

As if summoned by her thoughts, Cameron stepped up beside his horse. He put his hand on her leg and stroked her. The arrogant look upon his face, the gleam of expected victory in his eyes, gave Avery the impetus to move. She slowly smiled and wriggled her fingers at him. The look of total astonishment on his face was a delight to see. Then she kicked him in the face, sending him tumbling back onto the ground. Avery kicked the horse into a gallop even as she yelled Gillyanne's name. To her relief, her cousin responded immediately, and Avery only had to slow her pace a little to allow Gillyanne to leap up behind her. As they raced away, she could hear Cameron bellowing, and she laughed.

Cameron surged to his feet cursing loudly and viciously. It did not surprise him at all to see Avery control his huge stallion with an easy skill, or her cousin cleanly mount a horse on the move. He doubted anything those two did any more would surprise him, especially if it was something that would annoy him. Hoping he did not sound as crazed as he felt, he started bellowing orders, pleased to see Leargan already hurrying toward him with two saddled horses.

"Wasnae it ye who said they must be watched verra closely?" drawled Leargan as he and Cameron mounted the horses.

"One more word and I will cut your tongue out," Cameron snapped as he spurred his horse into a gallop.

Leargan ignored the threat as he kept pace with Cameron "I dinnae think ye will catch them. Your horse is the fastest amongst all we have, and the lasses show a true skill at riding."

"They dinnae ken the area, dinnae ken where to go."

"Mayhap not, but they merely have to stay out of reach and hide."

And that was just what Cameron feared. If the girls had no set destination then there was no way to know where they were going. That meant he would soon be reduced to tracking them—a slow process that gave them the advantage. Worse, he would not be surprised if they had learned ways to hide their trail. The Murray lasses had already revealed that they had skills that most well-bred lasses did not. He was determined, however, not to be defeated by a pair of skinny lasses, even if he had to trail the brats right up to the gates of Donncoill.

It was noon before Avery felt it was safe enough to take a rest. She and Gillyanne slid off the horse, both groaning softly. The small copse they had found was perfect, however. Shaded, cool, with a small brook trickling through it and plenty of fresh grass for the horse. Gillyanne helped her wipe the horse down, water it and tether it. Then they both collapsed beneath a tree. It was several moments before either of them had the strength to search the bags on the horse for some food and drink. To Avery's delight, she also found Cameron's map, and she studied it as she and her cousin nibbled on oatcakes and sipped at some wine.

" 'Tis hard to ken where to go when we dinnae ken where we are," Gillyanne murmured, slumping against the thick trunk of the tree and closing her eyes.

"True, but as soon as we find out where we are, this will be a great help." Avery relaxed next to her cousin.

"Do ye think Cameron will hunt us for verra long?"

"Longer than we may like. He is a stubborn oaf."

"And, we stole his horse."

Avery grinned. "Aye, we did that. Howbeit, I think he

will hunt us down mostly because he willnae be able to stomach being defeated by two wee lasses.''

Gillyanne nodded. ''That would sorely sting a mon's pride.''

''And Cameron has a lot of that.''

''I was a little surprised that ye were so quick to flee.''

''Nay that quick.'' Avery sighed. ''I hesitated. Then he gave me that look.''

''What look?''

''That arrogant *I ken I am winning* look. So, I kicked it off his face.''

She smiled faintly when Gillyanne giggled. ''So, this is all his own fault. If he had nay looked so cursed sure of himself, I would probably still be sitting there trying to convince myself to flee. There was a verra large part of me that wanted to stay right there, close to him. All I could think of was how, if I succeeded in escaping, I might ne'er see the mon again.''

''Dinnae sound so disgusted with yourself.'' Gillyanne patted Avery's hand. ''Considering your feelings for the mon, 'tis only natural ye wouldnae want to leave him, especially fearing that it might be forever. Payton would understand.''

''Aye, he would, but I am nay sure it would ease my guilt much. 'Tis sinful, but my greatest regret is that I didnae give in at least once ere I left him.''

'' 'Twould be mine.''

''Truly?''

''Truly. Such a fierce passion is a rare thing. Our parents have told us so. So has Elspeth. 'Tis what we all search for. That passion coupled with love. We want what our parents have. Ye could see a chance for it.'' Gillyanne winked at Avery. ''Try to soothe yourself by recalling that 'tis all Cameron's fault ye cannae try to see if that fierce passion is the seed of love.''

"It was in me," Avery whispered, fighting the urge to weep. "And aye, 'tis all that fool's fault. His sister's, too. Mayhap 'tis indeed best that we escape, for I could act verra rashly if I e'er have to meet Payton's accuser."

Avery stood up and brushed herself off. "Best we start on our way again. We can travel slowly now."

"Are ye certain?" Gillyanne asked as she followed Avery over to the horse.

"We havenae seen Cameron or Leargan for a long time. That means they must track us now and 'twill slow them down." Even as she mounted, Gillyanne quickly getting up behind her, Avery caught the glint of something through the trees. "Curse it, I cannae believe he has found us." A heartbeat later, Avery realized that those glints were from the sun touching on armor, and there were far more of them than could be produced by two men. " 'Tisnae them."

Gillyanne clutched Avery's waist as her cousin urged their horse across the brook and into the thick trees on the other side. "Who is it?"

"I dinnae ken. Looks to be an army. So now we hide."

"Hide? Wouldnae it be better to just ride away, verra swiftly?"

"They are close enough to hear or see us if we bolt," Avery whispered as she nudged the horse into a thick stand of trees, the shadows comfortingly deep and concealing. "I think we should also get some idea of who else roams these woods."

Avery leaned forward enough to keep her hand on the side of her mount's head near his nose, prepared to muzzle him with her hand if the need arose. She could see the small army through the thick branches of the trees now as they paused to briefly water their horses. The pennant one carried was of the most interest to her, the arms upon it making her blood run cold. It was the DeVeaux, and

she had the chilling feeling they were armed and ready
for something that would mean trouble or grief for her.

"Avery," Gillyanne said, the soft hint of a question
in her voice

"Hush. 'Tis still enough that I may be able to catch a
word or two which will tell me why these bastards are
here."

It was only a few moments later when Avery decided
she had heard more than enough. DeVeau wanted his
money back and cared not if he slaughtered every MacAlpin to get it. It had been foolish to think, simply because
the man had not immediately set after them, that he would
be willing to let so much of his coin leave his hands. As
she watched the men ride away, Avery knew she was
faced with a hard decision. Did she and Gillyanne continue
on in their escape, or did they ride back and warn the
MacAlpins? She sighed as she ruefully admitted the decision had been made the moment she knew about the
threat.

"The DeVeaux are going to kill them," Gillyanne said.

"I ken it." Avery shook her head. "I think we might
have actually been successful this time."

"We go back to warn them?"

"As soon as I can figure out the best way to do so
without tripping o'er the DeVeaux."

Gillyanne nodded. "I thought that was what ye would
decide."

"Why? Cameron means to use us against our clan,
against Payton. He means to ransom you and dishonor
me. He and his men didnae attack our French kinsmen,
but they were in DeVeau's hire. We should be wishing
the DeVeaux good luck and hying for a port." Avery
nudged her horse back across the brook.

"Aye, we probably should, and no one would blame
us—but we willnae."

"Nay, we willnae. We will put our own skinny necks in danger trying to save our captors. Misled as Cameron and the others are, they dinnae deserve to be slaughtered."

"Nay, they dinnae," agreed Gillyanne. "Think we can reach the camp faster than DeVeau's dogs can?"

"We can only try. And they dinnae look to be in any great hurry."

"Mayhap they dinnae ken where Cameron's camp is."

"They may not ken exactly, but they ken what port he heads to." She nudged her mount into a steady trot, heading back the way they had just come but in a straighter line. "It may be but a good guess, or one of the MacAlpins told one of DeVeau's men. Nay out of betrayal, simply nay kenning the depths of treachery his new master would sink to. Ye watch for any sign of a MacAlpin or that we have drifted too close to the DeVeaux. I will set my mind on getting us back to that camp as fast as possible."

As they rode, Avery prayed for success. Despite the situation Cameron had pulled her into, and his accusations against her brother, she certainly did not want to see him killed or maimed, or any of his people hurt, either. She suspected she would feel the same even if she did not care about the fool. Brief though the acquaintance had been, she liked the MacAlpins and did not wish to see them cut down by DeVeau treachery and greed. All she could do now, however, was try to keep herself and Gillyanne safe, yet reach the MacAlpins in time to save them.

"Jesu, took there, Cameron," said Leargan, his voice softened by both surprise and caution.

Cameron looked in the direction his cousin pointed, and swore. He was thrilled to see Avery and her cousin close enough to capture, yet was confused as to why they were. They had executed a skillful escape, covering their tracks well. He had just admitted to himself that he had lost them, yet here they were, riding straight back toward his camp and captivity.

"Think they are lost?" Cameron asked, doubting it.

"I would be most disappointed if it was that simple," replied Leargan.

"Yet why are they returning to camp?"

"Mayhap because they have decided that we are the lesser of two evils. They are being followed, cousin."

Cameron cursed and nudged his mount into a gallop even as the two men trailing Avery picked up speed. He was relieved to hear Gillyanne cry out a warning. Avery kicked his horse into a gallop, but it would be a close-run race. He signaled Leargan to take down the man on the left even as he headed for the man on the right.

Avery felt as if her heart had leapt into her throat when Gillyanne cried out a warning. She caught a brief glimpse of two DeVeau men rapidly approaching and kicked her horse into a gallop. It was going to be a race to see who reached the MacAlpin camp first, and Avery wished she could feel more certain of victory.

Then, Gillyanne cried out again and Avery glanced behind her, terrified briefly that the DeVeau men had gotten close enough to hurt her cousin. When she recognized the two men close on the heels of the DeVeau hounds, she was elated to be rescued, though she decided it might be wise to keep right on running.

" 'Tis Cameron and Leargan," Gillyanne said.

"I ken it," replied Avery.

"Cannae we stop running now?"

"Nay. The DeVeaux are clearly a lot closer than I thought they were, and Cameron will demand some explanations, if he e'en lets me speak."

"How far?"

"Ten, mayhap fifteen minutes at this speed."

"Weel, hie on, cousin."

"I intend to."

Cameron watched as the man he had just killed tumbled out of the saddle; then he quickly grasped the reins of the man's horse. He looked to see Leargan just doing the same. When he saw that Avery still raced toward camp, he swore and then hitched the man's mount securely to his. Leargan hurried to his side, also towing a horse.

"Why does she still flee?" Leargan asked, even as he and Cameron started to chase after the two Murray females.

"I begin to think the question we should ask is: Why are these DeVeau swine so close?" muttered Cameron.

"They are DeVeau's men? Ye are sure?"

"Verra. I recognized the one I just had to kill."

"An attack?"

"I fear it may be."

Leargan cursed fiercely for a moment. "The lasses are trying to save our hides."

Cameron just curtly nodded. This was going to cause him trouble. Avery and Gillyanne had obviously tossed aside their very good chance at freedom to warn him and his people. They had even put themselves in danger to do so. His people were going to think the lasses deserved to be rewarded because of that. Briefly, Cameron tried to convince himself that this was the only reason Avery was doing it—for freedom and a safe escort home—but he could not do it. His long-held cynicism refused to reach out and include Avery.

Despite that, he would continue with his plan. His sister's needs had to come first. Using Avery was still the best way to pay back the insult done to his sister, and to get her the husband she needed. It did not ease his guilt much to know that Avery would probably understand. She would never let him forget the debt he owed her, but she

would still understand why he could not reward her with
her freedom.

"Attack!" Avery cried as she galloped into the MacAlpin camp and reined her mount into a rearing halt. "The
DeVeaux are headed your way."

"But, they arenae our enemies," said Wee Rob.

"They are now," said Cameron as he rode up, dis-
mounting before his horse had come to a complete halt.
"They want their money back."

"How close are they?" asked one burly man.

Cameron looked at Avery. "Those men were forward
scouts?"

"Aye. I doubt Gilly and I gained much distance on
what looked to be a sizable DeVeau force. I would say
only minutes." Avery dismounted and helped Gillyanne
down.

"Or less," added Gillyanne, pointing to a slight cloud
of dust.

Avery and Gillyanne found themselves hurried away
with the other women, all of them grabbing what supplies
and goods they could carry as they fled. They were accom-
panied by three pages and two squires who brought along
the horses. But yards from the camp, sheltered by the
trees, they halted. It was their sad duty to watch, prepared
to flee if the battle turned against their men. Only one
small page would hold back, hiding until it was over so
that he could report the final outcome and let them know
if there were any wounded to collect. Avery did not ask
if they would bury or collect their dead as well.

As she watched Cameron's small force prepare to meet
one twice its size, Avery prayed. She prayed that the
MacAlpins would not pay too high a price for the folly
of dealing with a DeVeau. She prayed the DeVeau men
were not willing to sacrifice too many men just to return
the mercenary fee to their lord. She also prayed that, if

the worst happened, if the MacAlpins lost, she and her cousin would not find themselves back in the grasp of their old enemy.

When the attack came, it came hard, fast, and loud. Avery swayed as if she herself had withstood the first assault. A soft gasp erupted from the ones around her, and she knew she had not suffered that strange reaction alone. Avery doubted anyone could stand silent and still before such a display of force.

Cameron and his men had placed themselves upon a small rise. It was just high enough to give them an advantage, putting them at a height to more equally battle the men on horseback and putting the DeVeau force at a slight but welcome disadvantage. The MacAlpins formed a tight circle, a pair of skilled archers in the middle. If the DeVeau men were not too determined, Cameron's battle plan could easily win the fight. Avery felt the flicker of hope invade her heart.

It soon became impossible to watch every aspect of the battle, so Avery set her gaze on Cameron and kept it there. She held her breath each time the DeVeaux swarmed toward him, and let it go each time he repelled them. By the soft cries of those around her, she knew that some of Cameron's men had fallen, but never once did she take her gaze from Cameron. Instead, she simply prayed for the soul of the fallen man and hoped it was a mendable wound that had caused his fall and not the cold touch of death.

Although it felt as if she had stood there praying and watching for hours, Avery knew it was probably more like minutes before the battle turned in favor of the MacAlpins. DeVeau dead and wounded littered the camp, and the enemy suddenly seemed to become aware of how dearly the battle was costing them. One man helped a wounded companion to stumble away from the fight, then another did the same, and another, until it became a hasty retreat. It took all of Avery's willpower to stay where she was until the DeVeaux had disappeared into the trees; then she saw Cameron sink to his knees. Even as she started toward him, the other women also moved, until they were all running toward the men. Every step of the way, Avery prayed that Cameron was hale or only slightly wounded, that weariness had brought him to his knees and not the weight of impending death.

Chapter Six

With his gaze still fixed upon the dust of the fleeing DeVeaux, Cameron slowly sank to his knees. He found just enough strength to signal a man to follow the DeVeaux and make certain the retreat was a true one; then he slumped. The battle had been short and fierce, but he felt as if it had lasted all day. Leargan panted at his side, assuring Cameron that his cousin still lived, and Cameron decided he could take a moment to marshal his strength before seeing to his losses.

A soft touch upon his arm roused him from his exhausted stupor. Cameron looked up to find Avery looking at him with concern darkening her fine eyes. Guilt lashed him. He owed her his life and those of his men who survived the battle. He should let her go, but he knew he would not. His desire for her and his need to make things right for his sister would not allow him to.

"Are ye wounded?" Avery asked as she looked him over.

"I am nay sure," Cameron replied; then he began to join her in checking for wounds on his body.

"It appears that all ye have suffered is a shallow sword slash upon your arm."

"The others?" he asked as he let her tend to his injury.

"One dead, one who may be dying, three wounded but nay mortally if the wounds are tended weel." She frowned as, done with washing the wound, she smeared an ointment on it. After a close study she shrugged and began to bandage it. "I could stitch it if ye would rather. 'Twould lessen the scar that may remain."

"Let it scar."

Avery was not surprised by his reply. The same men who could leap into battle and face death and pain without flinching always quailed when faced with the prospect of needing a wound stitched. It never ceased to amaze and amuse her. She collected her things and stood up, ready to go help the other wounded. Impulsively she bent down and lightly kissed Cameron on the mouth. The look of total astonishment on his face made her moment of weakness worthwhile. She hurried away before he was able to shake free of his shock.

"Looks as if ye are closer to winning than I thought," drawled Leargan.

Cameron blinked and stared at his cousin for a moment before his wits returned. "Ye are still here."

Leargan snorted in disgust as he slowly, wearily rose to his feet, then helped Cameron stand up. "I may as weel have been a rock for all the two of ye noticed. Although at least the lass took a wee moment to be sure I wasnae wounded."

"She obviously has some skill in healing."

"Both of them do." Leargan nodded toward where Gillyanne was helping Avery. " 'Tis said that one of the

Murray women, Lord Botolf's wife, I believe, is a famed healer.''

"Of course.'' Cameron shook his head and nearly staggered. "I begin to think there is nothing a Murray cannae do. 'Tis annoying.''

Leargan chuckled, then grew serious. "They saved our lives.''

"Aye, they did.''

"They gave up a verra good chance of escaping.''

Cameron sighed heavily. "Aye, they did. Although, two wee lasses wandering about on their own could also have stumbled into a lot of trouble and danger.''

"Ye arenae going to give this up, are ye?'' Leargan snapped out the demand after cursing heartily for a moment.

"I cannae.''

"For your sister's sake?''

"Aye. Avery Murray could be as pure and sweet and giving as a nun and I would still do this. 'Tis my duty to restore the honor stolen from my sister. Avery Murray is the surest way to do that. Just as I cannae turn my back on my sister, so Sir Payton Murray cannae turn his back on his. I will, however, temper my actions.''

"Ye willnae try to dishonor the lass?''

"I cannae promise that.''

"Nay, I didnae think ye could?' Leargan shook his head. "Ye truly do fair stink of want for her.''

"Cover your nose, then,'' Cameron grumbled. He looked around. "We cannae stay here, but we cannae travel too far, either. I dinnae wish to risk the lives of the wounded.''

"I will tell the men to break camp, then go find us a new site.''

Cameron watched Leargan walk away and then turned his full attention to his people. The bodies of the DeVeau men were already stripped of all valuables and were being dragged away to be discarded in the wood. His men had acquitted themselves proudly, he decided as he reached the place where four of his men were laid out. One was already wrapped in a shroud, one was lying ominously still and pale, and two were complaining and cursing as the Murray women tended their wounds. Cameron felt sure those two would survive, and he knelt by the too-quiet, more seriously wounded man.

A pang struck him as he saw the youth of the soldier, probably not much past eighteen. It was Peter, a young man who had thought the journey to France would bring him wealth and adventure. Too young, Cameron thought. Too young to feel the chill of death, and to be cut down for so paltry a reason. This was no battle for king and country, but the attack of a dishonorable fool who did not want to lose the coin paid to mercenaries.

"He may yet live," Avery said as she stepped up and looked down at Peter

"Aye?" Cameron set his fingers against the vein in Peter's throat and felt a steady, if dangerously weak, pulse. "He doesnae look as if he can travel verra far."

"Nay, not now. Howbeit the wound did little damage to his innards. It but bled so freely, 'twas like to drain him. The bleeding has ceased. If it doesnae start again, and if he doesnae take a fever, he could heal quickly, at least to the point where he could survive a journey taken carefully."

"How soon could ye tell?"

"Two days. Mayhap less." Avery did not even blink at the harsh curse he spat out. She had heard worse.

"We will move to a new camp as soon as Leargan has found us one." He glanced at the shrouded body. "Who is the dead mon? Do ye ken?"

"One of the women said he was a mon called Adam."

"Ah." Cameron felt guilty for feeling a hint of relief that the man had been neither kin nor friend. "A mon who joined us as we traveled here, a mercenary who kenned he had a better chance to earn money as part of a group rather than alone. Why did ye come back?" he asked abruptly, meeting her gaze and silently cursing the fact that she had her feelings well shielded.

"I may wish to be free, but nay at the cost of others' lives."

"Ah, and here I thought it might be for love of my fair face."

"Your face is about as fair as a moonless night." She gently lifted Peter up until his face rested against her shoulder, and slowly began to feed him a drink, stroking his throat with her long, beautiful fingers to coax him to swallow.

"What is that ye feed the lad?" Cameron asked, finding himself ridiculously jealous of young Peter's position.

"An herbal drink that will strengthen him and will help him to replace all that blood he lost."

"Ye didnae give it to the others."

"Nay, they arenae hurt so badly. They are stoutly whining, a sure sign of health and quick recovery."

Cameron grinned. "If Peter begins to whine, ye will consider him cured, will ye?"

"Aye." She gently settled the young man back down on his blanket. "A mon facing death doesnae usually whine about twinges, itches, and foul-tasting medicines. If he has any wit or strength left to speak or think, he usually tries to recall all the sins he has committed, worries on what faces him after death, and begs for absolution."

"Ye have seen a lot of men die, have ye?"

"Too many," she replied in almost too soft a voice; then she rose and walked away.

An hour later they moved camp. A distance of little

more than a mile away was another small clearing with adequate water and grass for the horses. There was also a high hill close at hand that would allow a watch to be kept on the surrounding countryside. The DeVeaux would not be able to get close again without being seen.

By the time camp was set up, Cameron had bathed and eaten and was more than ready to seek his bed. He looked around for Avery. It annoyed him to see her and Gillyanne returning from the brook only lightly guarded. Even as she paused by the wounded men to check on them, Cameron strode over and grasped her by her wrist. He ignored the disapproving looks and mutters from his men as he dragged Avery to his tent. Clearly he had lost whatever support he had had for his plan. He wondered how they could so easily disregard his sister's needs—the insult done her and thus the whole clan. Cameron shoved Avery into his tent, followed her in, and went to pour himself some wine.

"I assume this means that my daring, gallant rescue today changes nothing," Avery drawled as she sat down on the furs that formed his bed and began to remove her boots.

"It cannae," he said flatly as he sat down on a heavy, dark chest that held his belongings. "Ye are needed to force your brother to do his duty by my sister, the lass he dishonored."

"Why dinnae ye just try to grab him? Drag him before the priest yourself instead of using me to lure him to his fate?"

"Iain told me that he had tried to do just that, but it didnae work. Your brother nimbly evades every trap."

"Aye, he would. He has learned that game verra weel."

"He makes a habit of seducing young lasses, does he?"

"Nay, ye thick-witted lout," she said very sweetly as she stripped down to her underclothes.

For a brief moment, Avery had contemplated sleeping in all her clothes, but she decided that she was sick to death of continuously trying to preserve some scrap of modesty. Her crisp linen shift and the delicate linen braies she had made for herself were modest enough. She did wish she had the courage to watch Cameron as she shed her gown, certain he would be stunned, but she decided he would see that as too much of a challenge. The abrupt, heavy silence in the tent gave her enough satisfaction as she made herself comfortable on the rough bed and tugged the blanket over her.

Cameron was astonished when Avery stripped down to her shift and those odd underbreeches she wore with such calm, almost as it he were her brother or some maid. As if he was a man she did not have to worry about, he thought with a spark of annoyance. He had been doing a fine job of seducing her since she had stumbled into his grasp, even making her shiver with need, and pant and moan. She ought to worry about him. She ought to worry about him a lot. His increasing irritation grew with a bound when he realized what she had just called him.

" 'Twould be wise for ye to keep a sweeter tongue in your mouth, lass," he growled, annoyed that simply saying the words *tongue* and *mouth* had him hard as iron.

"I thought I did speak sweetly," she replied.

She had, he mused. Her tone had been sweet as thick honey. Cameron decided to return to talking about her brother. She would be quick to argue with him, and that could well work to cool the lust now throbbing in his veins. He did not think he should try to seduce her tonight. After all she had done today, it would be discourteous not to give her at least one night's respite.

"Ye have called Sir Payton handsome, gallant, sweet. honorable, brave, clever, and a mon all the lasses slobber o'er. Are ye telling me he is also monkish in his habits?

That he hasnae used all these wondrous gifts to pull the lasses into his bed?'' Cameron could see that his sarcasm enraged her, and he almost smiled. He would certainly be getting that argument he wanted now.

''He doesnae have to pull any lass into his bed,'' Avery snapped. ''Nay, he often has to kick them out.''

If Sir Payton was not oozing vanity from every pore, it certainly was not because his sister kept him humble, Cameron thought wryly. ''He fair trips o'er lasses tumbling at his feet, does he?''

Cameron's sarcasm made Avery ache to hit him. ''Nearly so. Ye will see.''

''All I wish to see of your brother is his back as he kneels afore a priest to wed my sister and restore the honor he has stolen from her.''

''And I keep telling you that my brother would ne'er steal anything from a lass, has ne'er had to. And, if he had bedded your sister, he would ne'er deny it. Why, he e'en once faced a Douglas mon squarely and told him that he had bedded down with the mon's betrothed. Of course, Payton was warning the mon about the evil of the woman, and the Douglas mon didnae really want her because he thought she had already murdered three of his kinsmen—which she had, but that doesnae matter. The tale shows that my brother is a verra honest mon.''

Not knowing the whole tale, Cameron felt it could also show that Payton Murray was a reckless fool. One just did not go about confessing to bedding the betrothed of a Douglas man. Douglas men didnae take such insults well. There was clearly a great deal more to the tale, but he would drag it out of her later. Right now he had work to do. He had to get her so furious with him that she would neither look at nor speak to him but would try to stay as far away from him as her captivity would allow.

''Does it? I think it shows that he doesnae have much

care for the boundaries other men observe. If ye mean to make him sound the saint ye claim he is, telling me he bedded another mon's woman isnae the way to do it.''

He had a point there, Avery mused, but she knew she would rather pull out all of her fingernails than tell him so. "I keep telling ye that Payton is no saint, but he does stay away from virgins. I doubt your kinsmen made it a secret that they were seeking a husband for your sister, and Payton always takes care to avoid such maidens."

" 'Tis clear he has no wish for a wife.''

Since Cameron was stripping down to his loincloth, Avery suddenly found it a little difficult to talk. She also found it very difficult to hide her appreciation of his lean, dark body. It was not easy, but she forced her suddenly wanton thoughts back to the matter at hand: Cameron's insults to Payton.

"Of course he wishes a wife—somewhen. He has no objection to marriage, unless 'tis shoved down his throat and to a lass he doesnae want.''

"If he didnae want my sister for a wife, he shouldnae have bedded her.''

When he bound their wrists together and then sprawled on his back at her side, Avery fought the temptation to pummel him senseless. She kept telling herself it was good for him to have such faith in his sister, to want to aid and protect her. That faith was sadly misplaced, but she doubted she could get him to believe that.

For a moment she wondered why she even tried. He would not believe any wrong of his sister, just as she would not believe any wrong of Payton. Arguing with him about this problem was akin to banging her head against a stone wall, but she would continue to refute his accusations against her brother. If nothing else, she wanted her defense of Payton, all of her arguments in her brother's favor, to be planted firmly in Cameron's mind. She hoped to plant some doubt there, to raise a few questions in his mind, before they confronted his sister. It might help him finally see that the girl was lying.

"When was the last time ye saw your sister?" she abruptly asked.

Cameron frowned. "Just before I came here, o'er two years ago."

"Ah. Weel, I saw Payton but months ago."

"And?"

"It seems to me that I ken my brother, am closer to him, then ye ken your sister."

"No lass would claim such a loss of honor unless 'tis true," he snapped, angered by the fact that there was some good sense behind her claim. He could not honestly say that he knew his sister well at all.

Avery made a sharp, scornful noise. "She will if she thinks it will get her something she wants."

That was an opinion that matched his own far too closely to argue with. "And your sainted brother is such a wondrous prize, is he?"

"He is young, strong, too handsome for any lass's peace of mind, heir to some fine lands, and plump of purse."

Exactly what many a lass and her family would eagerly seek, he thought crossly. His plan was not working out as he had hoped. Avery had turned reasonable in her arguments and he was the one getting annoyed. Still troubled by guilt over the fact that he was not discarding his plans even though she had saved his and his people's lives, the very last thing he wished her to be was reasonable. That only stirred up his guilt to a highly uncomfortable level.

"Then he will make a fine husband for my sister even it he is a debauchee," he drawled.

Avery cursed. "Thick-headed oaf."

" 'Tis nay wise to insult your captor, lass.''

"I dinnae suppose ye considered ending this game in gratitude for my saving your wee life.''

"For a moment. Then I just decided to change my plan a wee bit instead. I willnae use whate'er happens between us to shame ye.''

"Ye intended to blacken my name?'' she asked, nearly breathless with outrage.

"I thought on it. Your brother has blackened my sister's name. But now I will keep this all verra private.''

"I am humbled by your generosity.''

Avery turned her back on him. She had not really thought too deeply on exactly how he intended to use her, beyond taking her chastity in exchange for his sister's and using her to bring Payton to heel. It hurt to learn he had thought to make her shame widely known, but she told herself not to be such a fool. He thought his sister had been shamed, and he might well have been told that her loss of innocence was no secret. Naturally he would feel that Payton ought to suffer the pain of a humiliated sister, too. For a brief moment, she was almost sorry he had changed his plan, for she would have liked to know if he would have been able to follow it through. She told herself not to be such an idiot. It was undoubtedly one of those things it was best not to know. Since he thought he was fighting to restore his sister's honor, it was a corner she had best never have to back him into.

There was one thing to consider, however. He was not going to use what might happen between them to hurt her family now, except, perhaps, in the most private of ways. It would now be a great deal easier to dull the sharp edge of that sword. Now, her telling her family that her innocence had not been stolen, but had been freely, if foolishly, given away, would be heeded. Now all she had to do was decide if she was willing to risk all to try and win Cameron's heart.

"Sleep weel, Avery," Cameron murmured.

"Have nightmares, Cameron," she grumbled, inwardly sighing when he just laughed.

She closed her eyes and reached out for sleep's calming touch. Her future was uncertain, but losing sleep over that would accomplish nothing. There was a hard decision to be made, and she wanted to be well rested, with her wits clear and sharp, when she made it.

Chapter Seven

Her blood was on fire. The inferno raging inside of her was being stoked by warm lips and big, stroking hands. A shudder of fierce desire rippled through Avery, dragging her into full wakefulness. She clutched the man sprawled on top of her, gasping with delight as he warmed her breasts with his hands. Aching and hungry she rubbed her body against his and heard him groan.

That deep, hoarse sound of desire broke through the haze of passion clouding Avery's mind. Cameron was seducing her and she was avidly participating. A very large part of her wished to continue to participate, but she struggled to grasp at some strand of sanity. Allowing oneself to be mindlessly swept away by passion was not the way to make a decision that could all too easily leave her with a shattered heart. She grabbed Cameron by the wrists, feeling both pleased and frustrated when he immediately ceased caressing her.

"Ye are a sneaky, lecherous rogue, Cameron MacAlpin," she said, her voice husky and unsteady as she struggled to rein in the passion still throbbing in her veins.

"Are ye telling me to stop?" he asked.

"Aye."

"Why? 'Tis clear that ye want me." He brushed his thumbs over the hard tips of her breasts and watched her tremble.

Avery felt his touch straight to the marrow of her bones "Arrogant oaf. Get off."

Cameron hesitated a moment, then cursed and rolled off her. He quickly undid the bonds tying their wrists together and got out of bed. He knew that if he did not put some distance between them, and quickly, his aching need could drive him to ignore her *nay*. Seducing her while she was still asleep was underhanded enough; he did not want to sink any lower to get what he craved. Cameron made note, however, of how swiftly and fiercely she had responded and how slow she had been to say that *nay*. It might be underhanded, but he knew he would try it again.

It did not help Avery to cool the heat in her blood to see Cameron standing so close and wearing so little. She breathed a hearty, if silent, sigh of relief when he began to get dressed. Subtly taking deep, slow breaths, she fought to calm herself, to rid herself of all signs that could tell him how badly she wanted him. The ache twisting her insides would undoubtedly take a lot longer to quell. When long minutes passed and he said nothing, mutely preparing to leave the tent, she frowned at him.

"Sulking, are ye?" she goaded him.

"Nay," he replied, looking at her. "I am trying to get out ere I forget that I should heed a lass's *nay* and return to that bed."

She slowly sat up. The look in his dark eyes told her that remaining sprawled on her back was more invitation than she wished to give him at the moment. Seeing how he desired her was also more temptation than she had the will to resist right now. His plan to put some distance between them—quickly—was a very good one, but his arrogance demanded some response.

"That *nay* would still be said."

"Would it? Oh, aye, I suspicion your mouth could still form the word, but the rest of ye would be loudly crying *aye*. Just as it was but moments ago."

" 'Twas naught but the mindless response of a body to a skilled touch. A response ye got only because I was asleep." She realized that goading him was not a particularly wise thing to do when he suddenly strode over, yanked her into his arms, and gave her a kiss that curled her toes.

Cameron was breathing hard when he set her back on her feet. His only consolation was that she was, too. It had been foolish to let her goad him. He had just begun to get his lusts under control and now they were raging mindlessly again. Yet he did not want her passion to be born of no more than a skilled touch. He wanted it to be for him, the man, and for him alone. Vanity, he told himself. It was just vanity. That claim rang hollow, but he clung to it

"Ye want me, lass," he said as he buckled on his sword. " 'Twill nay be long now ere ye decide that denying yourself the pleasure we can share isnae worth the ache ye are left with."

Avery took a deep breath to reply, but he was already leaving. There was a brief moment of amusing confusion as he tangled with young Donald, who was just arriving to help him dress. Once Cameron was gone, Avery let out a long, slow sigh of relief. The man could certainly heat up a tent.

As Avery washed up and dressed in her old, much-

mended gown, she tried to decide what her next step
should be. She did not need Cameron arrogantly telling
her that she wanted him, ached for him. It was a truth
she had lived with since setting eyes on the rogue. She
was also more than ready to surrender to that, to gamble
that his desire was born of more than lust. As Elspeth
had shown her, there were some men who needed to be
given everything a woman had to give before any of those
deeper, softer emotions were yanked free.

She would probably be memorable, Avery mused, if
she left Cameron with the worst case of unfed lust any
man had ever suffered. Unfortunately, that was a memory
that could easily be banished by a rousing night or two
in the arms of a skilled courtesan. She needed to fill his
mind and body with sweeter, more heated memories. If
he still sent her away, she wanted him to be unable to
forget how fierce their passion had been, how good she
had felt in his arms, even how she smelled and tasted.
She wanted him so soaked in the memory of her that no
other woman could fully banish her from his mind. If he
was going to ache after she was gone, it would not be
for what he had never had, but for what he had lost and
could find nowhere else.

The only problem was in how to give Cameron what
he wanted, yet not give him a complete victory. Seducing
him for a change was one possibility. It would certainly
shock and surprise Cameron if she became the aggressor
instead of simply responding to, then retreating from, his
advances. That alone made the plan an attractive one. It
would also make it clear from the beginning that she was
giving him what they both craved, willingly, freely; he
was not taking or conquering anything. He would probably still think of it as winning, but she could not worry
herself over the many vagaries in a man's mind.

Once outside, Avery saw Gillyanne with the women

preparing a meal for themselves and the men, and she hurried over to join her. Soon she was caught up in a round of chores, including the nursing of the wounded men. She found it mildly amusing that three of the women, Joan, Marie, and Therese, all looked remarkably alike, being short, plump, brown-haired, and brown-eyed. Only Anne, the wife of Ranald, one of Cameron's oldest soldiers, stood out—and in more ways than one. Anne was tall, dark, buxom, outspoken, and just a little commanding. The other three women needed a firm hand, however, being sweet but obviously not chosen for their sharp wits. As she and Anne tended to a rapidly healing Peter, Avery heard the three other women arguing in a bewildering mixture of French, Gaelic, and heavily accented English over who made the best oatcakes. She looked across Peter and shared a grin with Anne, grins that widened when she heard Gillyanne trying to sort it all out and calm the women down.

"I wonder how they can understand each other," Avery said, shaking her head.

Anne's steel grey eyes softened with amusement as she replied, " 'Tis only when they get agitated that they sound like a flock of noisy geese. The French lasses are learning the English verra quickly. Wee Therese can e'en say a wee bit in the Gaelic. When 'tis something they need to ken to survive or improve their lot, those two French lasses can show a surprisingly keen wit. They will make a firm place for themselves at Cairnmoor."

Seeing that Peter had fallen asleep, Avery studied Anne for a moment, then bluntly asked, "Do ye ken Cameron's sister?"

"Ah, nay weel, I fear. I am but the wife of a lowly mon-at-arms."

"Oh. Like that, is she?"

"I shouldnae speak ill of the laird's sister." Anne

sighed and shook her head. "Yet we owe ye and wee Gilly our verra lives. Since our laird doesnae seem inclined to reward that with your freedom, weel, mayhap 'tis only fair that ye ken exactly what ye are to face at Cairnmoor." She stood up and pulled Avery to her feet. "We will fetch ourselves some wine and sit in the shade, then have ourselves a wee talk."

Avery did not wait long once they were settled beneath a large tree to ask, "Is there something I need to ken about Cameron's sister? I cannae see how learning about her will change my situation much."

"It probably willnae change it much at all," Anne agreed. "It may help to explain a few things, however, and 'tis only right that ye ken something about the lass whose words have dragged ye into this trouble."

"Her lies."

Anne grimaced. "One cannae really go about calling her laird's own sister a liar. There are many among us, howbeit, who believe she may be, or, mistaken in her accusations." She smiled faintly when Avery rolled her eyes. "The lass has ne'er had a mother. The woman died verra soon after the lass was born. The old laird died whilst she was still a bairn. There is the aunt, but, if ye think those three squabbling women are light of wit, ye just must meet dear Aunt Agnes. A sweet, good-hearted woman, but she couldnae tell a lie or a deceit if it fell on her. Sir Iain, the laird's cousin, is a good mon, but he kens naught about raising a wee lass. Our laird did his best, but he was nay much more than a lad himself."

"So, Cameron was father and brother to the lass and nay doubt feels guilty, thinking that he didnae do either job verra weel."

"Nay doubt. Katherine is verra spoiled. She is a bonny lass, or was when we left. Barely sixteen and already had many a laddie playing the fool for her. When she wanted something, she got it. Her aunt and the laird didnae seem able to deny her anything.''

"And now she wants my brother.'' Avery frowned and took a sip of wine. "Being spoiled requires coin. I thought, weel, since Cameron has been selling his sword—''

"He was poor? Nay. He wished to leave Scotland for a while. Had a disappointment of the heart, 'tis said. 'Tis why he took a vow of celibacy.''

Avery blinked in surprise then suddenly recalled something she had heard on the day of her capture. "Just when did he take this vow?''

"Near to three years ago. Far as I can tell, he has stood by it.''

Dismay pushed its way through Avery's shock. Was that why Cameron desired her so much, simply because he had not bedded a woman for so long? Instinct told her no, but her confidence, weak as it was, was badly shaken. She started in surprise when Anne patted her hand.

'' 'Tisnae why our laird fair pants after ye, lass.''

"Are ye sure?''

"Aye. He has stayed cold to all the lasses ere now, and some have chased him hard indeed. He took one look at you and all that fine willpower disappeared in a blinking. Oh, being a mon, he probably tells himself 'tis naught but a long celibacy which makes him hunger so, but I doubt e'en he fully believes that. Nay, no matter what the fool lad tells himself, he lusts after ye simply because ye are ye. I dinnae think he will change his mind about trading ye for your brother, though, nay unless he discovers Katherine is lying ere the deed is done.''

"So, ye *do* think she is lying. Gillyanne seemed to think ye all wanted my brother to pay dearly for dishonoring the lass.''

"At first, but many just arenae so sure any longer. 'Tis one of those accusations one must think on for a wee while, and the more thinking we did, the less certain we all were that our laird has the full truth or the full tale.'' Anne smiled faintly. ''And, kenning ye and wee Gillyanne as we do now, 'tis hard to think ye would have a brother who would do such a thing or that ye would defend him so steadfastly if ye did. Still, 'tis only what the laird believes that matters, and he doesnae see too clearly when 'tis Katherine involved.''

''Nay, and now I ken why.'' Avery turned her thoughts to the reasons behind Cameron's vow of celibacy. ''A disappointment of the heart, ye said? It doesnae usually take a mon so hard nor the hurt linger for so long.''

''Oh, he isnae pining. Nay, nay. I am nay sure he was e'en in love. 'Twas the betrayal he suffered from, but the last in far too many. The lad has a true skill for setting his eyes on the wrong type of lass.''

''Humph. I ken the sort. Fair of hair, blue of eye, and fulsome. The sort who smiles, flutters her eyelashes, and makes verra certain that the appropriate parts of her lush body bounce and sway. The sort who uses finely honed skills and wee gasps to make a mon feel all mon.'' She could not fully restrain a smile when Anne laughed. ''The sort who believes her bonny looks and a clever use of her hands are all she needs to give a mon, and who expects far too much in return for her meager gifts. I would have liked to think that Cameron was much too wise to succumb to such wiles, to let beauty draw him in then deceive him.''

''No mon is too wise for that. Nay, not until he learns that 'tis what lies within the heart that matters. Aye, and e'en when they come to understand that truth, they will still cast an eye at the beauties of the world. A good mon willnae be unfaithful, but that doesnae mean he willnae still be done a fool by big blue eyes, golden curls, and ripe breasts.''

"Idiots." Avery sighed and stood up, idly brushing off her skirts. "Back to work."

"Do ye mean to give into our laird?" Anne asked as she, too, stood up.

"Give in? Sounds too much like surrender to me. A Murray ne'er surrenders. Weel, nay too often." She smiled slowly and winked at Anne. "Nay, I intend to bemuse and confuse his lairdship."

"I think ye have done a fine job of that already."

"Ah, but 'tis now time for the *coup de grace*. Now that he is suitably accustomed to *nays* and insults, I mean to turn up sweet and go on the attack." She left Anne laughing heartily.

Avery managed to avoid Cameron for the rest of the day. It was not very difficult. He busied himself with making sure their camp was well guarded and secured against attack. She helped with the chores and spent a great deal of time nursing young Peter insuring that he continued to improve with a heartwarming speed.

She slowly discovered that Cameron's people were no longer fully behind his plans for her. They felt she and Gillyanne were owed their freedom in recompense for saving nearly all their lives. Avery realized that she and Gillyanne could probably escape again and very few of Cameron's people would try to stop them. The problem was, she no longer wished to go.

That reluctance troubled her, for it seemed disloyal to Payton. She should be trying her best to flee so that she and Gillyanne could not be used to drag Payton into a marriage he plainly did not want. Avery knew Payton would never fault her for following her own heart, but she suspected she would blame herself, especially if she lost her gamble to win Cameron's heart. If she won, the whole problem was solved, for Cameron would not let her go, not even in trade. The question was, did she have the right to take even that gamble when Payton could share in the consequences if she lost?

"Now what has ye looking so troubled?" asked Gillyanne as she sat down beside Avery in front of Cameron's tent. "I was hoping to share my evening's meal with a much more cheerful companion."

"I was just thinking that we would probably be able to escape with some ease now, yet I dinnae want to do it," Avery explained. "Then I got to thinking how unfair, even disloyal, that was to Payton. He doesnae want Katherine, who is clearly a selfish, spoiled liar; yet, if I stay, I could be used to force him to take her."

"Aye, ye could be, yet 'tis nay your fault."

" 'Tis if I dinnae try to take that weapon away from Cameron."

"Only a wee bit. Ye love the fool and ye have a chance to make him love you. Payton would understand why ye stayed with Cameron. We also tried to escape—twice."

"I am nay sure that first attempt should count."

"There is one thing ye havenae considered as ye have argued with yourself," Gillyanne said quietly before filling her mouth with a bite of tender venison.

"And what is that?" asked Avery.

"We are but two wee lasses. Aye, we could probably escape. We almost made it the last time. Howbeit, if we succeed in fleeing Cameron we will be two wee lasses all alone, two wee lasses who must then try to find their way from where'er this is to a French port, get a place on a ship headed to Scotland, and then get across Scotland to Donncoill. I dinnae believe Payton would want or expect us to take such risks just to stop his marriage to Katherine. And think how horrible he would feel if anything happened to us whilst escaping."

The logic of Gillyanne's argument left Avery speechless. Then she wondered if she accepted it so quickly and completely simply because it allowed her to do what she wanted. Nay, she mused, Gillyanne was right. No one's life was at risk in all of this. Payton would not want her and Gillyanne to risk their lives just to save him from an unwanted marriage. True, marriages were forever but for the most part they were not fatal. He would indeed be devastated if anything happened to either of them whilst attempting to save him from an unwanted trip to the altar. Payton would most likely consider all of this his problem, and his alone to solve.

"Ye are right," Avery finally said, and then she began to eat.

Gillyanne laughed softly. "I think I must needs make some record of this miraculous moment."

"Impertinent child."

"Ye are *sure* ye love Sir Cameron, are ye?"

"Oh, aye, e'en when I want to strike him about the head with something hard and heavy." She exchanged a grin with Gillyanne. " 'Tis nay a blind, besotted type of loving. And I dinnae think all will be weel just because *I* love *him*."

"It should be. Love is a verra precious gift."

"Aye, and there is certainly joy in the feel of it swelling one's heart and in the giving of it. Howbeit, giving it doesnae mean one will get it back. And, if one doesnae feel love, one cannae always see it as such a wondrous gift when given to them. I doubt that person can e'en recognize it though it be staring him right in the face."

"Men can be verra foolish creatures," Gillyanne muttered as she shook her head. "I so wish ye to be happy."

"Oh, I will be, if only for a little while." Avery shrugged. "And e'en if I cannae win his heart, there will still be a part of me which will be happy, for I will have held him for a wee while. Once the pain fades—and it will—the memories will be sweet."

Watching a frowning Cameron approach them, Gillyanne murmured, "Somehow the word *sweet,* e'en if ye only speak of the memory of him, just doesnae sit weel on that mon."

Avery shared a laugh with Gillyanne. When their amusement only made Cameron frown more darkly and watch them warily, she laughed a little more. She could not help but find some pleasure in the fact that such a large, strong man would find her and Gillyanne a threat, even if it was only to his peace of mind.

She kissed Gillyanne on the cheek, watched her cousin walk away, and turned a bright, welcoming smile on Cameron. He could not fully hide his surprise and uncertainty. And this was only the beginning, she thought with an inner chuckle. Unless she weakened and Cameron somehow took the lead in the game they were about to play, she planned to make the poor man nearly dizzy with confusion. They would become lovers tonight, but Avery intended to take that step completely under her own power. Cameron might still try to claim a victory after tonight, but he was going to have to do some very twisted thinking to convince himself of it.

Chapter Eight

She was plotting. Cameron was certain of it. There was a suspicious gleam in her eyes, and she was being far too sweet. Since there was no way she could escape now that they were in his tent and soon to bed down for the night, he could not guess what her game might be—and it made him very uneasy. Perhaps there was something she wanted and she was going to try to use her feminine wiles to get it. Although that did not seem like something Avery would do, he frowned even more. All females were born knowing such games, he sternly reminded himself. She would find that he was not so susceptible to such ploys.

As she slowly began to undress, he felt his desire for her rapidly soar. This was taunting, pure and simple. He was sure of it. No woman could be so naive as to think she could shed even some of her clothing in front of a man without stirring his interest. After the long, torturous days and nights he had spent trying to seduce her, Avery certainty could not be so unaware of the effect such actions would have upon him. She was crippling him, and he was sure the little wretch knew it.

Well, two could play at that game, he decided. He might be half mad with an unsatisfied hunger, but he knew he had seen the gleam of interest in her eyes from time to time. He had felt the heat of her desire. She might be fighting it, but the hunger was there. Cameron was sure of it. And if she could torment him, then he could torment her.

Avery swallowed hard as Cameron started to take off his clothes. Her weakness for him was going to make it very hard to maintain the upper hand in this game. The sight of his lean, hard body heated her blood, made her ache to touch him, to taste him, to wrap her body tightly around his. With so many brothers and male cousins, she had seen many an example of the male form. It struck her as a little strange that seeing Cameron's should make her knees tremble with weakness, should inflame her lusts until she felt nearly dazed. She quickly averted her eyes, fighting for control of her errant desire. This was to be *her* game, *her* seduction, and she had no intention of letting her own weaknesses cause her to lose control of the situation.

Once stripped to her chemise and braies, she moved to wash up. It was not easy to decide what her next step should be. She really had little idea of how to seduce a man. It was not something she had ever done or ever even thought about. In fact, she had little experience with lusting or being lusted after. She was too slim and too strange-looking. She had occasionally caught a faint gleam of interest in a man's eyes, only to watch it fade as some full-breasted, pale-skinned lass tripped by. Men obviously liked a woman with some flesh on her bones, with breasts that bounced, and with nicely rounded hips that swayed as she walked. Avery suspected she would never have so lush a shape. She knew that Cameron's blatant desire for her too-slender form, a form too often ignored and occasionally ridiculed, only made it all the harder to resist him. It was heady indeed to be so desired.

Sensing that Cameron watched her, Avery unlaced her chemise a little. She slowly eased the damp rag she held inside to wash her breasts and under her arms. Cameron's breathing grew a little louder, a little uneven. Loosening her braies, she slid the cloth beneath them to wash her nether regions. Avery could almost feel the heat of his stare. Humming softly to herself, she took her time in washing off her arms and her legs. Although she was not sure how such a mundane activity could arouse a man, she had no doubt that Cameron was aroused. She could almost smell the hunger growing inside him.

"Are ye trying to bestir me to madness?" Cameron demanded, thinking that, for an innocent, Avery seemed to have an instinctive knowledge of what could make a man dazed with need.

His deep voice, raspy and thick with unmistakable passion, seemed to enter Avery's veins, heating her blood. "I but try not to take the stench of a day's hard work to bed with me."

"Ye didnae stink."

"Mayhap my nose is a wee bit more sensitive than yours."

"And mayhap ye taunt me."

Although Avery tightened the laces on her braies, she left the ones on her chemise loosened as she turned to face him. She fought the urge to look and see just how much of herself she was revealing when his gaze fixed upon her chest and stayed there. His black eyes gleamed with desire, his chest rose and fell heavily from the deep, unsteady breaths he took, and his hands were clenched into tight white-knuckled fists at his side. The knowledge that she, thin little Avery, could put such a beautiful man into such a state was an intoxicating thing. So heady and inflaming that she had to forcibly subdue the urge to fling herself into his arms. Avery sternly reminded herself that her plan was to seduce, not to surrender.

"Taunt ye?" she murmured. "I havenae said a word."

He grunted, a short, harsh sound rife with disbelief. "Ye have said more than enough, lass, though ye speak nary a word. Ye cannae be so naive that ye think ye can behave so right before my eyes and nay stir any response. Nay, no lass could be that blindingly innocent or ignorant of a mon."

"Innocent, ignorant and naive. Ye make it sound as if I am thrice cursed."

"I begin to think 'tis I who am cursed."

Avery decided she had made her resistance far too clear, for Cameron seemed unable to realize there had been a distinct change in her attitude. Seducing him was not going to be easy if he was going to blame her every move or word on naïveté, innocence, or ignorance, or some other less flattering motive. Avery tried to recall what she had heard some of the men in her family say they liked, what little she had managed to observe. Taking a deep breath to steady herself, she stepped closer to him and placed her hand on his broad, smooth chest.

Cameron broke out in a sweat. He looked at that small, delicate hand on his chest, the small tips of each long finger feeling like a brand on his skin, then looked at her. There was a look of innocence and curiosity in her lovely eyes, but there was also the gleam of a challenge there. Was she daring him to act upon the lust raging through his body just so she could then deny him? It was a game he had the misfortune of enduring before: the favors held just out of reach, offered then withdrawn until he promised some reward. Yet instinct told him Avery would not play such a game, if only because she had no idea how much power she could have over a man—over him. That left him uncertain of just what she was doing, however.

"Cursed, are ye?" she asked, her voice low and husky. "Have the black fairies set a spell upon ye, then?"

"I begin to think so," he murmured, and he could not stop himself from placing his hand over hers, holding her small warm hand where it was. "This is certainly a torment worthy of their ilk."

"I have been called many things, but ne'er a torment."

"Then the men about Donncoill are blind or complete fools."

"Flattery, Cameron? 'Tis a momentous occasion, this." She placed her free hand at his waist with what she hoped was an air of idleness, as simply a means to steady herself since he kept her other hand captive beneath his.

"Ye are an impertinent wee lass." He took a quick, sharp breath when she lightly stroked his side. "Ye play with fire, lass. In truth, I find myself most uncertain of just what game ye are playing."

"Who says this is a game I play?"

She trailed her fingers across his belly. His grip on her other hand tightened almost painfully as he trembled. It astounded her that she could so affect this man, but she quickly smothered a twinge of unaccustomed vanity. For all she knew, the man was simply hot of blood, easy to arouse, and there was his lengthy celibacy to consider.

For a brief moment Avery hesitated in her subtle assault on his senses. She dearly wished to believe Anne's assurances that Cameron's lust was stirred by Avery Murray alone, but that did indeed seem vain, especially since she had never stirred a man's lusts before. Nay. She inwardly shook her head. She would not falter now. Although she might not emerge from this first joining as the conqueror, she would still hold the honors of having approached him first, of having touched him first, of having stirred his desire to a feverish level ere he had even begun to stir hers. She would also hold the honors of being the first woman he had held in an intimate embrace for three long years. Avery circled his navel with one finger and felt his muscles clench beneath her touch.

"Jesu, lass, much more and I willnae heed any *nay* ye might think to utter," he warned, his voice little more than a groan of need.

"And mayhap I willnae utter one."

It was almost impossible to subdue a squeak of surprise when he suddenly grasped her by the arms and, in one tidy, graceful move, had her down on the bed, his long, hard body sprawled on top of hers. Then she was caught up in how good he felt there, her body welcoming the weight of his, his warmth seeping into her veins; and the faint tickle of fear she felt vanished. This was what she wanted. It might be nearly impossible to hold the upper hand in what was to happen now, but she knew she had pushed him to the edge, knew that no matter what lies he told himself later, a part of him would always know that she had not surrendered what he wanted, that she had given it to him.

Uttering a soft growl, Cameron kissed her. It was a hard, fierce kiss, which proclaimed his hunger as clearly as the hard length beneath his loincloth did. Avery wrapped her arms around his neck and returned the kiss with an equal hunger. She echoed the shudder that went through him. Avery wondered if such ferocity, such near desperation, was a good thing considering this was to be her first time; then he brushed his thumb over the hard, aching tip at her breast and she ceased to think at all.

Cameron struggled to unlace her chemise, his hands so unsteady that he was embarrassingly clumsy. His only consolation was that Avery appeared to be as desperate as he was—so desperate that she was blind to his awkwardness. Finally he slid his hands down to the embroidered hem of the thin chemise and began to edge it up her body, following its ascent with kisses, strokes of his tongue, and gentle, lightly grazing bites. When he finally bared her breasts, he was so enraptured by the sight, he had to shake himself slightly to recall the need to finish removing the garment.

He tossed the chemise aside and proceeded to look his fill, gently pinning her wrists to their rough bed when she tried to cover herself. Her breasts were not the large, ripe ones he had always favored in the past, but he deemed them perfection: high, firm, round as an apple, and topped with a large nipple colored an invitingly rich pink. His mouth watered.

Fighting to calm his need to a more controllable level from the blinding height it had risen to, he studied the rest of her lithe shape. Her skin was a warm, light-golden hue all over. Suddenly, frustrated by the small braies she wore, he clasped both her wrists in one hand, then wrenched that last piece of covering from her slender body. His breath caught almost painfully in his throat as he looked over the slim shapeliness of her hips and every inch of her surprisingly long, slender, faintly muscular legs. Then his hungry gaze settled on the neat triangle of golden-brown curls at the juncture of her beautiful thighs and he groaned. There lay heaven, and he knew it was going to take every ounce of his self-restraint to stop himself from taking her too quickly. He was shaking with the need to bury himself in her heat, immediately and deeply, but a lingering thread of sanity kept reminding him that she was a virgin, that she needed gentleness and preparation.

With his free hand he removed his loincloth; then he slowly lowered his trembling body onto hers. The feel of her silken flesh touching his left him struggling to breathe. Cameron did not think he had ever been so inflamed. He had never wanted a woman as badly as he wanted this one. Even the scent of her, the heady mix of lavender, clean skin, and feminine arousal, made him nearly mad with need. Seeing a hint of unease enter her passion-warmed eyes, he quickly kissed her as he released his hold on her hands. To his relief, she immediately wrapped her strong, slim arms around him.

The baring of her body had made Avery nearly cringe, but the heat of his gaze had swiftly burned away her shyness and uncertainty. His blatant appreciation of the shape so many had scorned made her feel nearly beautiful. The way his warm, taut flesh felt against her body had her fighting for an even breath. Instinct told her that, if she gained some control over her passion, it would aid Cameron in gaining some control over his. Although her body ached with greed for him, she did not want her first time to be too hurried, too frantic. Then he touched his soft, warm lips to her breast, and she wondered if she even had the strength of will to slow things down a little.

So sharp was the pleasure that raced through her when Cameron licked the hard tip of her breast Avery cried out. She clutched his strong arms in a vain attempt to steady herself as he laved and suckled greedily. An ache grew low in her belly and she felt compelled to rub against him. The feel of his erection against her mons only made her feel more agitated, more needy. She slid her hand down his side, then between their bodies to clasp him. He felt so hard, yet the skin there was silken smooth. Avery stroked him and was a little startled when he gasped out a curse, bowed his body away from hers, and pulled her hand away.

"Nay, lass, keep those wee hands to yourself or I will

be finishing this dance ere ye have had a chance to enjoy it,'' Cameron said.

Avery was not sure she understood what he meant. Then he stroked his big hand over her stomach and slid it between her legs. Avery doubted that she would notice now if he spoke nothing but gibberish. The feel of his long, callused fingers stroking her so intimately had her thrashing, fighting the feelings pounding through her, yet eager for them, afraid of what was happening to her, yet greedy for more.

"Jesu, lass, ye are already wet with welcome," he said, his voice hoarse and unsteady.

"Are ye just going to discuss it or are ye going to do something about it?" she challenged, not surprised to hear how thick and husky her own voice was, but only that she still had the wit left to speak at all.

Cameron laughed shakily as he spread her legs and positioned himself. " 'Twill hurt ye this first time.''

"Right now I think it will hurt me more if ye stop.''

"Oh, there is nay a chance of me stopping now, my wee cat.''

Her breath came in short gasps as he began to ease into her. A foolish part of her flared to life, panicked, certain he was too large, would never fit, and would damage her if he continued, but she ruthlessly silenced it. Cameron did feel large, filling her in a way that was both slightly uncomfortable and intensely pleasurable. When he stopped, she knew he had reached her maidenhead, and she tried not to tense in anticipation of the pain to come—something she knew would only make it worse.

"Lass, we could play this game without it costing ye your maidenhead," Cameron said. "A wee gentle ride. Nay too deep.''

"Now,'' Avery wrapped one leg around his trim waist,

"where would be"—she wrapped her other leg around him—"the fun in that?"

Using her legs and arms to force their bodies together, Avery impaled herself upon him. She echoed his startled curse. For a brief moment the pain of losing her maidenhead stilled her passion, but then she concentrated on how completely they were joined, on how a man and a woman could not get any closer than this, physically. She shifted slightly and gasped as her passion returned in a rush.

Cameron started to move, muttering hoarse words of flattery and encouragement against her neck. She clung to him, quickly adjusting to meet his thrusts. She slid her hands down his back to clutch at his taut buttocks, trying to push him deeper, to make sure that he did not even try to leave her now. A tension built inside her, and although she guessed what it meant, she found its strength a little alarming.

"Cameron," she cried, knowing she had just revealed her uncertainty, and briefly wishing that she could have been stronger.

"Nay, loving, dinnae fight it." He slowly edged his hand between their bodies to the place where they were joined. "Come with me, Avery. Give it to me."

He touched her, stroked her with his long, clever fingers, and Avery felt herself shatter. Waves of delight flowed over her. She clung to him as his thrusts grew fiercer. He suddenly plunged deep, his hands clenching on her hips so tightly it was almost painful. Cameron shuddered, groaned her name, and jerked against her a few times as if he no longer had full control of his body. She felt the heated rush of his seed deep inside her and shattered once more, only faintly aware of Cameron cursing in surprise and delight.

Avery did not come to her senses until Cameron had

cleaned them both off and was lying back down at her side. She felt almost too weak to move, yet when he pulled her into his arms, interest flickered to life inside her. Such greed, she mused, and smiled faintly as she rubbed her cheek against his chest.

True, she had not maintained full control, but she was satisfied. Even Cameron could not question that she had willingly stepped into his arms, that she had eagerly given him her maidenhead. He had actually hesitated to take it and she found that a little endearing. No matter what happened now, whether they had a future or not, she knew she would never regret becoming his lover. Innocent she might have been, and still was in many ways, but she knew in her heart that this was a once-in-a-lifetime passion. This was love, she thought, and she sighed, feeling the pinch of sadness, for it was an unrequited love. Avery promised herself that, even if it remained unreturned, she would still find joy in it.

Cameron heard her sigh and felt a quick, sharp stab of guilt. "Regrets?"

"Mayhap it would be wiser if we didnae discuss the whys, the ifs, or the wherefores of all of this," she said quietly as she stroked his chest, loving the feel of his taut warm skin, of muscles honed to smooth perfection. "After all, there is a verra good chance ye will say something that will anger me."

"And then ye will return to crying me nay?" Cameron tightened his grip on her, determined not to let that happen.

"Nay, then I will cut your heart out with a dull spoon and I think that might irritate your people."

He chuckled and stroked her back, from her slim shoulder to her nicely shaped backside. She felt good in his arms. The passion she had revealed in his arms had astounded him. So much fire in such a small, delicate woman. Even now, as he touched her only idly, he could feel her warm to him. She moved against his side in subtle invitation and her nipples hardened against his skin. Suddenly he knew, without a doubt, that it was going to be very hard to give her up. He was going to have to do his utmost to hold to his plan, to keep his sister's travails always in mind. And, he thought, trembling as he felt her tongue lightly play over his chest, he was going to have to keep his heart well guarded. Passion had made a fool of him far too often, and this passion was the strongest, the fiercest he had ever savored; thus it was a far more dangerous one. If Avery thought to turn him from his plans by feeding his desires, she would soon see that he could not be so easily manipulated. When she slid her hand over his belly and wrapped her long fingers around his manhood, he decided he would be a fool indeed, however, if he did not at least let her try.

"Ye should rest," he said, closing his eyes and savoring the feel of her stroking him to an aching hardness. "Ye will be sore come the morning."

"Nay more sore than I have been from riding a horse all the day, yet it ne'er stopped me from climbing back into the saddle the next morning." She combed her fingers through the thick hair at his groin, clasped the soft sack at the base of his erection, and gently squeezed.

A brief, surprised laugh escaped her when Cameron suddenly grabbed her, turned her onto her back, and sprawled on top of her. "Ye do move fast for such a large mon." She ran her feet up and down his calves, enjoying the feel of their sinewy strength. "Ye dinnae like to be touched?"

"I like it too much." He plucked at her hardened nipples with his fingers, then slowly licked each one, smiling with enjoyment over the way she squirmed beneath him "Mayhap in a week or two I will be able to savor more than one touch of those bonny hands."

She welcomed his kiss, for it silenced the words that had rushed into her mouth, the awkward questions about how close to Cairnmoor they would be by then, and whether he would still be eager to send her away. It would not be easy to banish such questions and concerns, but she would. Avery refused to allow such worries to steal away any of the delight she could feel in his arms. She simply promised herself that she would not allow that self-imposed blindness to become so complete that she fooled herself into thinking all was well. She would enjoy the heaven she found in his arms and pray that Cameron gained the wit to see what they could share, and see it clearly enough to want to hold fast to it.

Chapter Nine

Avery winced slightly as she stood up after helping Peter eat his porridge. She was feeling somewhat sore, although she was not really in pain. Clearly, making love stretched a few muscles she did not usually make much use of. Since she had woken up to find Cameron already deep inside her and herself in a fever of need, she had not really noticed her discomfort until now. What she needed was a long soak in a hot bath, but she decided she would wait until evening to have it. If she sought one now, she had the feeling that nearly everyone in camp would know the reason why.

When Anne asked her to gather some wood for the fires, Avery welcomed the chore, quickly collecting the small wood cart. With Gillyanne in tow and their guards ambling along behind them, she headed into the surrounding forest. It allowed her a respite from wondering if each person she caught looking at her was doing so because he knew what she had done. Avery knew it would take a while before she could feel comfortable in her place as Cameron's lover. The fact that everyone in camp knew Cameron had no plan to make their intimate relationship a permanent one caused her far more unease than she thought it ought to.

"So, how does it feel to be a woman now?" asked Gillyanne as she tossed some kindling into the little cart.

"How do ye ken that I have taken that step?" Avery asked a little testily. "Am I branded upon the forehead?"

Gillyanne laughed and shook her head. "Nay, ye look no different, which I find a little disappointing. Nay, 'tis just that ye told me ye meant to give in, and I can nae believe that braw mon of yours would refuse an *aye* when ye gave him one."

"Oh. Weel, he didnae. And it just feels odd right now. Whilst in his arms the delight is near to blinding, but, now I feel . . . weel, uneasy. I wonder how many ken what I have done, yet I dinnae feel any shame, just a wee bit of discomfort—mayhap embarrassment—that my personal business may nay be as private as I would like."

"That will probably pass. I dinnae think anyone here will think any less of ye for this." Gillyanne shrugged. "In truth, I think nay just a few of Cameron's people wonder if this trouble with his sister has rattled their laird's wits."

"That willnae please Cameron if he catches wind of it."

"Nay, but mayhap 'twill make the fool pause and think a bit."

"One can only hope."

"And just what do ye wish him to think of?' "

"That 'twill cost him most dearly to set me aside," Avery replied quietly.

"Mayhap a good sound knock on the head will help,"

Gillyanne drawled as she hefted a thick piece of wood in her small hands.

Avery laughed. "Aye, mayhap."

"And what will ye do if he doesnae gain the wit to see that he needs ye, wants to keep ye?"

Waste away, Avery thought. *Shatter into a hundred sharp, cutting pieces.* But she simply replied, "Survive," and was pleased when, after studying her closely for a moment, Gillyanne just nodded and returned to the chore of collecting wood.

"So, need I ask why ye are in such a fine mood?" Leargan asked Cameron as they saddled their horses, preparing to go on a hunt for food.

"Some things are nay any of your concern," replied Cameron, tightening the cinches on his saddle.

"Weel, if ye dinnae wish the whole camp to ken that ye have finally gained your prize, 'twould be best to stop looking at the lass so . . . er, warmly."

"Thought I had been looking at her that way for days now."

"True, but the look has changed some. 'Tis now one holding a knowledge of just what awaits ye there."

Cameron mounted, stared out over the camp, and sighed. Leargan was probably right. Instead of just looking eager, he now looked eager and knowing. He probably looked like a man who now knew he would find a welcome in the arms of the woman he lusted after. And he did indeed lust after Avery Murray. Only sheer strength of will had pulled him out of her arms this morning. A large part of him had ached to remain cloistered in his tent all day making love to her. In truth, several long, sweaty days of lovemaking would probably not be enough to take the edge off his greed for her. Just thinking about her had him aching.

"It shouldnae be a surprise to anyone," Cameron said. "'Twas my plan from the beginning. And, 'tis still none of their concern. 'Tis between me and Avery, none other."

Leargan mounted, following when Cameron nudged his horse into motion. "Nay? They like her and that wee impertinent cousin of hers. She saved our lives, helps their women, tends their wounds, and, 'tis because of her care that young Peter will live. Ye are their laird and they will follow with little question, but that doesnae mean that they are nae thinking of a few. They dinnae feel that she deserves to be used, shamed, and then cast aside."

"Do ye forget Katherine's plight?"

"Nay, but that is nae Avery's doing. The righteousness of your plan appealed to all of us until we came to ken the lass ye would use to accomplish it. Now it just doesnae set right. Ye could have left her be. Ye could have set aside the seduction part of your plan and just used her in trade, the ransom being Sir Payton."

"Aye, I could have. Howbeit, ye cannae blame this on me. Last night she seduced me." Cameron scowled at Leargan when his cousin released a snorting laugh of blatant disbelief. "She did. Aye, she didnae need to use many tricks, did she? 'Tis no secret I have lusted after her from the start. However, I was questioning the whole of my plan." He frowned. "I suddenly didnae want the bedding, if there was to be one, to be part of it all. But, *she* came to *me*. Jesu, at one point I e'en offered to leave her maidenhood intact, but she took that decision from my hands as weel."

"Weel, ye handsome rogue, ye have obviously driven the poor lass to madness." Leargan met Cameron's glare with a wide, unrepentant grin, then quickly grew serious again. "Marry her."

" 'Twould be verra difficult to trade Avery for her brother if I made her my wife, now wouldnae it?''

"Trade Gillyanne for Sir Payton.''

"If Avery was my wife, any threat I made against the wee lass wouldnae carry any weight, would it. The Murrays wouldnae believe that I would do anything more to my wife's wee cousin than glare at her. Jesu, they would ken that I would have to battle my own wife to e'en try to hurt that lass. And, I dinnae want a wife.''

"Every mon needs an heir.''

"I dinnae. I have you and any one of nearly a dozen other cousins.''

"And ye dinnae trust any woman as far as ye can spit, do ye?''

"Do ye blame me? A treacherous lot, women are. Sweet and soft when they want something, yet quick to stab ye in the back if the mood takes them or they find richer fields elsewhere. Right now, Avery is being sweet and soft, but 'twill nay last.''

Leargan shook his head. "Ye malign the poor lass without cause. Do ye mistrust all men because some have revealed a lack of honor? Nay. Yet ye spit upon the honor of all women because of the actions of a few.''

"More than a few,'' Cameron muttered, but the truth of Leargan's words could not really be argued away. "The only thing that matters, that cannae be ignored, is that Katherine needs to wed the mon who seduced her. If she is carrying a bairn, then that bairn needs his father. The way to get those things is with Gillyanne and Avery.''

"Ye are a stubborn mon, cousin.''

"Why? Because I feel a stronger loyalty to one of my own blood than to a wee lass tossed at my feet, to the sister of the mon who dishonored my sister? If matters were t'other way round, Avery would feel the same. She would stand firm by her blood kin, by her clansmen. And she would expect me to understand that.''

"Ah, but that would imply that she has a sense of loyalty and honor, and ye cannae seem to believe that any lass could have either,'' Leargan drawled. Then he nudged his horse ahead of Cameron's, signaling an end to the discussion.

Cameron cursed and followed his cousin. He had begun to see that, perhaps there were a few flaws in his beliefs about women. It was a change of attitude he fought against, however. His cynicism, his complete lack of faith in women, was part of his shield against the allure of Avery, and he was determined not to lose it.

He was pleased to have all discussion about Avery ended, too. Leargan's suggestion about marrying the lass was not one he wanted to hear too often, nor any arguments that would reveal it to be in any way possible. It was tempting, too tempting. Now that he had tasted her passion, he would like nothing better than to hold her in his bed, to have the right to reach for her any time he felt so inclined. To his utter dismay, he could all too easily envision a future with her, could even see the children they could raise together. Nay, even the word *marriage* was enough to start him thinking, and he could not afford to. Avery would be sent away. What they shared now was only a passing thing. For his own sake, and for Katherine's, he could not allow it to be anything more.

Avery sighed with pleasure as she eased her body down into the hot herbal-scented bath. She found it a little amusing that Cameron toted along the huge bathing tub as well as his feather mattress, although she was deeply grateful for both. Since they were settled in one spot for

more than one night, he had had his tub and his mattress
unpacked. The man plainly liked his comforts. She suspected he had also anticipated very little trouble along
the way, which was comforting.

As she lounged in the bath, letting the heat soothe away
each and every twinge, she thought about how she should
deal with Cameron now. He was her lover now, and it
would be hard to change that even if she had any inclination to do so. Cameron was a very stubborn man, and he
had his mind set on using her to force Payton to marry
Katherine. He also did not trust women. That left her in
the awkward position of having to prove herself to him,
of making him see that she was just what he needed. She
had saved the lives of him and his people, done her fair
share of the work of keeping his men fed, clothed, and
comfortable, and nursed his wounded men. Now she
warmed his bed, and she did not think it was vanity that
made her certain she did that very well indeed. As far as
Avery could see, there was not a whole lot more she
could do.

Briefly, she considered telling him what lay in her heart,
but she quickly cast aside that idea. Cameron would think
she played some kind of game. His distrust of women
would make him see her words of love as no more than
some attempt to get him to do as she wanted. That would
hurt—far more than she even cared to think about.

So, she mused, that left her with the passion they shared.
Although he did not seem to sense it, she put her love
for him behind every kiss, every touch, every sigh of
delight. Eventually that might work to soften his heart,
make him rethink his plans. That, and just continuing to
behave as she had been. Cameron was not stupid. At
some point, he had to realize that not all women were
like the ones whose betrayals had so soured him.

Avery grimaced as she started to wash herself. Perhaps,

if she did no more than soften his attitude about women, she could find some solace in that. It would not warm her lonely bed after he had set her aside, nor mend her broken heart, but it would be an accomplishment she could take some pride in.

Suddenly, Cameron appeared at the side of her tub, naked and grinning. Avery knew she was staring at him stupidly as he climbed into the tub, but she could not help herself. He was such a beautiful man, the mere sight of him was enough to stir her desire. She was also startled to realize that she had been sunk so deeply into her own thoughts that she had not even heard him enter the tent and undress.

"Are ye sure this tub can hold both of us?" she asked as he slowly sank down into the water, his long body crowding her up against the far end.

"Aye, although I may regret this." He scooped up a handful of water, sniffed it, and grimaced. "My men will think I smell far too pretty. Ah, weel, at least it is nae roses. And, getting all hot and sweaty afterward should dim some of the stench."

"And just what do ye plan to do to get all hot and sweaty?" she asked, although the heated look in his eyes gave her a very good idea. "Hunt? Train the men? Wrestle?"

"Wrestle. With ye. All night long," he added, drawing out each word as he plucked the soap and washing cloth from her hands. "Come, turn round, lass, and I will wash your back."

Even as she did what he told her to, she muttered, "I was almost done bathing."

"Ah, but ye have nae done your back yet, have ye?"

"Weel, nay," she replied, certain he had far more in mind than just assisting her in her bath.

Avery trembled slightly as he began to wash her back;

she was mildly disgusted with herself. He was not doing anything seductive. In fact, he barely touched her with his hands, yet the way he rubbed her with the washing rag was enough to stir her blood. Obviously, as concerned her passion for Cameron, there was little hope for control. Now that she knew the full delight they could share, her weakness for him had clearly grown tenfold.

"Stand up, lass, so that I can finish the back of you," Cameron said.

There was a trace of huskiness in his deep voice that told Avery he was not completely unmoved. She found some comfort in that. It was also a little sad, she decided as she stood up. One instinctively tried to guard oneself against such a weakness. It was possible that they could spend what little time they had together both fighting hard against becoming helpless victims of their own passions. Love would find a hard time taking root under such conditions.

She caught her breath as he began to wash her legs and backside. There was a change in the way he touched her. He was using his hands to soap her skin now, and he was stroking her. When he rinsed the soap away, she breathed a sigh of relief pleased that that torment was over, only to nearly stumble to her knees when he kissed her at the very base of her spine. She clenched her hands into tight fists when he took his kisses even lower.

"Turn around, loving," he ordered, grasping her firmly by the hips and gently forcing her to obey him.

It was hard for Avery to decide which heated her cheeks more: her rising desire or her embarrassment. She felt horribly exposed, yet the taut look of passion on his dark face kept her from trying to shield herself from his gaze. When he nudged her legs apart to wash between them, she grasped hold of his head, her knees so weak that she felt a need to support herself. She was shaking slightly by the time he rinsed the soap away, but when she tried to step away, he held her in place. A cry of shock and delight escaped her when he kissed the soft curls he had so gently bathed.

"Nay, Cameron," she protested.

"Aye, Avery. Oh, most definitely, aye."

With but a few strokes of his tongue, he silenced her embarrassed protests. Avery closed her eyes and gave herself over fully to the pleasure he was giving her. Very quickly she did not care what he saw or what he did, so long as he did not stop. With his fingers and his mouth, he drove her mad, pushing her to the edge time and time again only to draw back. He teased and tormented her until she was demanding that he end this torture.

He stopped her attempt to join their bodies, taking her to her release with his kisses. Even as she shuddered from the strength of it, he pulled her down onto his lap, impaling her on himself. He bent her back over his arm and turned his greedy, sensuous attentions upon her breasts. With his hands upon her hips, he moved her body on his until she felt her passion soaring again. This time when she cried out in release, he was with her.

Although several moments had passed, Avery was still dazed from his lovemaking when she let him lift her from the bath and dry her off. When he was done, she had recovered enough to snatch the drying cloth from his hands. She began to rub him dry, determined to push him to the brink of madness as he had done to her.

By the time she was kneeling in front of him, painstakingly drying his legs, Cameron was breathing hard. Her own desire rising rapidly, Avery meticulously dried his groin, savoring his every gasp and groan as she stroked him. She then tossed aside the cloth, placed her hands on his trim hips, and ever so slowly ran her tongue up the full length of his erection. The groan that escaped him seemed to shake his whole body.

Cameron stared down at her as she kissed and licked him. His hands were clenched into tight fists at his side as he fought for the control to enjoy her loving. When she captured his gaze with hers and then eased him into her warm mouth, he knew that was a pleasure he did not have the strength to savor for very long at all.

Finally, with a harsh cry that was a mixture of pleasure and disappointment over his own inability to control himself, he gripped her beneath her arms and carried her to the bed. Even as he thought to apologize for not being able to take the time to stir her passions to an equal height, he plunged into her and found her more than ready for him. That proof that she had been nearly as aroused as he by loving him only inflamed him more. What ensued was a frenzied mating, but Avery met and equaled his ferocity. When his release shuddered through him, she was but a heartbeat behind with her own.

He collapsed into her arms. Although Cameron suspected he was too heavy for her, he was too wrung out to move. After a few minutes, he felt her squirm a little beneath him and he mustered just enough strength to flop over onto his back and pull her up against his side. If they kept indulging their passion for each other with such ferocity, he would be entering Cairnmoor on a litter. When he recalled that reaching his home would signal the end of his affair with Avery, he swiftly pushed such thoughts right out of his mind. He did not want to think of endings when his body still thrummed from the delights he had just enjoyed.

"I think we need to practice some caution, lass," he said, brushing a lazy kiss over her forehead. "Much more of this greedy behavior and I willnae be able to sit a horse.''

''Dinnae have the stamina ye had when ye were young, is that it?'' she murmured, lightly rubbing her hand over his hip.

''Verra amusing. Ye should be too exhausted to be so impertinent.''

''I recover fast.'' She yawned and rubbed her cheek against his chest. ''Was that, weel . . . normal?''

Cameron laughed softly. ''Afraid ye may be excommunicated or something?'' He stroked her back, then began to fondle her backside, unable to stop touching her. ''If ye confessed all this, ye would probably have to do a penance or two since the church considers most all pleasures a sin. Aye, they scowl upon anything more than a hurried rutting in the dark whilst nearly fully clothed. Dinnae fret o'er it, lass. We havenae done anything many another hasnae done, and I dinnae think 'tis the devil leading ye along.''

Nay, just my loins, she mused, but she only nodded. From what she had occasionally overheard the men in her family talk about, most everyone was indeed indulging themselves whenever the opportunity arose. If enjoying such pleasures was enough to consign oneself to hell's fires, she would not be lonely, for most of her family would probably be roasting right alongside her.

''Humph, ye have gotten me all a-sweat,'' she mumbled, glancing toward the bath.

''Want me to scrub your back?'' he offered with a grin as she scrambled over his body and walked toward the tub.

Shivering slightly as she hastily washed up with the now-cooled water, she limited her response to one brief, thoroughly-disgusted look his way. She wrapped the drying cloth around herself and hurried back to bed. Even as she crawled back beneath the blankets, Cameron grabbed the drying cloth off her and went to wash up. She squeaked with surprise when he got back into bed a few minutes later and yanked her into his arms.

"Cameron, ye are cold all over," she protested.

"I ken it," he said, holding her even closer. "Ye will warm me up."

He slid his hand over her stomach and between her thighs. Her gasp of shock quickly turned to a murmur of delight. Cameron found the way she responded so swiftly and sweetly to him one of the greatest pleasures he had ever known. He hooked her leg back over his hip, opening her more fully to his touch.

"I am definitely feeling warmer now," he murmured against her ear.

Avery shivered, feeling the deep rumble of his voice all the way down to her toes "I thought ye were going to curb our greedy behavior." She gasped as he suddenly turned her onto her back and crouched over her, the size of his erection telling her that he was certainly feeling greedy again.

"I was thinking that our recent gluttonous behavior has fed my fever weel enough that, this time, I can go slowly." He dragged his tongue over her nipple. "I can savor you, play with you, linger over each and every delicious inch of you."

His soft, husky words made her skin tingle with anticipation. "Ye were worried about being unable to sit your horse," she reminded him.

"I can walk, or, mayhap I will just have Leargan carry me about." He kissed each of her hipbones.

When he settled himself between her legs and licked the inside of each thigh, she whispered, "Ye plan to drive me completely insane, dinnae ye?"

He hooked her legs over his shoulders, slid his hands

beneath her bottom, and touched a kiss to her nether curls. "Completely."

"Oh, sweet Mary," she groaned. She suspected it would be the last coherent thing she would say for a very long time.

Chapter Ten

" 'Tis the DeVeaux again."

Cameron stared at Leargan in utter disbelief, then softly cursed.

Although he and Leargan had ridden ahead of the others to make sure the trail they followed was safe, he had not really expected to find any trouble. They were making good time in their journey to the port they would sail from—such good time that they had almost made up for the four days lost waiting for the wounded men to heal enough to travel safely. In truth, he was undoubtedly pushing his people harder than was needed. He had heard a few grumbles, but he fought to ignore them. It was probably not completely rational, yet he felt that if he took his time, everyone would think it was because he wished to hold onto Avery a little longer. Since that was exactly what he did want to do, he strove hard to do the exact opposite. In his current state of emotional turmoil, confronting DeVeau's men was not something he wanted to deal with.

"After all the men they lost in the last attack, ye would think they would give up," Cameron said. "The mon didnae pay us that weel. Jesu, he would pay nearly as much now just to replace the men he lost."

"Aye, it makes no sense. Perhaps we should try to spy upon them for a wee bit. They may not even be looking for us."

After considering the idea for a moment, Cameron nodded. They rode closer to where the DeVeaux were camped, then dismounted and secured their horses. Slipping through the trees, they reached the very edge of the camp and crouched in the shadows. Cameron nearly cursed aloud when a familiar figure stepped out of a tent a few feet away. Sir Charles DeVeau rarely rode with his men. Cameron found the man's presence ominous.

As they watched, a small table was set up. A fine linen cloth was spread over it and it was set with rich plates, eating utensils, and a goblet. Cameron nearly grunted in disgust when an ornate padded chair was set before the table. Sir Charles sat down and a nervous little man hurried over to serve what was obviously the first course of a many-course dinner. Cameron doubted the man fed his soldiers with such care and bounty.

Sir Charles was into the third course of his elaborate meal and Cameron was thinking that he and Leargan were wasting their time, when one of the DeVeau soldiers marched up. "Where are the MacAlpins?" Sir Charles asked after dabbing at his mouth with a lace-trimmed linen napkin.

"Not far from here, my lord," the man replied.

"And the prize I seek?"

"Should be along shortly. Luck was with us. We gained the prize without even alerting the camp."

A chill snaked down Cameron's spine. He knew they were not talking about the coin. That was stored with the baggage and could not possibly be taken without someone being alerted, for it would be set in the very heart of his camp. His unease grew as he mulled over every other possibility, continuously coming back to the same answer. DeVeau had sent his men to kidnap someone and, recalling that there was an old, bitter feud between the DeVeaux and the Murrays and Lucettes, he had a bone-chilling idea of just who they might be seeking.

He looked at Leargan and found no reassurances in that man's dark expression. It was clear that his cousin had reached the same conclusion. Cameron silently asked, "Stay?" and Leargan nodded. Tense and fighting to stay calm and clearheaded, Cameron waited, all the while praying that he was wrong.

Avery slipped away from camp for a moment of privacy. She half smiled when her guard watched her leave, looked to see that Gillyanne was still in the camp, and returned to his work. The guards had obviously decided that, if she and Gillyanne were not together, there was little chance she would try to escape. Avery was a little tempted to make a dash for it just to stir things up, but she knew that Cameron would never believe she had only meant it as a tease.

Feeling a need to stretch her legs after riding all day, she walked slowly through the wood, keeping the camp within hearing distance if not always in sight. For a week now they had been riding steadily toward the port from which they would sail to Scotland. It seemed as if Cameron was pushing them hard. Although she could understand his need to return home to sort out his sister's troubles, or even because he missed Scotland after being away for so long, it still hurt that he would hurry so. As far as she knew, he still planned to be rid of her once they reached Cairnmoor. Despite telling herself not to be foolish, that it was vain to think everything the man did was somehow about her, and despite the greed with which he still reached for her in the night, Avery could not stop herself from occasionally thinking that he was in a painful hurry to be rid of her.

She often puzzled over how the problem of Cameron's sister could be solved without using her or Gillyanne. If the girl could be exposed as the liar she so clearly was, that would solve everything, but Avery doubted that could be accomplished easily. From what little information she had gathered about Katherine, the girl knew how to get what she wanted—and she wanted Payton. There was little chance that the man who had been her lover, if there even was one, would step boldly forth and claim responsibility. That left only the chance that Cameron would fall in love with her, would be so anxious to keep her at his side, that he would find some other solution to his sister's problem. Avery saw little sign of that miracle occurring.

Some ripe berries caught her eye and Avery hurried to collect them. They would add a nice sweetness to the camp fare that consisted mostly of meat and porridge. As she filled the hollow made by her gathered skirts, she sensed something that sent a tremor of alarm through her. She stared off into the woods but could see nothing. Just as she was about to turn to look behind her, a large, gauntleted hand was clamped over her mouth.

Avery dropped her skirts, scattering the berries, and started to reach up to try and remove that hand. She gave a muffled scream as her hands were grabbed, yanked behind her, and bound at the wrists. The hand over her mouth was removed, but she was gagged with a cloth so swiftly she did not even have time to draw the breath needed to scream for help. Despite her struggles, she was easily lifted up and flung over a broad shoulder, the thrashing of her legs stilled by the tightening of a muscular arm around them. She was painfully bounced along as the man who held her captive ran through the wood, away from the MacAlpin camp.

A few moments later, she was flung belly-down over a saddle, the breath knocked out of her. As she struggled to recover from that, her captor mounted and spurred his horse into a gallop. Avery set her mind to not becoming ill. She tried to see who held her, but gained only the knowledge that there were three men, their attire and fine horses marking them as knights, or at least, rather successful mercenaries.

It was not until they reached a camp that Avery got a better idea of exactly what kind of trouble she was in. Dazed, her head pounding, and her stomach bruised, she was dragged from the horse and set roughly on her feet. It was then that she saw the DeVeau banner. As she was yanked toward an ornate tent, she prayed this was some ploy to get DeVeau's coin back without losing any more men, and not because Sir Charles had discovered who she was.

Her gag was yanked off as she was set before Sir Charles, and she welcomed the wine that was poured down her throat, despite the fact that it was given to her so roughly it nearly choked her. ''This becomes tedious,'' she finally said, meeting Sir Charles's cold gaze and holding it. ''Is there yet another gambling debt to be paid? Or do you think Sir Cameron will pay to get me back?''

''Sir Cameron will not be given the chance to get you back,'' Sir Charles replied, studying her closely as he sipped his wine.

''Why? You did not think I was worth enough to pay

off Sir Bearnard's debt. Has my worth suddenly risen then?''

"Oh, yes, quite. You are a Murray."

Avery fought down the surge of fear that rushed through her and gave the man a look of pure, innocent confusion. "A who?"

"Very well done," Sir Charles drawled, almost smiling. "Do not waste your time and mine with that game. Your kinsmen, the Lucettes, have been demanding your return and that of your cousin. They refuse to believe that I do not have you—either of you."

"And what do you care about what the Lucettes want or believe?"

"I care nothing at all, except that the extent of their concern tells me that you could prove very useful to me."

"How?" Avery prayed that he would speak of some simple ransom or an exchange of prisoners. His reply made her heart sink into her boots.

"I am not yet sure. My only plan thus far was to remove you from Sir Cameron's grasp. Now that that has been accomplished, I must pause to consider all possibilities. I suppose the Scot has bedded you?"

"Sir Cameron has taken a vow of celibacy. He is returning me to my family."

"Ah, yes, to the murderess and the lover who aided her in escaping justice."

"My mother did not kill anyone. She was proven innocent; the real murderers were found and hanged."

"Or so the Lucettes would have us believe. It matters not. It is an old crime, although the bitch profited well by it." He tilted his head slightly to the side. "Now, there is a thought. I wonder how much Lady Gisele would be willing to give up to get her daughter back?"

"I think your king might frown upon your forcing her

to give up what he, and his father before him, have said belongs to my mother and the Lucettes.''

Sir Charles stood up and slowly walked around her. Avery cringed inwardly as he stroked her tumbled hair, patted her backside, and then, with an almost frightening coldness, placed one pale hand over her breast. She held steady, forcing herself not to reveal any of the deep revulsion she felt, and to meet his gaze with a cold stare.

''I wonder how your father and mother would feel if I sent you back to them with your belly swollen with my bastard,'' Sir Charles said as he returned to his seat and had another drink of wine.

''And I suggest that you try to recall how your cousin Michael died.''

''Think to geld me, do you?''

''In a heartbeat.''

''Such fire. It will be interesting to see how well it warms a man's bed.''

He languidly waved his hand at her guard. ''Secure her in my tent, Anton.'' He smiled faintly. ''And be sure there are no sharp objects about.''

Avery did not fight as she was taken into the tent, knowing it would be a useless waste of her strength. She shook her head when she found the inside of his tent furnished like an elegant bedchamber. Her guard untied her wrists and, with the help of Sir Charles's burly squire, tied her hand and foot to the large bed.

The moment the men left, Avery stared blindly at the fire in the center of the huge tent and tried to calm herself. She needed some strand of hope to maintain her strength. Cameron would come after her. What troubled her was the feeling that he would not really do so because he cared for her, but because honor and the fact that he needed her for his sister drove him to it. Then she told herself not to be such an idiot. The reasons why he would come did not really matter at the moment—only that he would come. She set her mind to praying that her rescue would not cost Cameron too dearly, and that it would come before Sir Charles had a chance to defile her with his touch.

Cameron took several deep breaths to calm himself, then signaled Leargan that he could safely release him now. When he had seen Avery brought before Sir Charles and heard the man's plans for her, rage had blinded him for a moment. Only Leargan's quick action had saved him from the fatal error of bursting into the DeVeau camp and relieving Sir Charles of the hand that had touched Avery. Cautiously, he followed his cousin back to their horses.

"I have to get her back," Cameron said as he stood by his horse, tightly gripping the saddle and struggling to further control his rage and fear.

"Of course ye do," Leargan agreed. "I wonder how his cousin Michael died?" he asked, thinking to divert Cameron long enough to help him regain some calm.

" 'Tis said that his manhood was cut off, shoved into his mouth, and then his throat was cut."

"Jesu," Leargan whispered. "How did ye find that out?"

"I asked why Sir Charles wanted to attack the Lucettes and learned a great deal about the feud. Avery also told me of her mother's side of the tale. Clearly there is a measure of greed involved in it all." Cameron mounted. "We shall need a few men."

Leargan mounted and followed Cameron as they slowly rode away, needing a little more distance from the DeVeau camp before spurring their horses into a gallop. " 'Twas easy to slip close to the camp, and Sir Charles's tent is foolishly set near the edge.''

"So, enough men to create a diversion, and a small number to raid Sir Charles's tent.''

"Aye, that should do it.''

"And we shall have to tell the others to break camp and move on. No point in sitting there waiting for the DeVeaux to try and retrieve their prize. I think I shall have to kill Sir Charles,'' Cameron added quietly, spurring his mount into a gallop before Leargan could argue the wisdom of that.

They found the camp in an uproar; Avery's disappearance was already discovered. Cameron fought against the urge to vent his tumultuous feelings upon Wee Rob. He had told the man to make sure that Avery did not try to escape, and the man had done his job. He had never considered the possibility that Avery might have enemies who would try to take her. That had been foolish. He had known about the feud, the old hatreds, between the DeVeaux and the Murrays. He should have considered the possibility that DeVeau would discover just whom Sir Bearnard had captured and would want the girls back. At least Gillyanne was safe, Cameron thought as he met her fear-widened gaze and nearly winced with guilt.

"Are ye sure that Sir Charles kens who Avery is?'' Gillyanne asked.

"Aye, I fear so, lass,'' Cameron replied. "I heard him say so myself. Leargan and I were close enough to hear every word said.''

"Jesu,'' Gillyanne whispered. She shivered. "He will hurt her.''

"Nay, lass, ye cannae be sure of that,'' Cameron lied, desperate to soothe her.

"Aye, I can, though I thank ye for the kind lie. Nay, DeVeau men hurt women. 'Tis their way. I wonder why

Avery didnae sense the danger,'' she muttered, frowning slightly.

"Weel, they probably slipped up behind the lass, caught her by surprise.''

"That wouldnae matter. She must have been distracted.'' She smiled faintly at Cameron's look of confusion. "Avery is verra good at sensing an approaching threat. She gave us warning ere the DeVeaux attacked our kinsmen. There isnae much time to act upon her feelings or warnings, but that time 'twas enough to allow the Lucettes to fight, to make the DeVeaux attack a battle instead of a slaughter.'' She shrugged. "I suppose it doesnae always work.''

"She can *sense* danger?''

"Aye. 'Tis as if she can smell it in the air sometimes. Her father can, too. 'Tis a fine skill, e'en if it doesnae always work. Like this time.'' She saw the men beginning to gather around Cameron. "Ye are going to save her.''

" 'Tis our plan. I dinnae think her life is in any danger,'' he added, hoping to ease any fear she might still suffer.

"Nay, not unless she gets loose and tries to kill Sir Charles. God's speed,'' she said before hurrying off to help the women break camp.

Cameron led his men back toward the DeVeau camp. He tried to push Gillyanne's parting words from his mind, but he could not. Avery was not a woman to meekly accept her fate, to sit quietly weeping and pray someone would come to save her. He was not sure what one small, unarmed woman could do against Sir Charles, but he knew the man was a dangerous one to anger. For a brief moment, Cameron was sorry he had kept Avery's knife, then shook that regret aside. The fact that she was unarmed might be enough to keep her alive until he could get her out of there.

"Your plan to free her is a good one," Leargan said. "We will get the lass back."

"Aye, if she doesnae do something foolish like try to save herself," Cameron muttered.

"Ah, I hadnae considered that. Sir Charles ordered her weel secured. She probably willnae be able to try anything nay matter how much she may wish to."

"While the thought of that swine keeping her tied and helpless isnae one I care to linger on, 'twould be best for her if she is."

"The lass must be used to it by now."

Cameron was glad they were mounted, or he would have struck his cousin for that remark. And, the sad truth was, Leargan did not deserve to be knocked flat for stating a simple fact. He could only hope Avery did not see too many similarities between what Sir Charles planned for her and his own actions. Cameron knew he could never have hurt Avery, not physically, but he was not sure she knew it.

"Let us hope he, too, softens the sting of the ropes with silken underwrappings," Cameron murmured, feeling the need somehow, even subtly, to defend his actions. "And let us hope he is still eating his dinner."

"Do ye think he meant his threat? About setting his bastard growing in her?"

"I dinnae think he kens just what he will do with her, although the tone of his voice when he made the threat implied that he rather savored the idea."

The thought of Sir Charles touching Avery, possessing her, made Cameron almost ill with rage. Avery was his. It did not matter that he intended to set her aside, or that he staunchly resisted feeling anything more than lust for her. He was the first man to taste her passion, and until he set her aside, he intended to be the only man who enjoyed it. If Sir Charles raped Avery, he would soon be made to view his cousin Michael's death as a merciful one.

Leaving their horses at a safe distance with two men to stand guard over them, Cameron and the rest of his men crept closer to the DeVeau camp. Cameron tensed when he saw that Sir Charles was no longer outside his tent. He had to fight down the urge to charge into the man's tent, sword swinging. Quietly he ordered four of his men to slip around to the other side of the camp and enact their diversion. That left Cameron with Leargan, Wee Rob, and Colin. It also left him with the nerve-racking need to do nothing but wait.

"It willnae take them long to pull all eyes their way," Leargan whispered.

"Cease trying to comfort me, cousin," Cameron replied in an equally soft voice, wondering how he must look if Leargan kept feeling the need to try and calm him down.

"Weel, ye did look ready to charge that tent a moment ago, sword swinging, and a battle cry upon your lips."

"It was only a passing urge."

"Mayhap ye ought to ask yourself why ye have the urge at all. After all, 'tis only wee Avery Murray, the lass ye mean to toss back into her family's lap soon after we reach Cairnmoor. Ye still have wee Gillyanne to make your trade."

"And if ye shut your mouth right now, ye may still have a tongue to delight the lasses with."

Leargan rolled his eyes, but he shut his mouth. Cameron returned to staring at the tent, frustrated that he could not see inside, that there was no way to let Avery know he was near. Such waiting also left him with little more to do than think, and he cursed silently, when Leargan's words refused to be silenced or ignored.

He should not be so enraged that another man touched Avery. He should not be so angry and afraid because she was under threat that he nearly acted with reckless foolishness, even had to have help to stay calm. Somehow, he was failing in keeping himself aloof in enjoying the passion they shared but never allowing it to become some emotional entanglement.

Avery was fun, he mused, making him laugh—something he had done little of in the past few years. She was actually a very likable young woman with her own special, endearing wit and charm. Despite her higher station in life, she did not hesitate to work alongside, and even befriend, the wives of his men at arms. Avery was quick to rush to the aid of any injured or ill person. The journey across France had been rough, sometimes even grueling, but she made no complaint. In truth, the only thing they could not even discuss without anger was the matter of his sister's accusations against her brother.

Cameron decided that he did like Avery, enjoyed her company. It amazed him, but it did not feel odd to think of Avery as a friend as well as a lover. There was also the fact that he and his men owed her their lives. All good reasons to risk life and limb to save her now, he decided, easily dismissing the faint voice that told him he was fooling himself again.

To Cameron's relief, if only because it stopped him from thinking any more, his men gave him the diversion he needed. Two of the small carts at the far end of the camp caught fire. To add to the resultant confusion, the horses were sent racing through the camp. Smiling grimly, Cameron made his way to the back of Sir Charles's tent.

Chapter Eleven

It was not easy, but Avery hid the fear she felt when Sir Charles entered his tent. The way he looked at her splayed out on his bed like some ancient sacrifice, and then smiled, made her wish that she still had her knife. Killing the man, as she so dearly wished to do, would undoubtedly earn her a quick, brutal death, but, at that precise moment, it seemed worth it.

"Is this how your fine Scottish lover kept you at his side?" Sir Charles asked.

"Nay," she replied; then she recalled that she had to speak French. "He but secured one wrist to the bed. A braver man than you." She barely repressed a squeak of alarm when he suddenly drew his sword and touched the cold, sharp point to her throat.

"You should be more careful with your taunts, woman, especially considering your current position."

"You will stain your fine sheets, my lord."

"Ah, yes, there is that to consider."

Avery held her breath as he began slowly to cut the laces on her bodice. This DeVeau was obviously as cold and twisted as the ones her mother had confronted. Considering how long her mother had had to deal with such chilling insanity, Avery was surprised the woman was as sweet and happy as she was. It also explained why her mother rarely returned to the land of her birth. Despite how fond she was of her Lucette kin, Avery knew that, if she managed to get out of this trap alive, she would be reluctant to return to France, too.

"Do you mean to return me to my family naked?" she asked, proud of the calm way she spoke, her voice revealing none of the very real terror she felt as he carefully, almost idly, cut the clothes from her body.

"No, I would never be so lacking in chivalry," he replied. "I shall put you into a fine, elegant gown. One worthy of a DeVeau whore. One much like my cousin Vachel gave your mother so many years ago."

"And just how is dear Sir Vachel? Dead, I hope." She inwardly shivered as he flicked open her cut gown with the tip of his sword.

"Quite dead." He stepped closer to the bed and gently stroked her legs.

Avery forced herself not to flinch at his touch, but it was a lot harder to quell the nausea that afflicted her. "Died peacefully in his bed, did he?"

"In his bed, yes. Peacefully? I fear not. About ten years ago, it was. Some traitorous dog fed him a particularly nasty poison. It took him days to die—long, torturous days filled with pain."

The tone of Sir Charles's voice told Avery that, if Sir Charles himself had not killed Sir Vachel, he knew who had done it, how it was done, and why. Undoubtedly, he had profited nicely from the death. She thought it very hypocritical of the man to condemn her mother, who had been proven innocent, when he himself was obviously guilty of murdering a DeVeau. Clearly, the DeVeaux considered the killing of a kinsman their own personal privilege.

When he sheathed his sword and began to unlace her chemise, Avery had to bite back the pleas for mercy that rushed into her mouth. She would not give the man that satisfaction. It did strike her as strange, however, that the lack of any outward signs of lust, the lack of even the most feral warming in his eyes, made her more uneasy than did his touch. He was doing this to humiliate her, nothing more, and that realization chilled her to the bone. And she knew, at that moment, that he would toy with her for a very long time—quite probably until she was so mad with shame and fear that she would beg him to rape her just to get it over with.

Sir Charles opened her chemise and stared down at her breasts. He frowned slightly and tapped one long finger against his chin. Avery wished she could get her ankle free so that she could kick him—repeatedly—in the face.

"Your breasts are somewhat small," he murmured. "I have always favored lusher curves."

"If I had known you would be judging them, I would have made an effort to fatten myself up more."

"The nipples are perfection, however," he continued, ignoring her sarcasm. "Large, and a lovely shade of pink. I suspect they will service me and my bastard very well." He placed his hands on her breasts and rubbed his thumbs over her nipples. "Not very responsive, are they?"

"You want a response from me? Lean closer. I am quite prepared to vomit."

She bit back a cry when he slapped her face. It was done with the same cold, precise calm with which he did everything else. Avery was beginning to feel as if none of this were real, as if she were caught up in some nightmare.

Surely no man could be as lacking in feeling, good or
bad, as this one seemed to be? She tensed when he pushed
up the hem of her chemise, exposing her braies. Under
other circumstances, she might have enjoyed his look of
surprise, as it was obvious that he rarely indulged in any
expression at all. All she could think of, however, was
how little now stood between him and the most intimate
part of her.

"Did you think such a garment would protect you from
a man?" he asked as he took a knife from his belt.

"They are warm," she replied, her voice flat, as slowly
her shame and fear was swamped by a cold, hard rage.

Sir Charles cut the side of one leg and flipped the front
of her braies back, exposing her to his view. "You are
gold all over. Intriguing. And you appear to be very clean.
I approve."

"I am going to kill you."

"Now? I do not believe you are in any position to
make threats."

"I am a patient woman when I need to be. I can wait.
Tomorrow, the next day, two years from now. It matters
not. When the chance comes—and it will—I will kill
you, and in a way that will make Sir Michael's and Sir
Vachel's deaths look like kindnesses."

Before Sir Charles could respond, there was an outcry
in the camp. "I had best go to see what those fools are
doing. When I return, you can entertain me with a recita-
tion of all the ways you plan to kill me." He gave her a
slow intimate stroke between her legs with his cold fingers
and then walked away.

Avery took several deep breaths to try and calm herself.
She felt ill, but was not sure if it was from the strength
of her anger or the feel of his cold-as-death fingers touching her flesh. Beneath her rage she knew her fear still
lurked, that within her was a woman cringing in terror

over the deeply personal abuse Sir Charles intended to inflict. Rage felt better, however, and Avery was determined to cling to it.

Suddenly, a strange noise, like something slowly ripping, penetrated her dark thoughts. She turned her head but could not see behind her, where the noise was coming from. When Cameron and Leargan suddenly appeared at her bedside, she was too relieved to feel any embarrassment over her nudity, and anger still bubbled wildly in her veins.

"Where is Sir Charles?" Cameron asked as he cut her free and Leargan tactfully turned his back on them.

"He went out to see what the trouble was," Avery replied, rubbing her wrists after Cameron freed them and waiting somewhat impatiently for him to free her ankles as well.

"Damn, I wanted to kill him. Leargan, keep a watch for the bastard." Cameron quickly relaced Avery's chemise, then tore several strips from the fine linen sheet upon the bed. "Did he rape you?" he asked as, after she removed her damaged braies and shoved them into her pocket, he tied her gown together.

"Nay. I believe he meant to torment me with the threat of it for a while."

"Jesu. How I do ache to kill that mon."

"Ye cannae."

"I ken it now, but—"

"Because I am going to kill him," she said as she grabbed the knife Cameron had set down on the bed and strode toward the tent opening.

Cameron quickly grabbed hold of Avery, but she was like a trapped wild thing in his arms. The fact that she was obviously careful not to hurt him with the knife she held told him that she had not completely lost her senses. They were, however, losing valuable time in which to make a successful escape. Finally, just as Cameron decided he was going to have to do something drastic, Leargan took the hard choice out of his hands. Murmuring an apology to Avery, Leargan gave her one quick, restrained punch on the jaw and she went limp in Cameron's arms. Cameron sighed and tossed her over his shoulder as Leargan collected his knife.

"Sorry, cousin," Leargan murmured as they both turned toward the rear of the tent.

"Ye had no choice," Cameron said as, rejoining the other men, they loped toward their waiting horses. "In truth, I was just about to do the verra same thing. There was no time to talk her out of her madness. And, although I, too, ache to see DeVeau dead, 'tis best that we didnae kill him. That could easily have set his whole insane family on our trail."

"Aye. Now we just have to worry about him, about how badly he wants Avery."

"The mon ne'er travels with his soldiers, yet he was there."

"So, we assume that he wants her verra badly indeed. Did he rape the poor lass?" Leargan asked quietly, holding Avery while Cameron mounted.

"Nay," Cameron replied as he took Avery back into his arms. "As she said, he wanted to torture her for a wee while with the promise of the crime. Constant insults to her person and the threat of more to come. Nay wonder she wanted him dead."

The moment all of his men were mounted, Cameron spurred his horse to a gallop, leading them all away from the DeVeau camp. It would now be a hard race to the port. DeVeau would not take the loss of his prisoner well, if only because the ease with which she was recaptured made him look the fool. He could only hope that either because of greed or embarrassment, the man would not bring any of his large, none too sane family in on the chase.

They caught up with the rest of their people two hours later. Cameron dispatched some men to cover their trail. He paused only long enough to reassure a worried Anne and Gillyanne that Avery was fine. They would travel hard for two more hours, he decided, and then camp, for, despite his comforting words to the women, Cameron was a little concerned about Avery.

Leargan had not hit Avery hard, yet she remained unconscious. Cameron accepted her word that she had not been raped, his own eyes having reaffirmed her claim after a brief but thorough look at her body. Yet she had been as enraged as he had ever seen a woman and—in truth, few men. What had Sir Charles done to her? Would she waken still angry and eager to kill the man, or would she be shocked, devastated, or terrified? She had been naked, her clothes cut free of her body, so DeVeau must have assaulted her in some way. Selfish though it was, Cameron could not help but wonder if her experiences would temper her passion, change how she responded to him.

By the time they stopped for the night, Avery was awake but a little unsteady. Cameron dismounted, then held her close as he ordered Leargan to set up his smaller tent. He then told Donald to lay out his rougher bedding of furs and blankets plus a change of clothes. He wanted the rest of his belongings left packed in the cart so that they could leave more swiftly come morning.

"I need a bath," Avery said as Gillyanne and Anne hurried over to her side.

There was something in her tone of voice that told Cameron he should not refuse her request, but he hesitated. "I did not really wish to light any fires," he began.

"I dinnae care if the water is naught but barely melted ice. I *need* a bath."

"There is water near at hand," Anne said. "A wee creek. Ye can bathe there. Me and Gilly will come along with ye." When Avery nodded, Anne told Gillyanne, "Take her to the creek, lass. I will be right along with soap, drying cloths, and some clean clothes. Go on, now." As soon as the two Murray women walked away, Anne looked at Cameron. "Was she raped?"

"Nay. She said he didnae rape her, and from what I saw of her, I believe her." He grimaced and ran his hands through his hair. "She was naked, howbeit. She wanted to kill him, fought hard to go after him, so hard that Leargan had to knock her out. That seems to say that the mon did something to her. I am just nay sure what."

"He made her afraid," Anne said quietly, sighing.

"Aye, I am sure he did. That would make her so angry, e'en nearly desperate to kill him?"

"It would me."

Cameron was too surprised to respond, and he just watched Anne walk away. A little concerned that Avery might still be desperate to cut Sir Charles's throat, Cameron sent Wee Rob to make sure that she did not try to slip away. He returned to frowning in the direction the women had gone, puzzling over Anne's words, until Leargan rejoined him.

"The women, Anne and wee Gilly, will set the lass right," Leargan said; then he shook his head. "I have ne'er seen a lass so verra eager to spill a mon's blood."

"Anne says it was because DeVeau made Avery feel afraid," Cameron said.

"Ah, aye, Avery wouldnae like that at all."

"Oh? For all of her dark threats, Avery has ne'er e'en tried to kill me."

"Weel, nay. She isnae afraid of you."

"Many women have been afraid of me, and, in some ways, I threaten Avery and her clan."

"Ye are a dark, brooding devil, true enough, and ye could afford to smile more often, but ye dinnae frighten Avery. Ne'er have as far as I can tell. Mayhap ye need to snarl a wee bit more."

"Shut your mouth, Leargan," Cameron said, almost genially.

"Mouth now shut. Weel, in a moment."

"Leargan," Cameron warned, frowning slightly when he saw the intent look upon his cousin's face.

"I dinnae intend to taunt ye this time. It concerns Avery and what has happened to her. Ye can be a hard mon, cousin, but yon lassie is going to need ye to be . . . weel, softer." Leargan cursed softly and dragged his fingers through his hair. "I am nay sure what I am trying to say, except dinnae expect that lass to be all better when the ladies have cleaned her up. She will need, weel, sympathy. For her to be so enraged, the mon had to have done something to her, and that something will probably be troubling her."

"Her cousin Sorcha was raped," Cameron said quietly. "Gillyanne's elder sister."

"Oh, hell's fires. Weel, that explains some of it, doesnae it?"

"Aye, I think it might. Go away, Leargan," Cameron said as he started to walk toward his tent. "I may not ken what to do to soothe a troubled lass, but I do ken that I cannae leave the lass alone."

"Nay, of course not."

"After all, she might still set out to kill the mon."

"Are ye calmer now, lass?" Anne asked as she helped a now well scrubbed Avery don her clean clothes.

"A wee bit," Avery replied. "I still want to kill that bastard, but the madness is gone." She managed a faint smile for Gillyanne, who began to brush out her still-damp hair. "And, I will have to make Leargan suffer just a wee bit for hitting me."

"Wince a little and touch your poor battered jaw now and then, and ye will have the poor lad on his hands and knees begging for your forgiveness."

Avery laughed softly. "I am nay sure I wish to torment him that much." She shivered slightly and wrapped her arms around her waist. "I thought bathing would banish the feel of his hands, but I swear I can still feel the coldness of them."

"Ah, poor wee lass." Anne gave her a brief hug. "He didnae get inside of ye. Find some comfort in that."

"Aye, I will. Jesu, but his touch was so cold, I cannae help but wonder if he would have frozen my innards had he raped me."

"Now there is a thought that ye most certainly must push right out of your head," Gillyanne murmured as she finished braiding Avery's hair. She scowled toward the wood. "Why is that fool Wee Rob marching about o'er there?"

"I suspect he has been set to keep a watch o'er me," Avery replied.

"Cameron cannae think ye would try to escape after all that has happened tonight."

"Nay, but I suspect he fears I may pick up a sword and race back toward the DeVeau camp screaming for blood." She linked arms with Anne and Gillyanne, glad of their silent comfort. "I had best get back to Cameron and let him ken that I have come to my senses. I ken now that, if I had killed that bastard, the woods and roads of France would have soon teemed with DeVeaux seeking vengeance, or their hirelings seeking rewards. 'Tis what happened to my poor mother and she was innocent.''

Gillyanne nodded, then added softly, ''And, mayhap, if ye let Cameron hold ye, he can take some of the coldness away.''

''Aye, mayhap he can. Might as weel get some use out of the big oaf.'' She laughed along with her companions.

It was several minutes after she had entered Cameron's tent and was preparing for bed that Avery became aware of how closely he was watching her. Stripped to her chemise, she turned to look at him. He was sprawled on his side on the bed, beautifully, unabashedly naked. She was glad he had not changed his manner around her simply because of what had happened to her. Somehow, that helped to lessen the importance of Sir Charles's actions.

''If ye wait for me to begin foaming at the mouth, grab a sword, and run off into the night, ye will have a verra long wait,'' she said as she settled down on the furs by his side.

''It might have been vastly entertaining,'' he drawled.

''Only if I was naked and painted blue like our ancestors.'' When he said nothing, she looked up to catch him leaning over her and grinning. ''Ye find that amusing?''

''Actually, I was trying to think of a private place we could sneak away to and just where I might be able to find some blue paint.''

''Lecherous rogue,'' she muttered, but with no condemnation in her voice, and she sighed with a mixture of pleasure and relief when he tugged her into his arms.

''What did that bastard do to ye, Avery?'' he asked quietly.

''Ye mean aside from tying me to the bed, cutting up my clothes, and threatening to put his bastard in me?''

"Aye, aside from that, although that alone makes me eager to cut his heart out."

"Only if ye let me help." She idly stroked his chest, savoring the warmth of his skin. "He touched me a little. 'Twas the way he did it and what he said that drove me near mad. He was cold, empty, and his words were as cold as his touch." She stared fixedly at Cameron's chest as she repeated the things Sir Charles had said. "I dinnae think I e'er fully understood what madness my mother had to deal with until now."

"She is obviously a brave and resourceful woman." Cameron said, fighting to subdue the rage he felt over all she had told him.

Avery kissed his chest and felt his immediate response, yet he was obviously holding himself in tight control. She could not allow that, although she appreciated his consideration for her sensibilities. What she needed now, however, was his passion, his warmth. She needed him to make love to her to banish fully the ghosts of Sir Charles's touch. She wanted her last memory of the day to be of the heated delight she could find in his arms.

"Are ye nay going to kiss me good night?" she asked, rubbing her foot up and down his calf.

"Ah, my wee cat, if I kiss you, I willnae be stopping there. Now that I ken the fullness of your passion, 'tis nay easy to resist the allure of it."

She slid her arms around his neck and tugged him closer until she could brush her lips over his. "Banish the cold, Cameron."

He studied her face for a moment, then kissed her. Avery gave herself over completely to his lovemaking. She greedily accepted every touch of his hands, every brush of his lips, soaking up the warmth of the desire they shared. She clung to him as he possessed her, urging him on as they sought the heights together. Avery continued to cling to him as they both struggled to recover from the ferocity of their releases. When Cameron finally flopped onto his back, she did not wait for him to pull her close, but curled her body around his. In his arms, she felt not only warm again, but safe.

"Did that help, lass?" he asked, touching a kiss to the top of her head.

"Oh, aye. Ye did indeed banish the cold." She tried to smother a yawn behind her hand.

"Get some rest, loving. Dawn isnae so verra far away."

"Ye think we will need to race to the port? That he will give chase?" When he hesitated to reply, she said, "Nay, dinnae try to think of a comforting lie. He will, if only because he thinks he can use me to gain hold of some of the property and wealth my mother gained from her first marriage."

"Aye, there is that. Dinnae worry, lass. I willnae let the bastard get you."

Avery thought it a little odd that a man who wished to use her for ransom would risk so much to save her from another man who wished to ransom her, but she decided not to point that out. Cameron was not acting out of greed. Nor would he ever hurt her—not purposely or physically. Cameron might break her heart, she mused, but Sir Charles DeVeau could easily destroy her very soul.

"We are even now," Cameron murmured.

"Even?" she asked.

"Aye. Ye saved our lives and we just saved yours. The debt is cleared. Now everything is back to the way it was."

Avery decided she was simply too tired to hit him.

Chapter Twelve

As they approached the river they needed to cross, Avery began to feel uneasy. She looked all around but could see no sign of danger. None of the men acted as if they had seen anything, either. Yet the sense of something wrong did not fade.

"Something troubling ye, Avery?"

Avery glanced back at her cousin, who sat behind her. She had been surprised when Cameron had set them both on the same horse, but had quickly noticed how his men had nearly encircled her and Gillyanne as they rode. It was not a guard set out to stop her and Gillyanne from trying to escape, but one to protect them from the DeVeaux, so she found it easy to tolerate. It was certainly the most efficient way to keep her and Gillyanne safe. Cameron had quickly guessed that Gillyanne could well be in as much danger as she was, for Sir Charles knew that her young cousin was with her.

"The river seems a wee bit full and fast," Avery

replied, studying the rapidly flowing water as they drew nearer to its banks.

"Aye, but 'tis still crossable, I think."

"Most like, if only at this fording point. I just feel, weel, nervous." She looked around again, still seeing no threat.

"The DeVeaux are still far behind us. And, unless they ken a faster way to reach the port, they will stay far behind."

"Ye are probably right. 'Tis but the fleeing from them for three long days that has wearied me, made me prone to seeing shadows where there are none. And we do approach Scotland much faster than we might have if the DeVeaux werenae chasing us. Scotland, then Cairnmoor, and then the results of this huge gamble I have taken."

"Ah, aye. Ye are losing time in which ye could make yourself important to that dark laird. I dinnae think ye are unimportant. He rescued ye from Sir Charles and now works verra hard to keep ye safe."

"He needs me—us—to get Payton to marry his sister."

"Aye, but I think 'tis far more than that which drives him."

Avery sighed. "So do I, at times. Yet it isnae what ye and I think which matters, but what Cameron believes."

Gillyanne nodded against Avery's back. "Men think differently than women do, 'tis certain. Weel, that doesnae mean that he willnae come to his senses, at least ere it is too late to mend things. Sometimes a mon has to think he has lost something ere he realizes just how much he values it."

"I fear that if Cameron senses that he values me in any way, he will push me e'en further away from him. I begin to think I have chosen a mon who guards his heart as fiercely as he now guards us."

"No one can completely guard his heart."

"Weel, no sense in worrying about it all now." Avery
frowned as they all gathered at the river's edge and prepared to cross it. "A bridge would have been nice."

"The river truly bothers ye, doesnae it."

"I dinnae ken if 'tis the river or the crossing of it, but
I cannae shake free of this deepening unease I feel."
Avery frowned as she watched Donald scramble onto the
back of the cart holding some of their belongings. She
turned to Cameron, who had just reined in at her side.
"Mayhap young Donald should ride across on a horse."

"The lad will be fine, Avery," Cameron assured her,
somewhat touched that she should show such concern
over the safety of his squire. "There is a lot he can hang
onto in the cart."

"Aye, that is true enough," she agreed, yet she found
herself tensing as the cart entered the water with Wee
Rob struggling to control the nervous horse.

Avery turned to speak to Cameron again only to discover him gone. She silently cursed, then looked back at
the river. She had just begun to convince herself she was
being foolish and had nudged her mount forward to join
the others crossing the river, when she looked at the
baggage cart one more time. Her heart leaped into her
throat as she watched the cart suddenly tip precariously
to one side. Avery suspected the back right wheel had
sunk into a hole. The jolt was hard enough to send a
screaming Donald into the river, where the swift current
was dragging him rapidly downstream.

No one leaped in after the boy, which told Avery that
there were no swimmers among the MacAlpins. A few
men tried to ride through the water to reach the boy, but
the depth of the river beyond the fording place made the
horses useless. Two men nearly joined the flailing boy
before they could get their mounts back on a surer footing.
Avery cursed again and nudged her mount into the water.

"Grab the reins," Avery ordered Gillyanne as she yanked off her boots and tossed aside her heavy cloak.

Cameron was quickly making his way toward her. Avery knew he was going to try to stop her, just as she knew she was probably the only one who could save poor Donald. Moving so that she sat sideways in the saddle, Avery hastily pulled her skirts up between her legs and secured them at her waist. Cameron was just reaching out for her when she leaped into the cold water and began to swim toward Donald.

"Colin, get everyone across," bellowed Cameron as he urged his horse back onto the bank. "Leargan, with me. That fool lass is going to get herself killed," he muttered as he rode along the bank, keeping Avery and Donald in sight.

"Avery can swim verra weel," cried Gillyanne as she, too, followed Cameron.

Cursing when he saw the girl close behind him instead of crossing the river with the others as she should, Cameron yelled back, "Aye, I can see that. But, how weel can she swim trying to hold onto a terrified boy who is bigger than she is?" Cameron was not really pleased with the fact that Gillyanne had no answer for him.

It was not easy, but Avery ignored the biting cold of the water even though it felt as if it were seeping into the very marrow of her bones. Her clothes were heavy enough to sap her strength faster than was probably safe. Avery kept her gaze fixed firmly upon Donald as she swam. He was just ahead of her, flailing wildly, yet that seemed to be helping him to keep his head above the water most of the time and to slow his rapid progress down the river. When his gaze met hers, Avery knew he saw her and recognized her, yet his expression was still one of intense fear. Avery cautiously approached the boy, knowing how easy it would be for such a terrified person to become a serious threat to the very one trying to save him.

"Donald," she called to him, staying just out of reach until she was certain he would let her help him.

"Avery, I dinnae want to drown," he gasped; then he coughed violently as water splashed into his mouth.

"Ye willnae drown if ye do everything I tell ye to. Can ye do that, Donald?"

"Aye."

"Easy now, I am swimming closer and ye dinnae want to hit me by mistake, do ye?"

"Nay. 'Tis cold, Avery."

"Oh, aye. 'Tis that, right enough."

She swam up behind him and quickly put her arm under his and around his chest. "Lie back, Donald. Calm, now." She was a little surprised at how quickly he obeyed, seemingly putting his complete trust in her. "Gently kick your legs. That is the way. A wee bit more gently. Aye, aye." She caught sight of a knot of branches caught against some rocks in the heart of the river. "Now, ye will feel my body coming up beneath yours. Very slowly, keep kicking those legs." Despite how well he was taking her commands, she knew she could not go very far while holding him since she was doing most of the swimming for both of them. "We are going to swim o'er to those branches right o'er there."

"Shouldnae we go to the bank?" he asked.

"These are closer and we can hold onto them until someone can get a rope out to us. Ye are a wee bit bigger than me, Donald, and though I can keep us above the water, I cannae drag ye too far."

"I can see the laird," he stuttered.

"Good. He will soon toss us a rope."

Once they reached the small dam of wood, Avery made sure Donald was holding onto it tightly before she let him go. Wondering if her teeth were chattering as loudly as his were, she then clung to the wood herself and looked toward the bank. To her great relief she saw Cameron, Leargan, and Gillyanne there. Cameron held a stout rope in his hands.

"I will grab the rope when 'tis thrown to us," Avery told Donald. "Dinnae ye let go of this wood, e'en if it starts to shake free and float away. Dinnae fear. We will chase ye down and a stout piece of wood will keep ye afloat until we do."

"But ye may need my help to tie the rope round yourself," Donald protested.

"Ye will go first. Nay, dinnae argue," she said when he began to stutter out a *nay*. "I can swim, Donald. Ye cannae. So ye will be pulled to safety first."

It took two tries before Avery caught the rope Cameron threw out to her. The rock he had tied to the end to weight it caught her hard against the shoulder. It would undoubtedly leave a colorful bruise, although she suspected she already had far too many for one more to be noticed.

"While I tie this rope round your chest, I want ye to take deep breaths, then let them out slowly," she advised Donald as she began to secure the rope around him, praying her cold fingers could make the knots tight enough to hold firm. "Now when I cry 'ready,' ye take as deep a breath as ye can and hold it tight. 'Twill be a rough ride to the shore, but a quick one, and holding that breath will help ye. Understand?"

"Aye, m'lady," he whispered.

"And try to flop onto your back when ye feel the first tug upon the rope. 'Twill make the ride easier for you if ye can. Ready!"

Avery was pleased to hear Donald take a huge breath even as he was yanked away from the branches. The youth's ride to the bank was indeed impressively fast and, she was certain, a little terrifying. She flexed her fingers, concerned over how stiff with cold they had become, and waited for the next toss of the rope. When her rapidly numbing fingers refused to grasp the rope tight enough to keep hold of it, Avery felt her concern swiftly turn to fear.

"She cannae hold the rope," Gillyanne said, yanking off her boots.

"This next time—" began Cameron, his eyes widening slightly when Gillyanne began to take off her gown.

"Her hands will be e'en colder by then, e'en more clumsy."

"Lass, ye cannae mean to go in after her."

" 'Tis exactly what I mean to do," Gillyanne snapped as she finished stripping to her chemise. "Is there enough of that rope to tie it round me yet leave a length free that I may use it to tie Avery to me?"

"I cannae let ye do this."

"Ye have to. Neither of ye can swim, and if Avery's hands are too cold now to hold the rope, in a verra short time they will be too cold to hold firm to that branch she is clinging to."

Muttering curses over his lack of choices or the time to come up with another plan, Cameron tied the rope around Gillyanne's tiny waist, leaving her what he felt was plenty of rope for her to lash Avery to her. "If I e'en think ye might be in danger, I will yank ye back in."

"Fair enough," Gillyanne said, and she dove gracefully into the water.

"Jesu," muttered Leargan as he wrapped a blanket around a violently shivering Donald. "I guess we can add swimming to the lengthy list of odd skills those Murray lasses have." He shook his head as he watched

Gillyanne race toward Avery, cutting through the rough waters with clean, strong strokes. "Mayhap one or two of us should try to learn."

Cameron just nodded, his gaze fixed upon Avery and his hands tight upon the rope. He understood what had made Avery go after Donald, was pleased that the youth had not drowned, and could even deeply respect the bravery displayed by both of the Murray lasses. However, if Avery survived this, Cameron decided that he would throttle her.

"Gilly?" Avery whispered as her cousin swam up beside her. "Ye shouldnae be taking such risks."

Securing the rope around Avery's waist, Gillyanne just shook her head. "Neither should you."

"The water proved colder than I thought it would be."

" 'Tis probably being fed by melting snows, ye great fool. Ready?" Gillyanne asked after rechecking the knot she had just made.

"Aye."

Avery had barely enough time to take a deep breath before Gillyanne signaled Cameron. The next she knew, she was on her back in Gillyanne's thin arms and both of them were being pulled toward the bank at an alarming speed. When they hit the bank, she released with a grunt the breath she had been holding.

Nothing was said as she and Gillyanne were yanked from the water and wrapped up in blankets. Despite the cold and utter exhaustion afflicting her, Avery could feel the anger in Cameron as he held her in his arms while they rode to join the others. He ought to be thanking her for saving Donald's life, she thought crossly; then she decided she was more concerned with getting warm and dry than with understanding his moodiness. If he was going to yell at her, he could wait until she had rested a little.

She was more asleep than awake when she was handed over into Anne's care. Anne and the other women worked fast to get her and Gillyanne dry and dressed in warm clothes. A still silent Cameron set her in his baggage cart next to Gillyanne and covered them both with one of his heavy furs. Avery could hear Donald talking and decided the youth would be fine, that he was obviously a lot stronger than he looked.

"I dinnae need to rest," protested Gillyanne as Cameron tucked her in.

"Ye are there to help your fool cousin get warm again," Cameron snapped.

Avery managed to open her eyes enough to see Gillyanne make a face at the departing Cameron's back and she almost smiled. "I do feel a wee bit cold, Gillyanne."

Gillyanne turned onto her side, her back to Avery, and said, "Then curl your skinny self round me. 'Twill help. That ill-tempered lout ye fancy is right about that. Ye dinnae feel verra cold," she murmured as Avery held her close.

"Inside I do. I think Anne rubbed the outside of me so hard, 'tis a miracle I wasnae set alight."

"She said she wanted to get your blood flowing again."

"Oh. Weel, 'tis flowing, but it, and my verra bones, feel chilled. Donald sounded recovered, though."

"Aye. I think some people arenae as troubled by the cold as others. Or, he was thrashing about so furiously, he kept himself warm enough."

Even though Avery was feeling a little warmer, she still felt completely exhausted and knew she would soon be asleep. "I wonder why Cameron is so angry."

"Weel, if I try to think like ye do, then I would say 'tis because his pawn nearly drowned herself. But I, being so much cleverer, think 'tis because he nearly lost his lover, that he wasnae thinking of his sister at all at that moment. He is angry because ye took a grave risk and, mayhap, because he couldnae do anything to help Donald himself. Men dinnae like being helpless or having lasses rush to the rescue.''

"A lot of people cannae swim,'' Avery murmured, too tired to take issue with Gillyanne's pert replies.

Gillyanne nodded then yawned. ''I think my wee swim did tire me some after all.''

"If that is a ploy to try to get me to rest, dinnae trouble yourself I am already more asleep than awake.''

A moment later, Gillyanne glanced over her shoulder and saw that Avery was fast asleep. She doubted her cousin had stayed awake for much longer than it had taken to finish her sentence. Just as she was about to turn away and indulge in a little nap herself, Cameron rode up, reached down, and lightly brushed his knuckles over Avery's cheek.

When Cameron raised his gaze to meet Gillyanne's, he felt a little embarrassed to be caught doing something that could be seen more as a tender, caring gesture than one of idle concern. ''She has lost that deathly chill.''

"Aye, though she says the cold has set deep,'' replied Gillyanne, turning slightly so that she was more comfortable while talking to him.

"Who taught the two of ye to swim like that?''

"The ones in our family who had already learned took turns teaching us. Our fithers kenned how and felt it was a good thing to learn. My mither kenned how, too. She saved my fither once.'' Gillyanne looked down at Avery, then back at Cameron, and, thinking to save her cousin a lecture later, said, ''Kenning she might be able to save

Donald, she couldnae just set there and let the river take him.''

Cameron released a deep sigh and, with it, much of his lingering anger over the risks Avery had taken. "Nay, of course not. 'Twould be beyond the will of a Murray lass to do anything else but hurl herself into a raging river to save the life of a lad she barely kens."

"It wasnae raging. Just tumbling along a wee bit faster than it should."

"Ye are an impertinent brat who wasnae dealt a stern hand often enough."

"So I have been told. Aye, my own fither says it now and again, but he spoils me. He says 'tis because I look a lot like my mither—and he spoils her, too."

"And who does Avery look like? Her brother?"

"Nay, her fither, my uncle Nigel. Payton looks a wee bit like both of his parents. Payton is . . . weel, beautiful. A maid once told our cousin Elspeth that Payton is so bonny that he but needs to walk by and he rips a sigh of longing from the heart of every woman who espies him, young or old." Gillyanne laughed softly at Cameron's look of disgust. " 'Tis how most men react to that bit of nonsense. But he is bonny. The only other men I have e'er seen who might be said to be as bonny are my fither and my cousin Elspeth's husband, Cormac."

Cameron was annoyed by his own curiosity, but he felt almost compelled to ask, "And just what makes him so verra bonny?"

"Weel, he has lovely hair, the perfect blend of red and gold, thick and soft as silk. He has beautiful skin of a pale golden color, much akin to Avery's. He isnae as tall or as broad as ye are, but tall enough, lean, and verra graceful. His features are nearly perfect and he has beautiful eyes—a warm golden brown with shards of emerald green." She shrugged. "He is my cousin. I can see the beauty, but nay as another woman might.'' She quirked one brow. ''Nay as your sister might—as a mon she would do most anything to have.''

After staring at Gillyanne for a moment, Cameron ordered, ''Watch for signs of a fever,'' then rode away.

Even though he tried to immerse himself in the work of guarding his people and searching out a safe place to camp for the night, Cameron could not shake Gillyanne's words from his mind. Avery and Gillyanne had claimed that Payton was the sort of man who did not need to seduce a lass, that he was too bonny to need to, yet he had shrugged those claims aside with ease. He was not sure why a description of the man should suddenly make that difficult. Although Cameron knew he could not claim to know just what women liked, it certainly sounded as if Sir Payton Murray held a lion's share of such qualities.

Could Katherine have seen the man and decided she had to have him? Even he could not deny that his sister was spoiled, used to getting anything and everything she wanted. Mayhap Payton had not returned her interest and she had lashed out, falsely accusing him in her fit of pain or hurt pride over such a rejection. Katherine might not have expected matters to become so complicated and, now, did not know how to untangle the mess she had made.

Cameron cursed himself for what felt far too much like disloyalty. If he followed that line of thinking too much further, he would be thinking his sister the sort of woman who would callously destroy any number of lives just to get what she wanted. He refused to believe his own flesh and blood would do such a thing.

In all fairness, however, he eased his condemnation of Sir Payton. He realized he could not make himself believe the charge of rape, and now even the charge of a heartless seduction began to look questionable. That change of

opinion was aided by coming to know Avery and Gillyanne. Although a lot of families had a bad seed, he
could not believe those two would so staunchly defend
a man who would rape a woman or who was a heartless
user of women.

That left him with the possibility that Sir Payton and
his sister had had an affair. It did not match with Avery's
insistence that her brother would not bed a virgin, then
refuse to wed her. It also left Katherine still looking like
a liar with her claims of rape, but that could have come
about because the affair had been discovered and she had
panicked. That could be a forgivable sin, especially if she
had already begun to suspect that she was with child.

He shook his head and rode back to the cart holding
Gillyanne and Avery. No matter what the truth was, his
sister needed a husband. She claimed Payton as her lover,
possibly the father of her child, and that claim was now
widely known. Although he could accept the possibility
that Katherine had spun a tale to try to salvage her reputation, he could not believe that she would lie about everything. Sir Payton had bedded Katherine and he would be
made to marry her. What Cameron wanted now was a little
more information about this man, even though Payton's
cousins made him sound far too good to be real. It would
help him decide the correct approach to take to resolve
the problem awaiting him at Cairnmoor. After all, it would
not do to offend or anger too deeply the man who would
soon be his brother by law.

When he reached the cart only to find both Anne and
Gillyanne kneeling by Avery, Cameron forgot all about
his sister and her problems. "Something wrong?" he
asked, hoping he did not sound as terrified as he suddenly
felt.

"We are going to have to stop running for a wee while,
laird," Anne said.

"Anne," he snapped, "what ails her?" He tensed as Anne's expression told him he was about to hear something he did not want to hear.

"Fever, Laird," Anne whispered, uttering a word that made Cameron's blood run cold.

Chapter Thirteen

"Hot."

"Aye, lassie, I ken it." Cameron dipped the rag into the bowl of cool water and gently bathed Avery's face, just as he had hundreds of times in the past three days. " 'Twill pass."

Avery opened her eyes and tried to fix her gaze on the owner of that familiar deep voice. "Cameron? 'Tis too hot."

" 'Tis a fever ye suffer from, lass." He began to bathe her arms. "Your wee swim in the river has left ye fevered."

"Fever. Ah, I am to die, then."

"Nay," snapped Cameron. "Ye will conquer this."

"Nay, I am too tired. Where is my mither and Aunt Maldie? Aunt Maldie will fix this."

Cameron winced, dismayed that she was not thinking as clearly as he had first thought. Although she was not as alarmingly delirious as she had been from time to time since the fever had taken her, she was still badly confused. He mixed up some of the herbal drink Gillyanne insisted he use, sat beside Avery, and put his arm around her shoulders. As he supported her against him and forced her to drink the potion, the heat of her body alarmed him. Nothing they did seemed to break the fever's tight hold on her. He could not believe such a delicate, slender woman could last much longer; in fact, he was surprised that she had the strength to fight it for as long as she had.

"Did Aunt Maldie make that?" Avery asked as he settled her back down.

"Nay, loving. Your aunt isnae here. We are still in France." He frowned when she suddenly looked terrified.

"DeVeau!" she gasped. "Dinnae let him touch me."

He grabbed hold of her hands. "Never, lass. I will keep him away. I swear it!" He sighed when she looked at him, silent tears running down her face. "DeVeau will ne'er get hold of you. I willnae allow it."

"But ye mean to leave me."

"Nay, lass, I will stay right here and guard you."

"For now. Then ye will leave me. I havenae had the time I need. I havenae made ye want me."

Cameron brushed a kiss over her forehead. "Of course I want you. Havenae I shown ye that truth often enough?"

"For rutting with, but nay for the rest. I need time and I dinnae have it." She closed her eyes and muttered, "There just isnae enough time left ere ye leave me. I havenae been able to make ye love me as I love you. 'Tis so unfair. Elspeth won her gamble. Why cannae I? If ye love someone, shouldnae they love ye back? That would be only fair."

"Aye, loving, that would be only fair," he said softly, but she was already asleep.

Slowly he stood up, poured himself a large draught of wine, and gulped it down. It was the fever talking, he

told himself, just as he had every time she had spoken
of loving him. She was caught fast in dreams and memories—perhaps even confusing him with someone else.
The very thought that she might be speaking those words
to someone else, even a man existing only in her dreams,
twisted his innards into painful knots. Even that was
preferable to believing in her avowals, however. Not only
did he find the idea that Avery might love him much too
tempting, but the possibility presented him with far more
problems and doubts than he could deal with. After all,
to help his sister he had to return Avery to her family,
had to force her brother to marry his sister, and did, in
fact, have to threaten her family to bring all that about.
Cameron doubted that was something even a woman in
love would be able to forgive too easily.

"If ye use her words against her, I will cut out your
tongue."

Turning around, Cameron was not really surprised to
see little Gillyanne there, although the coldness of her
words and the fierce look on her small, pretty face was
a little startling. "Avery is delirious, suffering the fancies
of a mind gripped by a fever. I dinnae take anything she
says now verra seriously. 'Tis all naught but babble."

The noise Gillyanne made was rife with scorn. "If it
makes ye feel better to think that, I willnae argue with
it."

"How kind." Sometimes, Cameron mused, it was difficult to recall that Gillyanne was not a woman grown,
but a girl of barely thirteen.

After placing her small hand on Avery's forehead, Gillyanne took a deep breath to steady herself. "The herbs
dinnae seem to be working."

"She is nay any worse."

"Nay, but I had hoped it would break by now. Anne

is having a cold bath brought. We are going to sink her whole body in it.''

"Do ye think that wise?''

"My aunt Maldie says it can help.''

Cameron knew better than to argue. Soon after Avery had become fevered, he had discovered that whatever Aunt Maldie said about healing was treated as God's own truth. Since Maldie's knowledge had kept Avery alive this long, he had to concede that the woman must have some skill. He was just not sure that plunging Avery into cold water, the very thing that had apparently brought the fever on, was the way to make it go away.

"Leargan is preparing to ride out to look for DeVeau,'' Gillyanne said, watching him with that knowing look that made him so uneasy at times. "He would welcome your company, and we will be all done ere ye return.''

"I think she might like her hair cleaned,'' he said, and he felt himself color faintly when Gillyanne gifted him with a little smile.

"Aye, she would. We shall tend to it.''

Afraid he would soon reveal far too much of his confusion to this young girl if he stayed any longer, Cameron hurried away to join Leargan. Cameron told himself it was ridiculous to feel so uneasy around a girl who was more child than woman. Despite that sensible scolding, he could not fully discard the feeling that Gillyanne saw people all too clearly, could see right through whatever emotional armor a person wore or whatever guise one tried to hide behind. He was almost tempted to ask her what she saw when she looked at him, just to see if her opinions would ease some of the confusion he was trapped in.

After curtly replying to Leargan's inquiry about Avery's health, Cameron rode away from camp with his cousin. The chore of searching for any sign that DeVeau had found them or was close at hand did not work to keep his thoughts off Avery as he had hoped it would. Thoughts of her served only to keep his emotions in an uncomfortable state of turmoil.

The chance that she could die absolutely terrified him. That told him that he had not done a very good job of protecting himself, that his emotions had definitely become entangled with his passions. Cameron did not dare examine just how deeply and completely he had been captured by Avery. The fact that he found her delirious claims of love a source of bitter joy made him think he probably had no chance of drawing back now—at least not emotionally. He also knew that he would not be able to stay out of her arms, either. His passion for her, his hunger for her touch, would not be denied. Somehow, he was going to have to shield himself better than he had before.

"The bastard has either given up the chase or will be waiting for us on the docks," said Leargan.

"I ken it. We have lost our lead," Cameron said, sighing as they headed back to camp.

"Weel, it cannae be helped. We will just have to approach the port and whatever ship we can find verra cautiously."

"True. And it will probably be days yet ere we can travel. E'en if the fever breaks by morning, Avery will need several days of rest ere she is strong enough to travel, and several more days of traveling verra slowly so as not to dangerously weaken her."

"All of which is necessary, I ken it, but it will also give DeVeau plenty of time to prepare for our arrival."

"Then mayhap I will have the pleasure of killing him at last. He haunts her. Her fear of him comes out in her delirium," he said quietly. "I spoke aloud the wish that I might find what was needed to ease that fear. Her bloodthirsty wee cousin suggested she go, hunt the mon down, and bring Avery his head.'' Cameron was able to smile faintly when Leargan laughed. "Wretched brat. Worse, I think there is a small part of her which was completely serious.''

"Probably more than a small part. The few times the lass has mentioned DeVeau, her voice holds a cold, hard, and verra mature fury. 'Tis because of the rape of her sister. I think none of those Murrays have an ounce of mercy in their hearts for a rapist.''

Cameron nodded. "I ken it, so ye need not begin to lecture me. S'truth, I began to doubt Katherine's claims of rape soon after meeting Avery and Gillyanne. Whilst they have a tendency to make Sir Payton sound like one of God's own sainted angels, I dinnae think they would defend him if he was a mon who treated women poorly.''

"If Katherine lied about that, could she nay have lied about the rest?''

"Who kens for certain. I cannae. Nay until I speak to her. E'en if all that happened between them was a brief affair, one ended when Sir Payton's interest waned, her name had been blackened. He must make amends for that. And if she carries his child, he needs to give it legitimacy.'' He held up his hand to stop Leargan when his cousin began to speak. "Nay. There is naught to be gained from chewing o'er Katherine's troubles. What e'er the truth is, her reputation has been sullied and she needs a husband. Sir Payton is as good a choice as any, finer than many, and I have the means to get him.''

"But to gain that prize for Katherine, ye must give up Avery, and I dinnae think ye are as easy about that as ye were at the beginning of all of this.''

"No mon would wish to send away a lass who warms his bed as wee as Avery warms mine.'' Cameron inwardly cringed to hear himself speak of Avery in such a way, but he told himself it was for the best, that such an attitude would help him to regain the aloofness he needed.

"Of course," Leargan drawled, the sarcastic tone of his voice clearly revealing his lack of belief in Cameron's callous words.

"Such a rich feasting after almost three years of naught can confuse a mon. When everything is settled, I will find myself a skilled leman."

"Aye. I am certain some mercenary whore is just what ye will need to forget Avery."

Cameron glared at his cousin, thinking that Leargan had become far too skilled at the chore of being his conscience. "And a sound knock offside your fat head is just what ye need to get ye to keep your mouth shut."

Leargan rolled his eyes but was quiet. Cameron knew it would not help all that much to keep silencing Leargan. Unfortunately, he could not silence his own thoughts as easily. The last thing he wished to confide to Leargan was that he was having to fight a constant, fierce battle to stop himself from holding tight to Avery. He had to make himself believe that it was just lust, combined with a comfortable liking for the woman Avery was, which made him hesitate, however briefly, to do as he knew he must. That there might be more than liking and passion between him and Avery was not a possibility he dared even consider. Therein lay a bitter tragedy.

When they rode into camp, Cameron saw all his people gathered in front of his tent. "She has died," he whispered, too afraid of what he would hear or see even to dismount.

"Or recovered," said Leargan as he dismounted. "There is only one way to discover what is happening, Cameron."

It was the last thing he wished to do, but Cameron dismounted and walked toward his tent. He came to an abrupt halt but a step away from the crowd. Cameron knew he was gaping, but a quick glance at Leargan told him he was not alone in that.

Someone was singing. And yet, he thought, that word was simply not enough to describe the sound coming out of his tent. That voice, the strength of it, the perfection of the tone, and the rich emotional power of it, made it something far more than singing. He could fully understand how it held his people enthralled. Cameron felt the same sense of utter wonder.

The song was a fairly common one. A French ballad of an ill-fated love, it was something Cameron had always scorned as little more than minstrels' babbling. He could not scorn it now. In fact, he could all too easily understand why Wee Rob was weeping and why no one taunted the big man for doing so.

Just as the song ended, a hand was thrust out through the tent flaps. It waved about a few times before being yanked back inside. Leargan and Cameron were nearly knocked down as everyone who had been standing in front of the tent suddenly turned and hurried away. Despite the confusion, Cameron managed to grab hold of Donald.

"Who was that singing?" he demanded of the boy.

"Gillyanne," Donald replied.

"That voice came out of wee Gilly?" Leargan asked, making no effort to hide his complete astonishment.

"Aye. I dinnae ken where she hides it. It always makes Wee Rob weep."

"Why have I ne'er heard her before?" Cameron asked.

"Because she has only done it since Avery got ill and only when ye are away from camp. Anne says it calms Avery, but wee Gilly is shy. So, Anne told her we would-nae trouble her about the singing or be asking her to do more. Anne made us all promise we would ignore it, but

I dinnae think she realized the beauty of it. So we just pretend to ignore it.''

"Ah, and so 'twas Anne's hand I saw poked out of my tent. She was telling ye that the lass was done and 'twas time for ye to move along.'' When Donald nodded and cast a nervous look toward the tent, Cameron almost smiled. "Go on, then, laddie. Go fetch me some food and water to wash in. I will be in my tent.''

The moment Donald was gone, Leargan said, "Do ye think the wee lass kens what she sounds like?''

"Probably not,'' replied Cameron. "Gillyanne probably kens that she can sing weel, but I suspect she doesnae ken why it should make grown men cry. 'Tis hard to explain, so all flattery undoubtedly sounds like little more than polite compliments.''

"True. Weel, I had best slip away so that I, too, can act as if I have nay just heard an angel sing.''

Cameron smiled briefly, then strode into his tent just as Gillyanne was preparing to leave. She blushed slightly when she saw him, and Cameron knew she suspected he had heard her sing. He found it a little astonishing that someone with such a gift should be so shy about it.

"How is Avery?'' he asked. "Did the cold bath help her?'' He stepped close to the bed and brushed his fingers over Avery's cheeks. "She feels a wee bit cooler.''

"Aye,'' agreed Anne. "If it shows itself to be a true help, we may do it again e'en though the lass didnae like it at all.''

"She roused enough to complain sensibly?''

"Oh, aye, and some harsh words she had for the ones who would set her down in a cold bath.'' Anne laughed as she took Gillyanne's hand in hers. "The lass has an interesting way with a curse.''

"Of course, she was feverish,'' Gillyanne said as Anne

tugged her out of the tent. "One doesnae heed what a person beset by a fever has to say, does one? Nay, that would be verra foolish."

Cameron watched the girl follow Anne out of the tent. He resisted the urge to give her tiny backside a sharp slap. When that lass finally became a woman, she was going to cause some poor man a great deal of trouble, he decided, almost wishing he would be around to see it. That, he suspected, would never happen. Despite the fact that he intended to make Sir Payton Murray marry his sister, Cameron doubted he would ever be welcomed as a member of the family.

As soon as he finished the meal Donald brought him, Cameron washed up. Wearing only his loincloth, he stared longingly at the bed. He had unpacked his fine feather mattress for Avery to rest on. Anne had spread an oiled cloth beneath Avery to protect the mattress from the damp caused by constantly bathing her fevered body. There was plenty of room for him to lie down on the soft bed, yet he had to wonder how long he would be allowed to sleep this time. Since Avery had fallen ill, he had managed only to snatch short rests, his sleep often disturbed by her bouts of delirium. But short rests were better than no sleep at all, he finally decided, and crawled into bed beside her.

He settled himself on his side facing her and curled his arm around her waist. She was almost too hot to sleep near comfortably, but he wanted to be sure he would feel it if she tried to get out of bed. Looking her over, he noticed that she was starting to take on the sharp edges of someone who was not getting enough food. The occasional broths poured down her throat were not enough to replace what was being used up by her battle with the fever.

"Ye willnae die, Avery," he whispered as he kissed her cheek.

Just once, he decided, it would not hurt to give in to some of the feelings tearing him apart inside, especially his fear that she could die. Even though he did not—could not—plan to keep her at his side, he wanted to be able to think of her as alive and happy. True, he did not want to think of her happy with another man, but it might be pleasant now and again to think of her content with her family. He could not bear to think of the vibrant, clever woman he had come to know turned cold and silent by death. It just did not seem right or fair that Avery should die before she had had the time to really live.

"Nay, loving, ye cannae let this cursed fever win. I need to ken that ye are alive somewhere, laughing, arguing, and spitting insults at some fool who deserves a few. E'en kenning that some rogue may hold ye, wed ye, and give ye bairns to love would be easier to bear than thinking of all your fire doused forever and set deep in the cold clay. So live, Avery Murray, if only to make my life a misery."

Cameron touched a kiss to her fever-dried lips, then settled his head back down on his pillow and closed his eyes. He needed some sleep almost as badly as Avery did, but he had to force himself to relax enough to succumb to its pull. There was a large part of him that feared that, while he slept, Avery would slip away.

A dampness against his skin pulled Cameron from his sleep. He grimaced, afraid he was about to discover that Avery had wet the bed; then he realized that dampness came from her skin. His heart pounding with hope, he sat up and lit the candles set on the chest next to the bed. Cameron was not really surprised to see his hand shaking as he reached out to place his hand on her forehead. He closed his eyes against the strength of the emotion that

surged through him when he found her cool to the touch—
cool and covered in sweat.

He scrambled out of the bed, donned his plaid, and
went to get Gillyanne and Anne. The two slept but a few
feet away from his tent so that they could be fetched
quickly if needed. Cameron was pleased to discover that
they were easy to wake and immediately alert. He was
not pleased, however, to be forced to wait outside his
own tent while they tended to Avery.

"Ye can come in now," Anne called out just as Cameron was preparing to march into his tent and see what
they were doing.

"How kind of ye to invite me," he snapped as he
entered the tent.

"Wheesht, ye wake up in a foul temper, dinnae ye?"
Gillyanne murmured as she tucked a blanket around a
soundly, peacefully sleeping Avery.

" 'Tis chill out there." Cameron looked at Anne. "Has
her fever truly broken, then?"

"Aye. She woke long enough to take some broth and
medicine," Anne replied. "We have cleaned her and put
on a warm, dry nightdress. She should sleep through the
rest of the night. The worst is over, I am certain of it.
Food and rest is all she will need now—plenty of both
to give her back the strength she has lost."

Once the two women were gone, Cameron shrugged
off his plaid, snuffed the candles, and crawled back into
bed. He pulled Avery into his arms, savoring the coolness
of her body. She did need some fattening up, but despite
her loss of weight, she felt perfect in his arms. She felt
beautiful. Beautifully alive. He kissed her shoulder.

"Cameron?"

"Nay, 'tis Leargan," he murmured as he kissed her
ear, unable to fully suppress the joy he felt over her
recovery.

"Oh, aye? Odd. I hadnae thought ye would be as hairy as Cameron," Avery drawled.

"I am nay hairy." Cameron gave into the compelling urge to hug her lightly, pleased by her sarcasm—that sign that her spirit was already returning.

"Of course not." She sighed. "I have been sick, havenae I?"

"Ye have been fighting a fever for three long days, lass, but it appears that ye have won the fight."

"Oh. Weel, that is good to hear, but if I have been abed for three days, I suspect we havenae traveled verra far."

"Nay, and we will probably set right here for a few more days, until Anne says that ye willnae suffer from a journey."

"And so we have lost the race against DeVeau."

"Dinnae fret o'er that, loving."

"Easier said than done."

Cameron kissed the side of her neck. "Rest Avery. That is what ye need now. Rest and food. We can discuss that swine later, when ye are strong again. We watch for him and we ken that he may be waiting for us when we reach the port. 'Tis all that need be done now. So sleep."

"I should like to argue with you, but I fear I am much too tired." She yawned, then snuggled closer to him.

"I will be ready to argue with you when ye are stronger," he said, smiling when she responded with a sleepy giggle.

As he felt her relax in his arms, he wondered if he was confronting the problem of Avery and his errant feelings for her in the wrong way. She made him feel good, dangerous though that was. Perhaps he should just enjoy their time together and cease fighting her allure. After almost losing her to the fever, wasting what little time they might have left together trapped in a morass of doubt and wrestling with his own fears seemed foolish. Cameron decided he would give the matter some serious consideration—as soon as he had had a good night's sleep.

Chapter Fourteen

Avery smiled faintly as she watched Cameron wash up before getting dressed. This would be the last full day they spent in camp. She had already cost them a week between suffering the fever and then struggling to regain the strength needed to travel. There was a devious, desperate part of her that was tempted to feign a lingering weakness, even a small relapse, but she strongly repressed it. It would do her no real good, however, and could, in fact, severely hurt her cause if Cameron caught her at it.

All malingering would gain her was more boredom as she was kept confined to her bed, more distasteful potions to swallow, and even less time spent with Cameron. As if that were possible, she thought crossly as she sat up a little straighter against the plumped-up pillows. He left early in the morning and slipped into bed very late at night. She was lucky if he peeked into the tent once or twice during the day. Despite the hardness she could feel pressed against her backside as they slept, she could not completely stop herself from worrying that, at some time during the celibacy imposed by her illness, Cameron had lost interest in her.

When he stepped up to the bed to pick up the shirt Donald had laid out for him, her gaze settled on his taut stomach. She smiled faintly as she saw the little star-shaped birthmark below his navel, only partially hidden by the light dusting of hair there. Every time she saw it, she wanted to kiss it.

It was a surprisingly familiar urge, Avery suddenly realized, which made no sense at all. She did not make a habit of kissing men's bellies. She gasped as, suddenly, a clear memory of kissing a little boy's belly came to mind. As distinctly as if it was happening at that very moment, instead of over a year ago, she could see herself laughing, see the little boy squirming and giggling as she noisily kissed the little star-shaped birthmark on his round little belly. A dark little boy with rich, black hair, mysterious black eyes, and dark skin. Little Alan, she thought as she stared at Cameron. Cameron was little Alan as a grown man. The way Cameron started to frown at her told Avery that some of her shock must be showing on her face, and she struggled to calm herself down.

"Are ye alright, Avery?" Cameron asked as he felt her forehead. "Ye look a little pale and unsettled."

" 'Tis naught," she said. "Could ye send Gillyanne to me?"

"Ah, of course."

A little embarrassed when she realized he thought she needed someone to help her see to her personal needs, Avery nonetheless took advantage of his conclusions. She stared down at her hands until she heard him leave; for once she was far too upset to feel piqued over the lack of any kiss or touch in farewell. Even as she slumped back against her pillows and began to curse heartily, Gillyanne hurried into the tent.

"Do ye need some help?" Gillyanne asked.

"Nay." Avery got out of bed, waving aside her cousin's attempts to assist her. "Just give me a moment to see to my morning's ablutions and then we must talk."

Gillyanne sat down on the bed as Avery went behind the blanket that had been strung up to provide her with a privacy screen. "Ye look a little pale. Are ye sure ye arenae sickening again?"

"Verra sure. I have just had a wee bit of a shock."

Avery was just scrambling back into bed when Donald arrived with her morning meal. To her dismay, the youth was feeling talkative and stayed as she ate her food. By the time he left, Avery was nearly squirming with her need to talk to Gillyanne.

"Now ye are looking a wee bit flushed," Gillyanne said, reaching out to feel Avery's face.

Muttering a curse, Avery pushed her hand aside. "I am flushed because I am beginning to get irritated. I have had a shock, Gillyanne. I think I have just discovered something verra important, but I need to ask ye a few questions first. Do ye recall wee Alan, the bairn Elspeth and Cormac found and have taken in?"

"Oh, aye, that poor wee lad. 'Tis so hard to believe that anyone could just set a child out in the wood to die. Every time I think about it, I want to weep. He was blessed, though, for our Elspeth was sent to care for him."

"And he is verra dark, isnae he."

"Aye. Verra dark. Black hair, black eyes, dark skin." As Gillyanne spoke, her eyes slowly widened. "Nay."

"And Alan has an odd wee marking, doesnae he?"

Gillyanne nodded warily. "A wee star set low on his little belly."

"Curse it!" Avery flopped back against her pillows. "I do believe I have found wee Alan's father."

"Cameron?" Gillyanne whispered, and she gasped when Avery nodded. "Are ye sure?"

Ignoring the way Gillyanne blushed, Avery explained how she had reached her startling conclusion. "Do ye think ye can recall exactly what Alan's wee mark looked like?"

"Of course. Most birth spots are just that—spots or blotches. 'Tis rare to see one that actually looks like something. If Cameron's is the same, I will ken it. Ye want me to look at Cameron's belly?"

"I dinnae ken what I want."

"He should be told, Avery. He would want to be told."

"But what of Elspeth, Cormac, and young Christopher? They love that bairn. By now Alan is old enough to be thinking they are his family."

" 'Tis sad, but they also ken that he isnae theirs. They ken that he has a father somewhere." Gillyanne sighed and shook her head. " 'Twill cause pain, right enough, but e'en they would say that Cameron should be told, that he has the right to ken about Alan. I am certain of it and I think ye are, too."

Although she dearly wished to argue that, Avery knew Gillyanne was right. "Weel, go see if the fool is still in the camp and bring him here. I best do this ere I lose my courage."

"Dinnae ye think Cameron will want the lad?"

"Aye, he will want his son. What troubles me is that I am about to tell him that there was obviously one lie, one dark betrayal, he didnae learn about."

"Oh, dear."

"Aye, quite. This news will re-stir all of that old bitterness and mistrust. All I can do is pray that I have softened his attitude enough so that 'twill only be a temporary relapse.''

When Gillyanne left, Avery poured herself some wine, hoping that a drink or two would give her some much-needed courage. She could almost wish that Gillyanne would not be able to find Cameron. It did not surprise her, however, when they both entered the tent only a few moments later. Avery decided morosely that it was probably best to get the matter settled.

''Go ahead, Gillyanne,'' she ordered her cousin as she poured Cameron a goblet of wine and Gillyanne began to tug up his shirt.

''Here, now, what are ye about?'' Cameron demanded, yanking his shirt back down.

The look of shock on Cameron's face and the hint of a blush in his cheeks were almost enough to make Avery smile. ''Such modesty. I just want Gillyanne to look at your birthmark.''

''The lass shouldnae be gazing upon a mon's belly.''

''Sweet Mary,'' muttered Gillyanne as she tried to pry his hand off his shirt. ''I have been traveling with an army. And, although your men are surprisingly modest for soldiers, I have seen near every belly in this group. I also have more male cousins and brothers than most lasses could abide. I willnae swoon. Let me look.''

''Cameron,'' Avery said. ''please, can ye just trust me for a moment? 'Tis important that Gillyanne have a look at it.'' She handed him the drink as he sighed and released his grip on his shirt.

''There, ye didnae need to be so shy,'' said Gillyanne as she lifted up his shirt. '' 'Tis a handsome belly.''

''Brazen wench,'' Cameron muttered, but he smiled faintly and sipped at his wine.

When Gillyanne just stared at Cameron's stomach, saying nothing, Avery finished off her wine and asked, "Is it the same?"

"The verra same." Gillyanne finally replied, "right down to the odd bluish color of it."

Gillyanne and Avery stared at each other for a moment, then looked at Cameron. He began to feel uneasy as he fixed his shirt. Their expressions were an odd mixture of trepidation and sadness. Cameron was suddenly sure that they had something they had to tell him, and they knew he was not going to take it well. He finished off his wine and held his goblet out for more. It did not help him in his efforts to calm himself when Avery refilled his goblet and then her own. Avery did not normally drink much, and she had just finished one full goblet of wine. The news had to be very bad indeed if she felt the need for so much false fortification.

"Whatever ye are about to say isnae going to make me happy, is it?" He sighed when they both shook their heads. "Best spit it out, then."

"I must start this by asking ye a few questions first," Avery said, sipping her wine to soothe a sudden dryness in her throat. "There are just one or two wee things to verify ere we are sure we are right. Did ye e'er ken a Mistress Anne Seaton before ye left Scotland?" The cold, hard look of anger that settled on his face was really all the answer Avery needed.

"Aye. She was my leman for a while ere I came to France."

"A long while before or shortly before ye left?"

Avery briefly hoped he would say it was a very long time before. Alan was a beautiful little boy, and she knew Cameron would be a good father to him. She just did not want to have to tell Cameron that he had been the victim of a far greater betrayal than the one dealt his pride. The whole tale was far uglier than that of a woman denying a man his son, and she knew it would re-stir every bad feeling he had concerning women. She did not deserve to suffer for that woman's crimes, but she had no doubt that she would.

"Shortly," he replied. "I left her when I found her abed with another mon, and left for France within the month."

"And this Anne Seaton lived in a wee village on the road to where the king ofttimes holds his court?"

"Aye. I bought the whore a wee cottage just outside of the village. What is all this about, Avery?"

"Please, Cameron, a little more patience." She took a deep breath to steady herself, for she did not really want to hear the answer to her next question; but she knew it was important. "Ye said ye visited her and found her with another mon? So ye didnae bed her, then?"

"I had just ended a wee visit with her, bedded her that verra morning, then left for court. I forgot something at the cottage and returned to get it. The fool she was lying with must have been just waiting to see me ride away."

"Did ye take care when ye bedded her?" Gillyanne asked.

Cameron's shock over the young girl's blunt question came and went quickly as a chill snaked down his spine. As far as he knew, there was only one good reason to ask if he had taken care when he had last bedded the woman. He looked at their solemn faces as he prayed that what he was thinking was wrong, but he found no reassurance there.

"Nay," he snapped. "She told me she was barren."

"She wasnae barren, Cameron," Avery said quietly. "She had a son. A wee lad with black hair, black eyes, dark skin, and a wee birthmark shaped like a star very low on his little belly." Avery was surprised that Gillyanne could study Cameron so calmly for the anger in the man was making her decidedly uneasy. "That last bedding was obviously a potent one."

"How do ye ken all of this? How do ye e'en ken who Anne Seaton is?"

"I dinnae ken her, have only just heard the tale. 'Tis my cousin Elspeth who learned all about the woman, although no one kenned who had fathered the bairn. It seems the only ones in the village who e'er saw ye clearly were Anne, the laird ye bought the cottage from, and the poor, terrified fool ye found in her bed. My cousin was captured by Sir Colin MacRae and held captive in that cottage for a wee while."

"Anne's cousin, a verra distant one, but a highborn relation she liked to boast of to prove that she was better than the others in the village." He shook his head. "I think she believed that touch of highborn blood would actually make me consider marrying her. Do ye think she holds the lad thinking to make me wed her for his sake? I wouldnae have thought her so foolish, yet she is vain."

"Cameron, she is dead." She saw no sign of pain in his look—simply shock, then a touch of confusion. "She was hanged, then burned after being decried a witch. Elspeth believes it was done more because she bedded one too many husbands and was brazenly arrogant about the sin. Although she was nay a witch, it was soon learned that she weel deserved her punishment. In the back garden were found the bodies of two men and three wee bairns. It seems that, if she couldnae rid her body of the bairn, she simply murdered it when it was born."

"Sweet Jesu," Cameron whispered, sickened by the thought that he had been intimate with such a woman. "My bairn?"

"She let him live, although no one can say how long she would have continued to do so. She thought ye would return to her. Oh, she was verra angry with you. In

revenge, she neither christened nor named the lad, thinking that, if he died, she could taunt ye with the fact that
your son had died unblessed and unshriven. She said as
much to the priest.'' Avery wondered just when all that
anger she felt building inside Cameron would break free
of the bonds he fought to keep on it

"The vicious bitch.'' His eyes narrowed as he studied
Avery. ''There is more.''

Avery nodded and was comforted when Gillyanne
clasped her hand, silently offering her strength as an added
support. ''This rest has naught to do with Anne Seaton,
though her actions were to blame in a way. After she was
executed, the villagers set your lad in the wood, left him
alone and exposed, left him to die.'' She was not surprised
when he paled, for it was a chilling tale. ''Elspeth and
Cormac found him. They have taken him into their home,
christened him, and named him Alan.''

"Then I will ask for him, too, when I trade ye and
Gillyanne for your brother.''

That cold reminder that she was little more than a pawn
in his plans made Avery want to weep, but she fought to
stay calm. Pride kept her from wanting him to guess how
easily he could hurt her. There was also Alan to consider.
She had to try and make Cameron understand that he
could not simply claim the child, collect him like some
forgotten cloak left behind at a trysting place. He had to
be made to see that Alan was too young to be abruptly
snatched from the only family he had ever known.

"Ye cannae do that,'' she said, and she was not really
surprised when he turned some of that wild fury churning
inside him onto her.

"He is my son,'' Cameron said; then he finished off
his wine and threw his goblet across the tent in a vain
attempt to ease some of his anger. ''Unlike the whore
who bore him, ye dinnae have e'en the smallest right to

decide his fate. I willnae allow yet another woman to play her games with my own flesh and blood as her pawn. I will have my son."

"Ye willnae just take him," she snapped, her own anger rising. "Try to think of something besides your own poor wee sense of injury, your own poor wee bruised pride. Alan is a wee bairn. By the time ye return to Scotland, he will have been with Elspeth and her family for o'er a year. They are the only family he has e'er known."

"*I* am his family."

"Aye, but he is too young to understand that. Ye cannae just strut into his life and claim your rights with nary a thought to him."

"Why would your cousin try to claim my bastard son?"

"Ye insult her and us with your suspicions. Think ye she needs your bastard child? She has her own husband's bastard and a wee daughter of her own now. She took your son in out of the kindness of her heart, as has her husband. If Alan's father had ne'er been found, they would have raised him, loved him, and done weel by him. They havenae forgotten there is a father somewhere, however—one who was ne'er told of his son—and they ken that he might appear, might want the lad. They will not, however, let ye just snatch him from the only family he kens. They will expect ye to understand that that will hurt him badly. It must all be done slowly, carefully."

"And, of course, they will ne'er see that they have a fine pawn to use against me when I try to make your brother do right by my sister," he said, his voice thick with sarcasm. "Do ye think me a fool?"

"At this moment, aye."

When he glared at her for a moment, then strode out of the tent, Avery cursed and slouched back against her pillow. Gillyanne appeared to be deep in thought, and

Avery used the time to try to calm herself. She was hurt and angry. While he had not said too many hurtful things, his whole attitude had been an affront. Although she had expected the tale would re-stir all of his old bitterness, mistrust, and anger, she realized she had not fully expected so much of it to be aimed at her. She had thought she had proven herself to him, yet the actions of a woman from his past had so swiftly caused him to eye her with suspicion, she knew she had only been fooling herself. That he could think even for a minute that she would use his own son against him showed her that she had not really touched any more than his passion. And, she thought sadly, his passion could well prove as fleeting and tenuous as his trust.

"The day just continues to improve," she muttered when an obviously angry Leargan strode into the tent and glared at her.

"What in God's name did ye do to Cameron?" demanded Leargan. "He just strode out of here as if all the beasts of hell were yapping at his heels."

"Ye tell him, Gillyanne," Avery said. "I believe I will just lie here and brood for a wee while."

Despite the strong urge to indulge in a hearty sulk, Avery found herself watching Leargan as Gillyanne told him all they had just told Cameron. The expressions that flickered over Leargan's open face were fascinating. When Gillyanne finished, he dragged his hand through his hair and muttered a long string of curses.

"That cursed bitch has managed to reach right out from the grave to make him miserable," Leargan muttered.

"Did he care for her then?" Avery asked.

"Nay. Weel, aye, a wee bit. Nay more than a mon usually cares for a bonny, skilled leman."

"And he trusted her to be faithful whilst he paid her upkeep only to be made a fool of."

Leargan nodded. "When he found her with another mon but hours after he had left her bed, that was bad enough. In the ensuing confrontation, however, she took great delight in letting him ken just how wrong he had been to think he could trust her to be faithful e'en for a day. Not only had she bedded near every mon for miles about, but she had taken several of his friends to her bed as weel, making sure that they heard all about what a fool he had been. She told him she had lied about being barren and had rid herself of one of his bairns. He didnae believe that, but now?" He shook his head. "I wouldnae be surprised if he fears one of the bairns buried in the bitch's garden was his. And I daresay he is thoroughly sickened by discovering just what sort of woman had succeeded in making a fool of him. I mean she wasnae just a faithless whore; she was a murderess, a killer of bairns. She was cold, heartless, e'en purely evil."

"Aye, she was," agreed Gillyanne. "I suspect he is feeling mightily sullied at the thought that he bedded down with such a woman."

"I certainly would," said Leargan.

"And so he is probably off somewhere trying to scrub that stain away e'en though 'tis three years old."

Leargan stared at her for a moment, then shook his head. "The way ye do that, lass, 'tis purely unsettling." He looked at Avery. "I had thought him cured of it all, that he had overcome the past and come to his senses. It would appear that this news has brought it all back."

"It would appear so," Avery agreed.

"I am sorry, lass."

"So am I, Leargan. Now go find the fool. He isnae in any condition to be watching his back."

"Mayhap 'tis just the shock and this relapse willnae last long."

"Mayhap, but then, it doesnae have to last too long

ere all my chances of benefiting from a change of heart are gone, does it?''

He hesitated, opened his mouth to say something, then shook his head ''Aye, I had best go and find the fool.''

The moment Leargan left, Gillyanne looked at Avery. ''That didnae go verra weel, did it.''

''Nay,'' agreed Avery, and she sipped at her wine. ''Not verra weel at all.

''I dinnae think he really believed those accusations he made. 'Twas the anger talking. He was verra, verra angry. 'Tis hard for a mon to ken that he can be so easily fooled by bonny smiles and an ache in his loins. I think Cameron believes he should be above that sort of foolishness, should be wiser, should be able to see more clearly. To discover Anne Seaton's crimes went so far beyond mere vanity and faithlessness makes him feel even more foolish.''

''Which makes him even angrier.''

''Aye. Weel, 'twill pass. How long can a mon brood o'er such a thing, anyway?''

''Gilly, 'twas Anne Seaton's faithlessness that was that last betrayal, that one which made Cameron turn his back on all women, the one which prompted his trip to France and his vow of celibacy.''

Gillyanne frowned, then gaped. ''But, all of that happened nearly three years ago.''

''Exactly. Cameron is a verra stubborn mon and, I feel 'tis safe to say, a champion brooder.''

''Oh, dear.''

''Quite.''

Chapter Fifteen

"Is he still brooding?"

Avery turned to smile at Gillyanne as her cousin climbed into the cart and sat beside her. Although, despite nearly a week of travel, Avery felt more than able to ride a horse, she was forced to stay in the cart. She was also forced to spend most of her time staring at Cameron's back. The man rarely came into the tent, never slept at her side, and barely spoke to her. He had just left with Leargan to spy on the port they lingered on the edges of, and she had not even been able to wish him Godspeed.

"Aye," she replied. "He does little more than glare or grunt and sleeps outside with his men."

"The idiot. Weel, Leargan has no new bruises, so mayhap his temper is easing a little."

Poor Leargan, Avery thought, and she smiled again. He had found Cameron that day, bathing in the river just as Gillyanne had said he would be. Avery doubted she would ever be able to learn who had said what to whom

to start the fight. There was even the possibility that
Leargan had started it on purpose, knowing that it was
what Cameron needed. Avery was not sure why, but
occasionally, men did seem to have need of a good, rousing fight. Leargan and Cameron had returned to camp
bruised and bloodied, but a lot of Cameron's anger had
apparently been pounded out of him.

The man was still brooding, however. Avery wondered
if there was any chance Leargan could pound that mood
out of him as well. Very soon she might be tempted to
do it herself. Their time together was rapidly fading away
while he sulked over a crime three years old. *Perhaps a
few knocks on the head with a stout cudgel,* she mused,
glaring in the direction he had gone.

"Are ye sure ye arenae brooding, too?" asked Gillyanne.

"Nay. Weel, not constantly," Avery confessed. "Just
now I was wondering if bashing Cameron o'er the head
would restore his senses."

Gillyanne laughed and shook her head. "It would probably only help ye to feel better. Cameron just feels things
verra deeply, I think, and he doesnae want to. He would
like to be emotionless, yet he is actually verra emotional."

" 'Twould be nice if he would direct some of that
emotion my way."

"Oh, I think he does. In truth, I wonder if some of this
brooding is being used to place a distance between you.
He is mon enough to foolishly believe that distance is
enough to kill any longing or need."

"Sometimes, Gilly dear, ye sound as if ye think men
are nay verra bright."

"When it comes to emotions, to love, to matters of the
heart, men can often be verra blind and verra dim-witted.
Women, too. Just nay as often. Some of the trouble with
men is that they see love for a woman—a need for her—

as a weakness. No mon willingly accepts, acknowledges, or welcomes a weakness. I adore my fither and uncles—think they are brilliant, strong, loving, and all that can be good in a mon. Yet, from the tales I have heard, when they were courting our mithers they were nay the brightest stars in the sky.'' She laughed along with Avery, then grew serious again. ''Just think on this, Avery. If a mon can be so wounded, so angered, by the betrayal of even his leman, a woman he didnae e'en love, he is undoubtedly a mon who does indeed have a heart—a verra big heart.''

''I have considered that possibility myself. And?''

''Did I say and?''

''Nay, but I could hear one in your voice. And?''

''And . . . mayhap sitting about waiting for him to get o'er his sulks isnae the best thing to do, especially not if he is using that mood to hold ye away from him. Since ye have so little time left to be with him, mayhap ye should try to get in his way, refuse to let him ignore you.'' Gillyanne briefly chewed on her lip, then warily continued, '' 'Tis the betrayals and faithless ways of women which have soured him, e'en made him afraid, though he would probably ne'er actually admit that. 'Tis nay fair that ye must suffer for the less-than-honorable actions of others or that ye must prove yourself, but 'twould nay help your cause if ye stood on your pride and refused to do so. And, keep in mind that soon he will find he has been betrayed and lied to yet again—by his verra own sister.''

''I ken it.'' Avery groaned softly. ''That could weel be the *coup de grace.*''

''Not if ye and your love still lurk fresh in his mind. Not if ye have refused to allow him to e'en try and put ye out of his mind and heart. If ye keep yourself in his thoughts by keeping yourself in his arms, in his life, then he willnae be able to help but recall such things as how ye ne'er lied to him, how ye stood loyal to your brother, how ye saved the lives of his people despite all of his unkind plans for you, and how ye told him the truth about his son. He will also recall that your passion was as honest as ye are.''

"So I should fling *myself* at his head instead of a rock."

Gillyanne laughed even as she nodded. ''Aye. I would.''

"Then I will, as soon as he returns from finding out where DeVeau is lurking in the town.''

"Do ye think DeVeau is there waiting for us?"

"I am certain that he is," replied Avery. "I swear I can almost smell the mon.''

"Do ye sense some danger?''

"Nay, and I pray that is a good thing.''

Cameron cursed and slouched against the wall of one of the buildings forming the shadowed alley where he and Leargan were hiding. He had known DeVeau would be waiting for them, but he had nursed the small hope that the man would have tired of the game by now. The man had his soldiers scattered all over the busy port town. It was not going to be easy to get his people to the ship he had just bought room on. In truth, that he had found a captain willing to take them all on, and with a ship able to hold them all, was the only bit of luck he had had. He felt sure he could trust the captain not to alert the DeVeaux, but Cameron could see no way to sneak his people, their horses, and all of their baggage safely onto the ship before it had to sail.

"We will need to reduce the number of his men," Leargan said as he leaned against the wall opposite Cameron.

"Aye." Cameron frowned across the road at the inn

DeVeau was staying in. "Pick a route and then close the eyes all the way along it."

"And do it verra close to sailing time so that we dinnae need to hold our place on the ship for long." He followed the direction of Cameron's gaze and smiled faintly. "I fear there willnae be enough time for ye to slip in there and cut his throat."

"I hadnae planned to make his death that easy."

"Still angry that he touched the lass ye have ignored for a week?"

"I have decided that I was wrong to break my vow of celibacy."

"Of course."

"Since we will soon be at Cairnmoor and I must then trade Avery for her brother, I have decided 'tis best to end the affair now, to clear away that small entanglement."

"If ye say so."

Cameron glared at his cousin. "Ye dinnae need to make your scorn quite so clear to hear."

Leargan shrugged. "I have decided that ye are too stubborn and too thick-witted to heed any of my great wisdom. If ye wish to let the past taint the rest of your life, who am I to stop you? I do, however, reserve the right to beat ye later for insulting Lady Avery by comparing her, e'en fleetingly, with the traitorous whores ye have dealt with in the past."

" 'Tis your right," Cameron snapped. "Just as 'tis my right to beat ye later for being such a continuous pain in the arse."

"Agreed."

"Now, we had best return to camp. There is a great deal of planning to do."

* * *

Avery listened in utter dismay as Cameron and Leargan described how the town was swarming with Sir Charles's men. Their plan to reduce the number of those men while most of the others tried to slip onto the ship was very risky. While it was true that the MacAlpins had every right to consider the DeVeaux their enemies now, it was also true that they faced this current danger because of her. As she opened her mouth to suggest that they simply give her back to the man, Gillyanne abruptly spoke out.

"Ye need a diversion," Gillyanne said softly.

"That would help, lass," Cameron agreed, "but since we used that trick when we freed Avery, DeVeau is surely watching for it."

"He looks for the usual soldier's diversion such as stampeded horses and burning supply carts. Ye need one that he willnae immediately suspect is your doing. Mayhap e'en something that could get some of your people and goods onto the ship right beneath the mon's nose."

Cameron's eyes widened and he nodded. "A verra good idea, yet I fear I havenae any thoughts on just how to do that."

"Many people take pilgrimages to holy places in England."

"Gilly, ye are astoundingly clever at times," Avery said, and she grinned briefly when Gillyanne blushed.

"I will confess that I sometimes possess a rather devious turn of mind," she murmured; then she looked back at Cameron. "There must be some of your people who arenae weel kenned by Sir Charles and his men—ones who would need little more than a somewhat concealing cloak to pass by the DeVeaux unrecognized."

"A small group," Avery continued. "Mayhap a half dozen and one heavily laden cart, plus a few of the more common horses. One woman and Gillyanne."

"Me?" Gillyanne squeaked at the same time that Cameron said, "Nay."

"Aye. A wee group of pilgrims willnae draw interest for long. Howbeit, a lass who has vowed to sing all the way to the holy shrine will surely hold most of the village's attention."

If Gillyanne sang her way through the town, Cameron doubted even the men on the ship would notice the people slipping aboard. It was a perfect diversion. Unfortunately, it could all too easily put Gillyanne in a great deal of danger.

"I cannae risk the lass," he said, struggling to ignore the murmurs of disappointment he heard.

"And I cannae sing in front of so many people," Gillyanne protested. "And, in truth, why should that hold anyone's attention for verra long?"

"Gilly, ye ken that ye have a voice people like to hear," Avery said. "And, for most people, the chance to hear a verra fine singer is as rare as a too-hot day in Scotland." She looked at Cameron next. "I dinnae think Gillyanne will be in any greater danger than if she was trying to slip aboard a ship encircled by verra alert DeVeau soldiers."

The argument that ensued did not last very long. Cameron's only real objection was that he did not want to put Gillyanne in any danger, but Avery was right. Gillyanne would be in as much danger, if not more, if she tried to sneak aboard a well-guarded ship. Cameron and the few men he would take with him could not close the eyes of all the DeVeau guard, and that guard would be the heaviest and the most alert around any ship prepared to sail. He reluctantly agreed to the plan, but only if some of the "pilgrims" were men who could fight if the need arose.

As Avery helped Anne—who had been chosen as one of the pilgrims—and Gillyanne to prepare, she tried not to regret that she could not be a part of the adventure.

Anne's husband, Ranald, and three other soldiers chosen for their rather ordinary appearance would also go. Donald was going to play the sickly lad the pilgrimage was intended to cure. Cameron and Leargan were busily packing the horses and cart with as much as they could carry. The abundance of goods carried by the pilgrims could be easily explained. Penances, indulgences, and blessings did not come cheaply.

"I wish I hadnae thought of this," Gillyanne muttered as Avery pinned up her hair.

" 'Twas inspired, Gilly," Avery said.

"Aye, by the fact that ye were about to suggest they just hand ye o'er to that swine."

"How did ye ken I was about to do that?" Avery had to admit that sometimes Gillyanne's insights could be rather unsettling.

"Ye had that this-is-all-my-fault look upon your face. I ken that Cameron wouldnae have done it, but I didnae e'en want to hear the argument that would ensue. And what is my reward? I must sing my way past a horde of strangers."

"Wheesht, lassie, it cannae be any worse than what I must do," said Anne as she pinned on her head-covering. "I must try to keep from laughing o'er the mere thought that my mon is playing at being a priest."

"He did ken a great deal of what a priest should say," Avery said. "Prayers and blessings. And, he speaks French as if he was born here."

Anne shrugged. " 'Tis just a skill he has. I do swear the mon recalls every word he has e'er heard uttered, and he is a fair mimic. Acting pious will certainly put a strain upon him, however. The rogue." She laughed along with Gillyanne and Avery, then straightened her shoulders and brushed down the skirts of her dull brown gown. "Let us be off, then. Sooner begun, sooner ended."

"Just where did Ranald get all of those priestly things, anyway?" Avery asked, and she was not really surprised when Anne's reply was to grab Gillyanne by the arm and hurry away to join the other false pilgrims.

Avery joined the group that would enter the village at the opposite end of where the pilgrims were to enter. They were almost done emptying the carts that would be left behind. Their supplies and belongings were packed onto the horses and their own backs. The horses were going to cause the most difficulty, Avery thought as she secured a heavy pack upon her back with Therese's help. A horse could not creep aboard like a person could, and it was not easy to quickly hide it away. Cameron's plan to unpack them at dockside, then at the last moment have two men take them aboard as if they were horsetraders was a good one, but the presence of the animals in the venture still made her uneasy.

She was disappointed that she got no chance to say anything to Cameron before he, Leargan, Wee Rob, Colin, and two other men left to slip into town and silence as many of DeVeau's men as possible. A brief exchange of waves was all she managed with Gillyanne before each of their groups went their separate ways. Every step of the way into town, Avery prayed that she was right to feel so confident in the plans that had been made. It was terrifying enough to know that if it all failed, she would end up back in Sir Charles's hands, but even more so to think that Gillyanne could fall into his grasp as well.

Cameron released the man he had just killed, sighing as he then dragged the body into the deeper shadows at the back of the alley. He did not like killing a man this way, slipping up behind him and striking without warning. Most of the guards he had silenced with a sharp, solid knock on the head, then left them tied and gagged. This man, however, had caught sight of one of his people slipping aboard the ship and had been about to cry out an alarm. It had been necessary to swiftly end that threat but Cameron much preferred a face-to-face battle to stealthy throat slitting.

Then, almost as if to ease his troubled soul, Gillyanne's remarkable voice cut through the air. He grinned when everything suddenly went still. Cameron mused that he would not be surprised if even the scavenging dogs had suddenly sat down to listen. He just hoped that his men were now accustomed enough to be able to ignore Gillyanne and go about their work, although he doubted anyone could ever listen to that voice with only a casual interest. There was just something about it that reached deep inside a person and grabbed hold.

As he kept Gillyanne's little troop in sight and watched for any more of Sir Charles's men who might need their eyes closed, Cameron began to make his way toward the ship. He had caught the occasional sight of his people boarding the ship and could only pray that they were all aboard by the time he and the "pilgrims" arrived. When he caught sight of a shadowy form inching closer, he tensed, then relaxed with a sigh when he recognized Leargan.

"Nearly everyone is on board," Leargan reported. "They will begin to load the horses in a minute. That wee lass has everyone's attention fixed firmly upon her. 'Tis as if they are all bewitched. E'en the bastard ye ache to kill," he added with a nod toward the inn.

Cameron followed the direction of his cousin's gaze and silently cursed. Sir Charles did look spellbound, but the way the man's attention was fixed so intently upon Gillyanne and her group made Cameron nervous. He could not feel completely certain that Sir Charles would not recognize any of them. There was also the chance that Sir Charles might simply decide he wanted Gillyanne, wanted to possess that beautiful voice for his own personal enjoyment.

Avery stood beside the burly captain, who leaned on the ship's railing, sighing with pleasure as he listened to Gillyanne sing. Everything seemed to be going very well, but Avery was not sure she should trust in her own sense of safety. Her uncanny ability to sense approaching danger had not been completely reliable lately. She suspected that the emotional turmoil she was in was the cause. When Gillyanne paused in her singing, Avery smiled at the captain, who was wiping the tears from his cheeks.

"My cousin sings like an angel, doesnae she?" Avery said, patting his arm. "Her father, Sir Eric Murray, laird of Dubhlinn, is so verra proud of her."

"Sir Eric Murray? He is kin to the MacMillans of Bealachan, isnae he?"

"Aye, their nephew. They have given my cousin a wee piece of land as a dowry so fond of her are they."

"I am a distant cousin, ye ken."

Since his name was MacMillan, Avery had already suspected the possibility of a connection, but she feigned surprise. "Weel, it does ease my mind to learn that we will be guided across the waters by a kinsmon." She sighed and shook her head. "I just hope my cousin can make it aboard safely."

"Why shouldnae she? Is she in some danger?"

"I cannae be sure, but the mon who seeks to use me for his own gains may weel try to grab her in my stead. He may e'en think to rob Scotland of that beautiful voice and hold it captive for his own selfish enjoyment."

"Thieving French," Captain MacMillan muttered, and he signaled to his men.

It was hard, but Avery bit back a smile when the sailors all armed themselves. Cameron's men already stood by the ship's railing armed with bows and arrows. Now they would have the added strength of over a dozen hardened sailors. The captain had been sympathetic enough to allow them to sail with him and not turn them over to DeVeau, but now she had given him reason enough to fight for them, too.

She watched as Cameron and his men arrived. The others slipped aboard while Cameron and Leargan helped Anne and the others get the cart and the horses onto the ship. Gillyanne stood on the dock, singing sweetly while Ranald blessed the sea and the vessel. Avery was just starting to relax when suddenly, Sir Charles and four other men came up behind Gillyanne. Before Ranald could stop him, Sir Charles grabbed Gillyanne and held a knife to her throat. Ranald faced them, sword drawn, but there was nothing he could do. Cameron and Leargan stood at the base of the ship's loading ramp, swords raised, but equally as helpless.

"Did ye think I would be long fooled by this game, Lady Avery?" called Sir Charles.

"Aye," Avery replied with a calm she did not feel. "Just how did ye guess?"

"Sir Renford here," he nodded to the man on his right, "suddenly recognized the girl. A man often recalls well a woman he hungered for but did not have the chance to possess. Now, I suggest you bring your sweet self down here if you ever wish to hear this little bird warble another tune."

When Avery moved as if to obey that command she was halted by Wee Rob, who stepped up behind her, grabbed her by both arms, and kept her pinned against the railings. Cameron never took his gaze from Sir Charles as he signaled to his men. Avery looked from one side of her to the other to see Cameron's men with their bows drawn, the arrows aimed steadily at Sir Charles. All the sailors also had their weapons raised—some with bows, others with swords or cudgels. Even Sir Charles, in all his cold arrogance, had to see that he would be dead the moment he drew one drop of blood from Gillyanne. Avery prayed that he was not insane enough to think that he could somehow escape, or worse, that he might decide to take Gillyanne down with him in some twisted act of revenge. She stood tense and afraid in Wee Rob's hold as Sir Charles's companions talked to him.

"Let the girl go, DeVeau," Cameron said in French. "There is no winning this game."

"My men . . ." began Sir Charles as he slowly took the knife away from Gillyanne's throat.

"Most of them are dead or tied up. I doubt you can muster any more than the four fools now cowering behind you."

"I am not fond of losing," said Sir Charles, but he shoved Gillyanne toward Ranald, who picked the girl up under one arm and ran for the ship. Sir Charles then bowed toward Avery. "Until we meet again."

"I do believe I have seen enough of France," Avery replied; then, released from Wee Rob's grip, she hurried to greet Gillyanne.

Cameron stood at the railing, watching Sir Charles as the ship pulled away from the dock. "That was a verra close call."

"Aye," agreed Leargan, standing at his side. "Fortunately, Sir Charles loves himself more dearly than he loves to win." Leargan glanced toward Avery and Gillyanne, deep in conversation with the captain. "Did ye ken that yon captain is a kinsmon of wee Gillyanne's?"

"Not until a few minutes ago." Cameron tightened his grip upon the railing as the ship began to gain speed. "Do ye think the lasses will try to get him to help them escape from us?"

Leargan also held the railing tightly as his face began to turn a greenish-grey. "I suspect it has occurred to them, but 'twill also occur to them that someone could get hurt, and they willnae wish that to happen."

Feeling himself break out into a cold, uncomfortable sweat, and knowing that he probably looked as bad as Leargan, Cameron laughed shakily. "I dinnae think we would be able to put up much of a fight, do ye?"

His cousin's only reply was an agonized groan, and a heartbeat later, Cameron heard himself echo it.

Chapter Sixteen

"Ah, weel, I can see that this journey isnae going to be the romantic interlude I had hoped for."

Cameron started to turn over and look at Avery, only to frown when he could not. "My wrists are lashed to the railing."

"Aye." Avery knelt down next to Cameron, thinking that she had never seen a man look quite so miserably ill. "Wee Rob was afraid ye might fall into the sea right along with the contents of your belly."

"Leargan?" Cameron looked from side to side but could not see his cousin.

"Anne and Gillyanne have already untied him and taken him to a bed."

"How can that help him? The beds move."

"True, but we have a potion that will help. We have made a lot of it, for near half your men fell ill."

He looked at her, noticed that she looked no more

than attractively windblown and sun-kissed, and deeply
resented it. "Have ye been taking this potion?"

"Nay." She brushed the sweat-matted hair from his
pale forehead and decided that he needed a wash as well
as another dosing.

"Of course not," he grumbled. "Why should I be surprised that Murray lasses are all accomplished sailors?"

Avery started to untie his wrists. "Actually, Gillyanne
and I havenae sailed much at all. Just on the trip o'er to
France."

"Ye arenae making me feel any kindlier toward ye."

"Tsk, and after Wee Rob and I worked so hard to get
those doses down your wretched throat."

Cameron could faintly recall someone pouring some
evil tasting brew into him; then he realized that he was
actually sensible for the first time since the ship had set
sail. "Just how long have I been lashed to this railing?"

" 'Tis near the end of the second day," she replied as
she put her arm around his waist and helped him stand
up.

He frowned down at the top of her head as she half
dragged him toward her cabin. "Ye shouldnae get so
close. I probably stink."

"Ye do that, but 'tis why I have had a bath prepared
for ye in my cabin."

"Dinnae I have my own cabin?"

"Nay. There are only a few and the captain gave them
to the women, although they are somewhat crowded with
sick men now." She struggled to hold him steady with
one arm as she unlatched the door to her tiny cabin. "Now
ye will be crowding mine."

Cameron wanted to protest that, but he was feeling too
ill to argue about anything. He stood unsteadily as she
handed him a goblet of some herbal concoction and then
began to take off his clothes. This arrangement was going

to ruin his plan to keep his distance from her. Then he decided he was probably too sick to be entrapped by his own passions, and he relaxed.

The potion tasted horrible, but he finished it and gratefully accepted the wine Avery gave him to cleanse the taste of it from his mouth. As he sank down into the hot bathwater with a sigh of pleasure, he realized he had not felt his stomach clench in quite a while. Vile-tasting though it was, the potion obviously helped.

"I think your potion is working," he said as she washed his hair.

"It usually does after the fourth dosing," she replied as she tilted his head back and, with a pitcher full of clean water, carefully rinsed the soap from his hair. "Ye have just downed your sixth."

" 'Tis so foul of taste, I am surprised it doesnae make me even sicker."

Avery laughed softly as she scrubbed his back. Leaving him on deck for two days had been one of the hardest things she had ever done. He had been so wretchedly ill, she had ached with her inability to do any more than force her potion down his throat and wait for it to begin its work. Now, however, she could see some advantage to having the worst of it pass before bringing him into the cabin. He now had a clean, fresh-smelling place in which to regain his strength.

And, she thought with an inner smile as she washed his feet and legs, he was somewhat at her mercy at the moment. She had decided that Gillyanne was right. It was foolish to allow him to keep a distance between them. If nothing else, she could not allow him to steal away what little time she had left to gather a few memories in his arms. If he still sent her away after they reached Cairnmoor, he would be stealing most of the joy from her future. She would not let him steal the joys and pleasures of the present as well. The definite signs of arousal he revealed as she finished bathing him told her that he still desired her and that it was time he ceased to hide from the passion they could share.

"I think I have recovered enough to dry myself," Cameron said as he stepped out of the bath.

Avery handed him the drying cloth and went to answer the knock at the door. Two men came in, set a tray of food down on a small table at the far end of the little cabin, then dragged the tub away. By the time they were gone, Cameron was dressed in the robe she had set out for him and was sitting at the table, eyeing the food a little warily.

"Ye can eat something," she said as she went to a large basin filled with hot water and began to take off her gown. "It willnae hurt, though I would go slowly. Your innards are undoubtedly a little tender."

"Undoubtedly," he whispered, his voice a little choked as her chemise fell around her feet followed by her braies.

He chewed on a thick slab of bread as he watched her wash herself. The sight of her slim, lovely back had him aching for her. Clearly, he was much improved, he thought, as he took a deep drink of wine that did nothing to cool his blood.

She was acting as if they were still lovers, he realized, frowning. That made no sense, for he had almost completely ignored her for a week. She should have seen nothing less than a cold, clear rejection. Of course, the way his errant body had reacted to her bathing him gave the lie to his pose of disinterest. Perhaps, he mused, he needed to tell her very bluntly that the affair was over.

Cameron stared at her as she joined him at the table dressed only in her robe, her thick, dark-golden hair tumbling wildly over her slim shoulders. She smiled sweetly at him. For reasons of her own, she was apparently going to treat his actions of the past week as nothing more than a sulk, a bad mood. As they ate, he continued to watch her, feeling arousal tighten his body, and an anticipation of the sweetness he could find in her arms setting all his nerves to tingling. The more he watched her, the more his passion rose and the more he began to think himself an idiot to give up what she so freely offered until it became absolutely necessary.

"What game are ye playing now, lass?" he finally asked, made wary by her good humor after she had suffered the sharp end of his bad mood for days.

"Game?" Avery asked as she crossed her legs. She made no move to adjust her robe when it fell open to expose her legs all the way up to the middle of her thigh. "Why do ye think I play some game?"

Tearing his gaze from her slim legs and trying to forget the urge to lick them from toe to hip and back down again, he gave her a mildly disgusted look. "Because, after the way I have acted this last week, a lass with your spirit ought to be wanting to bash me o'er the head. Instead, ye cure my illness, clean me up, feed me, smile at me, and tempt me."

"Ye were being ill tempered for a purpose, were ye? I thought ye were just brooding."

"I wasnae brooding."

"Oh? What do ye call it, then?"

"I was just reminding myself of the treacherous nature of women." He was not surprised to see anger sharpen her gaze.

"One could be unkind and point out that if one deals only with whores and adulteresses, one is a fool to expect honor and truth."

"A good, sharp hit, lass."

"Thank ye."

He realized that her words did not anger him because

he had already reached the same decision himself. The thought that she might think him a fool, even only in passing, pinched quite sharply, but he shrugged it aside. Men and women had been made fools over each other far too often. Cameron took comfort in the fact that he had at least learned from past failures.

"They were nay all whores and adulteresses," he felt compelled to tell her. "One was the lass I was betrothed to, a lass of high birth and, supposedly, a chaste body and sweet nature."

"Ye were married?" Avery wondered why, when she could shrug off the thought of lovers from his past with relative ease, she should find the thought of his betrothal or marriage so deeply upsetting.

"Nay, only betrothed. She seemed accepting of the marriage. A fortnight ere we were to be wed, she came to stay at Cairnmoor with her mother, her servants, and a few of her kinsmen, including a distant cousin named Jordan."

"And?" she prompted when he fell silent and scowled into his goblet of wine. "They were lovers, her and this Jordan?"

"Oh, aye, and he was no cousin, either. Nay, he was the son of an old, bitter enemy of my father's. The two of them planned to use the wedding celebration to slip his men into my keep and take it from me. My family, most of my men, and of course, myself, the poor besotted groom, were to be killed. They had already slipped a half dozen of his men into my home and begun their dark work. Six of my people were missing ere I noticed something was wrong. Later we found their bodies weighted with stone at the bottom of the moat."

And ye blame yourself for each one of those deaths, she thought, wishing she could take his guilt away. "How did ye find out what they were planning?"

"I went to her bedchamber, saw Jordan slipping inside, and set my ear against the door."

She winced. "And discovered those who say eavesdroppers nay hear any good about themselves were right?"

He smiled faintly. "True. I heard their plans and the fates of my missing people. I also heard that my bride was verra pleased it would all be accomplished ere she actually had to wed or bed me. She was terrified that this dark, scowling devil might actually touch her fair skin ere he was killed."

"Ouch. I suppose she preferred fair-haired, bonny young knights who cut the throats of the ones who welcome them into their homes." She was pleased to see him grin at her sarcasm. " 'Tis sometimes difficult to see beneath the smiles and sweet words. The flattery feels so nice, one likes to believe in it. At least when I learned how easy it is to see what isnae there, I didnae have to worry about saving my clan as weel as my pride. What did ye do?"

"Shut the gates, gathered up the traitors, and, when his people arrived, hanged the lot from my battlements. His people left."

It was harsh, but she knew he had given them a far more merciful death than many another would have. "E'en your betrothed?"

"Nay. I put the fear of the devil in her and her womenfolk and sent them home." He studied her closely for a moment, then abruptly asked, "Who lied to ye, then, lass?"

"Oh, just a lad. Just before I went to France, my parents took me to court. I think they hoped I would find a mate there. Let us just say that I didnae have the laddies tripping o'er each other to kiss my slippers. There was one lad, however, who showed me a marked interest and, ne'er having been wooed and flattered before, I will confess that I was moved by it. I heard some talk of his being one to seduce and abandon a lass, a rogue who spent more time rolling about in a lass's arms than in doing any work at all." She shrugged. "I told myself that all young lads indulge themselves in such ways ere they settle down with a wife."

Cameron knew how this tale would end and had to resist the urge to tell her not to finish it. He knew his tastes were not odd in any way, so he could not understand how other men failed to see her beauty, to see the promise of a rich, passionate fire in her lithe body. It did not really surprise him to feel an urge to find the young man she was speaking of and beat him soundly. After the incident with Sir Charles, he had come to accept that he felt very protective of Avery.

"That wasnae the way with this lad?" he asked.

"It may be, but I wasnae the lass who would be stopping his wandering ways. He wasnae verra discreet, was carrying on with a wedded lass e'en while he wooed me. I chanced upon them trysting in the garden. She expressed some jealousy o'er his attentions to me. It was soon revealed that his attentions to this too-thin lass with the strange eyes were due to the beauty of her dower." She smiled when he winced faintly. "I decided that what I wanted was not to be found at court."

"And, of course, he was fair and verra bonny."

She laughed softly. "He had black hair, skin as fair as milk, and blue eyes. I discovered that fair skin bruises most lividly," she murmured. "The lady's husband asked me if I had seen her when I returned to the great hall from the garden."

"Wicked lass." He toasted her with a brief lift of his goblet.

"Aye, though 'twas wrong to let my wretched pride

lead me. The husband might weel have killed them both. The lad took a dangerous beating as it was, for he was neither tall nor strong."

"Odd. The lasses usually favor the tall and the strong."

"Ah, but from what I heard said that day, he had something else to interest the lady. His lover said he had a verra big—"

"Avery," he warned, giving her a repressive look even though he felt like laughing.

"Dinnae fear. I didnae take a look to confirm her claim."

"How weel-behaved of you. Ye arenae too thin, lass, and those eyes of yours may be an odd color, but they are beautiful."

"Thank ye, kind sir," she said. Her voice was light and playful, but a faint blush stung her cheeks. "And I find I have a true weakness for braw, dark knights." She winked at him.

He set down his goblet and held out his hand. It made him feel dangerously good when she put her hand in his. With a sigh that was a mixture of pleasure and resignation over his weakness for her, he tugged her down onto his lap.

"Ye are feeling better, are ye?" she asked, her voice wavering slightly when he began to stroke her legs.

"Aye, much better," he replied as he licked the pulse point on her neck.

"Nay more brooding?"

Leaning back, he sighed and shook his head. "Nay. Ye cannae expect a mon to take it weel when ye tell him that someone hid his child from him, didnae e'en christen or name the poor wee lad."

Avery supposed that was Cameron's attempt at an explanation for how he had been acting, and probably the closest to an apology she would get from him. "Nay.

It was cruel. And crueler still for those people to set a bairn out in the wood to die.''

''Because he was as dark as the devil, so black of hair and eye he had to be the devil's own child, and the mark upon his belly was the proof of that curse.'' Cameron's voice was harsh, rough with a bitterness he could not hide.

That, she suspected, hurt most of all. She would not be surprised if it stirred up memories of hurts, insults, and rejections from the past. Cameron was certainly not the bonny, blue-eyed knight many a lass dreamed of. He was dark as sin, moody, and not very good at giving a lass sweet words and flatteries. It would probably surprise many to learn that she could love such a man, but she did—probably far more than was wise. He was her black-eyed knight, her dark-as-sin chevalier. She stroked his strong jaw and wondered how women could fail to see the beauty of his strong, dark features or be intrigued by the mystery of his dark eyes.

''Then I must be a verra big sinner,'' she murmured, ''for every time I see that wee mark upon your fine belly, I feel nearly compelled to kiss it.'' She felt him tremble faintly beneath the hands she had placed upon his chest.

Cameron had to clear his throat before he could say, ''Ne'er let it be said I denied my lady whate'er she wished.''

Avery liked the way he called her ''my lady,'' she decided as she slid out of his lap and knelt between his long legs. ''My lady'' was how she wanted him to think of her after he sent her away. My lady who made his bones melt with her passion. My lady who, with every touch, every kiss, revealed her delight in his big, strong, dark body. It would be a nice legacy, she mused as she kissed her way up one strong leg. It could also be a memory sweet enough and strong enough to last even when he had sent her back to Donncoill, compelling enough to make him find some way to get her back.

She stroked and kissed his legs until she felt a fine tremor ripple through him. Raising herself up on her knees, she untied his robe. Avery kissed his taut stomach, his hips, his ribs, the top of his strong thighs, everywhere but where she knew he wanted her to. Finally, with a light tug upon her hair and a few hoarse mutterings, he let her know that he had had all he could endure of her sensual teasing. She laughed softly and gave him what he wanted.

Cameron clutched the arms of the chair as he watched her love him with her mouth. She was getting very good at it, instinctively knowing how to keep him teetering precariously at the very edge of a sweet madness. The way she so freely gave him this pleasure, so obviously felt pleasure in the giving of it, only enhanced the delight. He wished he had the strength to enjoy it for far longer, but after only a few moments, he knew he had to stop her.

A soft gasp of surprise escaped Avery when he stood up, grasped her under the arms, and set her down in the chair. She murmured with pleasure as he pushed open her robe and feasted on her breasts. His hands and lips became the tools of a sensuous torture. Only when he knelt before her did she feel modesty cast a faint, cooling shadow over her passion.

"Nay. Too bold," she protested softly as he gently stopped her from pressing her legs together.

"I didnae deny ye any part of me," he said against her inner thigh.

"Men are a brazen lot, I think."

"Ah, lass, ye are beautiful here. All gold and silk and sweet, sweet honey."

It took little more than a stroke of his long fingers and

a kiss or two to banish her modesty. He took her to the heights with a ruthless speed. Avery quickly realized he had done so on purpose so that he could now toy with her as he pleased. She closed her eyes and struggled for control. Shameless and wanton though it was, she loved his intimate play. Once more he drove her to the pinnacle all lovers strive for. When it seemed as if he was going to do so a third time, she protested. Delightful as this sort of loving was, she needed to feel him inside her, craved the union of their bodies. She did not want to go it alone again.

Cameron grabbed her by the waist and pulled her out of the chair. Slowly he set her down upon him, easing himself into her body as if he had all the time in the world, as if they were not both shaking with need. Avery looked at him as she clung to his broad shoulders. His eyes were closed and his head was thrown back. There was a look of such pleasure upon his face, an expression of such intense anticipation, that she felt her own passions soar. By the time he had completely joined their bodies, her release was already beginning to swamp her. With a few hard thrusts, Cameron soon joined her in that paradise.

Avery collapsed in his arms, not surprised when he sprawled onto his back on the floor. She felt so wrung out, she was amazed she had the wit left to keep on breathing. If this was the sort of thing her parents had been indulging in for over twenty years, it was a wonder they were still alive. It did explain the large size of her family and, she thought with a little smile, those heated looks followed by unexplained disappearances. A sharp rapping on the door yanked Avery from her thoughts, and she suddenly stared at the door in horror, praying she had remembered to bolt it.

"Avery," called Gillyanne, "come and look at the stars."

When she heard Gillyanne skip away without even waiting for a reply, Avery collapsed back into Cameron's arms. "I think I already saw them, just now," she murmured; then she smiled when Cameron laughed, causing her to bounce gently on his chest.

"Come along, lass," he said as he sat up, set her aside, then stood. "I want to go out there and test this potion of yours."

As she started to get dressed, Avery said, "Where ye stand on the ship doesnae make any difference. If ye drink the potion thrice a day until we reach land, ye should be fine."

"Do ye have enough herbs to make such an amount? Ye said that nearly half my men are ill."

"A large amount can be boiled up using but a few handsful of herbs, and not all of your men were as ill as ye and Leargan. Some just need a day, mayhap two, to become accustomed to a ship. A dose or two was all they needed. Anne recalled the ones who were quick to settle as weel as those who suffer for the whole journey."

" 'Tis a vile cure," he said as, once dressed, he moved to help Avery finish lacing up her gown, "but 'tis nay as vile as the illness." He lightly braided her hair, then tied it with the ribbon she held out to him. "Come, let us go and see why Gillyanne feels we must look at these stars."

Avery let Cameron take her by the hand and lead her out of the cabin. He had returned to being passionate, playful, even friendly. His brooding was evidently over, and if it had been his intention to hold a distance between them, he had obviously changed his mind. It was not easy, but Avery held her tongue. Her pride rebelled at the way she was allowing him to apparently set her aside and pick her up again as the mood struck him, but she bludgeoned it into silence. She promised herself, however, that, if she and Cameron ended up together, she would teach him that explanations and apologies would not really hurt and left no scars. Women who did not get them from the men in their life, however, did.

Chapter Seventeen

"I hadnae realized just how deeply I had missed Scotland," Avery said as she stood on a rocky hill beside Gillyanne and surveyed the surrounding countryside. "I swear, but one day here and I e'en feel different."

"Hmmm. Cold," Gillyanne drawled, hugging her cloak more tightly around her.

"Ye have no romance in your soul."

"I do. It just doesnae tolerate being frozen by a north wind."

"What ye need is some more fat on your wee bones."

Gillyanne rolled her eyes. "Look who is giving me that advice. A lass who could be knocked over by a good strong wind."

"I am still standing despite being pounded by this gale." Avery tucked back behind her ear a strand of hair that had been tugged free by the light breezes. "I think I must have gained a few pounds."

"Oh, aye. Why, if I didnae ken that ye had your woman's time whilst ye were ill, I would think ye were with child, ye have grown so plump.''

"Do ye ken, I think someone could truly be hurt if they were pushed down this hillside." Avery gave Gillyanne a narrow-eyed glare, but her cousin just laughed. "I wish we were headed to Donncoill," she added softly as she watched the MacAlpins set up camp.

"I ken it." Gillyanne slipped her hand into Avery's. "We travel to Cairnmoor first."

Avery nodded and fought down an urge to weep. "I havenae changed his mind."

"Ye cannae and ye ken it. He thinks his sister a woman wronged and our Payton the one who wronged her. Unless Payton has willingly come to marry the lass, ye will be used to bring him there. Our fathers and brothers, all of our kinsmen, would do the same. The only difference here is that we ken that this girl lies. She will use her brother's sense of honor and love for her to get her our Payton as a husband. I hate to keep slapping ye with these hard truths, but ye must keep them in mind or ye will only add to whate'er hurt ye suffer o'er this."

"Then why am I trying so hard to make him love me?"

"Because ye love him. And, for what will happen afterward. For making his heart ache enough to look for answers, open his eyes enough that he may see that his sister is lying. For making him want to come after you no matter what happens between Katherine and Payton."

" 'Tis going to hurt," Avery whispered.

"Oh, aye, I suspect it will," agreed Gillyanne, and she lightly squeezed Avery's hand in sympathy. "Just keep telling yourself that for all the hurt ye may suffer, ye may also end up with all the glory our parents have. That is what I intend to have."

"Ye deserve nay less. I just pray ye dinnae have quite so much trouble gaining the prize."

"Ah, but how often does the greatest of prizes come easily?"

"What do ye think they are plotting up there?" Cameron asked Leargan as he watched Avery and Gillyanne standing on the hill.

"Finding a verra big rock and rolling it down on you?" Leargan replied. He met Cameron's disgusted look with a grin.

"Ye have been in irritatingly high spirits since we docked yesterday."

"I hadnae realized how much I missed this land. The heather, the hills, the rocks."

"The thistles, the cold, the rain."

Leargan laughed and shook his head. "Come, admit it. Ye are glad to be back. Ye missed it, too."

Cameron smiled faintly. "Aye, I did. It will be good to see Cairnmoor again." He frowned at Avery and her cousin again, knowing there would be at least one shadow on the joy of his homecoming.

"I really dinnae think they are plotting anything, Cameron. Mayhap they have just missed Scotland, too."

"And mayhap they are trying to decide in which direction lies Donncoill or the keep of any of their vast multitude of relations."

"Worried that your plans could pull us into a war?"

"Nay as long as I have the two lasses to trade for the lad. And I am nay threatening the lad's life, just making him marry Katherine."

"To some lads that may look to be the worse of the two fates. Just marriage," Leargan added hastily, "nay marriage to Katherine specifically."

"True." Cameron shrugged. "I cannae see the Murrays

and their various kinsmen shedding blood o'er the matter.''

''Nay, probably not. Ye do ken that, although ye can force the marriage, ye cannae make it a good one.''

''I ken it. Yet there must have been some spark between them if they were lovers.'' He grimaced. ''And surely the verra bonny, verra good, much-adored Sir Payton Murray could be nay other than a verra perfect husband.''

Leargan laughed. ''Ye sound almost jealous, cousin.''

''Perfection can be verra irritating.''

''Just how old is this oh-so-bonny-and-perfect knight?''

Cameron frowned. ''I dinnae ken. I believe he has been a knight for several years, so he must be near our age.''

''He could have gained his spurs at a particularly young age.''

''Please, God, nay,'' Cameron grumbled as he turned and strode toward his tent. ''If I discover he was knighted young for some great heroic deed, I believe I just might gag.''

Avery sat beside Cameron and watched him sleep. If the weather remained fine and the trail they followed was safe and clear of obstacles, they could be at Cairnmoor in four days. And then, she thought sadly, Cameron would trade her for Payton, send her away, and cut the very heart out of her. She did not think she could bear it.

She did not really understand how he could do it either. The matter of pride, of honor, of loyalty to his sister, she did understand. Yet despite all they had shared, he did not even seem to be considering any way of getting the husband he felt his sister needed and keeping his lover by his side. At times, Avery was certain he had come to care for her. Surely no man could make love to a woman as he did to her and not care, at least just a little. But perhaps a little was all it was. Too little.

And that, she admitted, was what she feared to learn. She was prepared to be traded for Payton and had accepted Cameron's reasons, ones she knew her family would also agree with even though it was all based upon a lie. What she feared was that he would trade her and send her away with no more emotion than he would feel if he traded some horses. She wanted him to be torn by his actions, and she very much feared that he would not be.

Cautiously she stood up, moved away from the bed, and started to get dressed. She could not stay and watch him sully all they had shared. She could not allow him to destroy the beauty of her memories. Avery desperately needed to be able to cling to the joy she had found in loving him, however briefly, but she now saw how easily he could destroy that. If she was not around to see him coldly discard her, she would still be able to treasure her memories, would still be able to see their passion as a beautiful thing.

After hastily packing a small sack with clothes and a few supplies, she crept out of the tent. No one stood guard near the tent, for no one expected her to flee Cameron's bed. There were a few guards set out to watch for thieves or anyone else eager for some bloodletting and looting, but she knew where they were. Taking a deep breath to steady herself, Avery slipped into the shadows of the surrounding wood.

Just inside the wood, she paused to look back at the camp. It troubled her to leave Gillyanne behind, but she knew that her cousin would understand. There was no possible way she could stealthily get Gillyanne out of camp, and Avery could not be sure there would be a chance for them to flee together in the next few days. The only thing she was certain of was that no one would hurt Gillyanne, and she knew her cousin shared that certainty and so would not be afraid.

She started away from the camp at a brisk walk, wondering how far she could get before dawn. Unless Cameron woke up and reached for her before then, Avery felt sure her absence would not be noticed until morning. If she judged it right that gave her about three hours, maybe more. It might be enough if, she thought with a sigh, she was headed in the right direction.

Once she reached her family, she could let them know that Gillyanne was safe, that no matter what Cameron said, he would not hurt the girl. Avery knew that, even if Cameron was angered enough to briefly consider it, his own people would stop him. In her heart, however, she knew Cameron would never lay a hand on a woman or a child. That knowledge would be enough to give Payton some choice in what he would do. Avery could only hope that Cameron did not see her actions as just another in a long line of betrayals.

"What do ye mean ye cannae find her?"

Hearing his bellow echo around the tense, too-quiet camp, Cameron took a deep breath and tried to calm himself. When he had woken up to find Avery gone from their bed, he had assumed that she had slipped away for a moment of privacy. Although a little disappointed that he would not be able to start the day by making love to her, he had not thought her absence suspicious. By the time he was dressed and Donald had brought his food, however, he had begun to worry. There were a lot of unseen dangers in the wood. Now, however, after an hour of searching for her, he was not only worried; he was suspicious and angry.

"Some of her things are missing," Anne announced quietly as she stepped out of Cameron's tent.

Cameron looked at Gillyanne. "She wouldnae escape without you."

Gillyanne shrugged. "Since the last time we tried to flee, we are always verra closely watched when we are together. And at night, I am usually weel encircled. She wouldnae have been able to rouse me without rousing someone else."

"Where would she go?"

"Donncoill."

"She doesnae ken how to get there from here."

"Avery had a long talk with Captain MacMillan. I think he may have given her a good idea of which way to go."

He had not considered that possibility and he cursed his blindness. "Ye dinnae seem verra concerned that she has left ye behind." Cameron fought against the urge to avoid the girl's sharp gaze.

"Ye willnae hurt me," Gillyanne said, her confidence clear to hear behind each word spoken. "*I* am in no danger."

"Neither was she," snapped Cameron. "I would ne'er have harmed her."

"That depends upon what ye consider harm." Gillyanne's smile was tinged with sadness. "I think poor Avery just decided that she didnae want to wait around and watch ye spoil everything."

Cameron was not sure what she meant, but before he could ask, Leargan stepped up beside him to report, "There are none of the horses missing. She is on foot."

"Then she should be easy to find," Cameron said as he strode toward the horses. He paused when he realized Leargan was following him. "I will go alone."

"Are ye sure that is wise?" Leargan asked as he moved to help Cameron saddle his horse.

"Who can say, but I will go alone. Ye can see to it that everyone continues on the trail we have chosen. When I find that fool lass, I will come and find you."

"Why not just let her go? What difference can it make?"

"If by some miracle she reaches any of her kinsmen, she will let them ken that any threat I make against Gillyanne can be ignored."

"And if ye find her, then bring her to Cairnmoor, ye are going to break her heart."

"She has kenned my plans from the beginning." Cameron said tersely as he mounted. "I have ne'er lied to her."

"Mayhap not in words," Leargan began, but then he shook his head and stepped away from the horse.

"Think on this, Leargan. 'Tis a three-day hard ride to Donncoill from here. God alone kens how long it would take to walk it. A wee lass alone on the road for days is in a lot more danger than she could e'er be with me. Someone could easily find her and do far more to her than bruise her poor wee heart."

Cameron kicked his horse into a gallop. He headed in the direction of Donncoill, hoping Avery was indeed following Captain MacMillan's directions. The time she had almost escaped in France, she had found her way back to his camp well enough and fast enough to give them a timely warning about the DeVeaux, so she obviously had some sense of direction. It was going to be difficult to find one small woman in a countryside with so many places to hide, even if she stayed on the right path. It would be impossible if she got herself lost.

She didnae want to wait around and watch ye spoil everything.

Although he did not want to, Cameron found himself thinking over Gillyanne's words and beginning to understand what she had meant. Avery was no amorous widow, adulterous wife, or skilled courtesan. She was a young highborn woman. She had been a virgin. A woman like that did not indulge in light, easily forgotten affairs. And, he thought with an inner grimace, most affairs ended because the passion had faded, not because one's lover used one in trade for a husband for his sister. Despite his cynicism and his need to keep his emotions well guarded, he could not deny that what he and Avery shared was beautiful. He could understand how she might not wish to see it ended in the way he planned, that a romantically minded young woman might find it all upsetting enough to flee from.

I havenae been able to make ye love me like I love you. If ye love someone, shouldnae they love ye back?

He cursed as he recalled her fevered words. For the most part he had managed to shove them into a dark corner of his mind, but they had slipped forth now and again to tantalize him. Telling himself that it was only vanity that made him want those words to be true had not completely dimmed their allure. Now he found himself wondering if Avery really believed them. It would be easy for an untried girl to confuse passion with love. If Avery believed she loved him, then he could easily understand how she could think leaving him now was far more preferable than waiting for him to cast her aside, to send her away with no promises of a future.

The cynical part of him jeered at his conclusions, scoffing at his attempts to explain Avery's actions by thinking she was in love. There was another explanation for her attempt to reach Donncoill. She wanted to save her brother. Avery hoped to let her family know they could ignore his threats, that Payton did not need to marry Katherine because Gillyanne was in no real danger.

It made perfect sense. She was going to betray him to her family. There was even the possibility she would use their affair against him, paint him as guilty of the same crimes he accused her brother of. Cameron realized that he had no idea of just how much information Avery might have gathered on him, his clan, and Cairnmoor. She could prove a threat to far more than his plans to get his sister a husband.

A moment later, Cameron cursed and shook his head. Fool that he might be, he could not make himself believe all that. He did not doubt that if she reached her clansmen, she would do her best to ruin his plans concerning Katherine and Payton, but he could not really call that a betrayal. Avery had as much right to protect her brother as he did to protect his sister. In his heart, he knew she would do no more than try to keep Payton from entering into a marriage he did not want. After all, if Avery had wished to harm him or his people, she could simply have ridden away the day she discovered the DeVeaux' plans to attack his camp.

The only thing that really mattered now, he told himself sternly, was finding Avery. At the moment none of the problems between them were of any importance. She was a tiny woman alone. Whether she had the sense to know it or not, the dangers she was courting were almost too numerous to count. He had to find her before something worse did.

It was nearly high noon before he finally found her, and by then he was so knotted up with fear for her, he did not know which he wanted to do more: kiss her or throttle her. As he topped a small hill, he saw her sit down on the bank of a creek. She tugged off her shoes and stockings and stuck her feet in the water. Her whole body reflected the relief she felt as the cool water bathed her feet. *Good,* he thought as he dismounted and secured his horse, *I hope she has blisters.* With as much silent caution as he would use to approach the deadliest of enemies, he crept up behind her.

Avery carefully eased her aching feet into the water. They felt both startled and soothed by the chill. She had been walking for a long time, but she was still surprised at how badly her feet hurt. When she considered how far it was to Donncoill, she feared she would arrive there with no more than bloodied stumps where her feet used to be.

"Mayhap I should have taken one of his horses," she muttered.

"Then I could have had ye hanged as a thief."

It did not really surprise her to hear that deep, familiar voice right behind her. Avery decided that she had been expecting his arrival nearly every step of the way. Either that or she could simply sense when he was near. At that moment, she did not consider that a very good thing. She did not want to be so deeply bound to him.

"Ye couldnae trade my pale corpse for Payton," she said without turning to look at him.

Cameron decided to ignore her petulant reply. He needed to give voice to some of the anger churning inside him. "Did ye e'en pause to think ere ye walked away from my bed?"

"Oh, is the poor mon nettled because he didnae have the chance to indulge in a morning rut?"

A soft screech of surprise escaped her when he suddenly grabbed her by one arm, yanked her to her feet, and tugged her around to face him. One look at his expression made it difficult to face him calmly. Cameron was furious.

"One: ye will ne'er again call what passes between us rutting." And why he thought that was the most important command to give her, he did not know. The woman was making him insane. "Two: ye are ne'er to go off alone again."

"I am nay going back with you."

It was hard, but Cameron resisted the urge to shake some sense into her.

"If I have to tie ye up and toss ye o'er my saddle, ye are going with me." He dragged his hands through his hair. "Ye are nay a stupid lass, but this? This is stupid. It could take ye a week, mayhap e'en a fortnight, to walk to Donncoill. Ye will be lucky to make it there alive. I doubt ye can make it there unharmed. Ye arenae that long cured of a fever, and Scotland's weather can be most unkind. Ye didnae steal enough food to last ye for more than a day or two. There are wild animals to worry about, and I doubt every person ye may chance upon will be a kind, gentle soul. There is also the chance ye could injure yourself, and ye would have no one about to help you."

"Enough," she said quietly but firmly. "Ye need not beat me o'er the head with every danger existing in field and forest." She crossed her arms over her chest and glared down at her cooling feet. "I did, mayhap, nay consider everything as carefully as I should."

There was no sense in trying to explain her actions. Even if she bared her heart and soul, Avery doubted Cameron would understand what had made her flee his side. If he did not feel what she did, he could not understand how his actions could hurt her, or how desperately she wanted to avoid that pain. It had been foolish to flee into the night, to even attempt such a journey alone and unprotected, but even if she had considered all the dangers, she was not sure that would have stopped her.

"My feet are all dirty now," she muttered.

Cameron almost laughed despite the strange ache in his heart. Avery looked an odd mixture of sad and cross. Although he shied away from considering just how deep her feelings for him went, he knew he was hurting her. He did not really want to hurt her.

The lingering cynic within him tried to mock him. After all, he had not asked any more of Avery than her passion. He had certainly never promised her any more than that. If she had let her heart lead her into deeper waters, it was her own fault.

He sighed and urged her to sit back down on the grassy bank while he bathed her feet with his own hands. It was true that he had not asked her for any more than passion, but he was beginning to believe he was being given more—a great deal more. Cameron wished he could make it easier for her, but he was bound by family duty and honor to continue with his plans. He also knew he was a selfish bastard, that he would greedily accept all she had to give right up until he had to send her away.

After he dried her feet with the edge of his cloak, he took it off and spread it on the ground. Their gazes locked, but she made no protest as he relieved them both of their clothes. He made love to her slowly, gently, cherishing every little sigh and gasp. When he joined their bodies, he paused to stare down at her. He wanted to hold fast to the feel of her tight heat surrounding him, to the look of passion on her face.

"Ye willnae be sad," he said as he began to thrust into her.

"Is that command number three?" she asked as she wrapped her legs and arms around him.

"Aye. Ye will nay let me make ye sad."

She threaded her fingers into his thick hair and tugged his face down to hers. "As ye will, my dark-as-sin cheva-

lier. When we can share such delight, how can I be sad?''
she whispered, and she kissed him, freeing herself to soar
to passion's heights along with him.

The moment the lingering heat of desire left her, Avery
felt her sadness return, but she fought to hide it as she
and Cameron got dressed. It served no purpose except to
dim what they could share in the little time they had left
together. Cameron had obviously guessed that she felt
more for him than passion. That he was concerned about
making her sad and did not wish to hurt her revealed that
he was not without some feeling for her. It would not
change things, but she would try to find some comfort in
the knowledge.

Cameron led her to his horse and set her on it. He
kissed her thigh before tugging her skirts down, then
mounted behind her. He then nudged his horse in the
direction of Cairnmoor. When Avery snuggled back
against him, he smiled faintly and kissed the top of her
head. Cameron dearly hoped that she was as resigned to
her fate as she seemed to be.

''I will understand if ye feel ye cannae share my bed
again,'' he felt compelled to say, though he knew it was
a lie.

Avery snorted softly as she closed her eyes. She could
hear his reluctance to make that concession behind every
word he spoke, but she had to respect him for even making
it. He realized that things had gone too far, had gotten
too complicated, and he was trying to set things right.
Ending their affair now would change nothing, however.
It would only mean that, when she had to leave, she would
be not only heartbroken, but filled with regret for every
lost chance to spend that one more night in his arms.

''One cannae go back, Cameron.''

''Nay, I suspect not.'' He sighed, relieved that she
would remain his lover, yet saddened over the thought

that it would probably cost her dearly in lost pride and added pain. ''I would change things if I could, but I must do as honor and duty command.''

She did not reply but only nodded, and Cameron fancied he could almost feel her disappointment. Or perhaps what he was feeling was his own.

Chapter Eighteen

Cairnmoor was huge. Avery stared at it and barely kept herself from gaping as they rode up to it. It seemed to rise up out of the very rock it was built upon. A small loch bordered it on one side and a wide moat, drawing its water from the loch, encircled the other three sides. It was as dark and forbidding as its laird. Even if her family got the mad idea of trying to fight to free her and Gillyanne, one look at this place would bring them to their senses.

Her attention was drawn from the keep by the sounds of the hearty greetings that assailed Cameron and his group as they rode toward the keep. It was evident that the people of Cairnmoor had no fear of being ruled over by such a dark knight. They obviously saw only a laird with the strength to protect them well and—for she carefully studied the clothes and the appearance of the people she saw—with enough coin to keep them well fed and warmly dressed.

When they reached the inner bailey and Cameron helped her dismount, Avery found herself pushed aside as his people hurried up to greet him. She felt a little less alone and ignored when Gillyanne reached her side to take her hand in hers. Although she was happy for those who were so joyfully reunited, Avery suddenly ached to see her own family. The sheen of tears in Gillyanne's eyes told her that her cousin felt the same. Even the thought that seeing her family would mean losing Cameron could not fully banish the longing she suddenly felt.

A tall, elegant gentleman approached Cameron, smiling widely. The touch of grey in his black hair and the lines upon his face were nearly all that kept him from looking exactly like Cameron. Avery was not really surprised when Cameron greeted the man as his cousin Iain. She tensed slightly when Cameron brought the man over to meet her and Gillyanne. There was no telling how those at Cairnmoor felt about the things of which her brother had been accused.

"Ah, have ye finally taken yourself a wife, lad?" Iain asked as he kissed first Avery's hand, then Gillyanne's.

Cameron felt himself blush, and after glaring at Avery and Gillyanne in a vain attempt to banish their identical smirks, he said, "Cousin Iain, may I introduce Lady Avery Murray and her cousin, Lady Gillyanne. Ladies, my cousin, Sir Iain MacAlpin."

"Murray?" Iain frowned at them, but Avery saw no anger in his look. "As in Sir Payton Murray?"

"Aye," replied Cameron "Avery is his sister."

"Ah. I think there is a tale I need to hear, and Katherine will be eager to see you, Cameron. Do ye ladies wish to be shown to your rooms now, mayhap have some hot water brought to you?" Iain asked.

"Nay, thank ye kindly, sir," replied Avery, "but we all stopped not a half hour's ride from here to tidy ourselves up. I think everyone wished to be looking their best when they were reunited with their kinsmen." When the man just nodded, she and Gillyanne followed him, Cameron, and Leargan into the keep.

"This place is huge," whispered Gillyanne. " 'Tis clear that this branch of the MacAlpin clan kens how to make a coin or two."

Upon entering the great hall and seeing all the rich tapestries on the wall, Avery had to agree. They were seated at the head table on Cameron's left, opposite Iain and Leargan. Avery helped herself to the bounty of bread, cheese, fruit, and cold meats that were set out as Cameron told Iain her tale. A few of the more personal parts were excluded, but the intent look upon the older man's face told her he had probably begun to guess what he was not being told.

Just as Iain seemed ready to ask her a question or two, there was a soft gasp at the door, which drew everyone's attention. Cameron murmured, "Katherine," and Avery knew she was about to meet the woman who was trying to entrap Payton. Avery studied the young woman who gracefully hurried to Cameron's side and, when he stood, flung herself into his arms.

Katherine was tall and fulsome and had the same rich, black hair that Cameron did. Her skin was the flawless ivory that poets rambled on about, and Avery noticed when the woman glanced her way several times, her eyes were a lovely deep blue. What troubled Avery was that within those glances there had been the expected curiosity, but there had also been the gleam of calculation. Worse, try as she might to accept Katherine's effusive greeting as one of honest sisterly affection, Avery could not suppress the sense that it was all for show. A quick glance at Gillyanne's still, watchful expression did not ease Avery's suspicions.

"Come, sister, join us at table," Cameron said, wondering why Katherine's loving greeting had not warmed him very much.

"But that woman is sitting in my chair," Katherine protested, pointing at Avery.

"Katherine," Cameron said, a little surprised at what sounded a bit too much like petulant rudeness, "ye can sit next to Leargan."

"I can move," offered Gillyanne. "I think I have the strength left to move down a seat despite the long journey I have endured. Then Avery can shift her weary body down one, too. And then Lady Katherine will be able to put her bonny ar—"

"Gillyanne," Cameron snapped, and then he sent a brief, repressive look at Leargan and Iain, who both looked close to laughing aloud. "Katherine will sit next to Leargan." He nudged his sister toward the seat. " 'Tis nay so far away that it will impede conversation."

"Thank God he didnae tell her to sit next to me," Gillyanne muttered.

"Did ye have something to say, Gilly?" asked Cameron, his eyes narrowed in a look of sharp rebuke.

Quickly shoving a slice of apple into her cousin's mouth, Avery replied, "Nay. Gillyanne was just complimenting the food." Avery wished the table were not so wide, for she badly wanted to kick Leargan to get him to stop grinning.

"Just who are these women, Cameron?" demanded Katherine as she sat down next to Leargan and glared at Gillyanne.

Cameron introduced the women to each other. The way Avery and Gillyanne nodded curtly at Katherine, and Katherine did the same back to them, made Cameron sigh. The battle lines had clearly been drawn. Although he and Avery no longer spoke of the accusations against her brother, it was obvious that both Murrays were still certain that Katherine was lying.

He studied the cool, smug look on Katherine's face and realized he did not feel the same great confidence in her that the Murray lasses obviously felt in Payton. His sister was a complete stranger to him, a young beautiful woman whom he did not know at all. That made him feel both sad and guilty. If they were strangers, it was his fault, Cameron decided. When he had been at Cairnmoor he had been too busy to have much to do with her, and then he had fled to France, leaving her in the care of others. Now that he was home, perhaps he could mend that and build the sort of relationship siblings should have.

"Are they related to my Payton, then?" Katherine asked, although her tone implied she already knew the answer to that question.

"Aye. Avery is his sister," Cameron replied.

"Really?"

It was only one word, but its tone and the look upon Katherine's face told Avery what was not being said, just thought. How could such a skinny, odd-looking female be related to the beautiful Sir Payton? The way Cameron was frowning at his sister made Avery wonder if he was hearing the same hidden message that she was.

"Aye." Cameron watched Katherine very closely as he asked, "Are ye still claiming that Sir Payton Murray seduced you?"

Katherine stared back at Cameron, one dark brow raised. "I believe the word I used was rape."

Out of the corner of his eye, Cameron saw Avery clamp a hand on Gillyanne's shoulder to hold the girl in her seat. " 'Tis a harsh accusation to fling at a mon's head, lass. Are ye sure?"

After holding her brother's gaze for a moment, Katherine turned away and heaved a shuddering sigh. She tugged a fine lace-trimmed linen cloth from her pocket and dabbed at her suddenly moist eyes. Then she looked at Cameron again from beneath partially lowered lashes, her full mouth trembling ever so faintly.

"I may have misnamed the crime," she said in a weak, unsteady voice. "In my despair o'er being so callously used and cast aside, I may have struck out blindly, wishing to hurt him as he so deeply hurt me."

A gagging noise sounded on Cameron's left, but by the time he looked at the Murrays, Avery was gently patting Gillyanne on the back and the younger girl was dabbing at her mouth with a napkin. Both looked suspiciously innocent. "Something wrong?"

"Gilly just got a wee piece of apple stuck in her throat," Avery replied.

Turning back to his sister, Cameron said, "I am sorry for your pain, Katherine."

" 'Tis nay your fault," Katherine replied. "I had hoped to overcome my shame and hurt, but"—she smoothed her skirts over her belly, revealing an unmistakable roundness—"I fear my perfidious lover has left me with child."

"Curse it," Gillyanne whispered as Katherine sniffled into her linen square, "that looks real."

"Aye," agreed Avery in as soft a voice, "but we both ken it isnae Payton's. He would ne'er disclaim his own child, which means he refuses her because he is absolutely certain that bairn cannae be his."

"So, the question which needs answering is, just whose can it be?"

"First we must try to discover how far along she is, then when she was at court."

"And, if it appears that she got with child while she was at court?"

"Then we need to try to discover who she saw whilst there. We can only hope Katherine isnae the sort who inspires undying loyalty in her servants, for they may weel hold the answers we need.''

"Ladies?" Cameron called, ending their whispered conference. "Is something troubling you?"

Realizing that Katherine had ceased sniffing out her tale of betrayal and heartbreak, Avery looked at Cameron and shook her head. "Nay. Gillyanne and I but shared a moment of understanding and commiseration o'er the sad plight of women used and cast aside by their lovers."

To his dismay, Cameron felt himself blush, then glared at Gillyanne, who looked far too amused by his discomfort. "Ye will nay suffer from this folly," he said to Katherine, then signaled to a page. "Bring me quill and paper," he ordered the boy. "I shall write to Sir Payton."

"That is so good of you, Cameron," said Katherine, "but it willnae matter. He has coldly refused all of our entreaties."

"Aye, but ye had naught to hold out as a lure aside from your love and your beauty, which he has proven foolish enough to refuse." Cameron was sure he heard Avery muttering something about wasting his flattery on the vain, but he decided to ignore it. He picked up the quill when the page set the writing materials in front of him. "I wish it could be otherwise for ye, Katherine, but I do have the means to force your lover to do as honor demands." He winced when Avery and Gillyanne stood up so abruptly that their chairs banged against the floor, and he knew he had just been unwittingly unkind. "Avery?"

"I believe I should like to be shown to my quarters now," Avery said, her gaze fixed upon Iain.

Cameron grasped her hand. "Ye kenned I was going to do this, that I have to do this."

"Aye." She snatched her hand away. "I kenned it, but

I ne'er expected ye to make me watch it.'' She looked back at Iain. "My room?"

"Place her in my mother's chambers," Cameron softly told Iain, "and wee Gilly in the room next to that." He watched Iain lead Avery away, then looked up to find Gillyanne glaring at him. "Gilly?"

"I hope ye put your eye out with that quill," Gillyanne snapped.

"Gilly," Avery called, pausing in the doorway to frown back at her cousin. "What were ye doing?" she asked as Gillyanne hurried to her side.

"I was but thanking Sir Cameron for the fine meal," Gillyanne replied.

As soon as the door shut behind Iain and the Murrays, Cameron relaxed, only to then glare at Leargan, who laughed softly. "Ye find something about this amusing?"

Leargan touched the missive Cameron was about to compose. "About this? Nay, naught at all. But Gilly? Aye. She is an endearing wee brat. If I wasnae already more than twice her age, I might be tempted to wait until she finished growing and marry the girl."

"But Leargan, her eyes dinnae match," said Katherine, obviously shocked. "And her hair is so untidy."

"Katherine, perfection isnae always as beautiful as uniqueness!" Leargan spoke, as if trying to teach something to a particularly slow-witted child; then he shook his head when she just continued to look at him as if he were the witless one. "Cameron, do ye ask for your son as weel?" he asked as he turned away from Katherine.

"What son?" demanded Katherine. "Dinnae say that skinny whore claims she gave ye a child?"

"Ye insult Lady Avery," Cameron snapped, his voice hard and cold.

"Do I? Have ye placed her in the room which adjoins yours so that ye may guard her more closely, then?"

Katherine suddenly gasped and placed her hand upon her chest. "Oh, brother, ye do this for me? As I have been used and shamed, so shall she be. 'Tis a great sacrifice ye make for me."

Although he told himself that Katherine had a right to feel no kindness toward a Murray, the excuse did not cool Cameron's fury over her words much at all. "What does or doesnae happen between Lady Avery and myself has naught to do with ye, Katherine. 'Tis nay your business, and I would be verra displeased if ye tried to make it anyone else's." He held her angry gaze until she gave him a curt nod of agreement; then, in what he hoped was a calmer tone, he explained, "The boy Leargan refers to is a bastard child born of a woman I kept as a mistress about three years ago. In one of those odd twists of fate, Avery's cousin Elspeth and her husband, Sir Cormac Armstrong, found the child abandoned and took him in."

"Weel, I suppose that was kind of them. It relieves ye of that burden. Aye, ye should express some thanks, I suppose."

Cameron stared at her, blinked slowly, then looked at Leargan. He was relieved to see that his cousin was looking as dumb-struck as he himself felt. It was impossible to know what he should conclude from his sister's surprisingly callous attitude toward his son. Illegitimate the boy might be, but he was of her blood—her own nephew. Cameron decided it was best to concentrate on an answer for Leargan and the wording of his message to Sir Payton Murray.

"As far as concerns wee Alan, Leargan," he told his cousin, "I believe I will simply mention that Avery and Gillyanne have presented me with the strong possibility that the boy is my son. I will politely but firmly stress that I consider the matter of the boy one that must be settled carefully and should in no way become entangled with this other issue.''

"Ye intend to take in this child?'' Katherine asked in astonishment.

After staring at Katherine for a moment, Cameron decided he was too weary and too burdened with his own concerns to try and understand her now. "I think ye should go and rest, Katherine. 'Tis obvious that the bairn and the excitement of the day have dimmed your usual fine spirits. We can speak again later. Mayhap at the feast this evening.''

The moment Katherine left, Cameron concentrated on composing the message he wished to deliver to Sir Payton Murray. He knew Leargan was waiting to say something, but he ignored him. Once the missive was finished, he called Wee Rob and Colin to his side and instructed them to take it to Donncoill. Finally, he leaned back in his chair, downed a full goblet of wine, and wondered why he did not feel better—relieved, as if he had accomplished something. He refilled his goblet and looked at Leargan.

"So, 'tis done,'' Leargan murmured.

"Aye, 'tis done.'' Cameron mused that he should feel at least a little triumphant, for he had just taken a large step toward restoring his sister's honor; yet he felt empty and had a strong urge to get staggeringly drunk.

"Mayhap ye should have waited a wee bit.''

"Why?''

" 'Tis somewhat clear that Katherine lied when she accused that mon of rape.''

"So, she may have lied about other things?'' Cameron softly cursed when Leargan nodded. "She may have. Howbeit, she still claims Sir Payton was her lover and is the father of the child she carries.''

"If she lied about the rape, mayhap she lies about the

true father of her child. Mayhap ye should more closely consider Sir Payton's claim that the child isnae his.''

"Mayhap I should," Cameron agreed softly, "but I cannae. I must accept Katherine's word on this. She is my sister. The bairn already rounds her shape. There is nay time to waste. She points her delicate finger at Sir Payton and I must act upon that claim or condemn my own sister to utter ruin.''

"I was rather hoping Lady Katherine was lying about being with child," Avery said as she sprawled on her back on the huge bed dominating the room she had been given.

"She is lying about everything else, though," Gillyanne said as she sat down on the foot of the bed.

"I ken it. Payton is firm in denying the child is his, and the only way he could be so sure it isnae is because he ne'er bedded down with her. We ken Payton, so we have kenned that truth from the start. Cameron has ne'er e'en met my brother, doesnae ken him at all, and what he does ken of our family is only what he has learned from us. We cannae exactly be considered unbiased judges of Payton's character.''

"But Cameron didnae e'en think it over. He greeted his sister and sent out his demands to Payton.''

And that hurt, Avery mused as she struggled to bury her pain. Cameron had done exactly as he always said he would. That he could do it right in front of her was what hurt the most, but a small part of her could even understand that. He had just been presented with the proof that his unwed sister carried a child. It was hardly surprising that protecting the tender feelings of his lover had not been the first thing on his mind.

"Gilly, my love, his only sister grows round with a bastard child."

Gillyanne slumped against the bedpost. "It isnae fair. Payton will be made to accept a child which isnae his and, if Katherine bears a son, make it his heir. And ye and Cameron shall be parted. All because bonny Katherine spread her legs for some poor stable lad or the like, but wants our Payton for her husband."

"Ye could have put that a wee bit less crudely," Avery murmured, but she completely understood Gillyanne's sense of outrage.

"Nay, I couldnae. Do ye think there is any way Payton could escape this marriage later?"

"There may be some way, but one shouldnae set any hope on that possibility. Katherine isnae a virgin, nor can there be any claim of consanguinity. And instinct tells me bonny Katherine wouldnae hesitate to hold to her lie e'en if made to swear to it upon holy relics."

"I got that feeling, too. She is ruthless."

"Aye, she is." Avery sighed. "She will make poor Payton's life a complete misery. She might e'en drive him into another woman's arms, and though he may find love there, he will suffer o'er the breaking of his marriage vows. I think I could actually forgive her if she did this because she loved him, but she doesnae. I truly believe she acts out of stung pride and vanity. She just wants a bonny, rich husband, a husband other women will envy her for having."

A knock at the door broke the heavy silence that followed Avery's words. When Anne and Therese entered, Avery was only slightly disappointed that it was not Cameron. Still, it was probably for the best that some time passed before they spoke again. After Therese led Gillyanne away, Avery looked at the lovely gold and green gowns draped over Anne's arms.

"Are those for me?" she asked.

"Aye." replied Anne as she laid the gowns out on the bed. "The laird thought ye might wish a fine gown for the feasting."

"Oh. There is to be a feast?"

"Aye, to celebrate our safe return. Ye will look so bonny in this gold one. They used to be Katherine's."

"Katherine is a wee bit larger than I am, Anne," she briefly glanced down at her small breasts, "in many ways."

"Nay when she wore this."

"Please, dinnae tell me just how young she was at the time. I dinnae need my mood made any darker than it is."

Anne sighed, sat down beside Avery, and hugged her. "I heard what happened. The mon is a fool."

"Aye and nay." Avery stood up and let Anne help her remove her gown. "He is a mon faced with an unwed sister carrying a child. If he doesnae get her a husband, she will be utterly ruined. The men in my family would act much the same. The only problem here is that Katherine is lying. A part of me thinks Cameron a bit of a fool for not being able to see that, but then, she is his sister."

"Ye were hoping he would find a way to solve this without sending ye home."

Avery nodded. "But in truth, I dinnae think I really believed she was with child. If Cameron e'en considered thinking o'er his plans or taking a wee while to be sure Katherine isnae lying, that wee round belly of hers stole all chance of it away."

"I notice he has put ye in the room next to his."

"Aye, with the verra big unlocked door between them. Nay verra subtle of him." She looked at Anne after the woman finished helping her into the dark-gold gown. "Do ye think I should . . . weel, lock that door?"

"I wouldnae. If I loved the mon, I would cling tightly right up until I was set upon my horse. Wheesht, I would love him so hard that, the first night he crawled into his empty bed, he would still be able to smell me there upon his sheets. And upon his skin, nay matter how hard he tried to scrub it away. Aye, I would do my best to make sure he couldnae forget me, nay for one minute of one day, until he came to his senses and brought me back."

Avery smiled. "That was my plan."

"Good. The gown is a near fit. A few stitches at the bosom and waist and 'twill be perfect." Anne tugged the gold gown off Avery and helped her into the green one. " 'Tis the same with this. Ye shall have this one for the morrow."

When that gown was also removed and Anne sat down on the bed to immediately sew the dark-gold gown, Avery eyed her friend with growing suspicion. "Katherine is being surprisingly generous."

"Aye," Anne muttered without looking up from her sewing. "I have several others that I will measure against the green. Ye will have some bonny, rich gowns to wear during your stay here."

"Anne, did Katherine truly give these gowns to me, or e'en lend them for my use?"

"Ye ken she didnae. She gave o'er one at her brother's command—a rather ugly brown thing. Weel, her maid showed me where the selfish child had all of the gowns she had outgrown packed away, and Therese and I helped ourselves. Gillyanne will be looking verra fine as weel."

"Which will be nice, but nay necessary."

"Oh, 'tis necessary." Anne looked at Avery. "Ye are a lady born as is wee Gilly. Ye will dress as the ladies ye are."

"To impress Katherine?"

"There is that."

"I dinnae think she would be impressed if I was draped head to foot in fine jewels."

"Nay, probably not, but at least her natural scorn will lack some bite if ye ken that ye are looking verra fine indeed."

Avery nodded in understanding. " 'Tis armor to give me the strength to ignore any barbs about my appearance."

"And to make our laird remember just who and what ye are," Anne said firmly. "Ye are a lady, a young lass of good blood whom he has bedded. He talks a fine show about saving his sister's good name. Weel, 'tis time he recalled that ye have one, too."

"I dinnae want him coming to me out of a sense of honor, either mine or his. I want him to come after me because he cannae abide the aching for me for one more night, because he cannae abide walking through another day without me in it."

"Oh, he will certainly come after ye for that, lass. None of us who have traveled with ye, have watched the two of ye together, doubt that for a moment. But men are odd creatures." She smiled briefly when Avery laughed. "They may recognize those other feelings, but hesitate to speak openly of them. They would act faster if they could hold up a good, monly sounding reason like doing the honorable thing. Then he can do as he wants to, grab ye back acting bold and daring in the doing of it, and have all the other men slapping him on the back and proclaiming him a fine lad. 'Tis then up to the lass, when she and her mon are alone, to get him to speak of more than how he so kindly did right by her."

"And what if that lass doesnae think there is any more than honor behind his actions?"

"Avery, I am sorry ye cannae see it and that, mayhap right now, neither can that fool lad, but, trust me, 'tis there. If naught else, no mon could act like such a fool around a lass and nay have some deep feelings for her.''

"So ye think that, if he comes after me, I shouldnae bristle and balk if all he speaks of is honor and duty? Ye think I should just beat my poor pride into silence and go along with him?'' Avery sighed when Anne nodded. "Since I will be doing all the aching and the longing I want him to feel, I suppose I must.''

"Aye, and once ye get him alone, take a stout cudgel to his stubborn pride until ye get him to spit out the words ye need to hear.''

Avery laughed. "I will heed your advice, Anne. Now, with a plan set firmly in mind, all I need do is pray that despite all that will undoubtedly go wrong in the next few weeks, fate will be kind enough to set it all right again.''

Chapter Nineteen

"They are alive?"

"Aye, *Maman,* and unhurt."

Payton smiled faintly as he watched his parents and his aunts and uncles. The women cried and hugged each other, then turned to the men for more hugs. The men fought to control their own emotions even as they dried their ladies' tears. He was not surprised when everyone took extra time and care with his aunt Bethia. After what had happened to Sorcha, Payton had been astonished at how well Bethia had stood firm during this latest trouble, during weeks of not knowing the fate of yet another one of her daughters. It had to have felt like an unending torture to the woman, yet this was the first time he had seen his aunt Bethia anywhere near collapse. She was a tiny, sweet woman, but she was obviously a lot stronger than he had ever realized. This overabundance of emotion, however, made him glad he had left the two messengers with the soldiers and brought this news to his family himself.

"Where are they?" demanded his father.

"At Cairnmoor, in the care of one Sir Cameron MacAlpin," replied Payton.

"Why did he not send them home?" asked his mother.

"Because he wants something for them."

"A ransom? How much does he want?" asked Sir Eric. "I dinnae favor giving into ransom demands, but"—he looked at his wife, Bethia's tightly clenched hands, picked them up in his, and brushed a kiss over them—"we will do anything to get our wee Gilly back."

"And your sister," agreed Sir Nigel as he studied his son closely. "How much?"

" 'Tis not a matter of how much, but of who," Payton replied quietly.

"Who?" After a moment of frowning deeply, his mother's eyes widened. "MacAlpin. *Merde*, 'tis that wretched girl, is it not?"

"Gisele, is there something ye have forgotten to tell me?" Nigel spoke calmly, but his anger was clear to see as he stared at his wife.

"Nay, *Maman,* let me explain," said Payton. "The last time I was at court, there was a young lass who attempted to work her wiles on me. Since she was a maid of good family, brought there to find a husband, I did my best to avoid her. There were a few times when she forced me to make my reluctance a little clearer than I liked, and it was verra clear that she wasnae a lass used to being denied anything. Still, I returned here and felt that was the end of it. Then I received word from her guardian that she claimed I had raped her." Payton held up his hand to silence the vociferous protests, although they pleased him. "He also demanded that I come to Cairnmoor immediately to marry the lass I had despoiled—one Lady Katherine MacAlpin.''

Nigel cursed. "I begin to see our problem."

"My problem," Payton said, and he hurried to continue his tale. "I replied that she was lying and dared the mon to bring on his witnesses who could claim otherwise."

"Not verra conciliatory."

"Nay, but I wasnae feeling too kindly toward the lass. Then came the claim that I had left the lass with child. I adamantly denied that, too. Weel, it went on for a while, then it all stopped. I had thought that the truth had finally come out and gave it little thought except to occasionally feel that I was due some apology." Payton looked down at the letter he held. "It seems the lass's guardian was merely awaiting the arrival of her brother, Sir Cameron."

"And now Sir Cameron accuses ye of rape?"

"Some truth must have come out, for nay, he doesnae. Katherine does, however, still claim me as her lover and the father of her child. If I go to Cairnmoor and accept his sister as my bride, he will give us back Avery and Gillyanne."

"How did he get his hands on our lasses?"

"It seems he was in the service of one Sir Charles DeVeau." Payton grinned briefly at the imaginative curse his mother spat out. "He refused to join the attack on the Lucettes and was preparing to leave, sick of the DeVeaux and France. Our lasses were handed o'er to him in payment for a gambling debt. He says there is more to the tale, but the lasses can have the telling of it when they return home."

"Confident bastard," muttered Nigel.

"And why shouldnae he be? He holds the stoutest cudgel."

"Do ye think he would hurt the lasses?" asked Bethia.

"Nay," replied Payton. "There is something in the

way he writes, e'en to calling our Gillyanne 'wee Gilly', that tells me he willnae hurt them. In truth, there is nary one threat against them here. Howbeit, he willnae return them either.''

"Then mayhaps we should just go and take them back," said Nigel, but there was the hint of a hesitation behind his bold words.

"I think that, it we start spilling the blood of his clan, he just may make those threats and mean them," said Payton. "Nay, I will go to Cairnmoor."

Giselle reached across the table to grasp her son's hand. "But he will make you wed that woman and you do not love her. Your firstborn will not even be your own blood."

"True, but I cannae leave my sister and Gillyanne trapped there. And who is to say the threats will not come in time? Or that he may e'en take this trouble to the king? I will go. And just because I go, it doesnae mean I will end up marrying the lying wench. I might be able to pull the truth from her, but I cannae e'en do that if I stay here, can I? There is one other thing Sir Cameron mentions." Payton looked at his uncle Balfour and aunt Maldie. "He says both Avery and Gillyanne have presented him with the verra strong possibility that he is wee Alan's father."

"Oh, dear," murmured Maldie. "Elspeth will be both pleased and verra hurt."

"If he wants the boy—" Gisele began, but then she nervously bit her lip.

"Nay, *Maman*," Payton said. "Sir Cameron asks that we nay make the bairn a part of this and deal with that matter separately and carefully. 'Tis tempting to think on the possibility, for I dinnae want to marry Katherine. But to use Alan to gain my freedom, we would have to tear him from the arms of the only family he has ever known. I cannae do it. If Sir Cameron is Alan's father, they belong

together, but for Alan's sake, it must be something done
with the utmost care.''

"I know. 'Tis just, this marriage will be so wrong. It
is based upon a lie and this Katherine sounds a most
wretched girl.''

Payton patted his mother's hand. "She is one of those
who is bonny only on the outside, true enough. Dinnae
fret. I can be most persuasive. I will get the truth out of
her.'' He slowly grinned. "And if I ken my sister and
wee Gilly, they are already hard at work trying to ferret
out that truth.''

The moment that Avery and Gillyanne left the great
hall, Cameron slumped in his seat and had a large drink
of wine. His sister had left but moments before, and
although he had the strong suspicion there was going to
be a confrontation between the women, he was going to
play the coward and stay out of it. Any time spent in the
presence of all three women was a test of endurance. He
was not about to put himself between them willingly. Let
them sort it out, Cameron mused. He would just sit back
and pray there was not too much blood spilled.

It had only been a week since he had made his demand
of Sir Payton, but Cameron decided it had been the longest
week of his life. He could almost look forward to the
man's arrival, which he felt would come in another day
or two. Sir Payton's arrival would clear the battlefield
the women had made of his home, but it would also mean
the loss of Avery.

Who was playing her own games, he suddenly thought,
frowning in the direction she had gone. Although he had
put her in the room adjoining his, he would not have been
surprised to find all the doors tightly barred against him.
Instead, Avery welcomed him into her arms with a smile

and all the passion any man could wish for. She was always dressed in a way that was a feast for the eyes; she acted as if nothing was wrong between them, as if the end of their affair were not looming on the horizon, and she was delightfully amorous, never refusing him no matter where he sought her out. It had to be some plot. He just could not figure out how it worked or what she could think to gain.

"Are those lasses driving ye to drink, then, lad?"

"'Tis a consideration, Iain," he muttered, and he smiled faintly at the older man. "Each time we sit down to a meal, I expect them to leap at each other, slashing away viciously at each other with their eating knives."

Iain nodded. "Trying to eat with all that feminine fury in the air does wreak havoc on a mon's digestion."

"'Tis wearying."

"Aye, ye do look tired, lad."

Leargan laughed and shook his head. "'Tis nay just avoiding the raging war between the lasses making our laird tired. If he isnae running away from that, he is rolling about with—"

"Leargan," Cameron growled, a little surprised that Leargan would say anything that was less than flattering about Avery.

"Ah, cousin, ye ken I would ne'er insult Avery. 'Tis probably envy ye hear. I would give my fine warhorse for a lass as sweet and warm as she seems to be, one who is both willing and passionate. 'Tis nay often ye can find a lass who truly enjoys the loving," Leargan winked, "or so it sounded in the stables this afternoon." He laughed along with Iain when Cameron blushed faintly.

"Obviously, I need to be a wee bit more discreet." Cameron frowned and drummed his fingers on the arm of his chair. "Actually, I think Avery is plotting something."

"Oh, for God's sake," Leargan muttered, laughter thick

in his voice "And what might that be? Wearing ye out so that ye are useless to any other woman for years after she leaves?"

Cameron decided to ignore his cousin's sarcasm. "She is being too amiable." He glared at his cousins when they both rolled their eyes. "I am sending her away. I am making her brother marry a woman he has repeatedly said he doesnae want. 'Tis hardly foolish to wonder why she acts as if nothing is wrong, why there is no anger or argument, and, curse it, why she still welcomes me in her bed. Avery is a proud lass with a goodly temper. Why is she being so *amiable?*"

"Weel, she certainly isnae being amiable to Katherine," said Iain.

"True. I occasionally wonder if I should put a guard o'er them to be sure they dinnae try to kill each other." Cameron dragged his hand through his hair. "Yet I expected some—e'en a lot—of that anger to be directed my way."

"Mayhap Avery understands that ye had no choice."

"Aye, yet I sometimes got the feeling she waited for me to find one, to discover some other way to solve this problem."

"That was probably before she saw that Katherine is definitely with child," Leargan said.

"A child Avery insists isnae her brother's," Cameron reminded him

"But it meant ye were confronted with a sister, unwed and already rounding with some mon's child. There really isnae any time to see who is right and who is wrong, or e'en if some lies have been told. Katherine needs a husband. The bairn needs a father. Katherine points her finger at Sir Payton. Ye have nay choice but to get the mon to the altar as soon as possible. Whate'er else Avery might feel, she has the wit to ken the truth of that, to ken that ye have been shoved hard into a corner." Leargan took a long drink of wine, then said quietly, "She saves her anger for the one who dragged ye both into this mess—the one she believes is lying."

"Do ye think Katherine is lying, Iain?" Cameron asked, hoping the older man, having spent more time with Katherine, might have some insight.

"I cannae say one way or the other. I just dinnae ken," Iain replied. He grimaced. "She is certainly capable of lying."

"Aye, o'er the week I have been home, I have seen that." Cameron shook his head. "I have failed the lass."

"We all have in some ways, but I refuse to wallow in guilt o'er it. Aye, we all spoiled her, but a child is said to learn from the examples set for her. I like to think we have all set good examples for her. Nay perfect, but good. Yet . . ." He shrugged. "Yet she isnae only spoiled, she is vain, and, from what I have seen, nay too kind to those she considers beneath her. And I cannae think of anyone here who would have taught her vanity and snobbery."

"Nay. She certainly would ne'er have gained such attitudes from ye and Aunt Agnes, and the pair of you have had much of the raising of her. Did ye e'er meet this lad Sir Payton?"

"Only briefly, and then I did little more than glimpse him from time to time."

"I hear he is bonny."

Iain grinned. "Oh, verra bonny indeed, or so all the lasses claim. In truth, I could see it, too. And the way the lasses swarm about him is a wonder. I wouldnae doubt it, when the laddie goes to the privy, there is a lass there offering to lend him a hand."

"That bad?"

"That bad. Yet, I ne'er heard any ill said about the lad. A few grumbles from jealous men, easily seen for what they were, but naught else. Not e'en that he takes an excessive advantage of the lasses who fling themselves at his head. I will confess, I was surprised when Katherine claimed him as her debaucher, but I had to believe her, didnae I?''

Cameron nodded. ''Ye had no choice. Did ye e'er believe the charge of rape?''

''Nay completely. 'Twas nay only the sure knowledge that the lad had no need to force himself on any lass, but, in truth, Katherine ne'er acted like a woman touched against her will. I have kenned a lass or two who were raped, and though they were strong enough to o'ercome that tragedy, there were scars, especially in the weeks and months that followed. Katherine acted as she always does, yet she held to her claim. In my mind, however, I began to think of it as a seduction she had let go too far.''

''Weel, only Katherine can clear up this confusion, and she holds fast to her tale of seduction and desertion. I do wonder from time to time if I am being used to get her the husband she thinks suits her best, and nay the mon who should be wedding her.''

''Then dinnae force the wedding too quickly,'' said Leargan.

''I cannae hold back too long,'' Cameron protested.

''A week or two willnae make much difference.''

''Nay, true enough. I hate it, but I do begin to doubt Katherine. I tell myself I but give into my own selfish reasons for wanting her to be wrong, but it doesnae still all the doubts. Curse it, I find myself listening at doors, having long conversations with Katherine and weighing her every word. I dinnae want to believe that Katherine would play such a game, yet I cannae stop myself from thinking she might be doing just that. And then I find myself trying yet again to prove my own sister a liar. Worse, I am nay doing a verra good job of it.''

"Then leave it to the lasses."

"Ye think that is what they try to do?"

"Oh, aye, no doubt of it."

"But, if they discover the truth and yet Katherine clings to her story, I still face the problem of believing two lasses who are eager to help Sir Payton, or standing loyal to my sister and believing her."

"Then keep your ear to the door, lad," said Iain, "and hope ye hear the truth ere it is too late."

"Dinnae ye two have somewhere else to go?" snapped Katherine, looking up from her needlework to glare at Avery and Gillyanne.

"Nay," replied Avery as she sat down opposite Katherine.

Avery looked around the ladies' solar. It was a lovely room, especially in the daytime when the sun's light poured in through the windows. It could have been a weak point if some attacker managed to get past all of Cameron's other formidable defenses, yet she suspected that had been considered and probably compensated for. She glanced toward Aunt Agnes to see that, as always, the plump, greying woman was sleeping in the chair in front of the fire. Avery doubted the sweet lady had ever been much of a chaperon for the willful Katherine. When Gillyanne sat down on the padded bench Katherine sat on, Avery almost laughed. Gillyanne knew Katherine both disliked her and found her unsettling. It was just like Gillyanne to take full advantage of that.

"I have heard it said that if a liar drinks holy water her tongue will turn black, rot, and fall out of her mouth," Gillyanne said, and she held a goblet of cool water out to Katherine.

"Peasants' nonsense," Katherine muttered, but Avery

noted that the woman did not accept the drink. "What are ye about?" Katherine slapped Gillyanne's hand away when the younger woman began to poke at her belly.

"Just making sure it isnae a pillow," Gillyanne replied. " 'Tis Sir Payton's child and ye ken it."

"Nay, it isnae."

"Oh, nay, it couldnae be Saint Payton's, could it. Ye both refuse to accept that he is a heartless seducer, that he could just use a lass and callously toss her aside, just like every other mon."

"Payton is no saint," Avery said, keeping her voice calm, her anger hidden, for she knew that annoyed Katherine. "He wouldnae, however, seduce a virgin, nor would he refuse to acknowledge his own child."

"Are ye saying I wasnae a virgin?" demanded Katherine, flinging aside her needlework.

Avery thought it very interesting that Katherine could so quickly discern that particular accusation in her words, especially since it had not even lurked there. She had not even considered the possibility that Katherine had had more than one lover, and yet, glancing at the softly snoring Aunt Agnes, Avery knew the younger woman had had ample time and opportunity for dalliance. For a brief moment, Avery wondered if there might be someone right at Cairnmoor, but she quickly decided Katherine was too smart for that. There were few secrets at a keep like Cairnmoor, and Katherine would be very careful to protect her guise of innocence. If there had been lovers right here at Cairnmoor, her tale of being an innocent maid seduced and cruelly cast aside would not have endured for as long as it had.

"Nay, I would not insult ye so," Avery said. "I but say that your seducer wasnae my brother."

"Then why should I be willing to marry him?"

"Because he is bonny, nay poor, and most women ye

meet will envy you. I suspect your lover was lacking in a few of the things ye think ye need, such as coin.''

"So, now ye would accuse me of tossing up my skirts for some ragged beggar?"

"Many a fine gentlemon hasnae the blessing of a full purse. 'Tis why he must often wed himself to it.''

"I have a verra fine dower. I need nay worry if the mon is poor or nay.''

"So, why not wed the mon who got ye with child instead of dragging an unwilling mon to the altar?''

"Do ye find it so verra hard to believe your brother could have lusted after me?'' Katherine asked, the hint of a smirk curving her full mouth. "I have turned many a lad's head and heart.''

"I suspect ye have, for ye are verra bonny on the outside,'' Avery murmured. "Aye, I could believe Payton might cast a covetous eye your way, but he wouldnae have bedded ye. He would have kenned that ye were there to find a husband, and he doesnae want a wife—not yet. That would have been enough to cool any warmth ye may have stirred within him.''

"Mayhap the warmth I stirred was simply too strong, too tempting for him to resist.'' Katherine glared at Gillyanne when the girl made a rude noise rife with mockery. "At least I have what is needed to catch a mon's eye.''

"I hope Gillyanne doesnae, for she is too young to be stirring any mon's interest,'' Avery said. "And, ye, Katherine, should be smart enough to ken that this lie cannae hold firm forever.''

"But it doesnae have to hold forever, does it? Only until the priest finishes the vows. Then I am married to that fine, bonny knight, and no one can change that.'' She stood up abruptly and went over to her aunt and, somewhat roughly, nudged the woman awake. "We must retire now, Aunt Agnes.'' Katherine moved to stand in front of Avery as her aunt gathered up her things. "If ye think spreading your legs for my brother will stop this marriage, ye are a fool."

Avery held her hand out to stop Gillyanne's angry advance on Katherine. "Aye, ye might just end up married to Payton, but that marriage will be based upon your lies and treachery. He will ne'er forgive ye for that. So what kind of happiness can ye find?"

"The kind that comes from wedding a bonny mon, a much-praised knight, a mon with a full purse, lands in France, and many a highly placed friend at court, including the king himself." She grabbed her still-sleepy aunt by the arm and strode out the door. "He can resent me all he likes, but he is still a far better choice than some lowly squire with six older brothers."

Wincing a little as the door slammed shut behind Katherine, Avery stared at the heavily carved oak panels for a moment. She had never wanted to strike someone as badly—and repeatedly—as she wanted to strike Katherine. The girl was spoiled, vain, and selfish beyond words. It was hard to believe she and Cameron were related.

"She is definitely lying about Payton," Gillyanne said as she moved to stand beside Avery.

"Most definitely," agreed Avery. "In fact, she just revealed quite a lot. For one thing, I believe Katherine had herself a fine time at court, and perhaps a tussle or two with a braw laddie ere she got there."

"Do ye think there may be one of those braw laddies here at Cairnmoor?"

"I doubt it. Too great a chance of it becoming known. And, if there is one, he isnae going to step forward and admit he rutted with the laird's sister. Nor do we have the time left to find one if there is, for he wilt be keeping it a verra close secret."

"But she did have a lad or two at court, didnae she?"

"She certainly did, and I believe the one which should most interest us is a poor squire."

"With six older brothers."

"Exactly. Of course, we dinnae ken who was at court when she was there, and again, I dinnae think we have much time left to find out. It has been a week since Cameron sent his demands to Donncoill. Payton could arrive any day now."

"I am sorry, Avery."

"Nay, dinnae be. Right now the most important thing is to help Payton. We cannae allow him to marry that woman."

Gillyanne gave an exaggerated shudder. "Nay, most certainly not. She will make him utterly miserable." Gillyanne rubbed a finger over her chin as she frowned in thought. "A name would be best, but Katherine may be the only one who kens it."

"True, but there may be a few more facts we can gather. Payton spends a lot of time at court. If we can tell him enough about this squire, he will ken who it is. He may have e'en seen him and Katherine talking."

"But, could he get Cameron to heed him e'en it he got a name? Could Payton get Cameron to at least try to search out the truth?"

"I think so," replied Avery. "Just lately there has been a look in Cameron's eyes that makes me think he has some doubt about Katherine's claims."

"Yet he still drags Payton to the altar."

"Because of that bairn and the fact that no one has e'er given him any other possible choice of groom. The first person we must speak to is Katherine's maid."

"She has been avoiding us," Gillyanne said as she followed Avery to the door.

"One more try at cornering her ourselves and then we will get Anne's help."

Avery and Gillyanne stepped out the door and bumped into Cameron and Leargan. "Ye are looking for us?" Avery asked as she began to sidle around him, tugging Gillyanne along with her.

"Aye," replied Cameron, watching her closely.

"Oh, dear. Weel, I will see ye later, will I not? But, right now, Gillyanne and I have something we really must do."

Cameron watched Avery and Gillyanne nearly run away; then he looked at Leargan. "Are ye going to try to tell me that they arenae plotting something now?"

"Oh, nay," Leargan said, laughing. "They are definitely plotting something now. Where are ye going?" he asked when Cameron started to walk back to the great hall.

"To have a verra large drink. Mayhap more than one. And I dinnae think I will stop unless I hear screaming."

Chapter Twenty

"Has anyone seen Avery?" Cameron asked as he warily entered the ladies' solar.

He looked around the room and winced inwardly. It was a beautiful room and he was fond of sitting in it. Right now, however, the air fairly crackled with tension and dislike. Gillyanne sat with Anne and was obviously supposed to be sewing, but she was mostly staring at Katherine. Cameron recognized that stare. It was the one that made the recipient feel naked. Anne was calmly sewing but also keeping a close eye on Gillyanne and Katherine. Katherine paused in her needlework to glare at Gillyanne from time to time. Aunt Agnes was napping in front of the fire, sweetly oblivious to it all.

"Have ye misplaced your leman?" Katherine asked.

Cameron was just stepping closer to his sister to reprimand her when he heard a distinctly feral hiss. It sounded so much like Avery, he looked around, then realized the noise had come from Gillyanne. He sent her a repressive scowl, which apparently did not frighten her in the least, then turned back to Katherine.

"Correct me if I am wrong. Katherine," he said, his voice soft and cold, "but are ye nay sitting there unwed and swelling with some mon's child?" He nodded when she blushed. "Ye will keep a still tongue in your head concerning Avery. Now again: does anyone ken where Avery is?"

"Out in the gardens," Gillyanne replied, studying him for a moment and then asking, "Ye have had word of our families?"

"The way ye do that can be verra unsettling, lass."

"Ah, but ye being such a braw lad, it doesnae trouble ye at all, does it?" Gillyanne smiled and winked at him.

The way Anne's shoulders shook told him the woman was laughing. He briefly felt like doing the same, but recalling the message he had just been given stole the urge away. "Sir Payton will arrive in the morning."

"Oh, dear. We did think it would be soon."

"Aye. They havenae wasted any time at all, really. 'Twas only eight days ago that I sent my men to Donncoill." He sighed and started out the door. "I had better go and tell Avery."

"Cameron," Katherine called as he began to shut the door behind him.

"What?" he asked, leaning back inside the room.

"Tell that wretched brat to cease staring at me."

He rolled his eyes even though he knew how uncomfortable those stares could be to endure. "Gillyanne, cease staring at Katherine." He left before Katherine noticed Gillyanne had not promised to stop, and before he gave into the temptation to ask Gilly just what she saw when she stared at Katherine.

* * *

Avery yanked out a weed, tossed it onto the refuse pile, and wondered why working in the herb garden was not making her feel better. It always had before. But then, she mused, she had never so assiduously courted a broken heart before. She had certainly never had a lover before. She had never had to worry that her brother was about to be forced into a marriage that could make him miserable before, either. Yanking weeds was just not enough to help her still all her doubts and fears, even if just for a little while.

If she was wise, she thought, she would close her door to Cameron—kick the oaf right out of her bed. He still gave her no words of love, no promises of a future. She had every right to turn her back on him. She also knew she would not do so. Avery was a little disgusted by her weakness for the man, but she doubted she would ever completely conquer it. Also, kicking him out of her bed would only compromise her plan to love him so hard that he would crave her return. She just wished he would give her some hint that she was touching his heart. It would give her some glimmer of hope to cling to.

Glancing up at the sky, she realized she would not have much time to clean up for the evening meal. And, she mused with a half smile as she stood up and looked herself over, she would need a lot of cleaning up. Avery turned to go back into the keep and nearly walked into Cameron.

"I was just headed in to clean up ere the evening meal is set out," she said. She wiped her hands on her skirts, only to grimace when she saw that her skirts were not much cleaner than her hands.

"Is there any dirt left in the garden?" Cameron murmured with a grin.

"I was weeding, and since the weeds dinnae grow to e'en my unimpressive height, I have to get down into the dirt."

"Obviously."

"Did ye have something to say, or did ye just come out here to catch me looking my verra worst?"

"Ah, lass, I think ye look adorable."

When he leaned closer and then just frowned as he studied her face, she asked, "Is there something wrong?"

"Nay, I was just trying to find a clean spot to kiss."

"Wretch." She stepped around him and started toward the keep. "Did ye have something to tell me?"

"Your brother will be arriving come the morning," he said quietly. He watched her pace briefly falter.

"And will I be taken away at that time?" Avery was pleased with how calm and accepting she sounded as they entered the keep and strode toward the stairs.

"Aye, ye and Gillyanne will leave with what sounds like a verra large troop of Murray men."

"But nay my parents or Gillyanne's?"

"Nay. 'Twas thought best that Payton come alone. Your brother will enter with only Wee Rob and Colin, and ye and Gillyanne will be sent out to the Murray men."

She paused at the foot of the stairs and finally looked at him. "I should like a few moments to greet and perhaps speak with my brother ere I leave Cairnmoor. I havenae seen him in months, and all things considered, it could be months ere I have another chance to see him."

"Fair enough."

Avery turned to go on up the stairs, only to meet Katherine coming down. The woman leaned back, staring at Avery in horror. Katherine obviously never got dirty, Avery mused, not really surprised.

"Did ye roll your toy about in the mud, Cameron?" Katherine asked.

At her side Avery felt Cameron tense. Before he could speak, she clasped Katherine's face in her hands and, ignoring her gasps of horror, kissed both her cheeks and gave her a big, tight hug. Deciding that she had shared enough of her bounty of dirt, she released the woman.

"Ah, I shall miss ye, Katherine," she drawled, her eyes widening slightly at the foulness of the curse Katherine spat at her before fleeing back up the stairs. "Tsk, I guess that feeling isnae shared." She looked at Cameron and found that he was laughing. "I couldnae help myself."

"Ah, lass, if ye werenae still as dirty as a muckworm, I would kiss you. Go and clean up." He watched her start up the stairs, then asked quietly, "Avery, do ye want to sup with me in my chambers?"

There was only one reason he would want to do that. He wanted to spend their last night together making love, probably as often as possible, probably until they collapsed from utter exhaustion. Avery knew she ought to tell him to go and soak his head.

"Aye. I shall meet ye there in an hour." She glanced down at herself. "Better make that two."

Avery stood wrapped in the drying cloth and frowned at her chemise. She absently replied to Anne's knock and call at the door, mumbling her invitation to enter. It was going to be her last night with Cameron for a while. Avery did not even try to think the word *forever,* but it flickered there at the edge of her thoughts. She had to hold fast to some hope of the future, however, or she would spend her last night with Cameron doing little more than weeping all over his fine chest. She did wish she could spend her last night with Cameron dressed in something besides a chemise he had seen more times than she cared to count.

"Nay, not that," said Anne as she snatched the chemise out of Avery's hands and tossed it onto the bed. "Not for tonight."

"And why might tonight be important?" Avery asked, but she suspected that Anne already knew.

" 'Tis your last night here—until ye return—leastwise."

"Such optimism."

Anne ignored that. "And a verra fine meal has been sent to the laird's bedchamber. Candles and fires have been lit. And ye arenae going to be dining in the great hall."

"There is no privacy here."

"Verra little, but I will confess that most of us are especially interested in what happens between ye and our laird." She smiled when Avery blushed. "We like ye, lass, and think ye would make our laird verra happy." She held out a nightdress and robe. "So will this."

Avery gasped and tentatively reached out for them. They were more lace than linen, and the linen was very sheer. Both the gown and the robe were a rich golden color and trimmed with black embroidery and lace. They were scandalous, the sort of thing some rich courtesan would wear.

"Where did ye find such shameless finery?" Avery asked.

"Do ye ken how ye hinted to me that Katherine might nay be the sweet-maid-done-wrong she wishes us all to think she is? Weel, I think ye are right." Anne tossed the gown and the robe on the bed. "Those arenae the night things most chaste maids wear."

"Katherine's? My, my, my! Ye do find the most interesting things in her bedchamber. No mon yet, though, I suppose."

"Sorry, nay. If she has shared her bed with any of the

lads here, they are being most careful now that the laird is home.'' Anne tugged at the drying cloth Avery had wrapped around herself. ''Come along, let us get ye into these.''

''I dinnae ken about this, Anne. They are beautiful, but I will feel naked. And, if they are Katherine's, they willnae fit.''

''They will,'' Anne assured her even as she put the night dress on Avery. ''Now, on Katherine, this is probably meant to be verra open on the sides here where it laces. On ye, 'twill close tight. It doesnae matter if the robe is loose. Ye arenae that much shorter than Katherine, so they shouldnae drag upon the floor too much.'' She looked down at the same time Avery did. ''Weel, it looks as if it was meant to show off the lass's ankles and feet, too. Shameless.''

''Absolutely,'' agreed Avery, and she grinned along with Anne. ''Oh, verra weel. I will just try to fool myself into thinking that, since I am wearing a nightdress and a robe, I am nay naked. I do wonder what Cameron will think, though.''

''Lass, one look at ye in this and, I promise ye, that lad willnae be doing any thinking at all.''

Cameron sipped at his wine as he paced his room. He found himself fretting over whether he should have stayed dressed, if wearing nothing but his robe was too presumptuous, if he should stand or sit. It was as if this were to be his and Avery's first time together, yet they had been lovers for weeks.

But never again, not after tonight, he thought, and he had to grab hold of the bedpost to steady himself against a sudden surge of what felt like anxiety. He took a deep drink of wine. The best thing to do was not think about it. If Avery could act as if everything were fine, so could he. And it would be fine, Cameron told himself firmly.

The door between his chambers and Avery's opened and he turned to greet her but nearly choked on the words. She gave him a shy smile as she stepped into the room and shut the door behind her. Cameron did not know how she could appear shy when wearing such clothes—what little there was of them.

As she stepped closer, the light from the fire and candles revealed just how thin the nightdress and robe were. Every, slender, perfect line of Avery's body was revealed. That he could see her body so clearly even though she was wearing something stirred Cameron's passion more swiftly than anything he had seen before. He was not sure he would have found it as alluring if she had arrived completely naked, although he decided it might not be wise to test that.

"Where did ye get this?" he asked as he reached out to touch the shadow of a nipple and watch it harden.

"Anne brought it to me." Avery was not surprised to hear a trace of huskiness in her voice, for the way he stared at her, his eyes sparkling with desire, was rapidly heating her blood.

"I wonder where she found it." He touched the shadow of her other nipple, smiling faintly when it, too, hardened.

"Ye look disgustingly pleased with yourself when that happens." She crossed her arms over her tingling breasts.

"And why shouldnae a mon be pleased when his touch warms such a bonny lass?"

She shivered slightly with pleasure. When he spoke in that low, husky tone, his deep voice was like a caress that reached deep inside her. Avery found both delight and dismay in this further evidence of her weakness for the man.

''The lass might be e'en more warmed if the lad offered her a wee bit of the feast laid out before the fire.''

He laughed softly and led her to her chair, then hesitated. ''Take the robe off, loving,'' he said softly.

Avery blushed. ''There isnae much under it.''

''I ken it. I wish to drive myself mad as we dine.''

''A strange wish,'' she murmured, but, reminding herself that this was a night to make memories—his and hers—she took off the robe.

Cameron stared at her, from the blush upon her cheeks to her toes, and took a deep, shuddering breath. ''Oh, aye. That will do it.''

''Why dinnae ye take your robe off, too?''

''Ye wish me to sit there naked?''

''Ye have your wishes and I have mine,'' she said as she sat down.

He actually felt shy as he reached for the tie on his robe. It was such an odd feeling that he promptly shed his robe in defiance of it. When he sat down opposite her, he gave himself a brief nod of thanks for spending extra coin to have the chair seats padded. Having the fire built up was not such a bad idea, either, he mused as he started to eat his meal.

There was little said as they ate. Occasionally, they playfully fed each other food. Cameron found it difficult to keep his gaze off her sheer, linen-draped form. He noticed that she eyed him with the same hunger.

''Lass,'' he said as he leaned back in his chair to sip at his wine, ''the way ye look at me makes me think that being such a hulking, dark devil of a mon isnae such a bad thing.''

Avery stood up and walked around the table. ''Ah, Cameron, ye are beautiful,'' she said as she stood between his long legs. ''Such strength''— she smoothed her hands over his broad chest—''such perfection of form. Aye, ye are big and dark, but I find it so lovely, so verra tempting.'' She began to kiss her way downward from the hollow in his throat. ''Your skin is smooth and warm. What scars ye carry speak of victory and survival.'' She knelt before him to kiss and stroke his long legs. ''How can a lass nay find such strength beguiling?'' She peered up at him as she curled her fingers around his erection. ''Even this fine fellow has his own beauty. Long, thick, and delicious,'' she whispered, feeling him tremble when she kissed him there.

''Ah, Avery, 'tis a joy when ye do that for me,'' he said as he set his goblet down on the floor. ''I wish I could savor it longer ere I have to stop you.''

''And ye always stop me,'' she murmured against his inner thigh.

The mere thought of her doing otherwise nearly made him groan. ''It would disgust ye if I didnae.''

''But ye would like it if I continued?''

''Lass, I . . .'' He had to clear his throat before he could continue. ''I have never . . .''

''Never?'' she asked as she kissed his hard stomach, intrigued by the thought that she might be able to give him something no other had.

''Never.'' He combed his fingers through her hair as she looked up at him. ''In truth, that poor wee laddie has ne'er had more than a kiss or two, and that begrudgingly given. I have heard other men say, weel . . .'' he faltered, uncertain of how to finish his sentence without being crude.

'' 'Tis a night for wishes and dreams fulfilled,'' she said, kissing his chest. ''A night for shameless gluttony, for blind, sweaty exhaustion. A night for memories to be made and held close.''

''Ah, because on the morrow,'' his eyes widened slightly when she placed her fingers over his mouth.

"Nay, dinnae speak of it. That truth will direct our every step this night, but let us try to ignore it. Let us just selfishly take what we want, as often as we can. That truth will come with the dawn. Dinnae let it intrude upon this night of dreams, wishes, and memories."

"Wishes and dreams, eh?" he asked, and when she smiled and nodded, he whispered, "Then aye, dinnae stop."

He almost changed his mind when she kissed her way down his body again. If she was disgusted, it could ruin the rest of what could be their last night together. Then he felt her tongue stroke him. He gasped, closed his eyes, and decided that if she said aye, she meant it.

It was more than any man deserved, he thought, as he clutched the arms of his chair and fought for some control. She seemed to know just when to pause to allow him to catch his breath. Just as he thought he might be able to last a goodly while and truly savor this delight, he felt something cool and wet dripped over his heated groin. He looked down to see that she had dribbled honey over him. As she began to meticulously lick him clean, he groaned, closed his eyes again, and gave himself over to the pleasure she was giving him. By the time she ceased toying with him, he was nearly writhing in the chair. He shook all over from the strength of the release she gifted him with, then collapsed in the chair, savoring each lingering flicker of pleasure all the way down to his toes.

When he was finally able to move, he looked down at her. Her head was against his thigh as she idly stroked his leg. The occasional touch of her warm lips against his skin told him that she was not disgusted. He reached out grasped her beneath the arms, and stood her up in front of him. His mind was suddenly full of every dream he had ever had of her, of every little trick of loving he had ever heard of and he was more than eager to try them all.

"Fetch a pillow from the bed, loving," he said, and he watched her every step. "Ye do look bonny in that," he murmured as he accepted the pillow she gave him. "But 'tis time to take it off."

"What is the pillow for?" she asked as he undid the laces on the gown.

"So ye dinnae bruise your back against the arm of the chair." He tugged the nightdress off her, held her by her slim hips, and looked her over thoroughly. "Ye are so lovely, lass. Ye fair steal my breath away."

She gasped when he lifted her and settled her across his lap. Her back and head were against the pillow he had set against the arm of the chair. Her legs were draped across the other chair arm. A blush heated her cheeks, for she felt too exposed to his gaze—almost vulnerable. That blush deepened when he slid his hand between her thighs and watched himself stroke her.

"Cameron, I dinnae think," she ended up murmuring against his lips as he gave her a quick, hard kiss to silence her.

"I want to see your pleasure, lass. I want to see it begin, see it grow, see it overwhelm ye."

"Ye see that each time we make love."

"Nay, not truly. A wee glimpse. A moment here and there. But I fear my own pleasure steals the chance to watch yours."

He raised her up slightly and put his mouth to her breasts. As he licked, nibbled, and suckled her until her breasts ached, she began to lose some of her embarrassment. It was not as if he had never seen her naked, she told herself, closing her eyes.

"I want to see every blush," he murmured, eyeing her damp, hard nipples with satisfaction as he settled her back down. "I want to watch those bonny breasts as your breathing grows quick and hard. I want to see your bonny wee stomach clench as passion grips ye. I have felt those sweet tremors in your thighs when they are clasped about me. Now, I want to see them, too."

The way he was caressing her, the way his scandalous words heated her blood, soon had her relaxing her guard, welcoming his touch. Then he moved her legs further apart. "Nay, Cameron," she started to protest.

"Aye, loving, let me. Remember—dreams and wishes?"

"Dreams and wishes and shameless gluttony," she whispered.

And modesty had no place in such a night, she decided as she allowed herself only to feel, not think. He took his time, keeping her balanced on the blade's edge for a long time before he granted her release. His hoarse words of delight only enhanced the strength of it. She felt deliciously weak as he lifted her up, turned her to face him, and joined their bodies with one deep thrust. Avery collapsed against his chest, and he held her close for a moment before turning her face up to his.

"I have heard that one can kiss one's way to bliss," he said, brushing his lips across hers.

"Where do ye hear such things?"

"Men talk."

"Weel, I am nay sure that will work."

"We will just have to try it and see."

They did, and it did. When Avery next came to her senses, Cameron was supporting her with one arm and drying her off. She had obviously been too dazed to notice the washing. He wrapped the drying cloth around her and handed her a goblet full of mead. Avery had drunk over half of it before she recalled that mead tended to go to her head very fast.

"Strong drink, that mead," Cameron said, and he

grinned when she nodded, "We seem to be fulfilling only *my* wishes. Surely ye must have one or two."

"I only thought as far as seeing if I could survive making love all night long."

He gently urged her to drink some more. "That is verra close to one of my wishes, too. Tell me what ye like, then."

She took another drink and mumbled, "I do rather like your kisses."

"Thank ye, but we just did that. Finish the mead," he ordered gently.

" 'Tis making me a wee bit drunk."

"Good. That was my plan. So, tell me what ye like, besides kisses," he urged softly, kissing her ear.

"But I do really like the kisses."

"So ye said, and, so we did."

"Not those kisses. The *other* kisses," she whispered. She frowned at her empty goblet. "I hadnae meant to say that."

"So ye like my *kisses?*" He started to nudge her back toward the chair. "I am good at that, am I?"

"Humph. I am sure ye ken verra weel that ye are."

"Nay. 'Tis difficult to tell if one is good at something when one has ne'er done it before." He yanked off her drying cloth and spread it over the chair.

"Never?" Avery was so surprised by that confession, she did not protest when he gently pushed her into the chair but just stared up at him when he leaned over her. "Truly?"

"Truly. 'Tis just another one of those things I heard about." He brushed a kiss over her lips. "The women I have kenned in the past were, shall we say, weel traveled. And sometimes nay all that clean. Ah, but ye, my bonny Avery, have only been with one mon—me. And ye are nay only clean, but delicious."

She shivered with pleasure "And ye gave me mead because?"

" 'Tis said that, if one is just a wee bit drunk, one is more freely amorous, but that heady ending to the loveplay can be verra, verra slow to arrive."

"Oh, my." She frowned in confusion when he picked up a small bowl from the table. "Blackberry jam?" The smile he gave her in reply made her eyes widen. "I used honey."

"Ye are sweet enough, loving. Honey and ye together would probably make my teeth ache. A little tart will be better," he murmured as he slowly covered her nipples with blackberry jam.

"I think we may have gone beyond shameless gluttony," she said shakily, "and plunged right into licentiousness."

"*Licentiousness* is a fine word."

When he bent to touch his mouth to her breasts and began to slowly lick away the blackberry jam, Avery decided that he just might be right about that.

Chapter Twenty-One

The sharp sound of knocking and Leargan's voice were not what Cameron wanted intruding upon his dreams. He snuggled closer to Avery's silky, warm body and felt himself harden with interest. That made him smile. Considering the long hours they had spent making love, he should be more than well sated, he should be glutted. However, if he hooked her lovely leg back over his hip a little, he could probably ease himself into her tight heat—

"Curse it, Cameron, get your arse out of bed!"

"Go away, Leargan!" Cameron yelled right back, and he was a little surprised when Avery only muttered a complaint about the noise and went right back to sleep. He had completely exhausted her, he thought proudly.

"A certain Sir Payton awaits your company in the great hall."

Every hint of warmth left Cameron's body. He slowly eased himself away from Avery, even as everything inside him demanded he hold onto her. He reminded himself that Katherine was with child and needed a husband. That gave him the strength to get out of bed, although it was a struggle. Duty was banging at the door and he had to obey the call. He was not only Katherine's brother, he was her laird. He had no choice.

Easing the door open a crack, he told Leargan he would be down in ten minutes. He then went to tend to his morning ablutions, fighting to ignore all the signs of the long, sensuous night he had spent with Avery. To his dismay, by the time he was dressed, she was awake. It was cowardly, but he had hoped just to slip away. After all, what was there to say?

"Payton is here," she said as she sat up and brushed her tangled hair off her face.

"Aye, he waits for me in the great hall," Cameron replied, clenching his hands against the urge to touch her.

Avery held the blanket around her as she climbed out of his bed. "Will ye still let me visit with him for a few moments before I leave?"

"Aye."

"Good. Thank ye. I will wait for him in my room."

He watched her walk to the door, the blanket draped around her and trailing slightly on the floor. "Avery?"

She paused in the doorway but did not turn to look at him. "There really isnae anything to say, is there?"

"Nay. Nay, I suppose not." He rubbed his chest, wondering why it felt so tight. "I wish . . ." He hesitated.

"Ah, Cameron, so do I, but I do wonder if we wish for the same thing."

The sound of the door shutting behind her made him jump, even though she had shut it very quietly. He started to look around the room, then forced himself to fix his gaze upon the door to the hall. As he walked toward it, he decided he would get someone to clean the room thoroughly before he had to return to it.

A group of women were clustered around the door to the great hall, peering inside and sighing. Cameron began to get a very bad feeling as he nudged his way through them. He paused in the doorway and heard their skirts rustle as they all moved so that they could peer around him. And standing next to Leargan, sipping wine and chatting amiably with his cousin, was what they were all sighing over.

Sir Payton Murray was indeed bonny, Cameron thought with some irritation. He was not particularly tall nor broad of shoulder, but Cameron had no doubt that the man could hold his own in most any fight. What Payton Murray had were the lean, strong lines of a finely bred horse. He was dressed well, and his every move was graceful. He was just as Gillyanne had described him. He also looked very young. Cameron suddenly doubted that Payton was that much older than Avery.

"Just how old are ye?" Cameron demanded as he strode over to Payton and Leargan.

"I will be one and twenty in a month," Payton replied calmly.

"But, ye have been *Sir* Payton for several years, havenae ye?"

"Aye I did a small service for our king when I was but seventeen, and he gave me his spurs."

"Saved the king's son from drowning," Leargan cheerfully told Cameron.

"Of course." Cameron poured himself some wine from the jug on the table, only to pause in sipping it when he caught a grinning Leargan staring at him. "Ye want to say something, Leargan?"

"I was just listening for the gagging to start."

"Ye will have our guest thinking we are all madmen here."

"Oh, I think ye are doing that weel enough without my help. Sir Payton Murray? Meet our laird, Sir Cameron MacAlpin."

Cameron returned Payton's brief nod. Leargan was right. He was acting like a lunatic. Somehow he had to pull himself together, to fix his thoughts on one thing and one thing only: the need to get Katherine a father's name for her child.

"Payton, my darling!"

A quick glance toward the door revealed Katherine pushing her way through the women, and Cameron looked at Payton. "My sister, Katherine. I believe ye are acquainted with her."

"Vaguely," Payton drawled.

The lad had presence, Cameron decided, and he watched closely as Katherine ran up to Payton. The young man neatly circumvented her attempt to throw herself into his arms. A distinctly sulky look crossed Katherine's face when Payton murmured a polite greeting and briefly kissed her hand. What Cameron did not see was any hint of passion in either of them. If there had been any, it was gone now.

"Get out of the way. Wheesht, ye would think ye had ne'er seen a redheaded laddie before."

Katherine muttered a curse at the sound of that voice. "I thought the brat was still abed."

After giving Katherine a sharp, cold look, Payton turned his attention toward the door. "Gilly, m'love," he called. "Fight on."

At that moment Gilly managed to break through the knot of women and stumble into the great hall. "Payton, ye are a bleeding hazard," she grumbled then ran over to fling herself into her cousin's welcoming arms.

Payton hugged and kissed her, then set her on her feet and looked her over. "Ye are looking verra fine, brat."

"Aye." She winked at him. "My beauty has been undimmed by my many trials and tribulations."

"Verra true, love. It has only been enhanced."

"Oh, that was a good one."

"Thank ye. I do try."

"I thought ye were leaving," Katherine said, glaring at Gillyanne.

"Going to miss me?" Before Katherine could reply, Gillyanne looked at Cameron. "I guess she willnae be inviting me to the wedding. Just when is it to be, anyway?"

Cameron got the distinct feeling there was more behind Gillyanne's question than simple curiosity. "A week. Mayhap two."

"But Cameron," protested Katherine, "what about my bairn?"

"What about it? It isnae going anywhere."

Katherine looked shocked. Payton and Leargan stared into their wine as they obviously tried to compose themselves. Gillyanne fell against him, giggling. Cameron sighed, wrapped his arm around her thin shoulders, and gave her a hug.

"Why, Cameron," Gillyanne drawled as she grinned up at him, "I think ye might actually have a sense of humor."

"I must. I havenae strangled ye yet."

"Been endearing yourself to everyone as usual, pet?" Payton teased.

"One or two," Gillyanne replied. "Where is Avery?"

"Aye, where is my sister?" Payton asked, looking at Cameron as he placed his goblet on the table.

There was a hard look in Payton's eyes that impressed Cameron. The youth was bonny with fine, courtly manners, but Cameron suddenly had no doubt that he could be a formidable opponent as well. So far he had not found anything wrong with Sir Payton Murray, and oddly enough, that irritated him just a little.

"Avery wished a short visit with you ere she left Cairnmoor," Cameron replied. "She awaits ye in her bedchamber."

"I will take ye there, Payton," Gillyanne said, clasping her cousin's hand in hers. "I can collect my things then and bring them down. Ye can tell Avery that I will wait for her down here."

"It willnae be a long visit, love," Payton said. "Bowen said he would wait for two hours. One has already passed. Ye ken how your Bowen is when the ones he watches for dinnae show on time."

"Weel, if the second hour starts to draw to an end, I will go to the gates and tell him that I am fine, to just wait a wee bit longer." Gillyanne glanced back at Cameron as she and Payton started to walk away. "Bowen is just verra protective of me."

The moment Payton and Gillyanne were gone, Cameron looked at Leargan. "Just how many Murrays are sitting outside my walls?"

"Two, three dozen," Leargan replied. "I would assume we were just subtly told that if the lasses dinnae appear by the time two hours have passed, suspicions will be roused. 'Twould be best to ensure that doesnae happen."

"Aye," agreed Cameron. "The last thing I want is a battle."

"Really, Cameron, they couldnae take Cairnmoor with so few men," Katherine said. "There is nay need to worry."

"I would think ye would prefer it if I didnae slaughter Sir Payton's clansmen until ye are safely wed."

Katherine's lips tightened into a thin, flat line. "I can see that ye are in an ill humor. I will leave ye to it."

As Katherine walked out, Cameron moved to the head of the table and flung himself into his chair. He had been awake not much more than an hour, and the day already felt as if it had been far too long. Considering what was to follow, it was undoubtedly only going to get worse.

Avery sat on her bed staring at her small bag of belongings and trying not to weep. Anne and Therese had stopped to wish her a good journey. They both acted confident that she would not be gone for very long. Avery desperately wished she could share in that certainty; yet at that moment, all she could think of was that Cameron had never given her any words of love. Not once, not even in the heat of passion, had he given her the smallest hint that this was not the ending it appeared to be.

She looked up when the door opened, and there stood Payton. Her brother's presence was both a pleasure and a pain. She loved Payton dearly and was always glad to see him. Unfortunately, this time his visit signaled the start of her journey home, away from Cameron. Avery found that she was able to smile, however, and she rose to her feet to hug him in greeting.

"He gave ye a verra fine room," Payton said, looking around.

"Nay verra subtle of ye, brother dear," she murmured.

Payton grimaced, dragged his fingers through his hair, and asked, "Are ye lovers?"

"Aye. And ye can take that look of anger from your face. I went willingly into his arms."

"He didnae seduce ye for revenge?"

"Oh, in the beginning he did have such a wondrous plan. He was told that ye had raped his sister, and there was no one about save Gillyanne and I to try to tell him different. Not only had we been in France at the time of the supposed crime, but we could hardly be considered unbiased in our opinions.''

"He doesnae believe that any longer.''

"Nay. I am nay sure when his mind changed, but it did. His plans changed for me as weel. He went from wanting to shame me as he felt his sister had been shamed to making it just a matter between the families and on to . . . weel''—she blushed—''e'en offering at a particularly awkward moment to leave me my maidenhead.'' She blushed even more beneath Payton's steady stare.

"Wretched lass,'' he murmured, and he laughed briefly before growing serious again. "Ye love him.''

"Desperately,'' she admitted on a sigh.

"Yet he sends ye away.''

"I dinnae think he kens any other way to do this. Ere we arrived at Cairnmoor, I am sure he was hesitating; then he saw that Katherine was indeed with child and she was still pointing her finger at you.''

"The child isnae mine.''

"Ye didnae e'en have to say it, Payton. The moment he told me ye had denied the child, I kenned it wasnae yours. And, I kenned there was only one way ye could be so sure it wasnae yours, and that was because ye ne'er bedded Katherine.''

"But your lover thinks I did.''

"Aye and nay. He doubts, Payton. I am certain of it. So is Gillyanne.''

Payton muttered a curse and paced the room for a moment. "Yet he will still force me to marry her.''

"He has a sister, unwed and rounding with child. Cameron may have gotten her to cease claiming ye raped her, forced her to soften her tale to one of seduction and desertion, but she still insists ye are the father of that bairn. What else can he do?"

"Nothing," Payton whispered, then he added more firmly, "Nothing at all, and I do understand that. Of course, that understanding is often smothered by my horror of taking that woman as my wife."

Avery hugged him again "When will he make ye wed her?"

"In a week, mayhap two. Now why has that made ye look so verra happy?"

"Because it is proof that he doubts her," Avery said as she clasped her hands together and pressed them against her breast. "Oh, Payton, he doubts her, and nay just a little. He has given ye time, time in which to prove her the liar she is. Aye, and he has given himself time to do the same. In truth, he has given ye the chance to get free of her."

"I thought much the same, but I suspect I will be held close within Cairnmoor, so finding the truth could be verra difficult."

She dismissed his concern with a wave of her hand. "Ye will get the truth out of her. I have no doubt about that."

"I wish I shared your confidence in me."

"Ye will. Just make sure that ye are nay the only one to hear it or get a name from her. I believe that Cameron will now at least try to bring the other mon before him, to question him. And, what Gillyanne and I have learned will help."

Payton grinned. "I was sure the two of you would be working hard to ferret out the truth. 'Tis why ye asked for this visit?"

"Aye, that and wanting to be sure ye understood why Cameron and I became lovers. 'Tis no secret at Cairnmoor, so ye were sure to discover the truth. In fact, Katherine will nay doubt fill your ears with it, wishing to shame me and giving nary a thought to the trouble she could cause her brother. I love the mon. I went to his bed willingly. I just wanted to be sure ye understood that.''

''Do ye think that, when matters settle some, Cameron will try to get ye back, to marry you?''

''I dinnae ken,'' she replied softly, taking a moment to swallow the urge to cry. ''Everyone else seems to think I will return, but I have had no words of hope from him. No words of love. He desires me and I think he cares for me in his way. He is a mon with scars upon his heart, Payton, and I ken enough of his past to ken why they are there and sympathize. I am just nay sure I got past them. But that cannae matter now. Yours is the most pressing problem.''

''That and the fact that Bowen leads the men. He gave us two hours, and that time is nearly done.''

''Oh, dear. Weel, from wee things Katherine let slip, and from what we coerced out of her maid, ye are looking for a squire. He is bonny, tall, and quite strong. Red hair and brown eyes. He is also poor and has six older brothers.'' She saw how thoughtful Payton suddenly looked and she asked, ''Do ye ken such a mon?''

''There is something tickling at the back of my mind. 'Twill come. 'Tis certainly enough to start with.'' He picked up her bag, took her by the arm, and started out of the room. ''And now we must go ere Bowen tries to charge the gates.''

''Gillyanne, if ye dinnae cease staring at me, I will toss the table linen o'er your head,'' Cameron grumbled, frowning at the girl seated on his left.

Gillyanne just laughed. ''I will miss ye, Cameron.''

"Odd thing, I think I might be fool enough to miss ye, too."

"Ah, I hear Payton and Avery. Time to go." She stood up, leaned over, kissed him on the cheek, and said quietly, "Dinnae brood. Think and listen. 'Twill all come right in the end, but only if ye set yourself free of the past."

Leargan moved to stand by Gillyanne, draped his arm around her shoulders, and started walking her to the door. "Ah, lass, if ye were just a wee bit older, and I just a wee bit younger, I wouldnae let ye skip out of here. We would make a fine pair."

"Flatterer. I would drive ye mad."

"Aye, but 'twould surely be a sweet madness." He kissed her on the cheek and nudged her toward Avery, who had just paused before the doors of the great hall. "And Avery, ye beauty, I shall miss ye, too." Leargan tugged a shocked Avery into his arms and gave her a resoundingly passionate kiss, which was dimmed only slightly by the sound of something crashing to the floor of the great hall.

When the kiss ended and Leargan set her away from him, she glanced over his shoulder to see that Cameron was on his feet. A page slipped up behind his glowering laird and set his fallen chair upright again. Avery looked at a grinning Leargan and tsked.

"Ye do like to risk that bonny face of yours, dinnae ye?" she said quietly.

"Nay as much as ye think," he drawled. "My horse is saddled and readied for me to go hunting."

She was almost able to laugh, but then she looked at Cameron. He made no move to come and say farewell, nor to give her any sweet words she could treasure. Although he looked upset, even faintly tormented, it was not enough. She needed more to give her some hope to cling to, and he was obviously not going to give it to her.

Avery curtsied in silent farewell and then, after he bowed
in silent reply, she walked away.

There was a slight hesitation in their departure as the
Murray men greeted them. Bowen hugged them both and
seemed reluctant to let go of Gillyanne. When they were
finally mounted, Avery fought the urge to look back until
they were too far away for her even to catch a glimpse
of Cairnmoor.

"Ye must nay be sad, Avery," Gillyanne said as she
rode up beside her.

"He said nary a word, Gillyanne," Avery replied.

"There was no privacy, and the problem of Payton and
Katherine must still be sorted out."

"True, and mayhap he simply had naught he wished
to say to me. Mayhap he decided silence was the kindest
way to say farewell." She nudged her horse to a faster
gait, leaving Gillyanne behind.

"Where is Leargan?" Cameron asked as Payton
strolled up to the table and sat down on his left.

"He went hunting," Payton replied as he helped himself to some of the food set out for the morning meal.

"Wise of him."

" 'Twas just a kiss."

"Ye should have stopped him from mauling your
sister."

"Avery didnae seem to mind." He shrugged. "No one
else seemed able to bestir himself to give her a fond
farewell."

Cameron studied the younger man. Payton only occasionally met his stare as he calmly ate. There was a
hard anger visible in those glances, but also the glint of
amusement. Cameron wondered what Avery had told her
brother.

Just thinking Avery's name caused an odd, wrenching ache in his chest. Cameron told himself it was only sharp regret. In her slim arms he had found the sweetest, richest pleasure he had ever known. Any man would sorely regret losing that. After a while, when the memories eased and he would not be so apt to make comparisons, he would find himself a mistress. If he took care of his body's cravings, he would soon forget Avery Murray. He scowled into his wine when even the cynical part of him seemed to scoff at that plan.

"Ye said the marriage wouldnae take place for a week, mayhap two?" Payton asked as he sprawled back in his chair and sipped at a goblet full of cider.

"Nay," Cameron replied. "I need to fetch a priest, and there are plans that must be made. A week would require a lot of luck and hard work, so I shall set the wedding date for a fortnight from now." He frowned when he saw two maids briefly flutter around Payton until the youth was able to gently send them on their way. "Is it always like that?"

"I am new to them," Payton replied. " 'Twill fade."

"Many a mon would kill to be able to draw such besotted attentions, to have such bounty constantly thrust at him."

" 'Tis all shallow—fleeting and unimportant. My uncle Eric had the same problem. Still does, actually. As he says, what is it that they admire but a lump of flesh and bone that happens to be shaped in a manner which pleases the eye? It can be scarred by wound or disease, easily made positively repulsive. For all they ken, I snore loud enough to deafen them, have the manners of a pig, and am an utter coward or a terrible lover. Whene'er I think I might be succumbing to the taint of vanity, I go home. My family kens how to keep me humble, especially Avery."

The ache returned to his chest and Cameron cursed inwardly. Whatever the affliction was, he hoped it did not last long. Muttering some excuse about needing to check Cairnmoor's supplies, he left the great hall. Cameron realized that he found Payton's knowing looks as unsettling as Gillyanne's. The fact that Payton's eyes, so very similar to Avery's, caused him to think of saddling his horse, chasing Avery down, and bringing her back to Cairnmoor, was one he fought to ignore.

Payton shook his head as he watched Cameron stride away. The man was battling something fiercely, and Payton feared it was himself. Avery had indeed picked a troubled man to love. Payton was not sure Cameron MacAlpin knew how to accept such a gift, and he was certainly struggling hard not to return it. He was going to have to quickly sort out the tangle with Katherine, and not just for his own sake. Cameron had to be made to see what he could have with Avery before he convinced himself that he did not need her at all.

"Is he gone?" asked Leargan as he slipped into the hall.

"Aye." Payton grinned as the man sat down across from him and began to eat heartily. "I thought ye were going hunting."

"Realized I had forgotten to break my fast. Cannae hunt on an empty stomach."

As he chewed on a thick slice of bread, Leargan studied Payton. "Ye ken it all, dinnae ye."

"Dinnae worry. I willnae try to kill him. Cannae. Avery loves him."

"Aye, poor wee lass." He exchanged a brief grin with Payton. "I can only hope yon fool has the wit to get her back."

"He may need some nudging. And the matter of my proposed marriage to Katherine must be sorted out first."

Leargan sighed. "Ye arenae the father of that bairn, are ye?"

"Nay, but I think I ken who is. Tell me, do ye have much skill at listening without being caught at it?"

"Aye. If ye will pardon my lack of modesty, I will confess that I am verra good at it. Why?"

"Whene'er I am alone with my dear betrothed, I want ye to be listening."

"Think ye can get her to admit that she is lying?"

"Aye, but I am the mon caught in this trap. 'Twould be my word against hers. I need someone Cameron can openly trust to be able to stand behind what I say. Willing?"

"Verra," agreed Leargan. "Of course, discovering all this came about because his own sister lied to him may not help Cameron much."

Payton made a languid gesture with one elegant hand. "Dinnae worry. I will get him and Avery together."

"Oh, aye? Ye think ye are that persuasive?"

"I can be, but 'tis Avery who will be my best weapon. She loves the fool. What mortal mon could turn his back on that for verra long?"

Chapter Twenty-Two

Cameron yanked on his boots, stood up, and found himself facing the chair. No matter how often he told himself it was just a piece of furniture, he would spend hours staring at it, his mind crowded with heated memories. Every morning for a week now, he had woken up firm in his decision to burn it. Then he would find himself staring at it and trembling with memories and emotions he did not want. Every night he found sleep elusive as he sprawled in his painfully empty bed and stared at that chair.

For two days he had tried to smother the ache inside him with drink, to fill the emptiness inside him with wine. When he had roused from one drunken stupor to find himself actually sitting in the chair, Avery's name upon his lips, he had decided that drink was no cure. He did not even want to consider what maudlin things he may have said to Leargan, who had too often had to help him to bed.

And now he brooded, he thought crossly. Brooding kept him locked within his own thoughts, and he did not want to be there. Avery was there. Her smile, her voice, the way she looked when he gave her pleasure. He found himself thinking of what he could have done differently, if anything. Those words of love she had let slip while fevered haunted him. His memories constantly reminded him that she was the first woman who had ever made him feel handsome. And as if he were the best lover ever born, he thought with a familiar tightening in his groin.

The other problem with brooding was that at the edges of his mind was a truth that was increasingly strident in its demand to be recognized. Cameron blamed it for his headaches and for that ache in his chest that refused to go away. Worse, it made him afraid—afraid that, if he finally listened to it, it was going to completely devastate him.

Resisting the urge to kick the chair, he strode out of his bedchamber. What he needed was hard work, the kind of work that would leave him too exhausted to think of things like how soft and sweet Avery's skin was. He walked into the great hall where Payton and Leargan sat eating heartily and conversing like old friends. Grunting a greeting, he walked to his seat only to stop and stare at the little pot of jam set next to his scones. Blackberry jam. Spitting out a curse, he picked it up, hurled it against the wall, and strode out of the great hall.

Leargan stared at the shattered pot and the dark jam oozing down the wall. "I dinnae think I want to ken why that set off his temper."

"Nay, neither do I," agreed Payton.

"He is getting worse."

"Not getting much sleep at night, I suspect. At least he isnae drinking any more."

"True, although I wish he had gotten drunk just one

more time so that I might have discovered why that chair in his room bothers him so much." Leargan looked at Payton and they both laughed. "Ah, nay, we shouldnae laugh. Poor fool is hurting."

"He is indeed, and I think he is verra close to admitting to himself just why he is."

Leargan studied Payton for a moment, then asked, "And ye will accept him when he weds your sister?"

"Aye," Payton replied. "I confess, I am nay sure why she loves the great, black-eyed, brooding fool, but she does. 'Tis all that matters, to me and to my kinsmen."

"Do ye think she will still be willing when he finally comes to his senses?"

"Oh, aye. Her anger and hurt will need soothing, but it willnae have been long enough since she left for her to e'en begin to stop loving him. Truth is, Avery probably cannae stop. We Murrays tend to mate for life, and she has obviously decided that Cameron is her mate. And I intend that she have him. Soon."

"Soon? Are ye that close to the truth, then?"

"I am. I have had a pleasant chat with all the maids who traveled to court with Katherine's group, and they were most helpful." He grinned when Leargan rolled his eyes "I also had a lovely visit or two with Aunt Agnes."

"Aunt Agnes? She is a dear woman and I love her, but I wouldnae have thought ye would get much sensible talk out of her."

"One but needs to ken how to sort the wheat from the chaff. Some verra intriguing bits of knowledge are hidden amongst all that happy chatter. She was an abysmal choice of chaperon for Katherine."

"Obviously. So ye think ye have learned enough to get the truth out of Katherine?"

Payton nodded. "And I have decided to use a bit of advice Gillyanne whispered to me ere she left here. She told me to make Katherine angry, that the woman doesnae think o'er what she says when she is angry. Then she told me how to stir up a fine rage in my betrothed. Deny her.''

"But ye have already done that," murmured Leargan.

"Before, aye, but Katherine thinks me weel trapped now. She thinks she has won the game, has fooled us all. She had her braw but poor lover, and her brother will see that she has her wealthy husband. Gillyanne is right. 'Tis time to deny Katherine all she thinks she has won: me in her bed, visits to my French lands and the French court, visits to our king's court, where I am in some favor now, and my purse. The only place she will be able to parade her prize will be here or at Donncoill.''

"She will be enraged."

"Exactly," Payton said, and he stood up. "In response, I want her to taunt me with what she sees as her victories over we poor foolish men.''

"And when does this play begin?" Leargan asked as he, too, stood up and nodded a greeting to Anne and Therese when they arrived.

"Tonight. A walk in the gardens, I believe."

"Good choice. Lots of places for me to lurk unseen," Leargan said as he and Payton began to leave.

"Here, now, what is this mess?" Anne cried, causing both men to turn and look at her. " 'Tis blackberry jam." She scowled over her shoulder at Payton and Leargan. "Did ye do this?"

"Nay, mistress," Payton replied. "Your laird did it."

Anne shook her head. "I dinnae understand. I thought he liked blackberry jam, but this is the second pot gone to waste.''

"The second?" asked Payton.

"Aye. The day ye arrived, Sir Payton, Therese and I were cleaning the laird's bedchamber. He must have spilled a pot of it. Just like a mon to grab anything close at hand to clean up a spill. Used a fine, soft drying cloth. 'Tis ruined now. Fortunately the spots on the robes and sheets were nay too bad. There was e'en some on one of the chairs.'' She frowned when the two men stared at her for a moment, then burst out laughing so hard they nearly staggered out of the great hall.

"Men can be verra odd creatures,'' she said, looking at Therese only to find the woman frowning thoughtfully at the mess. "What is it?'' Anne thought over everything she had said and considered the looks upon the young men's faces before they had started laughing. "Nay, it couldnae be.''

"*Oui*,'' said Therese. "I think someone play with their food, eh? Fun play, *oui?* Love play.''

"My, my, and wee Avery with such a sweet face.'' Anne stared at the jam, then looked at Therese again. "I rather like clotted cream and my Ranald fair swoons o'er it.''

"Me, I like the honey. My man, too.''

Anne and Therese left the jam for someone else to clean up. They went over to the table and made their selections. As they walked out of the great hall, they met Katherine walking in. Hiding their stolen treasure in their skirts, they fled, giggling like young girls.

Cameron stared at his goblet of wine and wondered if he should try getting drunk again. Hard work had not helped much. He glanced at Leargan, Payton, and Katherine, then at his aunt Agnes and cousin Iain: the company at the head table would not give him much diversion. Payton and Leargan were again talking like old friends while Katherine pouted over being ignored. His cousin Iain was enduring one of Aunt Agnes's long, rambling conversations. He missed Avery, he thought with a sigh. He had missed her from the moment she had walked away, and it simply was not getting any better. In fact, Cameron thought it was getting a lot worse—painfully worse.

"Cameron," Katherine said, loud enough to interrupt Payton and Leargan, "I think ye need to speak to the servants."

"Why?" He knew he sounded curt and uninterested, but Katherine had far too many complaints, and most were petty ones.

"They are stealing food. And they are doing a poor job of cleaning."

"The hall looks clean and stealing is a crime, so ye ought to weigh your words most carefully ere ye accuse anyone."

"The hall is clean now, but there was jam all o'er the wall this morning, and it was hours before it was cleaned up."

"Jam can be verra hard to clean up," Cameron murmured, proud of how calm he sounded.

"Usually best just to lick it up," drawled Leargan.

"It was on the wall," Katherine snapped, and she shook her head.

Cameron began to get a very bad feeling—a feeling that sharpened when he saw the laughter in Leargan's and Payton's eyes. " 'Tis gone now. So what about the stealing?"

"When I came down to break my fast, there was no clotted cream or honey for my scones or porridge."

"That doesnae mean it was stolen."

"Nay? I am certain I saw Anne and Therese trying to hide something in the folds of their skirts as they hurried away."

"Anne and the clotted cream," Cameron heard Leargan murmur to Payton. "Ranald loves it."

"Then it must be Theresa's mon Hugh who has the sweet tooth," said Payton.

Slumping in his chair, Cameron took a deep drink of wine. Somehow, someone had discovered one of the love games he had played with Avery. He supposed he ought to be flattered that others had rushed to imitate him. He had never been an adventurous lover before. It should not surprise him that such pleasure carried some cost.

"And then at the nooning, I wanted some strawberry jam for my bread." Katherine frowned briefly when Cameron groaned, but she did not pause long in her complaint. "The page said there was none. I kenned that must be a lie, so I went down to the kitchens."

"I am surprised that ye e'en ken where they are," drawled Payton.

Katherine ignored him. "Cook said there was none left, but there was a pot of it right on the table. She said it had gone bad and wouldnae let me take it. I didnae think it could go bad."

Deciding it was a waste of time to pretend he did not know his secret was out, Cameron looked at Payton and Leargan, who shook their heads in denial. "It can, I suppose. Cook would know," he told Katherine.

"Then explain why, when I went out later to take an apple to my mare, I saw Maude, the laundress, hurry off to her cottage with that verra same pot of jam?"

Cameron pictured Big Maude in his mind, a woman nearly as tall as him and several stone heavier. He then pictured her wee, skinny husband. One glance at the wide-eyed looks on Payton's and Leargan's faces told him they were doing the same. It was not an image he wished to linger over. He was certainly not going to tell Katherine what he thought was the fate of that jam.

"Since these people are the verra ones who make the foods, one cannae begrudge them an occasional treat," Cameron said. "If it becomes too common, I will speak to everyone."

"And I will stand firm at your side if ye do, cousin," vowed Leargan, his eyes sparkling with laughter.

Cameron spared a brief glare for his cousin before having another deep drink of wine. Leargan knew he would never speak to his people about this. What could he say? Please stop playing love games with my food? He just hoped that in a few days the pilfering would decrease to an unnoticeable trickle. He then thought of those rogues Ranald and Hugh and their handsome wives and decided he might be wise to keep an eye on the supply of clotted cream and honey.

"A fine meal, Sir Cameron, as always," Payton said, standing up and bowing slightly. "In truth, I ate so much I believe 'twould be wise to have a wee walk about the gardens to help settle it all."

"Oh, that is a lovely idea," Katherine said as she stood up and hurried to Payton's side.

"Aye, it was," Payton murmured as he led Katherine out of the great hall.

Payton, Cameron decided, was doing very little to hide his dislike of Katherine. He turned to speak to Leargan about it only to see his cousin following the couple. There was in Leargan's movements a distinct air of stealth that roused Cameron's curiosity. He got up and started to follow his cousin.

"Ye dinnae have to go to the garden with those young lovers," Agnes said as Cameron started by her seat. "Leargan will watch them."

"Is that where he went, then?" asked Cameron.

"Oh, aye. He always follows them. And such a considerate lad, too. He always stays just out of sight, giving them some privacy e'en as he is ever ready to intervene if he must. So, ye can just go and rest. Ye worked verra hard today.''

Agnes took a deep breath to begin one of her long talks, and Cameron felt himself tense. He did not wish to hurt his aunt's rather tender feelings, but he needed to find out what Leargan and Payton were plotting. Then Iain asked Agnes how she liked the wine served with the dinner. Agnes took another deep breath to answer, and Cameron fled. Everyone knew one did not ask Agnes how she liked the wine, for the woman found it necessary to compare it to every other wine she had ever tasted and tell you where she had tasted them, why, and even how each one had been served. Iain could be trapped for hours. Cameron swore he would find a way to repay the man for his sacrifice.

As quietly as possible, Cameron entered the gardens, his mother's and then Agnes' pride and joy, which took up a large part of the rear bailey. He saw Payton leaning against the side of the small well around which the whole garden had been planned. Katherine stood in front of him, her posture revealing her growing irritation with her chosen groom. At the far end of the gardens, Cameron caught the glimpse of a shadowed form and knew it was Leargan. Cameron crept around the couple by the well and sat down on a rough stone bench tucked into an alcove of bushes. A part of him dreaded hearing some ugly truth, but he forced himself to stay and listen, just as he knew Leargan was doing.

''Now Payton, my love,'' Katherine said, ''dinnae ye think ye have sulked long enough?''

''Nay,'' Payton replied. ''I believe I will probably brood o'er this injustice for another year or two.''

''Such nonsense. Why cannae ye think of all we can

share, of all we can do together and build together? There can be some good found in this marriage.''

''Such as?''

''Weel, we shall be lovers. There could be such passion between us,'' she said quietly, her voice low and husky.

''Nay.''

Katherine's laugh held a hint of uncertainty. ''Nay? We will be married. Of course ye will come to my bed.''

''Nay, I willnae. E'en if I was knotted up with an ache for a woman, I wouldnae touch you, certainly not until ye have that bairn.''

''Oh? Do ye think the bairn willnae look like you?''

''Since I didnae father it, 'tis possible.''

''And how would ye gain by not bedding me? Ye cannae claim that I am still a virgin. 'Twould be your word against mine as to who took my maidenhead and when, and e'en to whatever claims ye may try to make about the marriage being unconsummated. And we will have been seen at court as mon and wife, mayhap e'en at the French court, for I heard ye must soon travel there.''

''Did ye? Ye must have taken some time to learn about me then, for that wasnae weel kenned about the court,'' he said. ''I am flattered. But why should ye think ye would be traveling to court with me?''

''I will be your wife.''

''And mine to do with as I please. It doesnae please me to drag ye around with me.''

There ensued a silence so heavy, Cameron could almost feel it weighing him down. He could see what Payton was doing and had to respect the cleverness of the plan. Unfortunately, Katherine was revealing all too clearly that it was neither love nor a deep, abiding passion that made her want Sir Payton as a husband. She wanted his body, his prestige, and his purse. She wanted to flit from court to court, basking in his honors and in the envy of other women. And deep in his heart, Cameron knew there would be even uglier truths revealed, for as Payton denied her every prize she craved, she grew angrier. And when Katherine got angry, she lashed out. That much Cameron had learned about her. Katherine would try to hurt Payton, and if what Cameron began to suspect was true, one way to hurt him now was with the truth—to show him just how thoroughly he had been entrapped and would be made to look the fool.

"Ye must take me with you," she said finally, her voice trembling with rage. "I will be your wife. Just where am I to go whilst ye travel from court to court?"

"Weel, ye could stay here with your brother. There is also my family at Donneoill."

"Ye cannae do that."

"I can do anything I wish to," Payton said, his voice hard and cold. "Ye will be wife, my chattel. At least until the bairn comes and then I believe I will be able to cast you aside."

"Oh, nay, ye willnae."

"The bairn isnae mine."

" 'Twill look enough like me or enough like ye to make your claims of not fathering it little more than a matter of jests."

"Aye, I think ye did indeed plan this all verra weel," Payton said. "Ye found yourself a lover with red hair and brown eyes. I have seen the lad, and we could be kin. And he proved conveniently potent, too, didnae he? Ye have made one serious mistake, however, Katherine."

"Nay, *ye* have. Ye should ne'er have scorned me, Payton. Now ye willnae be able to, for I will be your wife. And if ye think ye can just tuck me out of sight, ye had best think again. My brother willnae let ye shame me so."

"Ere the bairn is born or soon thereafter, your brother

will ken that ye shame yourself, that ye have done naught but lie to him and use him. Aye, spurred on by your own ruthless selfishness, ye have used all of us.''

"I dinnae ken why ye keep saying this bairn will prove anything. 'Twill have black hair or red hair, blue eyes or brown. 'Twill look like my family or one of that vast horde ye call kin.''

"Aye, Malcolm Saunders does have red hair and brown eyes. He also has a large birthmark on his buttocks.''

"Nay, he doesnae.''

"Aye, and ye should ken the truth of that better than anyone, but I fear ye must have failed to notice a thing or two about your lover. Mayhap ye didnae rut with him except in the dark, or ne'er took the time to look o'er that fine body ye were using. Ah, but he was just a poor squire. Ye ne'er intended to stay with the lad, just use him for your pleasure. He was but part of a plan.''

"Malcolm doesnae have a mark,'' Katherine nearly shouted. "How could ye ken such a thing, anyway?''

"My squire saw him when they were swimming once. Gil swore it looked just like Sterling castle. Near covers his left buttock. Mayhap your gaze was elsewhere, your interest more in his *stature*. I have heard 'tis most impressive.''

"Your Gil sees and hears the oddest things—for a mon, leastwise.''

"Oh, most everyone at court has heard a wee whisper about how weel endowed young Malcolm is. Is he?''

"Jealous? I have heard that ye may equal him.''

"Not that ye will e'er ken the truth of that. I willnae crawl atween your legs ere the bairn is born, and once it is, I will have the proof I need to pull your greedy talons out of my hide.''

"Curse ye, the bairn may not carry this mark. If there e'en is one. I think ye lie, try to trick me.''

"Nay. Believe it or nay, Katherine, but oftimes the truth works as weel, if nay better, than lies and deceits. The mark proclaiming your lies for all to see will be there. It appears on the firstborn Saunders without fail."

"Malcolm is a seventh son," Katherine proclaimed, relief and triumph sounding in her voice.

"True enough, except that he is also the firstborn of his father's third wife."

Cameron leaned forward and buried his face in his hands. His sister had lied to him, used him. She had used them all. There was even the strong possibility she had plotted this entrapment of Sir Payton from the first moment he had rebuffed her. Cameron had begun to believe that Katherine was lying, but he never would have guessed the game was this complicated or this sordid. And for the sake of this selfish, scheming, spoiled child, he had sent away the woman he loved.

And there was that truth he had struggled against, he realized, nearly groaning aloud. While he had sat caught up in the revelation of Katherine's perfidy, the truth had stepped forward from the dark edges of his mind. It would not be denied any longer, and he had been right to fear it. It was utterly devastating. He loved Avery, loved her with a depth and intensity that was frightening. And for the sake of a spoiled child, he had thrown Avery away— sent from his side the only woman he would ever love. He stood up and walked out of hiding.

"It doesnae matter," Katherine said. "My brother will take my word o'er yours. He willnae let ye cast me aside."

"Oh, aye, he will," Cameron said as he stepped up beside Payton and looked at Katherine, pleased to see that she had the sense to look wary of him. "At this moment, I am but one more revelation from casting ye aside myself." Out of the corner of his eyes he saw Leargan approach them.

"He tricks me, Cameron, tricks me into saying things that arenae true," Katherine protested. She took a step back when she clearly saw the fury Cameron felt. " 'Tis nay as it sounds."

"Shut up. Oh, I had my doubts, have e'en caught ye in a lie or two, but I kept trying to believe ye at least had some feelings for the lad here. E'en that ye may have been lovers, briefly, though as I have come to ken Sir Payton, that was a lie it grew e'er more difficult to believe. Yet, nay once in all the little explanations I gave myself, all the possibilities I envisioned, did I come near the truth. Ye see, I still stumbled o'er the foolish notion that there was some feeling in ye, some heart. There is none at all, is there, lass?"

"Cameron, ye must let me explain."

"Explain what? That ye dinnae care who ye hurt, whose life ye destroy, so long as ye get what ye want? Sweet Mary, ye started all of this by accusing the lad of rape. That could easily have gotten him killed. When I realized that was a lie, I should have put an end to all of this right then." He took a deep breath to calm himself. "Ye will get yourself from my sight and stay out of my sight until I can get young Malcolm Saunders to Cairnmoor to marry ye."

"But he is nothing—naught but a squire, landless and poor!"

"He willnae be so poor once he has your dower, will he? Go, Katherine, and quickly." He breathed a sigh of relief when she obeyed him, for he had begun to fear he would give into the overwhelming urge to strike her. "The two of ye have been plotting toward this end all week, havenae ye?" he asked as he looked at Payton and Leargan.

"Aye," replied Payton when Leargan just shrugged. "Avery and Gillyanne had unearthed a few clues to the truth ere they left here. I unearthed a few more. But to be honest, Malcolm Saunders was the result of a guess. A weel-founded guess, but still, just a guess.''

"Jesu." Cameron shook his head. "And there is no birthmark shaped like Sterling Castle, either, I should wager.''

"Nay. From what Gil once said, if there is one, ye would nay be able to see it beneath the pelt of bright-red hair.''

Cameron knew that, if he was not so sick at heart, he would probably laugh. "But weel-endowed."

"Hung like a stallion, so rumor has it."

"Ah, weel, ye are free now. And Leargan, ye will go and find this stallion of a squire and get him back here to marry Katherine. Considering her beauty, the richness of her dower in land and coin, I dinnae think he will give ye too much trouble.''

"Cameron, we need to talk," said Payton as Cameron started to walk away.

"About what?" Cameron paused and frowned back at the younger man.

"Avery."

Drawing his breath in so sharply he nearly choked, Cameron shook his head. "I think I have born all I can endure this day," he said quietly, and he strode away, intending to drink himself into oblivion. It might be only a temporary cure for the pain he felt, but at the moment, he needed it.

"Poor sod," Leargan murmured. "This had to be a gut-wrenching revelation.''

"Aye," agreed Payton. "Worse, I think he had more than the one about Katherine's perfidy.''

"How do ye ken that? Are ye another one like Gillyanne?''

"Och, nay. I just think the cut was deeper than it should

have been since he had already guessed or suspected a lot of what dear Katherine revealed tonight. Cameron looked mortally wounded. Weel, let us go prepare to fetch the bridegroom.''

"Ye are coming with me, are ye?" Leargan fell into step beside Payton as they strolled back to the keep.

"Aye. I think your laird is going to get drunk and stay that way for a wee while. And until dear Katherine is wed and gone, I am nay sure he will heed any talk of Avery.''

"Ye think he will listen to ye afterward?''

"Aye, e'en if I have to tie him in that chair he is so troubled over.'' Payton laughed along with Leargan.

Chapter Twenty-Three

Lifting his head very carefully from his hands, Cameron warily eyed the potion someone had just set down in front of him. He could not believe he had immersed himself so deeply in self-pity and wine, but four days of that had certainly left its mark. Glancing around the great hall, he realized that not only was Katherine's marriage completed, but the wedding feast had ended as well. The only ones left were his rather pathetic self, Leargan, and Payton. It was Payton who offered the potion, but both men looked sympathetic. It was that, something a little too close to pity for Cameron's liking, that gave him the strength to pick up the potion and drink it down.

"Jesu." Cameron shuddered and then drank down the watery cider Payton gave him. "Why cannae a cure taste good?"

"I have oft wondered the same thing," Payton said as he sat down next to Cameron and set a plate of thickly sliced bread in front of him. "Eat. 'Twill soak up the poisons and help the potion do its work."

"What are ye still doing here?" Cameron asked as he slowly began to eat the bread.

"I had to be sure Katherine was wed and myself out of danger."

"Weel, she is, and ye are, so ye can leave now. Leargan can see to sending a mon or two with ye so ye can get back to Donncoill hale and happy. Two strong men to fight off the lasses and clear ye a path home."

"Such a sweet-tempered, thoughtful host," Payton murmured, fighting a grin. "But I am nay ready to leave yet."

"Katherine isnae still here, is she?" Cameron asked, wondering if Payton was only waiting to see the whole disaster through to the very end.

"Nay," replied Leargan, smiling faintly when Cameron slumped in his chair with obvious relief. "She left a few hours ago, whining about being banished to such a remote property with naught but a lowly squire for a husband. So ye can cease soaking yourself in wine to keep from throttling her."

Since that had been some of the reason for his plunge into drunken oblivion, Cameron did not argue with Leargan's words. "Did I e'er meet young Malcolm the stallion?"

"Aye. Once your head clears a bit ye will probably recall it. He is a fine lad, good-natured and polite, yet I think Katherine will soon discover that he is also clever enough to see her for what she is and strong-willed enough to curb her ways. Dinnae frown. I doubt he will beat her or the like. And he was most pleased with it all. He has risen from being a lowly squire with little hope of land or gain to a knight with both, plus a bonny wife and a child on the way."

"When did he become a knight?"

"On our way to the court to collect Malcolm, we paused to tell his father about his son's good fortune," replied Payton. "This news decided Sir Saunders to bestir himself to get his bairn of three and twenty years a knighthood. Malcolm had earned it," Payton assured him, "but the laird he was squire to hates to train new lads and so denies the knighthood until complaints grow too loud. Sir Saunders was verra loud so Malcolm arrived at his wedding as Sir Malcolm, but he believes he may wait a while ere he tells his new wife the good news."

Cameron smiled. "The lad may just have what is needed to control my sister."

"And he will have the help of his Nana, a big, strong-willed woman who adores him, and his Aunt Grizel, who is much the same. Aye, her and her four daughters."

"And one of his brothers, his wife, and her sister," added Leargan.

"Jesu, can the demesne I gave them hold that many?" asked Cameron.

"Aye," replied Leargan. "Katherine complained that she wouldnae have her own bedchamber with so many of Malcolm's kin coming to share in the bounty she was giving him. Malcolm told her that her brother was the giver of that bounty and why would she need her own bedchamber when she had his magnificent furry self to curl up with every night?"

Cameron was surprised he could do so, but he laughed. "I am almost sorry I missed all of this."

"I really dinnae think ye missed as much as ye think. Ye were drunk, but nay that drunk, and ye held up weel. 'Twas understood that ye drank heavily to stay your hand from the lass's backside. Malcolm said 'twas sometimes the only thing a mon could do. His Nana said she wouldnae be quite so constrained and would see that the fine, generous Laird Cameron wasnee troubled by the lass again.''

''And,'' continued Payton, ''that the lass will learn how to be a good wife to Nana's dear lad. 'Twill be a while ere one can see if Katherine has the wit to change, but if she does, Malcolm will be all the mon she needs. The kin who are sharing in this bounty will certainly be working to bring her to her senses. It seems ye were lucky she chose to use him, for ye will have a good mon holding that land, an ally ye can count on. Him and his whole family. They ken weel that ye could have forced the lad to wed Katherine and tossed them both out without a farthing. They ne'er expected such gifts, and 'tis how they see them—as gifts.''

''I didnae want Katherine here, but I couldnae toss her out with naught,'' Cameron said quietly.

''And she will be taken good care of though she might think she suffers. She will soon learn the difference between what she thinks is necessary and what truly is. And Malcolm is now a knight and laird of a small holding, with his brother his right hand. Sir Saunders, a poor laird, has seen two of his younger sons gain far more than he could e'er give them or hope they could earn. So all is settled and most all are verra happy. Save *ye*. Save my sister. And, now, we will talk about that.''

Cameron looked at Payton and reminded himself that the man was eight years younger than him. It did not dim the force of Payton's words or expression. He wanted to tell Payton sharply that what had happened between him and Avery was none of his concern, but he knew that was a lie. Avery was Payton's sister, his blood kin. Payton was also a young man he had wronged, one whose life he had nearly ruined. He was going to have to endure a discussion about Avery and try to hide how badly it would tear him apart.

"There really isnae anything to talk about," Cameron said in a faint last-ditch attempt to stop the discussion that would stir up all the feelings deadened by too much drink and, now, by the sickness such excess brought on.

"E'en if my sister hadnae told me there was something, near everyone else at Cairnmoor would have. I fear your sister was most anxious to tell all. 'Tis a good thing Avery spoke to me first." Payton looked at Cameron, one brow quirked upward. "Some brothers might feel inclined to do ye some harm. I have no doubt my father would be most pleased to tear ye into wee pieces—slowly. There is a verra good chance *Maman* would help."

"I am still alive, however," Cameron murmured. "Since your father isnae trying to kick down my gates to kill me, I must assume Avery has said naught."

"She wouldnae. So, do ye want my sister?"

The blunt question startled Cameron into answering honestly. "Aye. It matters not. I sent her away with nary a word," he said softly. "And I acted upon a lie. I should have—"

"Nay," Payton said, holding up a hand to stop his words. "I am nay the one ye need to talk to about what ye should have done or said. She is." He leaned closer to Cameron. "Do ye wish to marry Avery?"

"Aye."

Cameron was surprised by the speed of his reply. He had stoutly declared he did not want a wife from the moment he had discovered his betrothed's treachery. There had not been a woman since who had made him even consider changing his mind. Not until Avery.

He had tried to banish her from his mind and heart from the moment he had sent her away, and he had failed utterly. For one week he had sought to convince himself that all they had shared was passion, that he was simply regretting the fact that their affair had ended before the passion had faded. That pretense had been shattered the night in the garden when he had learned all too well what his sister's treachery had cost him. All the misery he had suffered since Avery had left was suddenly explained, but what had sent him plunging into one of the darkest moods he had ever suffered was the thought that he could do nothing about it. Now her own brother was offering her to him. He would be an utter fool not to accept that offer.

"One last question," Payton said very quietly. "Do ye love her?"

Staring into his goblet of cider, Cameron decided he owed the man at least one more moment of complete honesty. "Aye," he whispered.

"Good." Payton sat back in his chair. "Now, here is my plan."

"Ye are brooding."

Avery turned from the window she had been staring blindly out of to smile crookedly at her cousin Elspeth. They had come to the well-lit tower room to work on their tapestries. Elspeth worked peacefully while Avery had stared blindly at needle and wool, then had come to the window to do more of the same. As she studied her beautiful cousin, Avery could not stop herself from wondering it Cameron would have fought to keep her if she had possessed some of Elspeth's beauty.

"Avery, have I done something to upset you?" Elspeth asked.

It could be irritating to have people in one's family who so easily guessed one's moods, feelings, or thoughts, Avery decided. "Nay," Avery said firmly as she sat down on a padded bench beneath the high-arched window. "I was just thinking of how bonny ye are with that black hair and those big green eyes. Wheesht, ye look more like my mother than I e'er have." She grimaced. "I was just feeling a wee bit envious, in truth. A beautiful brother, beautiful cousins. and I."

"Ye are beautiful," Elspeth said. "Aye, ye arenae the sort of beauty poets and minstrels warble about. Neither am I. Mayhap ye dinnae like the color of your hair, but try thinking instead that 'tis thick, soft, and verra long. Mayhap ye are thinking yourself too thin. Think instead that, whilst some fool men might ogle full breasts and rounded hips, ye are strong, healthy, and verra, verra graceful. Your skin is clear, soft, and sparks with good health and warmth!"

"And I have good teeth."

Elspeth laughed. "Aye, ye do. Avery, there are verra few of us who can equal those fair ones in poem and song. Have ye seen many men who do? Nay."

"Weel, Payton, your Cormac, and uncle Eric come close to what is said to be monly perfection."

"Too much red in their hair, though it ne'er stopped the lasses from slavering o'er them. Cormac told me that the first thing about me that truly grabbed hold of his attention was my voice." She shrugged and nodded at Avery's look of surprise. "Then my mouth. He told me other things, but though I am pleased beyond words that he likes them, I am nay sure they are flattering. Not all of them. The mon claims to like the way my hair always looks a bit untidy no matter what I do. And, he thinks I have adorable feet." She laughed along with Avery but quickly grew serious again. "The mon wouldnae have bedded ye if he didnae find ye bonny. Dinnae look so wary, Avery, 'tis nay so verra obvious."

"Then how did ye ken it?"

"Something in the way ye brood. It holds the longing

of a lass who misses far more than a bonny face. Has your mither guessed?''

''I think so. She does try to . . . weel, talk to me and studies me a wee bit too closely. 'Tis why I thought to go to visit ye. Told her ye might wish to learn what I ken about Alan's father. Then ye arrive here to visit whilst Cormac is at court.''

''Sorry.'' Elspeth took a deep breath and asked softly, ''He will be good to my Alan, will he not?''

''Oh, aye. I think he has shown that already, dinnae ye? He has every right to just take the boy.''

''True. He has agreed to take it slowly, which shows concern for wee Alan's feelings. 'Twill also help me let go, though I am thinking the boy will always hold a large place in my heart. And, is there nay a chance ye will be the lady of Cairnmoor?''

''I dinnae ken.''

''Yet Sir Cameron bedded ye.''

Avery leaned back against the cool stone wall. As succinctly as she could, she told Elspeth all about her time with Cameron. She told her how it had begun as a plan of revenge and how she felt it had changed. She also told her of Cameron's mistrust of women and why he clung to it. Then she waited as Elspeth thought over all she had just learned.

''My, three years of celibacy,'' Elspeth finally murmured and shook her head.

''Which could be explanation enough for his desire.''

''Nay. A simple rut or two would take care of that. From what ye say, 'twas more than simple rutting he indulged in with ye.''

''I like to think so. It certainly was on my part. And once, when I called it rutting, he got verra angry. Commanded me to ne'er call what passes between us rutting.''

"Ah, Avery, there are the words to hang your hopes on."

"Do ye really think so?" Avery had thought them important, but she was wary of trusting in her own feelings and conclusions.

"I do and I think ye do, too. Ye are just afraid to believe in your own opinions. A mon who doesnae feel much more than desire for a lass isnae going to care what she calls their lovemaking. If ye said it whilst angry, he might murmur a few sweet denials and soothing flatteries. He doesnae get furious and command ye like that."

"Yet he sent me away." Avery inwardly grimaced over the hint of a childish whine in her voice.

"He had to. Ye ken it. 'Tis just one of those things it is easier to grab hold of when one wants to feel sorry for oneself. 'Tis the getting ye back which could prove difficult. It will certainly look like a greater problem to him than it will to you," Elspeth murmured as she tapped her fingers against her chin.

"How much bigger can it get?" grumbled Avery. "He made Payton the ransom for me and Gilly and will make poor Payton marry that wretched, lying sister of his. Poor Payton may already have been plunged into that purgatory."

Elspeth grinned. "Very dramatic."

"Thank ye."

"Now, ye said Cameron had changed from thinking Payton capable of rape all the way to saying the marriage wouldnae take place for a week or two. He is giving Payton time to prove Katherine is lying and trying to trick them all to get what she wants."

"So why doesnae Cameron prove it himself if he already has doubts?" Avery snapped.

"Ye ken the why of that, too," Elspeth scolded, but her tone was one of gentle sympathy. "Ye would find it hard to believe any of us would act so dishonorably. Ye would fight believing it just as hard as he is fighting the truth about his sister. Aye, right up until ye heard the confession of it all.''

"I wish ye would stop doing that."

"Doing what?"

"Stealing away all my reasons for brooding."

Avery smiled faintly when Elspeth laughed. It was true, however. She did find herself dragging such reasons to the fore to explain her own deep hurt to herself. Brooding over such things kept her from thinking too much on Cameron's silence the day she left him and the days since. It kept her from courting too assiduously the devastating thought that Cameron simply did not want her. She was startled from her increasingly dark thoughts when Elspeth suddenly sat down beside her and hugged her.

"Ye love him desperately, dinnae ye?" Elspeth spoke the words as a fact, not a question.

"Oh, aye," Avery whispered in reply. "I feel as if a part of me is missing. That if I dinnae have him in my life, I will ne'er again fully enjoy the living of it."

"I ken the feeling. So he is a good lover, is he?"

"Wicked woman," Avery drawled, and then she smiled, "I think so. 'Tis odd. I got the feeling he wasnae so sure of that. The last night we were together, he did confess that some of what we did, he had ne'er done before, had only heard of. And, I got the distinct feeling that he has ne'er been as . . . er, adventurous as he was with me."

Elspeth nodded and folded her hands in her lap. "Cormac confessed something similar, about having few, er, adventures. Considering the whore he had tangled himself up with, I was surprised, but she did have the game of innocent, of victim, to play out. Couldnae be too skilled and scandalous, could she? Um, I dinnae suppose ye could give me a hint of what ye meant by *adventurous?"*

"Ye *are* a wicked woman," Avery said, laughing a little in surprise.

"Humph. Men talk. Why shouldnae women?"

"Verra true. Weel, tell me, have ye e'er played with your food?" Avery asked, smiling. The way Elspeth's eyes widened told her all she wanted to know.

Avery stared at the letter she held. It had been slipped to her but an hour ago. She had descended from the tower room with Elspeth in something approaching a good mood, only to have it swiftly destroyed by this very secretive message from Payton. After a hasty meal, she had crept back up to the tower room to read it, but she had not gathered up the courage to do so yet. She suspected any word from Cairnmoor would make her feel the same: an uncomfortable mixture of trepidation and hope.

"Just read it, for sweet Mary's sake."

"Elspeth!" Avery clasped her hand over her pounding heart and glared at her cousin. "Weel, I cannae now. Ye are here."

"So?" Elspeth sat down on the bench next to Avery. "I didnae tell anyone ye got the letter. If ye wish it, I willnae tell anyone what it says, either."

"Are ye sure? E'en if it is from Payton?"

"Aye. After all, he isnae in any real danger, is he? There is a sadness o'er what may happen to Payton, but no fear."

Although Avery nodded, she still hesitated to read Payton's message. Was he reporting that all was well, that he had proven Katherine had lied, and was still a free man? If so, why so secretive a message? Why not just come home himself? Had he been forced to marry Katherine after all? If he had, a message sent secretly still promised no good news. Avery realized that, aside from her unsettled feelings about even the smallest bit of news concerning Cameron, the secrecy surrounding the letter troubled her. The only reasons she could think of for such stealth were bad ones.

"Are ye afraid it will tell ye something about Cameron which will hurt?" Elspeth asked softly.

"There is that," Avery replied. "Yet what also troubles me is the secrecy asked for. Why is there any need for it?"

"Oh. Weel, ye ken Cameron and his people. Could Payton be in any danger at Cairnmoor?"

"Only from being deafened by Katherine's whining because he has denied her everything, all she thought to gain from this marriage. 'Tis what Gilly told him to do, for she felt it would anger Katherine enough that she might spit out the truth."

"In the midst of some glorious fit?" Elspeth asked, and Avery nodded. "It could work."

"It could," agreed Avery. "Payton would probably do it even if he doubted that. It does have the sweet taste of revenge for all the trouble she has caused him."

"True. Do ye think there is something in there which will steal away all hope of being with Cameron again?"

" 'Tis possible. If Payton is now wed to Katherine, he will be angry, and so will most of our clan. Can I go against all that ill feeling to be with Cameron, and would he e'en think he could ask it of me? If Payton has proven Katherine a liar, Cameron will feel verra badly about all he did, for he will ken it was all based upon a lie. He might e'en think himself the greatest of fools. Neither possibility will make him want to face me again any time soon."

"Guilt and embarrassment. Two verra strong emotions

no mon wants to suffer, and both strong enough to keep his feet nailed to the floor. Shall I read it for you?'' Elspeth asked, holding her hand out.

It was cowardly, but Avery nodded and gave her cousin the missive. ''In truth, I suppose it matters naught. After all, if the wedding occurred, Cameron will think we cannae be together, and he will think the same—if for different reasons—if there was no wedding.''

''Nonsense. There is always a way. And mayhap 'tis time we planned a few.''

''What do ye mean?''

''Let us see what Payton has to say first.''

Avery clenched and unclenched her hands in her lap as Elspeth read the letter. After a few moments, she began to wonder whether her cousin was a slow reader, or was reading the letter several times over. The latter possibility struck her as very ominous. So did the frown upon her cousin's face.

''There is something wrong, isnae there?'' Avery finally asked.

''Not wrong, but definitely odd. Payton wants ye to come to him, but he isnae verra clear about why. He says it has to do with the wedding and certain things he has discovered.''

''Do ye think he needs my help to ferret out the truth?''

''Mayhap, but I would think he could openly ask any of us for that. Oh, dear, I hope he hasnae discovered that the true father of that bairn is one of our own. Then he could weel wish to deal only with you, for 'tis ye who ken the most about all of this, would ken what to ask, and what to look for.''

''If it is one of our own, 'twould probably be best if he hies to Cairnmoor. Once the truth is out, he could find his welcome amongst the clan gone. *Maman* is nay happy about any of this. I suppose I must go, but how does he think I can get to him? 'Tis no short ride to Cairnmoor. E'en if we meet half the way there, 'twould mean I am gone for at least three days.''

''And, if Katherine is still unwed, the MacAlpins will-nae wish to let the only mon they have for her disappear for a few days, will they?'' reasoned Elspeth.

''Oh, nay, of course not,'' Avery murmured.

''He has arranged for ye to meet him at a wee church which isnae too far from Cairnmoor. He wants ye to sneak out tonight, and says there will be men ye ken waiting to bring ye to him. He names a Leargan, a Wee Rob, a Colin, his squire Gil, and two of his own men, Jamie and Thomas. I wonder how they have come to join him at Cairnmoor?''

Avery frowned, shrugging off Elspeth's idle question. She did not really want to draw so near to Cairnmoor, not when Cameron had not sent for her. There was also the matter of what, if anything, she should tell her parents. If, after all that had happened, she simply disappeared for a week, her family would be frantic.

''I am nay sure I can frighten my family so,'' she said.

''There is another letter which will be given to them ere they can begin to fear for your safety.'' Elspeth patted Avery's tightly clenched hands. ''If there is any upset, I will do what I can to ease it, e'en tell them about this letter if necessary. Agreed?''

''Agreed.'' Avery sighed and was briefly overcome by sadness. She fought the urge to weep, something she felt she had done far too much of since leaving Cairnmoor. It was obvious she had nurtured some small hope that Payton was going to tell her Cameron had missed her, or even that there was some plan afoot to get her back.

''Avery, it has only been a wee bit o'er a week,'' Elspeth said softly, ''and 'tis clear that matters with Kath-erine remain unsettled. Dinnae cast aside all hope yet.''

"I try not to, but I fight to keep hope alive with no sweet words or promises to feed it. 'Tis verra hard."

"The mon may not have whispered such things into your ear, but every instinct I have tells me he does care for you." Elspeth nodded and smiled her encouragement when Avery looked at her. "Men sometimes cannae sort this all out as easily as a woman can. Didnae Gillyanne feel confident that ye and Cameron would be together?" When Avery nodded, Elspeth said, "Ye ken ye can trust in her instincts. And, ye must try to trust in what your own heart tells you."

"My heart is feeling verra bruised just now, and what thoughts it puts in my head are far from clear."

"Weel, first ye must find out what Payton wants." Elspeth stood up and tugged Avery to her feet. "I shall help ye creep out of here. Then, depending upon what Payton has to say, ye may consider continuing on to Cairnmoor and confronting your big, dark knight."

"And make him speak to me, make him say what he didnae say the day I left Cairnmoor?"

"Aye. I would."

"And would that be before or after ye beat him o'er the head with a stout cudgel?" Avery smiled faintly when Elspeth laughed, for they both knew she was not completely jesting.

Chapter Twenty-Four

Nigel sat on the edge of the bed and warily watched his angry wife pace their bedchamber. It was late and he wanted some sleep, but he knew rest would not come until Gisele was calmed. He was not exactly sure why she was so furious. Avery was safe. Payton had assured them of that in his letter. Their daughter might not be pleased with her brother and Sir Cameron, but he doubted she would be angry for long. If he judged right the cause of the sadness that had weighed her down since her return home, she loved Sir Cameron. Payton believed she did, too.

Payton was still a free man, he mused as Gisele muttered away in French. Avery would soon have the man Elspeth said she called her dark-as-sin chevalier. The only cloud he could see upon the horizon was that someone had stolen the only pot left of dark honey—his favorite. Elspeth had looked suspiciously guilty when she had heard him complain about it, but she had disappeared with her newly returned husband too quickly for him to question her.

"Are you listening to me?" Gisele snapped as she stood in front of Nigel.

"Actually? Nay," he replied, and he almost smiled at the startled look upon her face. "I was wondering what happened to that last pot of dark honey."

"Our daughter has been stolen away to be wed to that black-eyed rogue and you fret over missing honey pots?"

"Dark honey is my favorite. Strange, but I think Elspeth is hiding something, might e'en ken what happened to it." He was not surprised to hear Gisele grind her teeth. "Love, Avery is quite safe," he said quietly, and he caught her when she flung herself into his arms.

"He sold his sword to the DeVeaux," she muttered against his chest.

"And soon saw the error of that. He didnae fight your kinsmen."

"*Oui,* though it is not because of his reticence that so many survived that treachery. It was Avery's timely warning that did that. That man tried to force our son to marry his sister."

"She told him the child was Payton's. I dinnae believe I would have acted any differently."

"I wanted to give her a lovely wedding," Gisele whispered, her voice thick with tears.

Nigel patted her on the back. "Ye can have a grand feasting for the christening of her first child."

"She is with child?" Gisele cried, staring at him in horror.

"Nay, not that I could see. But, we Murrays are a fertile breed, so I dinnae think it will be a long wait."

"I want to go and meet this man."

"In a fortnight."

"Why so long?"

"Because they will be newly wed and should have some time alone. Because they may have a few troubles to sort out between them, and we would only make that harder to do. Because the father in me still has a small inclination to beat him verra soundly, as I am sure he has bedded our lass. And, because ye are angry with the mon and need time to get o'er it."

"A week?"

"Nay, a fortnight."

"Oh, as you wish. But, we do not wait a fortnight to leave. We leave in ten days, so we arrive there in a fortnight."

"Agreed."

"Thank you." She kissed him and laughed when he tumbled her down onto the bed. "And, for being such a good husband, I will tell you what has happened to the dark honey."

"Elspeth took it?" He frowned with suspicion when she slowly smiled and reached out for a small pot on the table next to the bed.

"*Oui,* I fear she did. I saw her and pressed her to tell me why. She did and I had to agree that she had good reasons for her theft. I also know that you are very fond of strawberry jam, too."

Much later, Nigel weakly agreed that he was indeed very fond of strawberry jam, and he wondered sleepily why his wife laughed so hard when he suggested that next time they try blackberries.

"Are ye certain your parents willnae be hard on Avery's heels, screaming for my blood?"

Payton sighed as he sprawled in a seat near the back of the tiny church and watched Cameron pace back and forth in front of the altar. *"Maman* may consider it, but my fither will stop her."

Cameron paused in his pacing long enough to frown at Payton. "I would have thought your father would be e'en more eager to get his hands on me."

"Ye are wedding Avery. E'en if he guessed ye have bedded her, and he nay doubt strongly suspects that ye have, that will satisfy him. Avery has probably been brooding about at Donncoill, and he has guessed her feelings for ye."

As he walked to the door of the small stone church to look outside, just as he had dozens of times already, Cameron asked, "Are ye verra sure Avery has feelings for me?" After seeing the same people outside still waiting for Avery to arrive, just as they had been for the past hour, he started to walk back to the altar but stopped to frown at a softly cursing Payton. " 'Tis a reasonable question since I am about to marry the lass."

" 'Twas reasonable the first time," Payton said. "I might e'en accept the first half-dozen times as reasonable. I believe ye passed reasonable a long time ago."

Muttering a curse, Cameron sat down facing Payton and dragged his hands through his hair. Caught up in the heady thought of getting Avery back, of holding her again, he had readily accepted Payton's plan. His uncertainty had grown in the week since then. Although it could be argued that he was not really kidnapping Avery for his bride since he had her brother's full compliance, he was still tricking her and pushing her into something she had not yet agreed to. The only hope he had to cling to, the one to make him think she might agree, was the memory of her passion for him and some fever-bred declarations of love. With each passing day, that had begun to look like not very much at all.

Yet despite his doubts and his reluctance to tie Avery

to his side if she did not wish to be there, Cameron was not sure he would put a stop to this plan if given the chance to do so. He needed Avery, needed her in his bed and in his life. Although he had finally accepted that he loved her, there was no joy in it—not when she was no longer with him. In truth, until Payton had offered this plan, the revelation of his feelings for Avery had caused him nothing but torment. He needed to put an end to that, needed to hold her and tell her how he felt, perhaps even ask her for forgiveness. It might be right and fair to offer Avery some choice, but he did not have the strength to risk it.

Meeting Payton's steady look, Cameron did not think the man would welcome some act of noble sacrifice, anyway. Payton knew he and Avery had been lovers, believed Avery loved him. The tables had been completely turned. Now it was Payton doing what he could to get his sister a husband. Young Payton was being far more amiable and understanding than he had been, but beneath that good humor, Cameron felt sure there was steely determination. There was only one way he might be able to put an end to this, and that would be to tell Payton that he neither wanted Avery nor loved her, completely disclaiming his earlier declarations. Unfortunately, even if he could spit out such lies, he doubted Payton would believe him. Worse, if Payton did believe him, a challenge would be made, for Payton would quite rightly feel he needed to fight Cameron, if not to try to restore Avery's honor, then certainly to make her seducer pay for hurting her.

"I ken most men are uneasy ere they take their wedding vows," Payton drawled, "but ye look almost tormented. Ye said ye wanted her and loved her. From all I have heard, ye couldnae keep your cursed hands off her. So, what is the problem?"

"None with me," Cameron replied, "but she may not feel the same."

"She bedded down with ye."

"Passion."

"Which the women of my clan seem to be gloriously free with, but only with one mon. She told me she loves ye."

"She could have said that to keep ye from getting dangerously angry about the bedding."

"And what makes ye think I wasnae angry anyway?" Payton asked quietly, but he went on before Cameron could make any response. "My sister wouldnae have become your lover if she didnae feel a great deal more for ye than passion. True, the women of my clan arenae the delicate, blushing maidens men say they want, but they have verra high morals."

"I wasnae saying Avery has no morals," Cameron snapped, wondering if Payton was actually trying to start an argument.

"I wondered, since of course, she had the bedding before the wedding. That does seem to be the way of it for our women. 'Tis because they dinnae bed the mon until they decide he is the one they have chosen."

"What?"

"Avery chose you. She decided ye were her mon, shall we say. Once Murray women choose their mate, 'tis amazing how much nonsense they will endure to have him. For, quite expectedly, the men they choose dinnae always understand how fortunate they are, not right away. Avery has chosen ye, wants ye, and says she loves ye. So I will do my best as her loving brother to see that she gets ye."

"It might help me now if Avery had spoken of these things. All I e'er heard from her were a few confused declarations when she was gripped by that fever. She ne'er spoke of what she felt at any other time."

"I should trust more in her fevered ravings if I were ye. And, I suspect ye didnae invite such confidences. She was probably waiting for some sign that ye would welcome such words, and ye spoke only of her leaving."

He could not argue with that, Cameron thought morosely. If he had doubts now, it truly was his own fault. He may have been unable to resist holding her close in his bed, but he had held her at a distance in every other way. Considering how little he had given her in return for her gifts of passion, laughter, and love, he would not be surprised if she were reluctant to marry him now.

"I just dinnae want to drag her into something she may have decided she doesnae want," Cameron said softly.

"She wants it though she may be angry enough for a wee while to tell ye otherwise. Dinnae ye have any faith in her?"

"Aye," Cameron replied without hesitation. "That really doesnae help me believe this is the way to do this, however. Ye say she wants this and I have a few feverish mutterings to tell me ye may be right. 'Tis nay a lot to hang a marriage on."

"'Tis best this way," Payton assured him "Ye can woo her after the wedding. Ye being such a brooding, reticent mon, I am nay sure ye could woo her weel from a distance. And ye would have to confront my parents," he began.

"Which would be best done after I have wedded her," Cameron finished as he got up to resume his pacing. "Especially since I dinnae think ye are of a temperament to deal with parents who ken ye have bedded their daughter, then sent her away and tried to make me marry your sister. Then there are those troublesome accusations of rape."

"I wonder if all of those lasses who think ye are so verra bonny ken how irritating ye can be."

"Nay, I save my true troublesome nature for the pleasure of my kinsmen."

"And that could be reason enough to hesitate to marry into the family."

"But ye willnae hesitate?"

Cameron sighed and shook his head. "I cannae. E'en though it means I must needs claim ye and wee Gilly as kin."

"Ah, but ye have met only a verra small part of my family."

"How encouraging." He frowned and eyed Payton a little warily. "Your family is large?"

"By the time ye include all the allies and kinsmen added through marriage, aye. I have ne'er paused to tally the ones I could call close kin, including most of Elspeth's husband Cormac's brothers and sisters. His parents were infamous breeders, especially since so many were illegitimate issue. Young they are, and always about. Then there are uncle Eric's kin, the MacMillans, who seem to be ever visiting. Then—"

Cameron held up his hand. "Enough. I fear I begin to feel I cheat ye by bringing so few into the fold." He briefly grinned. "There is, of course, Leargan. Oh, and Katherine."

Payton made an exaggerated grimace, then grew serious. "Do ye think ye can e'er forgive her?"

"Mayhap, if she shows true remorse and changes some. I think 'tis best if we leave her to the care of her husband and his family for a while. I have begun to recall things about them and I do think they may work that miracle. At least I need not worry o'er her bairn. Malcolm and his family will raise it right. I just wish I could have done the same for Katherine."

"Mayhap ye could have done more for the lass, but I wouldnae suffer much guilt o'er how she turned out. Ye gave her what ye could and she had loving people in Agnes and Iain, and many another. Sometimes a person just takes their own path and ye cannae get them back. Jesu, no mon could have had more abysmal parents than Cormac Armstrong, and he is a good mon. So are his brothers and sisters, the legitimate and the bastards.''

''And my son lives with these Armstrongs?'' Cameron asked quietly.

''Cormac, Elspeth, and all the rest treat wee Alan as one of their own. God smiled upon the lad when He set him down in Elspeth's path.''

Cameron sighed and nodded. ''There is a small part of me that wonders if it is fair to take the lad away from that. After all, if Avery gives me a son, Alan cannae be my heir. Yet he is my son. I have ne'er set eyes on the bairn, but I want him.''

''He is of your own flesh. Of course ye do. 'Twill take time, but ye will have him. Elspeth and Cormac are saddened by it all, but they kenned there was a father somewhere who may want the lad. And, they will be verra pleased that 'twill be Avery's home, too, which Alan will eventually come to live in.''

''Avery and Gillyanne say he looks just like me.''

''Aye, though he isnae of such a brooding temperament.''

''Weel, soon mayhap I willnae be, either.'' He tensed when Anne suddenly appeared in the doorway of the church.

''She is coming,'' Anne announced. ''I have the brew all ready. Ye get that priest,'' she ordered as she left.

''I am still nay sure we ought to be giving Avery that mead potion,'' Cameron muttered.

''Avery may crave your dark, brooding self, but she will be angry o'er this trick and be wanting a few explanations and declarations from you. Do ye really want to be doing that now?''

Cameron did not hesitate. ''Nay. I just hope that brew wears off ere it is time to begin my wedding night.''

Avery frowned as they rode up to the church. It had been a long journey but not an unpleasant one. The weather had stayed fine and the men had been good company. What they had not been, however, was very forthcoming. She still did not know why Payton had sent for her. Her suspicions had begun to grow with every mile, no matter how often she told herself it was not fair and that these men did not deserve such unkind thoughts as she was beginning to have.

The sight of Anne and Therese at the door of the church pleased her. It also added to her suspicions. There was no reason she could think of for them to be there. She did, however, smile with honest delight when she dismounted and they hurried over to hug her in greeting. Thirsty from the ride, she readily accepted the drink they gave her, only to frown after taking a sip.

''This is, weel, different,'' she murmured. '' 'Tis something like mead.''

Anne nodded. ''There is mead in it, but nay verra much, for I ken that ye find it too heady a drink.''

''Verra heady, and I need a clear head to speak with Payton. Where is he?'' she asked, and she took another drink. It was not bad tasting and served well enough to quench her thirst.

''Waiting for ye in the church. He said we could visit with ye for a moment or two first.''

''That was kind of him.'' She smiled brightly at the woman. '' 'Tis verra good to see ye. I have missed ye both.'' She frowned at Therese, who was fluttering about and carefully brushing the dust from her skirts. "I shouldnae fret o'er it, Therese. Payton willnae mind a bit of dust and dirt."

Therese removed Avery's cloak and tossed it to a grinning Leargan. "God will."

It took Avery a little longer than she thought it should to understand what Therese meant. "Oh. Aye. I suppose one ought to look as good as possible before entering a church. Mayhap Payton should just meet me out here." She finished her drink, then tossed the goblet to Leargan, who neatly caught it even as she wondered what had possessed her to do that.

"Nay," said Anne as she began to unbraid Avery's long hair. "Ye will want privacy."

"God wants my hair down, too?"

"The headdress will look much prettier if your hair is down and brushed weel."

"Of course. That makes sense."

It made no sense at all, a small part of Avery's mind told her, but she did not feel inclined to heed it. Questioning the kind things Anne and Therese were doing could lead to discord, and quite suddenly, Avery did not want even the smallest hint of discord. For the first time since she had left Cairnmoor she felt happy. A part of her expressed some dismay over how sweetly, blindly happy she was, but since that tasted suspiciously like discord, she ruthlessly banished it.

"Do I look bonny now?" she asked Anne, lightly touching the wreath of flowers in her hair.

"Oh, aye, verra bonny," replied Anne. "Happy about that, are ye?"

"Verra happy. Odd, but I am verra happy about the sun shining, too. And how bonny the day is. And how nice Leargan looks when he is grinning like a fool. Did I just call Leargan a fool? That wasnae kind of me. Sounds like discord.''

Anne began to tug her toward the church. ''And ye certainly dinnae want any discord today.''

''Nay, none at all. Oh, look at that. Leargan is getting to the church before us. Is he going to talk to Payton, too?''

''He will be saying a word or two to the lad, to be certain. Come along, lass, ye can look at those flowers later.''

''But they are verra pretty.''

''Verra pretty indeed, but ye willnae wish to miss what awaits ye in the church.''

''Payton waits there.''

''More than that.''

''A surprise? I do love surprises.''

''I am glad to hear it. It may keep ye from wanting to throttle us all later,'' Anne muttered as she tugged Avery into the church.

''She is weel away,'' announced Leargan as he walked into the church and moved to stand next to Cameron.

''So she willnae be causing any trouble?'' asked Payton.

''Nay, she is happy as a lark. Doesnae want any hint of discord, she says.''

''Good. I believe I will get back to my corner ere she sees me. In her current state of mind, such a distraction could cost us precious time.''

Cameron grimaced and dragged his hand through his hair as Payton made his escape. ''I should have preferred her sensible.''

'' 'Twould have been nicer, but I think the lad is right

to have anticipated that she would be a wee bit cross. She began to get verra suspicious as we rode here.''

''Why are there so many people here?'' asked Avery as Anne brought her down the aisle. ''Are they all going to talk to Payton?''

Cameron tensed when Avery finally saw him. She stared wide-eyed at him for a moment, then gave him a beautiful smile that made his heart ache. He dearly wished she were greeting him so while she was sober.

''Greetings, Cameron, my dark-as-sin chevalier,'' she said as she skipped up to him. ''I think I am supposed to be cross with you.''

He wrapped his arm around her shoulders and kissed her lightly on the lips, fighting the temptation to help himself to more. ''But that can wait until later, cannae it, loving?''

''Oh, aye, we cannae have any discord in the church.'' Avery squinted at the priest standing in front of them. ''Oh, dear, have ye made me come to Payton and Katherine's wedding? I think that might cause some discord.''

''Nay, not Payton and Katherine's wedding,'' he murmured as he gently forced her to kneel beside him before the priest.

''Oh, good, then I can still be happy.''

''I hope so, lass,'' he murmured, and he signaled the priest to begin. ''I sincerely hope so.''

Avery frowned as the priest began to speak. It all sounded familiar, but she was beginning to have a little trouble keeping her head clear. Her happiness was fading into a fog, and although the fog felt pleasant, too, she wanted that happiness back. The priest asked her something and she looked at Cameron.

''Say 'aye,' lass,'' he urged her.

An irritating little voice in her mind urged her to hesitate, but she said, "Aye." Each time the priest looked at her, she looked at Cameron, then dutifully repeated what he told her to. The way he smiled at her when she did as she was told eased the sense of wariness that was trying to shove its way through her sense of utter contentment. Questions brought discord, she reminded herself, smiling at Cameron again.

When Cameron tugged her to her feet, she felt dizzy and leaned heavily against him. She murmured her delight when he kissed her, then frowned when he pulled away too soon for her liking. There was a lot of talking going on, but everyone sounded happy, so she ignored it. Out of the corner of her eye, she was sure she saw Payton grinning at her, but then he slipped from view.

She looked up at Cameron. "I think my happiness is slipping away."

"Ah, weel, mayhap we can do something to bring it back," he said quietly.

"Oh? Do ye have some blackberry jam?" she asked; then she heard someone start to laugh heartily. It sounded like Leargan, but as she turned to frown at him, she stumbled and was caught up against Cameron's chest again. "Oh, dear."

"Is something wrong, Avery?" Cameron asked.

She looked up at him, but could not see him clearly. "My happiness is starting to feel verra odd, Cameron."

He caught her as she slumped, and picked her up in his arms. They were married, and he was sure she had no knowledge of it at all. It was going to be just one more thing he would have to try to explain and, mayhap, apologize for.

"What did Anne give her?" he asked Leargan.

"Some brew that she uses to ease pain," his cousin replied.

"Mixed with mead."

"Makes it taste better."

Cameron stared down at his unconscious bride. "I hope it wears off soon and doesnae leave Avery with an aching head. I was rather looking forward to a wedding night."

Chapter Twenty-Five

Avery opened her eyes and looked around. This was definitely not her bedchamber. Her eyes widened when her gaze settled on a very familiar chair. Then memory began to return. She turned to look at the man standing beside the bed. Cameron looked decidedly uneasy. As more memories flooded her mind, she decided it might be wiser of him to look afraid.

"Ye got me drunk," she snapped as she sat up to glare at him.

"Nay drunk. 'Twas a brew to ease pain," he said as he handed her a goblet of cider. "We needed ye, er, amiable."

She snatched it out of his hand and sniffed it. "I am nay sure I want to drink another thing ye serve me."

" 'Tis fine, Avery. I want ye sensible now."

After tentatively sipping the drink, she decided it was no more than cider and drank it down. It cleared away the lingering taste of the last drink. By the time she thrust the goblet back into his hand, she remembered even more.

"Did we kneel before a priest?" she demanded.

Cameron nodded as he watched her. She was definitely awake and sensible now. She was also getting angrier by the moment. That she had slept through the wedding celebration would probably not make her any happier. He hoped she did not figure that out until they got a few things sorted out between them.

"And just why did we kneel before a priest?"

"He married us," Cameron answered.

That was what she had suspected, but she was still stunned. For one brief moment she was filled with joy; then she realized that she had never even been asked if she wanted to marry him. He had not given her any of those words of love she had wanted. There was still the chance that he had married her because honor demanded it. Once he had realized his mistake about Payton and Katherine, he had begun to feel guilty about their affair, to feel that he had to do what was right by her.

"The look on your face, loving, tells me that ye arenae thinking verra kindly thoughts."

"Kindly? Ye want kindly when ye trick me into coming here, then pour some poison down my throat to make me senseless, and marry me without even asking me? I am nay senseless now, and I am thinking that was a verra sly trick to play." She gasped. "And Payton was a part of it, wasnae he? I can recall seeing him there."

Cameron sat down beside her on the bed and tried not to be stung by the way she shifted away from him. "Avery, dinnae ye want me? I shall make ye a good husband." He slipped his hand beneath her tousled skirts and stroked her leg, finding comfort in the way she trembled at his touch.

Avery told herself firmly to shove his hand away, but

she only managed to place her hand on top of his, stilling it for a moment. The warmth of his hand against her thigh, however, was robbing her of her righteous anger, replacing it with the heat of a too-long-denied hunger. There was no denying that she wanted him, but this was wrong, she thought. A marriage had to have more behind it than his sense of honor and passion. While it was true that she brought far more than that to it, he needed to bring the same depth of feeling, or the chances of suffering from deep disappointments and unhappiness were great.

"Ye married me because honor told ye to," she murmured.

"Nay," he protested.

She ignored that and continued, "Ye knew I wouldnae accept a marriage for the reasons of honor and guilt o'er whate'er wrong ye think ye might have done me, so ye tricked me."

He pushed her down onto the bed and sprawled on top of her, lightly pinning her to the bed. "Nay. I married ye because I wanted to."

"Payton arranged all this, didnae he."

"Aye, he did. It was his plan."

"Because he felt ye should marry his sister since ye had bedded her."

"Lass, ye would ken it for a lie if I told ye that our being lovers had naught to do with this marriage." He cautiously began to unlace her gown. " 'Tis nay why I married ye, nay the whole reason. Jesu, Avery, of course I want ye back in my bed. I ne'er wanted ye to leave it."

Since he was talking openly, Avery let him continue to undress her. She ruefully admitted that she was so hungry for his loving, he could toss up her skirts and take her now and she would not complain. However, it would not be wise to interrupt him at the moment. There was the small chance that he might say some of those things she ached to hear.

"So, ye wanted the passion back," she said, trembling slightly as he opened the bodice of her gown.

"Did ye nay miss it, then?"

He stroked the tip of her breast with his tongue, dampening the linen of her chemise and making her shiver with want. "A wee bit."

"I swear, lass, I didnae marry ye just because honor demanded it." He pressed his face against her breasts as he slid his hand up her leg to find the heated welcome he had missed so much. "Avery, I want to talk; I want to tell ye why I did certain things; I even want to try and tell ye what I feel; but, Jesu, I do want ye."

That was promising, she thought. "Right now?"

"Aye, now, and every moment since two heartbeats after ye left Cairnmoor."

"And then we will talk?"

"Aye."

"Then, aye, Cameron. Please."

She helped him in their frantic removal of their clothes. When their bodies met, flesh to flesh, she nearly wept from the beauty of it. She tried to touch him everywhere as he tried to touch her, but their need was too strong, too insistent. A soft cry of pleasure and relief escaped her when he finally joined their bodies, but she looked up at him in confusion when he did not move.

"Cameron?" she whispered, tightening her legs around him to pull him deeper within her.

He shuddered. "I just wanted to savor the feel of ye. It seems as if it has been a lifetime since I felt this pleasure." He touched his mouth to hers and whispered, " 'Tis like coming home."

There was so much feeling behind those soft words, Avery lost what little control she had over her passion. Their lovemaking was fast, furious, greedy, and a little rough, but she kept pace with him. Their release was equally fierce, and as Avery felt herself pulled down into its turbulent waters, she heard and felt Cameron join her. She was only just returning to her senses when he finished cleaning them off and crawled back into her arms.

"My wee cat," he murmured against her throat, "do ye nay love me just a wee bit?"

Avery sighed and combed her fingers through his hair. There really was no turning back now. They were married and, if she was honest with herself there was no other place she would rather be. He may not have said any of those sweet words she ached to hear, but there was affection there. She could feel it in his touch, hear it behind his words. And perhaps, she mused, if she was honest with him, he might find the courage to be honest with her. He might not love her yet, but perhaps he needed to know she loved him; perhaps knowing it would free him to love her.

"Aye," she said. "Nay just a wee bit. More than ye probably deserve."

A tremor went through his body. Before she could decide what that might indicate about his own feelings, he kissed her with a fierce hunger that brought her desire stirring back to life. Then, before she could look into his eyes, he buried his face back into the curve of her neck. If she did not know better, she thought she would think Cameron was feeling just a bit shy.

"When did ye ken that ye loved me?" he asked, warming her throat with soft, warm kisses.

"Shortly before I let ye seduce me."

"If I recall that night—and I do, verra weel—I believe *ye* seduced *me.*"

"Then that should tell ye verra clearly that I am a complete fool for ye."

"Nay, loving." He teased the tip of her breast with his finger, then his tongue. "I hope ye ne'er feel yourself a fool for loving me. I ken I did things that hurt ye," he began cautiously.

"Ye did, but ye ne'er asked me for love. 'Tis nay your fault if I gave it to you."

"Mayhap not, but I kenned verra early in the game that ye were nothing like other women I had kenned o'er the years. I wanted the passion, loving. Jesu, I craved it. But I didnae want to need you. I lied to myself so many times." He began to toy with her other breast. "I wanted nay more than an affair. Then I would send ye on your way and, aye, there would be regrets, but they would fade."

"Ye did send me away."

"I did and I regretted it from the moment ye walked out those gates. Of course, fool that I am, I told myself it was because the passion hadnae faded yet. I told myself it was to be expected that I would miss these bonny breasts." He briefly suckled each one, then slid his hand between her thighs. "And what mon wouldnae miss this honey?" He slowly stroked her. "Or those soft sounds of delight ye make when I taste your heat?" he whispered, and he replaced his fingers with his mouth.

She tensed for the space of one heartbeat, then gave herself over to the pleasure he offered. He tortured her and she loved it. And when he finally gave her the release her body was shaking for, she heard him say three little words that sent her soaring even higher.

It was several moments before she could catch her breath, and she looked down at him. He was lightly kissing her belly and her fingers were still tangled in his hair. Avery wanted to deny what had just happened, what she had heard, but she could not.

"Did ye just say ye loved me?" she asked tentatively, wishing he would look at her.

"Aye." He began to kiss his way back up to her breasts.

"I cannae believe ye told me while ye were doing that," she gasped, torn between utter shock and an urge to laugh.

"Ever since I kenned I loved ye, I have thought about telling ye while in my favorite place."

Avery gasped with shock, then felt herself blush, then began to giggle. "Ye are a wretched mon."

He held her face between his hands and brushed his lips over hers. "But ye love me."

"Oh, aye. Madly. Desperately. Voraciously."

"That sounds much like how I love ye."

"When?" she demanded as she nudged him onto his back.

"When?"

Cameron sprawled on his back and watched her as she kissed and licked her way down his body. Revealing what he felt had not been so painful as he had thought it would be. The rewards certainly made a little discomfort worthwhile, he mused, when he felt her long, delicate fingers stroke him intimately.

"When did ye ken ye loved me?" she asked, teasing him with quick, feather-light kisses along the hard length of his manhood.

"When I discovered the truth about Katherine. I sat there in the garden hearing Payton pull and trick the ugly truth out of her, and the only clear thought I had was, this was what I lost the woman I love for? Worse, at that moment I didnae think there was any way to mend the mistake I had made." He closed his eyes as she eased him into the moist heat of her mouth. "I want ye with me, Avery," he managed to say before he lost the ability to talk.

She toyed with him until he was sweating with need. Then she straddled him and slowly eased their bodies together. He grasped a thread of control and held her by her hips, gently holding her still as he filled his eyes with the beauty of her.

"I swear, I woke up every night in a sweat, thinking I could see ye like this, feel your heat around me, and then nearly wept when I realized it was naught but a dream." He slipped his hand down to the place where they were joined and stroked her, watching her lithe body tremble with pleasure. "I do love ye, Avery."

"And I do love ye, my dark-as-sin chevalier." She leaned over him and lightly kissed his mouth. "And right now, I have a wish to ride."

"Hard."

"Verra hard."

Cameron opened his eyes to find Avery still sprawled across his chest. He stroked her back and felt her move slightly against him. It was going to be a long, exhausting night he thought with a smile.

"I want to do so much for ye, Avery," he murmured.

"Ye do wonderful things for me, Cameron."

"Thank ye. but I wasnae referring to this."

She propped herself up on her elbows and smiled at him. "This is quite enough to keep me happy."

He gently brushed the hair from her face, and tucked it behind her ears. "And I intend to make ye happy, to make sure that ye ne'er regret marrying this dark devil. I will give ye fine gowns and all the treasures a lass could want. I will.'' He frowned when she placed her fingers over his mouth.

"Hush," she whispered. "I want but four things from ye, Cameron MacAlpin."

"And they are?"

"I want ye to love me as I love ye."

"I do, lass, though I shall probably ne'er understand how I could be so lucky."

"And I want ye to need me as I need ye."

"I need ye as I need food and air." He lightly stroked her slim hips. "I need ye to just face each day and ken I can survive it. Jesu, I need ye at my side just so that I can sleep at night."

" 'Tis much the same with me," she assured him. "And I need ye to trust me as I trust ye, with my heart, my soul, my verra life."

He could tell by the slight tension in her body that his answer was important. It was easy for him to understand why. He had made his mistrust of women all too clear, even striking out at her with it. Cameron knew he had been able to trust her for a long time, even before he realized how much he loved her; but he also knew he had never told her.

"I trust ye, lass. I have for a long time."

Avery felt an urge to cry with the strength of the joy she felt, but she knew Cameron would not understand, so she just smiled. "And, I want ye to give me bairns."

"I believe I have already begun to grant that wish."

"Aye," she patted his chest, "and a verra fine effort ye have made. I want some lovely black-eyed lads."

"And I want a wee kitten or two." He studied her for a moment, knowing that she would probably never understand just how much she had given him, and praying that he would never give her cause to regret her gifts to him. "And naught else?"

"Weel," she laughed softly and gently nipped his nose, "a wee pot of honey now and then wouldnae be amiss."

He turned her onto her back and sprawled in her arms. "I think blackberry jam would be better."

"Oh, my. Now there would be a beautiful argument to try and settle o'er the years."

"And it will be years, my love. Long, delicious years."

Epilogue

"Cameron!"

That his tiny wife's voice was loud enough to travel all the way from their bedchamber to the great hall astonished Cameron. He moved out of the great hall to stand at the foot of the stairs, his cousins Leargan and Iain flanking him and looking equally as astonished. Cameron glanced behind him to see Cormac also staring up the narrow stairs and smiling faintly.

"Never thought wee Avery could make a noise like that," drawled Cormac. "Gillyanne, aye, but nay Avery."

"Mayhap I should go up to her," Cameron said.

"Cameron, ye bastard!"

"Er, nay." Leargan grabbed him by the arm, "I am nay sure it is safe."

"How much danger can there be? She is having a baby."

"My wee Gisele was in labor when she chased me round the room with a log."

Cameron flushed a little guiltily as he turned to find that Avery's parents had arrived. "Why did she do that?"

"Said she wanted to hit me in the stomach a few times to let me ken how it felt. I made the mistake of telling her some bit of soothing nonsense. Maldie wrestled her onto the bed and I fled the room."

"Must you tell everyone that tale?" grumbled Gisele as she took her cloak off and handed it to a waiting and obviously besotted Wee Rob. "They will think I am a terrible dragon of a woman. *Bon jour,* Cameron. Since you are giving me a grandchild to spoil, I think I will maybe forgive you now."

"Ye are verra kind, m'lady," he said, kissing her hand. "Avery is—"

"Is my mother here yet?"

"Very loud," murmured Gisele. "I am here, little one," she called up the stairs. "I am coming up to you now."

"Good. Ere ye get up here, could ye kick Cameron for me, *Maman?*"

"Now, Avery—" Cameron began. Then he yelled, "Ow!" He rubbed his shin and gaped at Avery's mother, who smiled sweetly, then kissed him on the cheek. "I cannae believe ye kicked me."

"One should do what one can to keep the birthing mother happy, eh?" Gisele started up the stairs. "I am coming, Avery." She paused in the doorway of the room where Avery labored. "Ah, *ma petite,* you are glowing."

"I am fat and sweating," snapped Avery.

"Ah. Well, the sweat gives you a nice glow. Is there anything you want?"

"Aye, I want a verra long, verra sharp knife, and when this is over, I am going to hunt Cameron down and cut off his—"

Cameron breathed a sigh of relief when the abrupt

shutting of the bedchamber door cut off the end of that
threat. He ordered Wee Rob to see that drink and food
were set out, and then sent the men into the great hall.
A large part of him wanted to be with Avery, giving her
what small support he could as she struggled to bring
their child into the world, but it appeared that it might
be best for the continued harmony of their marriage if he
stayed away. She had Anne, Gillyanne, Elspeth, and her
mother to help her. He did not need to fear that she was
not getting all the care she needed.

"Dinnae fret, lad," Nigel said as he helped himself to
some wine. "Most of the lasses in our clan prefer to be
with the women at this time. And occasionally, 'tis safer
for the men to stay weel out of their reach."

"Mama Vree is mad at ye, Papa Cam'ron?" asked
Alan as he moved to stand by Cameron's chair.

"A wee bit," he replied, ruffling the boy's thick black
curls. " 'Twill pass. Having the bairn hurts some, and
Avery feels a need to yell a bit, is all."

"Aye, that is what Mama Beth did, too."

He watched as Alan rejoined young Christopher, a
rather ugly cat named Muddy, and Nurse Agnes by the
fire. In the nine months since he and Avery had gotten
married, Alan had visited them three times, each time
with Christopher and Agnes. The boy had readily accepted
that his name was MacAlpin, but it was obviously going
to take time to detach him from his adopted family even
just a little. Alan clearly wanted both families. Cameron
doubted he would ever separate the child from Christopher, however. Avery was right. There was a deep bond
between the two boys who had been so completely
rejected by their birth mothers.

It was enough, however, that Alan accepted him as his
father, even though that honor was shared with Cormac.
Since Cormac and Elspeth had saved his son's life, raised

him as one of their own, and had been willing to continue to do so, Cameron knew he would never begrudge them a place in the boy's life or affections. This visit held promise, too, for Alan would be staying for several months since Cameron had offered to begin Christopher's training. The tenuous bond between him and his son would have time to grow stronger.

The thoughts of children and family drew his gaze back toward the stairs. Despite his confidence in the women tending Avery, he could not fully suppress his fears. Avery might be strong of spirit, but she was delicate of build. Looking at Cormac and Avery's father, Nigel, Cameron struggled to find comfort in the fact that Elspeth and Avery's mother, both small, delicate women, had survived childbirth. If Avery needed him, she would send for him. Since he did not really wish to see her suffer even the smallest of pains, he told himself it was foolish to feel slightly piqued that she had not asked for him.

"I suppose I shall have to apologize to Cameron for all of those curses and threats I flung at him," Avery said as, once she and the bed linen had been freshened, she took her new son into her arms to nurse him.

"No, do not," said her mother as she kissed Avery's cheek and then the child's.

"Weel, I was a little . . . er, harsh."

"Small price for them to pay for all the hard work you have done," she grumbled. "Men—they gleefully plant the seed, then think nothing of it until the poor woman is sweating and cursing as she tries to birth it." She exchanged a grin with the others, then patted the baby's back. "You did well, Avery. We Murray lasses are good breeders. Just remember—"

"I ken it. Nay too many too often. I think I would like

to see Cameron now. Ere I go to sleep,'' she added with a faint smile.

It was not long after the women left that Cameron arrived. He nearly ran into the room, then stared at her for a long moment. He then shut the door, slumped against the hard wood, and took several deep breaths before walking over to the bed. Avery patted the bed next to her, silently urging him to sit down. He did so with such care that she had to smile.

"I dinnae have a knife, Cameron,'' she murmured, pleased to see him grin. "Come, look at your son." She placed the baby across her lap and undid his wrapping. "Is he nay the bonniest bairn ye have e'er seen?"

Cameron stared at his child. He really wanted to agree. To his eyes, however, his son looked a great deal like a mottled old man, only smaller. A dark old man with black hair sticking up all over his head, dark skin, and a small bluish star on his belly. The child had all the appropriate parts, he noted as he struggled to think of something to say. Then he heard Avery laugh and looked up to find her grinning at him.

"He will be bonny and plump soon,'' she said. She kissed Cameron's cheek, then wrapped the baby back up in his swaddling. "The birthing is hard on them. Probably as hard as it is upon the mothers. Trust me, I have seen enough newborn bairns to ken that he is quite perfect."

"And, of course, motherly pride has naught to do with that opinion,'' he drawled as he sprawled at her side.

"Of course not." She held her child in her arms as she sidled closer to Cameron. "He has your black hair. I am a wee bit impatient to see what color his eyes will be."

"They are blue." He gently touched the hair on his son's head. "An odd blue."

"Those are newborn eyes. They will change. Have ye decided what name we shall give him?"

"Tormand, after my father, if ye dinnae mind."

"Nay, 'tis a good name." She lifted her head and brushed a kiss over his mouth. "Thank ye for my son, husband."

Cameron wrapped his arm around her shoulder and held her close. "Nay, I should thank ye. After all, I had the pleasurable part in his making. Ye did all the work. Are ye sure ye are weel?" he asked softly, finally voicing his fears.

"Aye. just tired." She yawned but continued to stare at her son. "I do think he will look like ye and wee Alan."

"Poor lad."

"Ah, nay, husband. There can ne'er be enough dark-eyed knights to keep the lasses happy."

"Ye are blind, loving, but I praise God for it daily." He tilted her face up to his and gave her a slow, deep kiss. "I love ye, my wee cat."

Avery reached up to stroke his beard-shadowed cheek. "And I do love ye, my dark-as-sin chevalier." She giggled when he suddenly groaned and buried his face in her hair.

"Ye ken what I want to do now."

"Oh, aye, no more than I do, but nay for a month."

"A month?" When he saw her yawn again, he settled her more comfortably in

his arms.

"A whole month. Four long weeks," she murmured, and she could no longer fight the closing of her eyes.

"Weel, I suppose I should look at it as time weel spent."

"Weel spent at what?"

"Restoring our supply of blackberry jam." He grinned when she giggled just before going to sleep.

As soon as he was sure he would not wake Avery when he moved, Cameron got out of bed. He took their son from her arms with equal care. Avery was right, he thought as he warily and very carefully carried his son to his cradle. There was a good chance Tormand was going to look like him. He felt proud that he had left such a strong mark on his sons, and he knew that pride was Avery's doing.

Her love and passion had eased a lot of old doubts and pains. When she looked at him, he felt vainly handsome.

"I shall tell ye a wee secret, laddie," he said as he settled the child in the cradle and tucked the blanket around him. " 'Tis the secret of happiness. Ye are going to look a lot like me, and some fools think that a bad thing. Ignore their whispers of the devil, their talk of how your dark looks hold a dark soul. Ye just keep looking about, laddie, until ye find that wee lass who looks at ye as if ye are the bonniest mon in the Christian world. Dinnae settle for less, my boy. Find the lass who smiles at ye, loves ye e'en when ye are acting the fool, and holds ye close in the night, and ye will soon see that being a dark-as-sin chevalier isnae such a bad thing after all." He looked back at Avery as he lightly caressed his son's black hair. "In truth, ye will soon feel verra sorry for any mon who isnae one, for it seems we black-eyed knights ken how to find paradise."

Please turn the page
for an exciting sneak peek at
Hannah Howell's newest historical romance
HIGHLAND HEARTS
coming from Zebra Books
in February 2002

Chapter One

"Come to gloat, have ye?"

"I beg your pardon?" Tess asked, surprised. It took a moment for her to still the alarmed beating of her heart. The man's deep, rich voice had scared her half to death. She had passed through her uncle's dungeons earlier and they had been empty. Cautiously, she edged closer to the cell, thrusting her candle forward to shed some light into the shadowy recesses of the prison.

She gasped. Chained spread-eagled to the wall was the most beautiful man she had ever seen. Even his bruises, blood, and dirt did not dim his handsomeness. Then she frowned. There was something familiar about the blond giant there, glaring back at her.

"When did you get here?" she asked.

Revan frowned. The piquant little face pressed to the bars was not the face he had expected to see. Neither were the big dark eyes, wide with surprise. He wondered if Fergus Thurkettle was playing some kind of game. For the moment, he would play along. "Oh, I just strolled by near to two hours ago."

"And decided to nap amongst the iron chains, hmmm?"

" 'Tis cleaner than that bed o'er there."

Glancing at the rat-gnawed cot in the corner, she silently agreed. What was her uncle up to now? Uncle Fergus, she mused, carried his pretensions to being lord and master of all he surveyed a little too far. It was no longer just a slight eccentricity; it had become an obsession and it was chilling.

"Ye would not say so if ye kenned what was hanging there just last week," she said lightly.

"Aye? Who was it?"

"Oh, some skinny man who hadna discovered the benefit of a wee bit of soap and water."

"What happened to him?"

"There is a funny thing. I dinna ken." She had some dark theories but decided to keep them to herself. "I saw him here, weeping like a bairn. From what little I could learn he hadna committed a crime. I decided I would let him out, but I had to get the keys. By the time I got back, he was gone."

"So swiftly?"

"W-well, it wasna quite so swiftly. It took two days. I couldna just take the keys, for that would be noticed. So I talked to Iain, the blacksmith. He wasna easy to persuade, but I finally got him to make me a set. By the time I got the keys, the wee man was gone."

"Where do ye think he went?"

"I dinna ken. Dinna ken why he was here or why he suddenly wasna here. And now, just why are *ye* here?"

"Ah, it seems I tried to reach beyond my station."

She noticed the bitterness tainting his fine voice, but

she did not really understand what he was referring to. Her uncle, while an unreasonable man, had never locked someone up for that before. Then Tess slowly grasped the thread of an idea, one she did not like much at all.

"Oh, were ye sniffing round Brenda, then?"

"Sniffing round? I was courting her." More or less, he mused, but he was not about to confess to this chit. Hand in hand with cuddling up to the voluptuous Brenda Thurkettle had been his spying.

"And that is why ye are hanging up in there?" There were a few times when she had contemplated similar punishments for the men who had courted Brenda.

"Aye." He felt only a small twinge of guilt over that half-truth, then wondered why he even felt that. Some madman had chained him to a wall, and now some curious girl was watching him. There was little doubt in his mind that Thurkettle meant to murder him. He should feel no guilt at all over lying through his teeth if it got him out of this mess. Yet something about those huge dark eyes made him feel guilty. He told himself not to be such a fool.

"Well, that is a sad and foolish reason to hang a man up like a gutted deer," Tess said, deciding her uncle had finally lost what tenuous grip he might have had on sanity. "He shouldna shackle a man for having the poor taste and judgment to pursue a woman like Brenda," she murmured, reaching into a pocket in her doublet to fiddle with her keys.

Revan almost laughed. Brenda Thurkettle was blue-eyed, auburn-haired, and had a form to make any man alive ache with lust. No one would accuse a man of poor taste for pursuing a woman like that. Except, he mused with an inner chuckle, another woman. Or, he thought an instant later, someone who knew the person beneath the beauty. Revan began to wonder about the woman he was talking to.

"Are ye meaning to free me?"

"Well ... are ye sure 'tis *all* ye did? Court the regal Brenda?"

" 'Tis all and naught more. Did ye expect some heinous crime like robbery or murder or something?"

She shrugged, slowly tugging her keys out of her pocket. "It can grow rather tedious hereabouts."

His gaze fixed upon the keys. "Ye live here?"

It did not really surprise her that he did not know her, but she was growing weary of being consistently unnoticed.

"Aye, I am Tess, the niece. I have lived here nearly five years." She stared at him, contemplating. "I remember you now. I saw ye strolling about with our Mistress Brenda, taking her for a wee ride upon those matched horses. Verra nice. Was that a new doublet?"

"Aye, it was. Well?" He gently shook the chains attached to his wrists and ankles.

"Dinna rush me, I am thinking." She rubbed her chin with one hand. "Ye are the manservant to that fat laird, Angus MacLairn. Aye, that wouldna please Uncle. Howbeit, if ye *owned* MacLairn's keep—"

"Are ye intending to let me out of here or not?"

"Oh, dinna fash yourself." She set her candle down and unlocked the cell door. "Here, now." She brought her candle into the cell and set it down on a small, wobbly table by the cot. "Ye werena caught *in flagrante delicto* with Her Highness Brenda or the like, were ye?" She was not sure she ought to free a man awaiting a forced wedding even if Brenda cast her favors to nearly every man for miles about.

"In what?"

"Ye ken what I mean—mucking about, tussling, rolling

in the heather. I dinna care to set myself into the midst of that sort of trouble.''

'' 'Tis nothing like that, I swear it. Why would ye even think that?'' He had the sinking feeling he had been thoroughly fooled by Brenda, had missed a perfect opportunity.

''Well, the thrice-cursed fool is certain to be caught soon. Ye canna do something as often as she does that and not get caught. Do ye want your legs freed first or your arms?''

''My legs,'' he grumbled, then scowled as she knelt by his feet to unlock the shackles. ''Ye are dressed like a lad.''

''My, ye do have a keen eye, Sir Halyard,'' she murmured as she freed his legs; then she stood up to unlock the shackles at his wrists. ''Hell's fire, wrong key.'' She moved back to the light to clearly study them.

''Here, hold but a moment. How the devil did ye get in here? I just realized I didna hear ye come down the stairs. Ye were just there.''

''Well, there is a secret way out. Uncle had it made to allow the family to slip away if the need arose. Aha! Here is the key.'' She returned to unlock the manacles at his wrists.

Once free, Revan slowly sat down, rubbing his wrists to start the blood flowing again. As he did, he covertly studied his rescuer. She was a tiny little thing, and the somewhat ill-fitted doublet and hose accentuated her slenderness. At a glance he would guess her to be very young, but something about her husky voice told him that guess would be wrong.

''They hung my sword, hat, and cape over there upon the wall.''

Even as Tess went to fetch his things, she asked, ''Ye always wear your sword when you go courting?''

"I was planning to take Brenda riding. I thought I might need it." He grabbed his boots from where they had been set by the damp stone wall and yanked them on.

She held his things out to him, watching as he slowly stood up. He was big: tall, broad-shouldered, and lean. The perfect male. Inwardly she sighed. He was every lass's ideal lover but definitely a man only the Brendas of the world could hope to win. As she watched him buckle on his sword, fixing the leather belt around his slim hips, she wondered why Brenda had not defended him to her father. This one had to be the best of her crowd of admirers. By far.

She considered asking what he had done to get on the wrong side of her uncle, then she stopped in horror. Someone was coming. She heard a door creak open and saw a glowing light on the stairs that led to the dungeon. Someone was coming to see the prisoner she had just released. She turned to warn Revan only to be grabbed by him, his sinewy arm wrapped around her upper body. Since the cold steel of his dirk was pressed against her throat, she made no attempt to fight as he dragged her out of the cell.

"Where is the way out?" he hissed in her ear as they edged away from the approaching men.

"Keep backing up," she whispered fiercely. "Ye will come to the wall. What looks to be a large rack of shelves is, in truth, a door."

"How do I open it?"

"A loop of rope hangs down on the left side. Ye pull it open." She tensed as much from the cold blade as from her uncle and his two closest men-at-arms, Thomas and Donald. The three men reached the bottom of the stairs, turned, and saw them.

"God's beard, what goes on here?" Fergus Thurkettle bellowed as he drew his sword and pointed it at Revan.

"Ye best not try anything, Thurkettle," Revan warned in an icy voice, "or I will cut your niece's throat from ear to ear."

"Your method of showing gratitude could use a wee bit of refinement," Tess murmured, wondering how she could have so misjudged the man now dragging her toward her uncle's private escape route.

"Curse you, Tess, how did the man get free?"

"Well, now, Uncle, 'tis a question worth pondering," she managed to reply.

"Ye stupid bitch, ye set him free. Didna ye ken he is a murderer? He murdered Leith MacNeill."

"Who?"

Revan cursed as he realized Thurkettle had planned not only his death but a way to blame him for a cold-blooded murder as well. "That wee man who didna like soap," he hissed in Tess's ear. "Ye will have to find another fool to blame that on, Thurkettle," Raven said as he reached the door, "because this fool is leaving." They were both pressed up against the wall. "Pull the door open," he ordered Tess.

It was hard to move since his grip had all but pinned her arms to her sides. Grabbing the small loop of rope in her hand, she tugged several times before she opened the heavy door enough for them to slip into the small stairway behind it. She could see her uncle and his men edging after them. She grabbed the large iron handle on the back of the door. Without waiting for his order, she yanked it shut after she and Revan were inside. Then she shot the heavy bolt to lock it. A sudden thumping told her that her uncle and his men took at least a brief chance at following them.

"Where does this come out?" Revan demanded as he

hefted her up slightly so that her feet were off the ground, then made his way cautiously along the dark, slowly rising passage.

"In the stables. What looks to be a large rack for hanging bits and tools upon is a door. Ye willna be able to saddle your mount and ride out of here dragging me about like this."

"Ye would be surprised."

"They will be waiting for you."

"Of that I have no doubt."

"This is the last time I will do anyone a favor."

"Shut your mouth."

Since she could not think of a reply that could prevent him from using her as a shield, Tess decided to obey his curt order.

Revan cursed as he tried to hurry without losing his footing. He was the lowest of scoundrels. There were times, he mused, when being on the right side did not feel all that right. Just before Thurkettle had appeared, he had nearly talked himself out of taking the girl to pry information out of her. Thurkettle had turned the decision around. Although Revan hated hiding behind the girl, she was his only means of escape from Thurkettle's keep.

When they finally reached the door, he ordered her to unbolt it, then kicked it open. At first the sudden light blinded him. Squinting tightly, then slowly opening his eyes, he looked out. He smiled grimly when he saw Thurkettle waiting, five armed men now flanking him. He edged into the stable, moving away from the open door.

"Toss aside your weapons." He smiled coldly when they hesitated. "Dinnae push me, Thurkettle. I have naught to lose in this venture." Slowly the men tossed aside their weapons. "Now, ye"—he nodded toward a lanky, gray-haired stable hand—"saddle my horse and dinna forget all my belongings—including my bow and shield." He waited tensely as the man obeyed.

"Ye willna get away with this," Thurkettle hissed.

"I am nay doing too badly thus far."

"We will hunt ye down."

"Will ye, now? Dinna nip too close at my heels. I will have this fair niece of yours."

"Ye canna hold the lass forever."

"Long enough." Seeing that his horse was ready, Revan signaled the man, with a jerk of his head, to return to his companions. "Now, get in there." He nodded toward the tunnel he had just exited. Hissing curses, Thurkettle led his men inside. Revan kicked the door shut, then pushed Tess toward it. "Bolt it."

Doing as he said, she told him, "If ye move swiftly, ye ought to be clear of the walls ere they can get out."

"Not clear enough." He grasped her by the arm and pushed her toward his horse. "Mount."

"Ye are taking me with you?"

"Mount."

She mounted. There had to be a dozen ways she could break free, but not one came to mind. He swung up in front of her, reached back, and grabbed her wrists firmly. He then quickly tied them so that she was bound to him. When he spurred his horse to a gallop, she hung on, praying the fool did not kill them by riding like some madman in the dark.

Charging out the door of his keep, Fergus Thurkettle saw his prisoner riding off. "Cut that bastard down," he ordered his archers.

"But, sir," protested Thomas, "we could kill your niece."

Fergus cursed viciously, then abruptly halted. "What day is this?"

"What?" Thomas asked in total confusion.

"What day is this?"

"Tuesday, the fifteenth day of March."

"Aye, so it is, and yesterday was her birthday, her eighteenth birthday," Thurkettle murmured. Suddenly he was smiling.

"What are ye muttering about?"

Ignoring Thomas, Thurkettle stood watching the pair ride away as he hastily mulled over his choices. Tess was eighteen. The fortune he had held in trust now belonged to her. If she died, he was the only heir. For five long years he had longed for that fortune. Now he began to see a way, a way to kill two birds with one stone.

"Go after him," he ordered his men.

"But, sir," Thomas asked, "what about Tess?"

"Dinna fret over her. Look, that craven dog kens too much about my business with the Black Douglases. Soon Tess will, too. So that makes her dangerous, nay? Now—ride."

Once his men had raced off, Thurkettle strolled back into his keep, whistling a merry tune. He went inside, poured himself a tankard of fine French wine from a richly carved silver jug, then silently toasted himself.

"I suppose there is little chance of Sir Revan being brought back alive," a voice said behind him.

Glancing over his shoulder, Thurkettle frowned at his daughter as she moved to sit at the table. "Very little."

"Ah, what a shame." Brenda studied the jeweled rings on her fingers with an air of boredom.

"Nay, a necessity. I canna risk allowing him to reach the king and tell what he has learned just so ye can get your claws into him. Ye should have played your virtuous game a little less ardently."

"I did that for ye, so ye could find out if your suspicions were correct. I have seen little sign of gratitude."

"Ye *willna* see any. Ye were protecting yourself as

well. If the man is dragged back here and is still breathing, I will let ye have him for a few hours ere I kill him.''

"How kind." Brenda frowned. ''Ye had best be very careful of how ye handle this in front of Tess. She isna quite as dumb as she looks.''

"There is no need to fret over Tess." Thurkettle curled his thin, bloodless lips into a faint smile.

"Nay? She is the one who set him free, is she not?''

"Aye, the stupid bitch. She also showed him how to escape. He now uses her to try and protect himself. Well, he will soon discover that willna work.''

Very slowly, Brenda's eyes widened as she realized what her father was saying. "Ye mean to murder Tess.''

Scowling at his daughter, Thurkettle snapped, ''Aye, what of it? Dinna tell me ye will miss her.''

"Most of the time I barely notice her. 'Tis not me ye will have to explain it to but that horde of kinsmen Aunt was mad enough to wed into.''

Fergus Thurkettle shuddered as he recalled his sister's marriage. "I willna have to explain a thing. 'Twill be a sad case of kidnapping and murder.''

"Which we swiftly avenged.''

"Exactly.''

"Isnae killing her a wee bit harsh? 'Tis true, she released Revan but—''

"Ye *can* think beyond what gown to wear, can ye not? She has to ken something about our activities. That bastard will soon get it out of her. Together they can hang us all. Aye, and hanging would be the most merciful death we could pray for.''

"Oh—aye, I suppose she would have *had* to have noticed something in the five years she has been here.''

"Just so. There is more to it than that, however. She was eighteen yesterday. Her fortune and land are now all hers.''

"Fortune? Land? Tess has money?"

"Aye, Tess has money. Half the gowns ye wear were bought with her money. I had the expense of rearing her and all," he murmured. "I was allowed to extract funds for all that. For five long years I have tried to think of a way to get that money, yet not bring Comyns or Delgados clamoring at my gates. I have it now. She gave it to me herself."

"Are ye saying ye get all that is hers if she dies?"

"Every last ha'penny. Aye, and there is a cursed large pile of them."

"Just how big a purse? Are ye sure 'tis worth the risk?"

"Does thirty thousand gold riders appeal to you as worth a wee gamble?" He nodded when she simply gaped at him. "There is also a fine, rich keep south of Edinburgh, as well as some land in Spain. The girl is wealthy. Very, very wealthy."

"I canna believe it. Where would that . . . that mincing portrait painter, Delgado, get that kind of money? Or the Comyns?"

"Most of it comes from neither. 'Twas my sister's. Our father wished to be sure she had something to live on when she came to her senses and left that mongrel she married. It grew over the years."

"So neither the Comyns nor the Delgados can lay claim to it?"

"Nay. 'Twas Eileen's, thus Tess's."

"Are ye sure 'tis a perfect plan? Very, very sure? Near half those Delgados and Comyns are in the military or the service of the king. Aye, and the law or the church. We certainly dinna wish them to look too closely."

"She was kidnapped and murdered. What can there be to question?"

Brenda still frowned. "I will hold my celebrating until

ye have the money in your hands and none of that mongrel, lowborn family of hers clamoring at your gates."

She watched her father shrug, and she silently called him a fool. The man was celebrating before the deed was done, and Brenda considered that the height of folly. Sir Revan Halyard was a clever man, and little Tess was not without some wit. The pair of them could prove far more difficult to catch than her father anticipated. It might be a good time to supplement her private funds, she mused. If her father stumbled and fell, she did not intend to join him.

"Ye worry too much, Brenda."

"Aye? I think ye shouldna be quite so free of concern. I will keep mine, thank ye very much, until I see Sir Revan Halyard and Tess buried."

"Then ye had best see to the airing of your mourning gown, dearling, for ye will soon be standing over their graves."

Chapter Two

Tess groaned as Revan pulled her out of the saddle. She did not even want to think about how long she had been on the back of that horse. For hours they had ridden in a tortuous, circuitous route in order to shake off their pursuers. There did not seem to be a part of her that did not ache.

Revan pulled her roughly toward him and neatly tied her hands to the pommel of his saddle. She cursed him viciously under her breath. He was cruel and inhumane. The rope was so short she had to stand on tiptoe, pressed close to the sweaty horse. At the first opportunity she was going to stick her dirk into the man. A stomach wound—agonizing, slow to heal, but not fatal, she mused with a viciousness born of her discomfort and fear.

"Your language could do with some refinement," Revan murmured as he moved to push aside a large rock from the low banking.

"Aye? Well, your ideas on how to treat someone who helped you could use some improvement."

"Sorry, lass, but if I hadna used you to get out of there, I would have been dead ere I had gone two feet."

"Well, then, I am even more sorry I wandered by." She watched him drag some brush aside. "Curse ye to hell and back, what *are* ye doing?"

"Readying a place to hide."

"Oh, ye mean we arenae going to gallop through the moonless night like some cloaked reiver any longer? I am devastated."

"My, ye are a bitter-tongued wee thing." He glanced up at the quarter moon, then at her. "And 'tis not a moonless night. There is enough light here to see what I am doing."

"Ah"—she glanced up at the sky—"of course. That moon. Its radiance was such that I was blinded to its presence."

It was certainly hard for her to see what he was doing, she thought crossly. The horse badly obscured her view, but she could hear Revan shifting a great deal of rock and bracken. Every time she tried to nudge the horse a little in an attempt to move the beast around, the animal nudged her right back. His horse was as ill-begotten as he was, she thought angrily.

"Come along, then," Revan murmured as he untied her from the horse and rebound her wrists.

"Where?" She tried to resist his tug on her bound wrists. It looked as if he was dragging her and his stubborn horse straight toward the wall of rock that banked the hills. Then she espied the fault in the shadows, the hint that the wall was not as flat as she had thought. When he pushed her in front of him, she saw the opening.

"A cave," she drawled as she stumbled inside. "How suitable."

Urging his horse into the roomy cave, Revan ignored her remarks. He grabbed the end of the rope that was around her wrists and looped it back around the pommel of his saddle. While he readied a campsite for them, he did not want to risk her fleeing. He could not risk her drawing Thurkettle's men to his hiding place. After what they had been through, he doubted she would want to see those men, either, although he dared not trust in that.

Once he had prepared the campsite, he untied her again, instructing her to sit in the back of the cave. Keeping a close eye on her, he then quickly covered the opening as best as he could from the inside.

Tess walked over to the campsite and wearily sat down on the bedding he had spread out. She knew she ought to try to flee into the waning night, but at the moment she was simply too tired, and he was too much on guard. Also, she was not fond of being out alone in the dark.

She had some difficulty believing the tangle she had gotten herself involved in. Much of it made no sense. She glared at Revan as he crouched by the fire and began to make some porridge.

"Ye murdered someone, didna ye?" Even as she accused him, she could not believe him guilty of such a crime.

"Nay. I didna even draw my sword ere I was seized by Thurkettle."

"Then ye stole something."

"Nay. Not a farthing."

"Now, see here, ye had to have done something more than gawk at Brenda—"

"I did *not* gawk."

She ignored his remark. "My uncle isna one to act like this for something as trivial or common as courting. Curse it, if he tried to kill every man who trotted after his daughter, there would be corpses piled knee-high all over Scotland.''

''Do I detect a note of jealousy?''

''Nay, ye do not. Are ye prepared to answer my questions or not?''

''I have answered them.'' He looked at her, studying her closely. ''Now ye can answer a few questions of mine.''

''Oh, I can, can I?''

''Are ye truly Thurkettle's niece? I dinna see much of a resemblance.'' He snatched the battered hat she wore off her head, then half-wished he had let it be. That action had loosened what few hairpins she had used to keep her hair up. A thick, glossy mass of wavy raven-colored hair tumbled past her shoulders almost to her waist. The way the light of the fire touched it only increased its beauty. He now understood how the floppy, wide-crowned hat had stayed on her head during their wild ride. The thick hair filling the crown had held it in place.

''If ye kenned the family well, ye would see one or two similar traits,'' she said scornfully. ''Will ye free my hands now?'' She held her bound wrists out toward him.

He gently pushed them back into her lap. ''I will think about it. What is your name—Tess Thurkettle?''

''Contessa Comyn Delgado.'' She found some satisfaction—but no surprise—in his stunned look. Her full name surprised everyone.

''Ye are Spanish?'' he mumbled when he collected himself. ''I didna think Thurkettle had such a connection.''

''He doesnae. My father did. Thurkettle is my mother's brother. When my parents died, I was sent to live with him.'' She inwardly grimaced, thinking of how she had gone from the wrenching tragedy of losing her parents to the continuous tragedy of living with uncaring relatives.

"My father's mother was a Scot, a Comyn, and his father was Spanish. My father wasna considered good enough for a Thurkettle, as he was only a painter at the royal court."

Revan had little doubt that Tess spoke the truth. Thurkettle was well known for his pretensions. He had discovered some tenuous connection to Robert the Bruce and often boasted about the fragile bond. If the senior Thurkettle had even half the self-importance the younger did, it must have required a lot of courage for Tess's mother to wed Delgado. Life could not have been too pleasant for Tess, either, since she was a walking reminder of her mother's choice of husband. The Thurkettles would certainly have had other more profitable arrangements in mind.

"But," he spoke his thoughts aloud, "that doesna seem cause enough to kill you."

"*Kill me?*" she said, astonished. "No one was trying to *kill* me. They were after you."

"And you. They were firing arrows thick and fast, not to miss."

She did not want to talk about it. Until now she had managed to push aside her own suspicions. Although Revan had taken her as a shield, not one of her uncle's men had taken any care not to hurt her. Deny it as she would, the truth in all its chilling ugliness refused to go away. They *had* been aiming for her with as much intensity as they had been aiming for Revan. It was the final rejection of her mother's family.

Yet, to kill her? That was so drastic. Her uncle had had five years to do it. *And he had tried,* a voice whispered in her mind. He had tried three times.

Furiously, she tried to shake away the insidious suspicion, but it refused to be ignored. The fact that three specific incidents came immediately to mind told her she had never fully believed them accidents; she had fooled herself into turning away from the clues.

"Ye are wrong," she snapped, turning her hurt into anger against him.

Smiling wryly, Revan shook his head. At first he had thought Thurkettle's men were merely stupid. They were indeed stupid; however, they would never do anything without exact instructions from Thurkettle. If they were shooting to kill with no thought to Tess's safety, it was because Thurkettle had ordered it. What he needed to know was, why?

And she knew, he thought as he poured them each a cup of wine. He could read the knowledge in her wide, beautiful eyes. He could also read her struggle to deny it. It gave her a touch of innocence he decided it was wise to ignore. He did not want to assume she was not part of Thurkettle's treasonous plots and intrigues. Not yet. Trusting her too quickly could get him killed.

"Nay, I am *not* wrong, and ye ken it," he said, "I can see it in your eyes."

She gave him a contemptuous look as she accepted the cup of wine he held out. "Read it in my eyes? How foolish. They are eyes, not a letter."

"Your eyes are as readable as any letter, the script clear and precise. Ye are trying to deny what ye ken is the truth."

"Of course I deny it. 'Tis a heinous accusation. Why would my uncle wish me dead?"

"I was hoping ye could tell me."

"Well, I canna for he doesna." She sipped the wine, annoyed to find it tasted good.

"I canna believe 'tis because he disapproves of your bloodline," he murmured, watching her closely.

"Disapproval can be easily accomplished through ignoring me. He doesna have to bloody his hands to

disassociate himself from me. Ye have been trotting after
Brenda for a while, and ye dinnae ken I was about, did
ye?''

"Nay. Ye came as quite a surprise."

"Aha! So, he didna have to commit murder to cut me
off from the family."

"True. So what is the next possibility? Murder can
have many motives. Jealousy? Nay. Unless there is some
lover's triangle I am unaware of."

"Dinna be such an idiot."

"Nay, in truth, I think love doesna enter into this family
quandary at all."

The truth of that hurt, but she tried to hide it behind a
look of disgusted annoyance.

Revan saw the brief flash of pain in her look and felt
a twinge of sympathy. He had kept a close eye on the
Thurkettles for weeks, yet had never known about Tess.
She had been thoroughly ignored by her own kin, tucked
out of sight like a shameful secret. The time she had spent
with her uncle could not have been pleasant. He quelled
his sympathy, however. He was still not sure he could
trust her, still did not know if she was an intricate part
of her uncle's intrigues.

"Money, then. Greed. Do ye have some money?" Considering her rough, unsuitable attire, he doubted it but
then saw a look of realization widen her beautiful eyes.

Money, Tess thought, and shock rippled through her.
It was the one thing her uncle loved more than himself.
And she had some—a great deal by most people's stan-
dards—now that she had turned eighteen. The painful
fact that her birthday passed unnoticed again faded into
insignificance. Her lands and money were all hers now.
Her uncle was supposed to relinquish all control to her.
The doubts she had struggled to hold onto faded. For
wealth her uncle would most certainly try to kill her.

Those "accidents" had been attempts to remove the only heir who stood between her uncle and her fortune—herself. He wanted her dead and had wanted it for years. What he had needed was a way to point the finger of suspicion away from himself. An even-tempered mount suddenly gone wild and a fall that could have broken her neck was one way. A simple errand that sent her trotting back and forth over a flood-weakened bridge was another. Then there was that loosened masonry that chose to fall just as she stood beneath it.

And now, she thought as she looked at Revan, there was a kidnapper.

It was perfect. She had been abducted and, it could be claimed, murdered by her abductor. Even if it was guessed that she had died in the heavy pursuit by Thurkettle's men, her uncle would look innocent. What choice had he?

"Well?" Revan pressed after letting her think it over for a moment. He was rather bemused by how clearly her changing thoughts reflected in her heart-shaped face. "Ye do have some wealth?"

"A bit." She was not sure why, but she was reluctant to tell him just how much she was worth.

"Now, lass, Thurkettle wouldna trouble himself this much for only 'a bit.' "

"A few thousand gold riders, a wee bit of land." To some people thirty could be a few, she told herself, defending her lie.

"Well, 'tis nay as much as I had expected, but enough to rouse Thurkettle's greed."

He sensed she had not told him the whole truth, but he decided not to press. The exact amount did not really matter as long as she accepted the truth. Although still not sure he could fully trust her, he did think she would now be less likely to try and run off. He took out his knife and neatly cut the bonds at her wrists, then re-sheathed his knife.

"I am free?" She eyed him with mistrust, wondering if he planned some trick.

"I think ye will gain little by running away."

"Aye, I believe ye may be right." She stared at her wrists as she gently rubbed them to ease the chafing of her bonds. "I seem to have an excess of people trying to end my life." She glanced at him. "I assume I had best not exclude you just yet."

"Ye assume correctly."

"Isna it a wee bit stupid to threaten me now that I am free?"

Shrugging, he tested the porridge. It was ready to eat. "I dinna gain a thing by killing you." He spooned some of the hearty if plain fare into a wooden bowl, then handed it to her, tossing a spoon on top. "Ye do exactly as I say, and ye will be fine. Thurkettle willna give ye the same chance."

Reluctantly admitting to herself that he was right, she tested the food. It was not her favorite fare, but as hungry as she was, it tasted good. However, she silently prayed that if they were going to hide out together for a while, there would be some variety in their menu. If she had to suffer porridge on a day-by-day basis, she was sure she would soon decide her murderous uncle was not so bad after all.

Her life, she mused as she ate, had gone from bad to wretched in the blink of an eye. The only hope of improvement she had was to reach her father's family. They would take care of Uncle Thurkettle. And—she glared at Revan—the kidnapping Sir Halyard as well. The problem was, they were many days' ride away, and there was only Revan's mount. Worse, she was not certain she could find her way to them unaided. The Comyns were not renowned travelers. It was said that her uncle Silvio Comyn could get lost climbing out of bed. It was an exaggeration, of course, but the truth was, she and her relatives did have a tendency to go the wrong way.

She had only one real choice. Somehow she had to convince Revan that it was in his best interest to take her to them. Inwardly she sighed. Moses probably had an easier time parting the Red Sea. Revan had kidnapped her and threatened to cut her throat. He would not be eager to meet her kinsmen after that. Still, she decided it never hurt to try. She certainly could not get into any worse trouble.

"Ye can cease all that plotting," Revan murmured as he took her empty bowl.

Startled from her thoughts, she frowned at him. "And who says I am plotting anything?"

"That sly look that came over your face." He casually sipped at his wine.

"Sly look?" she muttered as she helped herself to another drink of wine.

"Now that ye are comfortable—"

"As cozy as a rat in the meal."

"We shall talk about your uncle."

"What now? I should think we ken all we need to. He wants us dead. Now we ken why he is trying to put me to rest in the cold clay, and I dinna believe ye have yet explained why he wants to kill you. Shall we discuss *that?*"

"I ken a few truths about him he would like to keep secret."

"Those could fill a book."

"Aye? Such as what?"

"Well, there are a few wives who must pray nightly that he keeps a discreet tongue in his head. He flaunts that weak drop of royal Bruce blood, and the fools believe it. They think it makes him special.'' She shook her head in disgust.

''That wasna the sort of secret I was thinking of.''

''Nay? Well, mayhap ye should tell me exactly what ye are interested in. Ye tell me what ye think ye have, and I will tell ye if I ken aught that will confirm or deny it.''

''Will ye?'' He watched her closely as he added another stick to the fire. ''Why should I believe that? Ye would be betraying kinsmen.''

''True. Most of the time ye would have to torture me to madness to make me do such a thing. But this collection of kinsmen is determined to murder me. I believe that cuts all bonds. Only a fool offers blind loyalty to a man who wants to kill her.''

''And ye are no fool.''

''Not all the time. So, what do ye think ye ken that could make Uncle so determined to put ye in the ground?''

Revan thought over his answer. There seemed little reason to keep secrets. She was in as much danger as he was, and he did not think her so stupid as to believe she could make some bargain with Thurkettle. He just hoped he was not acting in response to a huge pair of rich brown eyes, eyes that pulled at the truth, demanding his honesty. Silently he promised himself that in the future he would be very careful about looking into those eyes of hers.

''I believe he is dabbling in many illegal activities,'' he finally answered.

''Hell's fire, I thought ye were meaning to tell me something I didna ken for myself.''

''Ye ken he is doing something illegal?'' He decided her skill with sarcasm was not only good but could grow very irritating.

''My uncle? I should be very surprised if he wasna. Exactly what do ye think he is dabbling in?''

"Treason. He plots with the Black Douglases against James the Second." He found the shock that transformed her face somewhat reassuring.

Tess nearly choked on her wine. She had guessed at her uncle's criminal nature a long time ago, but she had never thought her uncle into any serious treachery. Treason against their king? She shook her head. Surely her uncle could not be such a fool, would not taint their family with such a black crime. But then, she thought as she struggled to subdue her shock, Fergus Thurkettle was clearly trying to kill her and Revan. He was also, suddenly and inexplicably, closely entangled with the Black Douglases, who had openly defied the king.

"Are ye certain about that?" she found herself forced to ask.

"Aye, very certain. I but needed some more proof, a few facts."

"Proof and facts?" She looked at him in slight surprise. "Ah, so that is why ye were slavering over the regal Brenda."

"I wasna slavering," he snapped; then he sighed, ruefully admitting to himself that he had come close a time or two. "I did think I could gain a little information from her, something that might lead me to the proof I sought."

"Well, ye didna ken the queen Brenda very well, then."

"She was a bit duller of wit than I had expected."

"Nay. A lot sharper. Whate'er old Fergus is doing, his royal daughter kens all about it."

He sighed as he set his wineskin aside. "I wondered about that whilst I was dangling from the wall in the dungeons." He had been taken for a fool, and it annoyed him.

"Brenda is a sly one," Tess said. "One too many questions from you, and she would grow suspicious."

"And probably kept Thurkettle informed of every step I took," he muttered.

"There is no 'probably' about it."

"Ye dinna need to rub salt in my wounds."

"No need to be so thrice-cursed ill-tempered over the matter. Men," she grumbled, shaking her head. "Show them auburn curls, big blue eyes, and a couple of other very big things, and their brains turn to warm gruel and leak right out their ears."

There was some painful truth in that, Revan thought, but he fought to ignore it. "Are ye planning to tell me more about your uncle?"

"I canna be certain I have much to tell. I always kenned he wasna a good man, but I canna say I was witness to anything that carried the taint of treason." She rubbed her forehead with one hand as she tried to think, but exhaustion was gaining on her, clouding her thoughts. "Mayhap ye should have asked me earlier. I begin to have difficulty recalling my own name."

She did look tired, he thought, and he reined in his suspicions. He was feeling rather weary himself. There would be time enough after they had both rested to press her for more information.

"Ye can lie down where ye are," he said as he started to bank the fire. "We can talk in the morning."

Nodding, she yanked off her boots and neatly stood them by her hat. She settled herself as comfortably as she could on the thin bedding, tugging the blanket over her and turning her back to the fire. Despite all the trouble she was in, she knew sleep would come quickly. It was just weighting her body when she felt Revan slip under the blanket and lie down beside her. Wide-eyed with shock, suddenly alert, she turned to stare at his broad back.

"What are ye doing?" she squeaked.

"Going to sleep."

"Ye canna sleep here."

" 'Tis the only place to sleep there is. Wheest, I am too weary to bother with some fool lass's outrage. I am also too weary to be any threat to any female. So ye can just calm yourself down and go to sleep."

For a brief moment she gave serious thought to continuing the argument, then turned her back to him. He was fully dressed, and she knew he was telling the truth about being tired. She also suspected he meant to keep a close eye on her until he was more sure of her motives. As she closed her eyes, she decided she was also simply too tired to bother with propriety at the moment.

Revan heard her breathing soften and knew she was asleep. He knew he would soon join her, his body aching with exhaustion. For now he felt they were safe, safe enough to rest up and gain some much-needed strength for the dangerous days that stretched out ahead of them.

About the Author

Hannah Howell is an award-winning author who lives with her family in Massachusetts. She is the author of eleven Zebra historical romances and is currently working on HIGHLAND BRIDE, the third book in her new Highland trilogy focusing on the daughters of the Murray brothers from HIGHLAND DESTINY, HIGHLAND HONOR, and HIGHLAND PROMISE. Look for HIGHLAND BRIDE in October 2002. Hannah loves hearing from readers and you may write to her c/o Zebra Books. Please include a self-addressed stamped envelope if you wish a response.